D0791542

MARY MODERN

MARY MODERN

A

NOVEL

CAMILLE DEANGELIS

Shaye Areheart Books

NEW YORK

This is a work of fiction. Names, characters, places, and incidents either are the product of the author's imagination or are used fictitiously. Any resemblance to actual persons, living or dead, events, or locales is entirely coincidental.

Published in the United States by Shaye Areheart Books, an imprint of the Crown Publishing Group, a division of Random House, Inc., New York.

SHAYE AREHEART BOOKS and colophon are trademarks of Random House, Inc.

Grateful acknowledgment is made to the following for permission to reprint previously published material:
Alfred Publishing Co., Inc.: Excerpt from "Sugar in My Bowl," words and music by Nina Simone. Copyright © 1962 (Renewed) WB Music Corp. All rights reserved. Reprinted by permission of Alfred Publishing Co., Inc.
Music Sales Corporation: Excerpt from "Kookaburra Sits in the Old Gum Tree," words and music by Marion Sinclair. Copyright © 1934 (Renewed) by Larrikin Music Pub. Pty. Ltd. All rights administered by Music Sales Corporation for the western hemisphere. International copyright secured. All rights reserved. Reprinted by permission of Music Sales Corporation.

ISBN-13: 978-0-7394-9169-0

Printed in the United States of America

Design by *Lynne Amft*

For my grandparents:
Kathleen and Michael DeAngelis, Ted Colangelo,
and especially for my grandmother Dorothy.

MARY MODERN

Prologue

THE EIGHTIES THROUGH THE TEENS
25 University Avenue
New Halcyon, Massachusetts

THE HOUSE HAS NO NAME, though it is quite grand enough to warrant one. Joseph Dearthing, ancestor of our heroine, had it built in 1882 with proceeds from the sales of his two best-known inventions, an early carbon-monoxide-detection device and a piano-tuning apparatus constructed from a clothespin. When the house was new it had no street address, so mail was sent in care of the university a quarter of a mile away where he professed on Thursday afternoons. There had never been a question of naming the house, for its owner had come of age in a Five Points tenement and had little patience for the pretensions of other self-made men.

That said, he built the quaintest house his children could imagine. His son, Ambrose, spent many a sunny afternoon toddling through a labyrinth fashioned from a bay laurel hedge, though at the time no one taller than he could possibly have become lost within it. To flank the house's front doorway, Dearthing commissioned two stained-glass panels depicting a pair of stern-faced seraphim from one of the finest artisans in Boston, and he was so pleased with these that he asked for a set of full-length pointed-arch windows for the dining room. No fairytale element went unrealized; there was even a three-story turret at the northwest corner. Dearthing's daughter, Cecelia, fell asleep every night in a chamber shaped like the full moon.

The visitor finds a surprise on the far side of every door. A mosaic of kaleidoscopic design covers the foyer floor; its intricacy may be fully appreciated only from a vantage point on the second-floor landing. Richly colored William Morris paper covers the walls in every room. The first-floor study offers a choice of more than twelve thousand volumes, and in the dining room a twee Latin inscription spans the limestone mantelpiece. A series of smaller drawing rooms leads to the great room, where above the Carrara marble fireplace hangs a mermaid salvaged from the prow of an antebellum merchant vessel, her left breast cleaved in two. Dust never settles on the baby grand piano in the corner, and the heady stink of lilies in full bloom wafts through the conservatory door. One finds the watercolors on Cecelia's easel beside the edelweiss surprisingly accomplished.

The Dearthings will employ no other housekeeper once Mrs. Henry passes in her sleep in her attic bedroom in the autumn of 1914. Her wind chimes will hang from the crossbeam for a hundred years afterwards. From the attic door, a meandering passage leads down a set of five steps, past the third-floor turret room, and down a spiral staircase to the family bedrooms on the second floor and the kitchen on the first.

There is one secret passage known to Ambrose, his sister, and later his wife and three children as "the loop," and no other living person is aware of its existence. Beginning and ending in the basement, the loop is composed of two dark and narrow staircases that are wedged between rooms on the eastern and western walls, and that meet again in the open attic on the third floor. Entrances on each floor are known as "broom closets," and one cannot gain access with an ordinary skeleton key. Though it was seldom exercised, Joseph Dearthing wanted the ability to traverse all four floors undetected; the loop would come in handy in the event of burglars, querulous houseguests, or naughty little ones sneaking out of bed on Christmas Eve. Granted, the loop is of scant interest to anyone outside the household, but the young Dearthings, like all children, cherish even the most inconsequential secrets.

Most of the house's curiosities are modern in origin though antique in influence, all the furnishings but one piece: a towering eighteenth-century Dutch curio cabinet in the dining room, carved from wood darker than mahogany, that features a Last Judgment scene of sorts. At the top of the cabinet a host of heavenly faces beams above the glassed-in shelves; cherubs blow trumpets and Christ sits enthroned. The side panels depict the story of Original Sin, and at the base of the cabinet, beneath the last drawer, are carved gargoyles and unrepentant swindlers, the faces of the damned. Joseph Dearthing purchased this piece of furniture at a New York auction house for what was then an outrageous sum. He justified the expense by claiming the cabinet's presence would keep his children honest. In truth, it would only give them nightmares.

I

HOUSEHOLD GODS

MORRÍGAN (MOHR-E-GAN): *Celtic war goddess, usually of sinister aspect, an arranger of fates who appears on the battlefields of Irish mythology. Her various shapes include that of a raven or scavenger crow; a washerwoman of garments belonging to warriors who will soon meet their deaths; a numinous woman or triad of women who may be either young or hag-like. ETYMOLOGY: from* mor *and* rígan, *"phantom queen."*

—ROSEMARY HARGREAVES,
A Compendium of Irish Folklore (1927)

FRIDAY, 11 NOVEMBER 2005 ~ 8:28 P.M.

25 University Avenue ~ The Basement

Bonobos are the only other primates who do it face to face. Females dominate bonobo society and copulation is diplomacy in its ideal form. Promiscuity means peace.

But that's bonobos. Is it a mistake to invite a man to one's house on the first date?

"Oh, well," Lucy says aloud, smiling vaguely as she raises her wrist to her nose for another sniff of her new perfume. A DNA sequence, collected last summer from the wing of a Painted Lady, scrolls down her computer screen at a dizzying speed.

Too late now: the doorbell's ringing. She reaches for her inhaler, gives it a shake, and takes a puff on her way up the stairs, stashing it in the mail table drawer on her way to the door.

8:32 P.M.

The Front Walk

Long before his chance encounter with its owner in the 600 section of the university library, Gray knew the Queen Anne at 25 University Avenue as the house that changes colors. The siding is a peculiar shade of yellow that turns a dusty sap-green under the light of the streetlamp. The house is yellow in the morning on his way to campus and green on his walk home. The old carriage house, with its padlocked doors and grimy octagonal windows, gives him the willies no matter the hour.

As he comes up the front walk for the first time, he sees that the house is in a worse state of repair than he had discerned from the curb. Not shabby, exactly—not yet—but the front yard has the disconsolate air of a home that no longer merits a write-up in *Better Homes and Gardens.* There's a widow's walk along the western side he'd never noticed before, a curious feature considering the sea is a full hour's drive away.

The porch lamp is on, but there's no light coming through the fanlight above the door. Stained-glass panels flank the doorway, but he can barely make out their design: angels, he supposes. Three sets of wings apiece. Seraphim?

He rings the bell three times before she answers it, and in the meantime he can hear the chime echoing through the hall. "Sorry," she says, shivering at the gust of cold air that accompanies his entrance. "I was in the basement." He hands her the bottle of Cusumano and Lucy says, "How thoughtful—I love Sicilian wine—thanks ever so much."

Strung on a delicate silver chain, a diamond of fair size glitters in the hollow of her throat, and the candle on the hall table softens the sharp edges of her profile. She'd seemed somewhat plain under the harsh fluorescent lights at the library, but in her own home, slipped into something made of satin and three times as old as she is, Lucy is altogether lovely. He watches the gooseflesh fade from her arms as she hangs his coat in a closet to the right of the entryway. An ancient deerstalker cap hangs on the door hook.

The house appears cavernous on the inside, probably because most of the lights are turned off. A tableau of family portraits, most of them in black and white, eyes him from high on the foyer walls, and a genealogical tree in careful calligraphy hangs above the hall table. Through an open door to his left he hears Billie Holiday singing "There Is No Greater Love."

Every time she leaves a room she flicks a switch. "We're big on conservation in this house," she tells him.

Other photographs line an arched hallway into the kitchen: wedding parties and engagement portraits, mostly; a few family-reunion shots with three or four dozen people crowded into the frame; and a smattering of baby pictures, all of them too old to be hers.

She flips on the kitchen light and dons a quilted baking mitt. A ceramic salad bowl on the granite countertop brims with spinach and crumbled feta cheese. The oven speaks in a jolly bass: "Lucy-bear, I believe the cookies are ready." He laughs.

"That's my dad." She opens the oven door and examines a tray of chicken fillets (cooked in lemon and rosemary, by the smell of it).

"That oven must be state-of-the-art."

"Because it talks?" She laughs. "Nah, my dad was just handy that way. He added an audio chip to the timer." The chicken sizzles gorgeously as she pulls the tray out of the oven and assembles the side dishes on the dumbwaiter. "He'd let me bake on my own when I was small, but then I'd always end up engrossed in a book and burn everything."

"That's why I don't cook."

"Not at all?"

"Well, some," he says, "but let's just say Julia Child would be horrified."

She looks at him, stricken. "You aren't a vegetarian, are you?" He shakes his head. "Oh, good," she says. "I suppose I should have asked."

He picks up the salad bowl and follows her through a swinging door into the dining room, then gasps at what he finds: a great stone fireplace, wide as an altar; a cathedral ceiling; a trio of seven-foot stained-glass windows—eating in here will feel like going to church. Two places have been set at the end of a long mahogany table, in itself the length of a good-sized house. Through speakers mounted on the wall above a large china cabinet comes the last line of the Billie Holiday song. Along the sideboard there is a row of crystal decanters, each filled with a fluorescent liquid. Incredulous, he sets the bowl down and approaches the bar. "Is that . . . *absinthe*?"

"I put food coloring in the gin. It was too old to drink, anyway."

"I take it you don't drink much." He runs his hand over an inscription carved in the stone mantelpiece: MEMENTO MORI, SED COMMORABOR.

"Clever," he murmurs.

"My great-great-grandfather chose it. He built the house," she says as she lifts the door on the dumbwaiter and sets a bowl of garlic mashed potatoes on the table.

He stands behind his chair with his hands in the pockets of his corduroy pants. "This is a beautiful dinner. I didn't expect you to go to so much trouble."

Smiling, she uncorks the wine in one swift motion and fills two long-stemmed glasses the size of soup bowls. "It wasn't any trouble. Sit, won't you?"

On the wall opposite the windows is another row of black-and-white photographs. At first glance they seem chosen for artistic rather than sentimental value: street musicians, farmers' markets, and barefoot children picking dandelions on a grassy hill. "My grandmother took those," she says.

As he settles into his chair, Gray recalls he had delivered a lecture on the Roman household gods just that afternoon. *Larēs,* the spirits of the dearly departed. Each family member was protected by the spirit of a certain ancestor, embodied in an ivory figurine kept on the household shrine. If you needed to pray, you'd hold your own protector in the palm of your hand.

"You haven't taken a bite," Lucy says after a minute. "What are you thinking of?"

Something older than Billie Holiday is playing now, a set of honey-sweet voices on a scratchy recording. "Do you have some sort of central sound system?"

"My father installed it. Why are you smiling like that?"

"I was just wondering what you do if someone in another room wants to listen to different music."

She shrugs. "There are never enough people around to disagree." He watches her eat, the light from the chandelier flashing off the ornate cutlery between her nimble fingers. There is a wide crescent moon at the base of each thumbnail. At the curve of her neckline two rust-colored pinpricks mar the shoulder seam, from an old safety pin left in the fabric too long. Lucy goes shopping in her own attic: tweed suits (of which she only ever wears the jacket or the skirt), silk dressing gowns, and lace-up boots (routinely polished but rarely worn). She will tell him she descends from a long line of pack rats.

Lucy catches him eyeing the white-gold wedding band she wears on her left ring finger. "It was my mother's." She pauses. "I hope you're not a Freudian."

9:56 P.M.
The Front Hall

LUCY HAS FIVE BOARDERS, male graduate students with acute vitamin D deficiencies and a shared predilection for heavy black clothing. They nod in tacit greeting as they pass him in the corridor, their long, pallid faces bobbing up and down in the semidarkness (and this produces an uncannily disembodied effect).

"Come on," she says, as the boarders disappear into the kitchen. The last of them turns in the doorway, briefly, eyeing Gray with curiosity. "We'll light a fire in the study."

"I'd like to have another look at your photographs," Gray says. Turning on the hall lamp with his free hand, he takes another sip of wine. After peering in at a tiny diptych curio of Joseph and Mary Anne Dearthing ("great-great," Lucy murmurs, her cheeks glowing with pleasure), he points to a picture of a dark-haired suffragist in Edwardian dress, her ballot poised above the slot. "This is amazing."

"My great-grandmother was the first woman in New Halcyon to cast a vote," Lucy says, "and she died a few years later. She and her sister-in-law cofounded a new suffrage party, to address the National Women's Party's failure to admit African-Americans. Alice Paul said they only wanted to turn it into a racial issue, but my great-grandmother called them all hypocrites. In public, no less." She smiles. "Am I boring you?"

"Not at all. You sound like a museum guide."

"So I *am* boring you."

"You're not boring me!"

There is another picture of importance beside it, an eight-year-old Lucy on her grandmother's lap. Her grandmother smiles at the camera, but Lucy looks away, as if there's something of greater interest elsewhere.

"Why don't you have any of your own baby pictures hanging up?"

She shrugs. "I always had some sort of rash devouring my face."

In the most ornate frame on the wall, a young couple poses atop the dome of some European cathedral. "Your great-grandparents?"

"My grandparents, actually. Mary and Teddy."

The honeymoon, no doubt. Smiling serenely, Lucy's grandmother rests her head on her husband's shoulder. "She must have been quite tall."

Lucy shakes her head, her eyes still on the photograph. "She was standing on something."

The date is written in the bottom right corner of the photograph. "Wow," he says. "My grandmother was *born* in nineteen twenty-nine."

"We like to spread out the generations in this family," she says. "My mother didn't have me until she was forty."

He returns to the family tree done in careful calligraphy, confused by what seems to be the matrilineal inheritance of surnames. Then he notices that Morrigan is Lucy's middle name—she only uses it as her last. Does this anger her father much, or is he the sort of man who concedes to any feminazi laboring for the fall of the patriarchy?

Gray points to a picture of a young couple taken at a picnic. "Is this your dad?" She nods. Her father looks like a garden-variety eccentric: black-rimmed eyeglasses; somewhat emaciated, as though he found time to eat only on festive occasions like this; and a mop of thick dark curls he'd probably never combed through a day in his life. It's almost eerie, Lucy's resemblance to her mother.

But seeing as Lucy wears her wedding ring, he knows better than to ask. "Where is your father now?"

She pauses. "Do you remember that fire in the Kellman Building?"

Two years ago last month, four scientists had died in the basement laboratory. He remembers passing all the gaudy memorials on the quad, four ten-by-twelve university yearbook portraits in flimsy metal frames festooned with wilting pink and yellow carnations. "Your father was . . . ?"

She nods.

"I'm sorry."

Lucy turns out the lamp. "Thanks," she says, "but let's talk about something else."

10:04 P.M.
The Study

IN SILENCE HE TAKES in the floor-to-ceiling bookcases filled with leather-bound volumes, the amaryllis growing in a blue crackleware pot on the windowsill behind the desk, the stone fireplace, and the sofa upholstered in crimson velvet. As Lucy closes the door behind them, he regards himself sadly in the large silver-framed mirror above the mantelpiece: he's too young for these wiry gray hairs sprouting at his temples, but not even the priciest hair dye could banish the avuncular air hanging about him these days.

Beneath the mirror is a small butterfly collection, a dozen specimens pinned to the board inside a glass case filmed with dust.

Setting her glass on the coffee table, she kneels before the hearth to turn the gas knob, and in a few seconds a fire burns cheerfully in the grate. In the far corner of the study there is an arched doorway leading into another lightless room. "What's through there?" he asks.

She settles onto the sofa. "A few drawing rooms, and then the great room. Nobody ever uses it, though."

"Why not?"

"It's too big."

Five sets of footsteps fall heavily on the stairs as the boarders retreat to their bedrooms with their late-night snacks.

"How long have they lived here?"

"The boys? Only since September. Colin and Felix are doing their Ph.D.'s in philosophy and theology, Dewey is writing a thesis on the metaphysical poets, and Rob and Milo are each doing a master's in computer science." She pauses. "Why are you looking at me like that?"

"I just find it a bit strange, you living in your family home with a bunch of guys."

"What's so strange about it? They needed a place to live, and I needed some extra cash."

"Is that so?"

"Keeping a house of this age and size isn't easy, or cheap. As it is, I'm not doing as much as I'd like, if I had the time." She pauses. "And come to think of it, I like having them around."

"I'm amazed you can keep them all straight."

"It's just the clothes they wear. They're all quite different despite their common purpose in life."

" 'Common purpose'?"

"They're a cult," she says, wineglass poised at her lips. "The Seventh Order of Saint Agatha."

"They look more like anarchists than religious zealots."

"As far as I can tell, they're a secular order. But they've all taken a vow of celibacy. I don't know, some sort of new-wave male purity movement."

He shakes his head. "Weird."

"Saint Agatha was a virgin martyr. Your old friends the Romans, they relieved her of her breasts."

Next to the butterfly collection is a photograph of Lucy in a blue commencement gown, beside her a stern-looking woman with a Sontag-like silver streak in her thick dark hair. "That's Megan," Lucy says. "My father's best friend. I work in her lab."

"What sort of research?"

"Right now we're testing a new drug for Huntington's. If it works as well as we hope, it should delay the onset of symptoms for at least a decade."

He sits beside her on the sofa. "So you give injections and record the results? That sort of thing?"

"Do I torture baby mice?" She sets her glass on the table and purses her lips. "We don't test on animals, Gray." (Not in *her* lab, anyway.)

"Then how do you test the drugs?"

"Human neurons."

"Cadavers?"

She shakes her head. "They clone the cells in the lab next door."

"Brain tissue that doesn't belong to anyone?"

"It belongs to the university."

He wants to ask her if the brain cells in her petri dishes work the same as hers do, if they ever scuttle away from her needle in mouthless protest. "So that's all you're working on?"

"Isn't that enough?"

"You mentioned you have a lab downstairs . . ."

"That's right. For the extracurriculars, you might say."

"Meaning . . . ?"

She leans in and her lips brush his earlobe. "Suffice it to say, it's illegal."

"Stem cells?"

She nods.

"But I thought privately funded research was still . . ."

"What I ought to have said was, it won't be legal for much longer."

"So what are you doing with them?" he says in a stage whisper. "Cloning yourselves? I know *that's* illegal." Indeed, both houses of Congress had banned the practice of human cloning earlier that year, despite the adamant testimony of dozens of scientists. Human reproductive cloning is the stuff of pure fantasy, the scientists said over the feedback on their microphones. Liberal pundits clucked their tongues at all the time and taxpayers' money gone to waste on banning something that could never happen anyway.

"Actually, in the near future it will be quite a valid means of reproduction. We'll do a perfectly fine job propagating the species on our own."

"And men will be obsolete in another couple of generations, is that it?"

"Oh, it shouldn't take half that long." She takes a sip of her wine, looks at him, and laughs, her breath fogging the inside of the glass.

"I don't see what's so funny about it."

"Don't worry." She pats him on the arm as if comforting him over some petty disappointment. "We'll keep you around. You're still good for some things."

THEY FINISH THE Cusumano and Lucy brings out a bottle of Cossentino with a triumphant flourish. "More Sicilian! Picked it up this afternoon. Great minds, huh?" For two hours she babbles about the Neanderthals ("They interbred with Homo sapiens to become the ancestors of modern Europeans—no, no—I don't *care* what you read in *The New York Times*"); the *Encyclopedia Atlantica* ("By the time the Z volume arrived there'd always be a new edition coming out, and of course they said he had to have everything completely up-to-date—did you notice that a full sixty percent of the books in this room are encyclopedias?"); advances in reprogenetics and the bizarre ramifications thereof ("Just think of it—the genetic child of an aborted fetus!"). Gray also learns that Ian Wilmut's sheep was cloned from a mammary cell, which is why she was named after Dolly Parton.

Lucy tells Gray she read her grandfather's copy of *The Decline and Fall of the Roman Empire* when she was twelve ("I didn't retain most of it"), and she asks him about his classes. He tells her about the lesser among his students, those who spend their mornings sniffing Kool-Aid packets through truncated coffee stirrers. They arrive with more time elapsed than remaining in the lecture period, a fluorescent orange sheen on the flesh beneath their noses.

"I'll bet you have plenty more stories like that one. You could write a book called 'Misadventures in Latin 101.' "

"I could do with fewer misadventures." He grumbles. "No one takes it seriously. I could teach them pig latin and no one would know the difference."

"Did you know that Caligula appointed his horse consul of the Empire?"

"I did."

"Of course you did." She yawns. "And the horse's name was Incitatus."

" 'Speedy,' " he says soberly, and she laughs. At some point he notices that her head is resting on his shoulder, her dark, glossy hair spilling down his arm.

She tugs at the woven hemp bracelet he wears on his right wrist. "You really are a rara avis, aren't you?"

"Why's that?"

"Your passion for Roman history. It must be strange for you, working with a lot of pasty-faced fuddy-duddies."

Abruptly he removes his shoulder from beneath her head and she sits upright. "Poor Gray, the only darky in his department," he sneers. "We aren't all running around the African Studies wing in search of Kunta Kinte, you know." This is all he is to them, a hereditary member of the talented tenth.

"I'm sorry," she says. "I didn't mean it that way."

"Oh? How *did* you mean it?"

"It's just that there's . . . there's something . . . incongruous . . . about you."

"*You're* the one who stinks of mothballs."

"I do not!"

"And you'd be none too pleased if I called you a WASP."

"I'm not a WASP," she sniffs. "We're Catholic."

"Which makes you guilt-ridden and therefore defensive about being a WASP."

She throws back her head and laughs. "I'm lapsed," she says. "It's not the same."

In the pause that follows he can almost hear the faint murmurs of decades-old conversations still lingering in the air above their heads.

She finishes her wine and slouches forward to place the glass on the coffee table. Best to assume he's no longer offended; otherwise she'll never see him again. "Would you like to see the lab?"

He nods, and her confidence is restored. Leading him by the hand out the study and across the foyer, she produces a ring of keys with which she turns the one, two, five, six dead bolts on the basement door.

THE 1940s THROUGH 1 NOVEMBER 1986
25 University Avenue

LUCINDA MORRIGAN has known since early childhood that she will marry a scientist. It's the sort of family joke that, for all the levity with which it is made, is intended seriously. Her mother's grandfather had been an inventor (his dust-laden collection of awkward prototypes and aborted brainchildren renders the built-in wine rack in the cellar thoroughly unreachable, unless one happens to be a rodent). Both her father and her grandfather had been physicians.

You might argue rightfully that Lucinda could become a doctor herself and marry an artist, but the heart of her intellect belongs to the morbid poets, poor sods like Dante Gabriel Rossetti, who exhumed his wife eight years on to retrieve a sheaf of poems he'd laid beside her cheek. Lucinda receives a Ph.D. in English literature at the age of twenty-four, and the university press publishes her "musings" on the metaphysical poets the following year.

Lucinda also dabbles in photography; her mother's Rolleiflex is a treasured possession. Her work remains undistinguished, not for want of talent but for genuine lack of opportunity: she suffers perennially from one illness or another. The maladies are as grave as they are frequent: Hodgkin's disease, which nearly claims her life, as a small child; a bout of pneumonia, for which she is hospitalized for two months, as a teenager; three cases of bronchitis in as many years. Even the bloom of youth and the hardiest of spirits cannot compensate for a body so ravaged over time.

She is delicate, but other than abstaining from alcoholic beverages she does not treat herself as such. Her old friend Marcus Delaney invites her to the departmental Christmas party in the Fairbridge Dining Room on December 17, 1971. It is there that she first makes the acquaintance of a certain mop-headed young man explaining the structure of the double helix to an eight-year-old boy in red polka-dot suspenders, both of them helping themselves to refills from the punch bowl at regular intervals. The boy hiccups and Ambrose says, "You shouldn't be drinking this, kiddo. Come to think of it, I'm quite certain it's been spiked." Lucinda laughs and he turns to her, flashing a generous grin as he gestures to her empty glass with the punch-bowl ladle he still holds dripping in his hand. She shakes her head politely, returning his smile, and the boy in the polka-dot suspenders departs their company to follow a rumor of a great heaping plate of frosted gingerbread cookies.

WHEN IT IS determined that Lucinda's latest illness will be her last, her husband sets about extracting and preserving little bits and pieces of her—he freezes her eggs, snips locks of her hair, fills a dozen vials with her blood—all to save until such a time as, years after her death, advances in biotechnology will permit her to live again. Patiently she indulges him in this delusion, opening wide as he swabs the inside of her mouth with a long-stemmed Q-tip.

She is returned to the earth fifteen years to the month of that university Christmas party, survived by her mother, her husband, and her young daughter. Other orphans have sheaves of old love letters (tied together with velvet ribbon, perhaps), home movies, carefully labeled photo albums, and such, but Lucy has few of these. The most tangible memento of her mother's life is a decades-old cell culture tucked at the back of a laboratory refrigerator.

THURSDAY, 23 OCTOBER 2003
New Halcyon

LIVES FLASH AND FADE like sparklers on the Fourth of July, and what's left afterwards but a rod of charred metal smoking in the grass? Ultimately there is no mystery involved in this arduous process of living and dying. Lucy will tell you that a cell ceases to divide simply when the telomeres on its chromosomes have snipped themselves past the point of function, that three hundred milligrams of hydrogen sulfide per cubic meter will asphyxiate a fifty-eight-year-old man of below-average weight in approximately eight and a half minutes. She will tell you that any mystery for you here is the by-product of your own ignorance.

SATURDAY, 12 NOVEMBER 2005 ~ 12:25 A.M.
25 University Avenue ~ The Basement

TAKING THE STEPS to the cellar feels like descending into another century: the current one. The wrought-iron stairway drops them (in their stocking feet) into a long white room lined on three sides with brown corkboard. Through audio speakers, mounted in the corners beneath the ceiling and hooked to the main system, comes the cheerful percussion of a tune sung by Sarah Vaughan.

Day in, day out—same old voodoo follows me about . . .

LUCY BENDS OVER the computer monitor to raise the volume on the central sound system.

Yellowed memorabilia clutter the corkboard—postcards, movie-ticket stubs, newspaper clippings—alongside intricate diagrams of the respiratory and cardiovascular systems, a holographic poster of the periodic table, and a lot of images Gray doesn't recognize. There are even a few framed facsimiles of Leonardo da Vinci's mechanical drawings on the wall above.

Gray frowns at a color photograph of the reconstructed *Australopithecus afarensis,* christened Lucy after the Beatles' infamous ode to a certain drug of choice.

"My dad used to say he named me after her."

"That's cruel!"

Lucy shrugs. "It was only a joke. I'm named after my mother."

And there's the equipment, of course, the microscopes and test tube racks and all sorts of unidentifiable gadgets assembled on a white Formica counter running along the walls beneath the corkboard. In the center of the room the counter juts out like a peninsula into a sea of spotless ceramic tiles, and on this counter is the computer—four flat-screen monitors of varying sizes along with a central processing unit to put the Pentagon to shame. An old leather armchair sits in front of the keyboard.

To his right he finds an antique dartboard, every dart pinned inside the bull's-eye; beside this is a large blackboard on wheels covered in old equations and doodles Lucy may never have the heart to erase. At the center of the board, done in blue and yellow chalk, a grinning amorphous mass spouts a cartoon talk-bubble: "I'm the little amoeba who couldn't!" Scrawled at the bottom of the board in childish capitals: SALVE PATER! The date is printed beside it in Roman numerals in a surer hand. There is also a list of numbers, which Lucy explains are the percentages of DNA humans share with those creatures marked in the first column. BONOBO, 97%, it says. AMOS THE FIELD MOUSE, 96%. DROSOPHILA, 59%. SPINACH, 31%. SHOWER MOLD, 21% (!!!).

Half-hidden behind the chalkboard, as if out of excessive modesty, stands her father's most cherished possession: the skeleton of Claudine du Moyenne, the celebrated acrobat of nineteenth-century Paris, suspended from a wheeled metal stand. (Many a late night did Ambrose dance her around the room, his hand positioned most indecently upon the exquisite curve of her right pelvic bone.) The skull gleams beneath the fluorescent light; the clavicle is smooth as a dagger blade. Lucy points out to Gray the joints on the skeleton's wrists, elbows, and knees. Beside *la mademoiselle,* a small refrigerator and horizontal DeepFreeze, the contents of which one must never confuse with the edibles inside the kitchenette fridge at the opposite end of the lab.

As he turns again to face the room, he notes the demarcation between laboratory and junk room by a stodgy highboy dresser and a nearly empty floor-to-ceiling wine rack. (The remaining bottles are mementos of the happiest nights of her parents' marriage.) On the far wall, past the kitchenette (complete with space-age coffeemaker), he spots an object of peculiar shape hidden beneath a dustcover, something that reminds him of a funeral bier.

"That's the best part," she says. "You'll never guess what it is."

He approaches the shrouded shape in the corner, hesitating, like a child on Christmas morning convinced that the object of his nightmares is waiting for him beneath the gift wrap. "It's . . . it's a time machine."

"Not quite." She tugs at the dustcover and it falls at their feet.

"What is it?" He puts out a hand as if to touch, his palm hovering above the clear casing edged in polished chrome. It's too dark in here to see more than vague metallic outlines beneath the plastic, but he reads the labels on the row of digital gauges along the side of the contraption; there are oxygen, carbon, hydrogen, and dozens more elements, and under these is another row of dials and switches without labels. Gray surveys the thing: how right he had been to think it the length of a coffin! This could be the vehicle for some technological fairy tale, a gruesome convergence of cryogenics and Snow White.

An electrical cord snakes around the base of the machine and the plug lies at Lucy's feet. "It doesn't exist to you as soon as you leave this room, right?" she says.

Gray nods with his mouth still open.

"It's meant to be a womb simulator," Lucy says.

He laughs. "Building from scratch?"

"That was the idea. He worked on this thing for years—decades, maybe. He was obsessed," she says softly. "It doesn't work, of course." And now it never will.

"Well," she says brightly. "That concludes our tour this evening, ladies and gentlemen." She makes a sweeping gesture toward the stairway. "Shall we?"

As he follows her up the steps he admires the curve of her inner calf inside the fishnet stockings, the contents of her cellar forgotten for the time being. Footsteps sound outside the basement door, and Lucy holds up a hand. "We have to wait here until they go back upstairs," she murmurs.

"Why?"

"I don't want any of them catching a glimpse of anything down here."

"Oh," he says, still eyeing her fishnets.

"They think I'm a body snatcher," she whispers. "And that after I'm done with the bodies I bury them in the basement walls." She covers his mouth with her hand as he begins to laugh.

SATURDAY, 12 NOVEMBER 2005 ~ 10:55 A.M.
The Master Bedroom

NATURALLY THERE ARE more marvels to be found on the second floor, though dawn is breaking before he discovers the finest among them: a small stained-glass rosette in the slanted ceiling above the four-poster bed. Pools of colored light stain her face, her breasts, the bedsheets; and as the sun rises the brightening greens and golds render her a creature of another world entirely. For an hour or more he lies beside her, watching her sleep (nodding off again himself here and there), and when she opens her eyes she smiles at him so serenely that he is quite certain she isn't human.

"What is it?" she murmurs, bringing her fingers to her lips. "Have I been drooling?"

In the shower he tells her he really ought to be going, and she agrees only because she should. Then she bites down playfully on his lower lip, and he knows the day belongs to her.

While she's cooking him breakfast he notices the carvings on the curio cabinet, and as she enters the dining room with two plates heaped high with bacon and fried potatoes he turns to look at her, his appetite snuffed out by the evil grimaces whittled in the dark wood. When he tells her why he's looking so uneasy, she just laughs. He manages to eat most of his breakfast, though, and afterwards they spend the better part of an hour going through her father's record collection in the green drawing room.

As he reads the back of an Ink Spots album she's thinking of that night in the library less than a week ago. They'd been searching for a book on the same shelf, alternately reaching and excusing themselves, and just when the situation had gotten intolerably awkward he had pulled a ten-year-old *Penthouse* from between two outdated psychology texts. The look on his face had made her laugh.

"Pornography is an applied science, you know," she'd said, and he had laughed in turn. Some pinch-faced grad student had shushed them after a few minutes of flirtatious small talk, so they adjourned to the third-floor lobby. On their way out of the 600s she spotted a tome entitled *Principles of Lubrication* and tapped the spine as she smiled at him mischievously. She'd decided then that he was handsome, perhaps too handsome for her, but that there was also a kindness, a certain reticence in his manner that tempered any arrogance his looks might have engendered.

Gray places the Ink Spots record on the turntable and drops the needle. "What are you thinking about now?"

She just smiles.

AT DUSK THEY walk hand in hand back to his apartment above the garage of Mrs. Jonathan Tepplethwaite, antediluvian widow of the twenty-ninth vice chancellor. Lucy waits in the living room while he chooses a clean set of clothes. "It's so chilly and damp in here," she calls down the narrow hallway. "It's a wonder you haven't gotten sick."

On the walk back to her house she tells him how her father told her more than once that people believe in God because it comforts them the way her teddy bears had comforted her. "Teddy Ruxpin, too?" she'd asked, and he'd nodded. For years afterwards she believed that Teddy Ruxpin *was* God, or at least some manifestation thereof, and that if she listened to the toy's cassette tape from start to finish surely someday it would reveal to her all the secrets of the universe.

"And how long did that phase last?" he asks, holding her hand a little tighter.

"Too long," she says, then adds quickly, "but I'm not an atheist."

He shrugs. "You say it as though it were a disease."

She gives him a sly look. "*You* say that as if you *were* one."

At this he just smiles enigmatically, and so she pegs him as a Unitarian.

As they cross the lawn at 25 University Avenue the doors to the carriage house slam against the padlock as though someone were trapped inside. "It's just the wind coming through a hole in the back wall," Lucy says in response to his expression.

"I take it you don't keep your car in there?"

"I don't have a car."

"The garage is empty?"

"It's structurally unsound."

They talk for hours again tonight, through the leftovers, two more bottles of wine, and another round of show-and-tell in the downstairs rooms. More talk of Claudine du Moyenne leads Gray to tell Lucy all about the Capuchin crypt beneath a seventeenth-century church in Rome, and she listens eagerly as he recounts an intricate arrangement of human vertebrae and foot and finger bones forming the face of a clock. "The word 'cappuccino' comes from the color of the Capuchins' robes," he says.

She asks him so many questions about his time in Italy, Romania, Egypt, and Nepal that he gets a squirmy feeling that perhaps she herself has never been as far as Europe. This assumption turns out to be untrue, although a week in Berlin with her high school German class doesn't exactly qualify her for world-traveler status. "It's not that I have no interest in going," she says quickly. "I've always wanted to see more of the world. I know this is going to sound bad, but . . . I guess I was just loath to leave my father here alone for very long."

"It doesn't sound bad," he says kindly.

There are pictures of her ancestors in all the drawing rooms, too, and a snapshot of her grandmother Mary and her mother, Lucinda, beside a snowman in a deerstalker cap—the one still hanging on the hook in the coat closet?—prompts her to tell him about Mary's obsession with Antarctica. Growlers and sunspots, the otherworldly beauty of Terra Nova Bay (and the Italian research station there, where foreigners are surprised to find the espresso machine hooked up to the main water supply), the myriad differences between Adelie and Emperor penguins—her grandmother had always spoken of Antarctica as though she'd actually been there. That was another misconception it took years to dispel.

"How long has it been since she passed away?"

"Sixteen years." She pauses. "Why?"

"Sixteen years is a long time to hold a grudge," he says. "Even a small one."

"What do you mean?"

"The way you were frowning just now. You look like you're still angry with her for misleading you."

"I'm not angry," she says. "I was never angry. I just . . ."

"You just what?"

She sighs. "I just miss her. And I wish I could ask her why she let me believe she'd been there."

Lucy yawns, and he suddenly has a vision of her bending over the freshwater spring beside the Arch of Septimius Severus, her hair shining in the sunlight as she takes a long drink. Smiling, she turns to him, wiping her mouth with the back of her hand.

The vision fades with the sound of her voice: "Gray?"

"Yes?"

"What are you thinking about?"

She misinterprets the look on his face, but the kiss would have happened regardless.

NOVEMBER AND DECEMBER, 2005
25 University Avenue

THE HOUSE HAS never felt empty, not even during those two years between the laboratory fire and the advent of the Seventh Order. It has nothing to do with the supernatural; when she smells her grandmother's perfume or her father's aftershave she knows it's just old odors clinging to the curtains.

Still, being at home used to feel like being at a party where she'd exhausted all topics of conversation with every other soul in the room. Enter Gray into that gathering of stale acquaintances and she no longer notices the sensation she used to have in the evenings, the feeling of being watched—as a mother watches a child.

Four nights a week, he sleeps over. After dinner they play Scrabble in the parlor on a Parsons table by the fireplace, taking turns stunning each other with seven-letter double-scores, Lucy rewinding the gramophone at regular intervals as they listen their way through Ambrose's record collection.

Gray passes the evenings they spend apart in his windowless office on campus, his teacher's copy of the Elementary Latin textbook on the desk before him. Altogether he wastes at least an hour imagining how the following evening will pass with good wine and a home-cooked meal, John Coltrane and a well-thumbed copy of *Merriam-Webster's Collegiate Dictionary.*

Lucy goes up to bed early, only to struggle with the bedclothes, angry with herself for suggesting they not spend every night together.

WEDNESDAY, 21 DECEMBER 2005 ~ 2:55 A.M.
The Master Bedroom

WHEN LUCY WAS a teenager, the fact that she could count the people who would die for her on a single finger used to send her into weeklong fits of depression. Then there were none, and she could not afford to linger on it. Now Gray winds his arm tight around her waist, mumbling in his sleep, and she drifts off thinking maybe one is enough.

In her dream she stands beside her father on the widow's walk watching the sun set behind the conifers, and she asks him why he ignored the fire alarm until it was too late. All she gets from him is a sympathetic smile, as though she were a caged animal, and she can see the dust specks on the lenses of his black-rimmed eyeglasses.

This dream doesn't shake her. Other nights she's found him standing beside her mother's grave at Saint Lucy's downtown—though her mother *has* no grave, and neither does he—and it's raining, and the traffic passes mutely down the avenue as she reaches for his hand. Those nights she wakes up to him saying *You are your mother's daughter,* and it's those words that frighten her the most.

FRIDAY, 17 FEBRUARY 2006 ~ 1:05 P.M.
Primavera Vegan Grill ~ New Halcyon

THEY CHOOSE THE same booth by the window every Friday afternoon, Lucy's favorite time of the week. The restaurant is a five-minute walk from campus, and it is organic vegetarian, for Megan will not consume anything that once had a face. Lucy's father's best friend—*her* best friend—hasn't so much as prodded a poached egg in over three decades.

Megan leans across the table, shielding her words with the laminated menu. "Do you realize that the only reason we're still on this project is because the governor's wife is a carrier?"

"I expected it was something like that."

"I hate feeling like this, like I can't take a crap without some man in the back of an unmarked van making a note of it."

"Thanks for ruining my lunch before I've even ordered it."

Megan pauses. "I thought it was only fair that I tell you . . ."

"Tell me what?"

"I've been here twenty-two years, Lu. I'm thinking it may be time for a change."

"I'll go where you go, boss," Lucy says. "Just as long as you don't leave town."

"I'm serious, Lucy." Megan straightens up and opens the menu. "But we'll discuss it another time. This booth could be bugged."

Lucy laughs as she stirs three packets of raw sugar into her iced tea.

"Tell me more about your beau," Megan says. "When am I going to get a proper introduction?"

"I'll have you both over for dinner sometime," Lucy says, once the waitress has taken their orders.

" 'Sometime'! You and your 'sometimes.' Leave it to you and no one will ever get around to doing anything."

"Come to think of it, I can't remember the last time you invited *me* over for dinner."

"You know how Ralphie sheds! It would take me three full days to get the sofas clean."

"You should hire someone to clean for you."

"I've seen him in the tearoom from time to time."

"Who?"

"Gray, of course. He's usually by himself."

"Why don't you say hello, then?"

"Didn't want to make him uncomfortable. You've told me before how he is. But oh, is he a fine-looking young man! One of those guys who make you wish you were twenty years younger."

"I'm just glad he doesn't make *me* feel that way."

Megan smiles benevolently. It occurs to her, as it has on more than one occasion, that any casual observer would assume Lucy is her daughter. This thought suffuses her with a warm, solid pleasure. "You've been getting in later and later, you know."

The waitress brings their salads. "I was in at twenty past nine this morning." Lucy pokes at a raw Brussels sprout. "That's hardly late at all."

They wag their heads at one another, their mouths full of diced apples, walnuts, raisins, and other things that do not belong in a real salad. Working for one's closest family friend does have its drawbacks. Megan spears a cherry tomato with her fork, and Lucy watches the little red orb as it disappears between her lips. "I've asked him to move in," she says.

Megan gasps mid-chew, then swallows quickly and clears her throat. "Are you sure that's a wise idea?"

"I've thought about it quite a bit. It's sensible, all things considered."

"And which 'things' are these, pray tell?"

Lucy frowns. "Since when are you the pillar of Christian morality?"

"I'm sorry. I just can't help worrying about you."

"Why?"

"Just a belated maternal instinct, you might say." There is no particular reason, save one: Lucy is "alone in the world," all by herself in a cavernous house despite the five warm bodies ever making scarcities of themselves in the upstairs rooms. In the midst of such isolation it is usually unwise to cast about for something to heat one's bed. "I'll refrain from the snide comments," Megan says. "Promise!"

"You should *see* his apartment, Meeg. Smell it, I mean—"

"Look at you. So earnest! You look like you're about to adopt a flea-bitten orphan from a third-world country."

"You said you weren't going to—"

"And are you sure this smell doesn't originate with him?"

"It was there when he moved in, thank you very much!"

"That's what he told you. Sorry, sorry, go on."

"*Mold,* Meeg. It's dark and damp and I can see how miserable he is there. The rent is exorbitant, too. He's so embarrassed by it that I've only been there one time, and for just a few minutes." She pauses. "Anything to add before I go on?"

Megan shakes her head; her mouth is full.

"What I mean to say is, things are going well between us, so it would be more than a practical arrangement."

"But you've only known him, what, three months? Can't you give it a little more time?"

Lucy shrugs. "If it doesn't work out, it doesn't work out. But I really do have a feeling that it will."

"How do you feel about him?"

Lucy places her fork on her plate and folds her hands in her lap, bowing her head as though composing her reply in iambic verse.

"Well?"

"I can't quantify it."

"Cut the crap, will you? Do you love him, or what?"

"That word just isn't relevant to me. Do I enjoy talking to him? Yes, sure, we talk for hours. Do I *want* him?"

Megan clamps her hands over her ears. "Ygggh! My baby godchild fornicating? Ygggh!"

"Grow up, will you?"

"*You* grow up, and answer the question. Do you love him?"

"Love?" Lucy rubs her temples as though the mere sound of the word could trigger a migraine. "What does love do but drive people mad?"

"Such a romantic notion! You ought to have been a poet." Megan pauses. "You're frighteningly like your father sometimes."

"Don't you mean 'frighteningly like your *mother*'?"

Megan shakes her head. "Your dad wrote his share of bad poetry, way back when."

"But—"

Megan winks. "Burned every scrap." She eyes the waitress hovering over them. "You want coffee?"

Nodding, Lucy shifts uneasily in her booth. This isn't the first time she's wondered if Megan was ever in love with her father.

WEDNESDAY, 15 MARCH 2006 ~ 7:00 P.M.
University of New Halcyon ~ Yobanashi Tea Room

IT WAS THE CLASSICS Department secretary who hatched the ingenious idea of holding the book launch on the Ides of March, and as a consequence the only attendees are Gray's mother, his girlfriend, and a handful of elderly dilettantes in polka-dot bow ties. Most of his colleagues are spending spring break in Europe, or at least that's what they told him, and the lone waitress is sullen as a lab monkey. The tearoom is beginning to resemble a morgue.

The university press, claiming budget constraints, has allotted him a rhubarb tart none of the old men will touch, a hot-water dispenser, and an array of the cheapest teas on the menu. Worst of all is the book itself, a series of annotated translations and contextual essays of and on an obscure Silver Age poet whose very existence is a matter of dispute. Gray is proud of his work, of course, but he should have known from the start that no one would notice or care about it.

At least Lucy's presence has a mollifying effect on his nerves. With her index finger tucked in the pages of chapter five, she stands at the center of the room glowing like a firefly, chatting brightly with his mother and the aging classicists. Buoyed by her confidence, he gets through the reading without stuttering, and his mother claps so enthusiastically she makes the room sound twice as full.

"He called me from Italy almost every day," she tells Lucy, oblivious to his groans and eye-rolling. "At that time his research wasn't going so well, and he was terribly discouraged. But I said, 'Son, just keep looking, trust in God, and you'll find everything you need.' My, doesn't his name look wonderful in print!"

SPRING AND SUMMER, 2006
25 University Avenue

LIVING HERE FEELS like an extended visit at first, like spending every night in a museum whose janitorial staff has gone on perpetual strike. The excess of religious iconography unnerves Gray—the dining room windows, the crucifix over every doorway and the faded Sacred Heart prints in tarnished frames, the little plastic figurines of Saint

Francis or Saint Anthony that turn up in the most unexpected places (the spice rack, the medicine cabinet), the faces carved on the dining room sideboard not least of all—but over time the strange is made ordinary.

Three months after Gray joins the household, he and Lucy split the cost of a preowned Prius, silver (she informs him that cars of this color are statistically safer), two years and fifty thousand miles old. They will only ever drive it to the grocery store. Most mornings she drags him out of bed for a four-mile run through town, and he discovers that the exercise improves both his concentration at work and the quality of his shut-eye.

They alternate cooking dinner, except on Mondays, when he brings home Chinese takeout and they eat it from the good bone china. On Tuesday mornings Gray discovers that each leftover dish of vegetable fried rice or sesame chicken has been picked at by one or more sets of fingers, and every Tuesday morning he slams the refrigerator door in disgust. Lucy, oblivious, will consolidate the contents of the paper cartons for her own lunch.

That's not quite true about using the car only for trips to the grocery store. A handful of times they'll drive to the nearest shore, an hour away, for a moonlit stroll along the promenade, dozens of phosphorescent jellyfish visible beneath the crest of each incoming tide. Lucy holds his hand and turns her face to the night breeze coming in off the ocean. The ends of her hair tickle his nose and mouth.

At the close of those evenings he lies awake beside her, breathing in the smell of salty air that still clings to her skin. One time, seized by an uncharacteristic impulse, he edges closer to her, the bedsprings groaning beneath him, and runs his tongue lightly along her upper arm—yes, she *does* taste a bit like saltwater taffy!

From a dream-lit room in another wing of the house—and in another time altogether, perhaps—Lucy gasps in mild disgust. Wiping that patch of wet skin with a corner of the bedsheet, she cries in a voice of unharnessed affection, "Oh, Skippy, you filthy little thing! Shouldn't you be outside digging up the rosebush?"

An old family pet, he supposes, long since laid beneath the flower beds itself. Gray keeps meaning to ask her about Skippy—what sort of a dog was he?—but she's never in his company when the question reasserts itself. One day in between lecture and office hours he even calls her extension, but in the lab at the opposite end of campus the phone rings until he hears her voice mail greeting, crisp and professional. Then he hangs up.

These quirks of hers don't irritate him, but they don't endear her, either: how she'll pretend she doesn't see spiders rather than snipe them with a wad of paper towels the way other girls do; her tossing and turning into daybreak, punctuated by the gasp of her inhaler; how her mental calendar is littered with the birthdays of people she no longer cares for ("Today is Bennett Rhody's birthday," she'll murmur over coffee, only sighing when he asks her who the hell Bennett Rhody is); the way she shakes her head and clucks her tongue at the follies of her former selves, as though someday, some days, many other someones won't regard her in just the same manner.

Gray teaches two summer courses in elementary Latin in the evenings, so he is free to procrastinate during the day in his new office in the third-floor turret room at Lucy's house. Three months in Rome the previous summer yielded a second book's worth of research, but the sight of that stack of notes, photocopies, and friable Italian hardcovers only disheartens him. Many an afternoon he passes in the overgrown labyrinth in the backyard, the laurel brushing his shoulders as he ruminates over some complicated line, polishing his translation as he goes. Once he even alights upon a sturdy nest tucked in the hedge, from which a tiny sparrow is attempting its first flight.

When he reaches the center of the labyrinth, more often than not he finds one of the boarders reading on a bench by the old fountain. How remarkable that Dewey or Colin or Rob or Milo or Felix should spend the occasional afternoon out here in the sunshine and come inside again still looking like an albino. Gray mumbles a greeting and ducks back into the maze.

He begins an acquaintance with their closest neighbor, Mrs. Eugenia Delaney, a diminutive woman ninety-one years of age who invites him to tea whenever she spots him through the well-tended rose hedge (hers, of course) that demarcates the line between their properties. Her kitchen makes him feel embarrassed, ungainly somehow, and he watches her pour the tea with childish fascination: beneath her translucent rice-paper skin, her veins look like tributaries on a map of the Amazon. She addresses him as "Professor" without irony (at least none that he can detect). On his third visit he discovers that, three decades ago, his campus office had belonged to her husband.

Mrs. Delaney tells him every time he visits about how impeccably Lucy's grandmother kept her kitchen garden. "Tomatoes as big as a baby's head, and oh, the cabbage! Mary grew the nicest cabbages. She used to bring some over to me now and again. Always so generous." Mrs. Delaney shakes her head. "Such a shame that gardening doesn't interest her," she says sadly, speaking of his girlfriend.

Back in what remains of the Morrigan flower beds, he looks up and spots the windows of the room in which he should be laboring under the ever-looming threat of publish-or-perish. Shielding his eyes against the noonday sun, he notices a small window, about as wide as his forearm, tucked between the turret room and the back stairwell. His closet has no window, though that seems to be its location. Over the following week he spots half a dozen more such windows, all dark as pitch, and all on the house's eastern and western façades. What is their function, these roomless windows?

In the evenings, behind a closed door on the third floor, he juggles a few blood oranges from the Mediterranean market downtown, muttering to himself (*"Gallia omnis divisa in partēs trēs"*), lulled by the strains of British trip-hop and the occasional footfalls of Felix or Colin or Dewey or Rob or Milo—he can never remember which name belongs to which boy, let alone which of them haunts the second-floor turret room. Which two erected a wall made of cardboard to divide the commodious middle bedroom? Milo and Dewey? Dewey and Colin? No, it's Colin who's got the turret room, and the skinny bastard pounds on a typewriter well into the morning.

On those nights Lucy locks herself in the basement to sequence some new sample—one of the weeds in what used to be the kitchen garden, the dormant amaryllis on the library windowsill, or a Red Admiral butterfly to compare with last year's Painted Lady. Occasionally one of the boys will poke his head into the laundry chute and howl in an absurd falsetto that either amuses or irritates her, depending on how her "work" is going.

In the mornings, as she pours their coffee, he often notices small bruises on her upper arms, little purple-yellow supernovas he can't recall having caused.

She says, "What windows?"

AUTUMN 2006
The Front Hall

THE FULL BOWED MOUTH, the wide limpid eyes: hers is an antiquated beauty, the aura of gentle sincerity no amount of Yardley's lavender water or cameo brooches can emulate. He lingers before the picture in the foyer with increasing frequency, taking note of a new detail every time: the teardrop pearl earrings, the fine lace on her collar, the pigeon taking flight from the left-hand railing.

Beside her, a young man spared from handsome conventionality by an aquiline nose and a moodily drawn mouth. Edward Morrigan sure has that smug first-team all-American air about him. But these are not kind thoughts to be thinking of his girlfriend's grandfather, a casualty of war, clearly a loving husband to inspire lifelong widowhood. Mary Morrigan died placidly at a venerable age, but she died alone all the same.

Behind them, a medieval urban landscape of bell towers and crumbling apartment buildings dissolves into *sfumato,* a smudgy gray horizon beyond the arc of her right shoulder. Florence, probably. Looking at that photograph above the mail table in the foyer—the two of them so euphoric at the beginning of their life together—Gray decides he knows too much.

FRIDAY, 12 JANUARY 2007 ~ 10:45 P.M.
The Green Drawing Room

F-L-O-T-S-A-M, the last letter on a triple-word score. "Take that," he says, reaching for the score pad. The fancier the word, the prouder he is; the score itself is secondary.

"Thirty-nine points." Lucy makes a show of rearranging her tiles on the rack. "Very nice."

"I know that look," Gray sniffs. "You can't top that, but I'd like to see you try."

"Watch me, then." Using the M in "flotsam," she leaves him flabbergasted with M-E-D-I-O-C-R-E, the last E on another triple-word score. "Bingo."

All he can say is, "You don't get two triples for that."

"I *know* that, Gray." Sadly she watches him add her score to the tally, grumbling to himself; with those ninety-two points in her column he'll never recover. How pathetic are they, a pair of academics whose greatest accomplishments are made on the Scrabble board?

SUNDAY, 11 FEBRUARY 2007 ~ 1:44 P.M.
Checkout Line II, Acme Supermarket ~ Hilary Road, New Halcyon

SAUCER-EYED, wiggly-fingered infants and all their trappings belong in other people's universes. Don't they?

The little girl in the green nylon papoose shimmies her pudgy legs in the seat, grasping at the air in front of Lucy's face. A feathery shock of bright red hair and a smile to charm the devil: Lucy is enchanted. The girl is her father's daughter, all right; the man wearing her on his back looks like that comedian—what's his name?—Carrot Top. He casts a glance over his shoulder as he drops a bunch of bananas on the conveyor belt. "Imogen, are you casting your spell again? I think you are." He reaches back and tweaks her toes. "I think you are!"

"She's beautiful," Lucy murmurs.

"Thank you." Imogen's father beams. "We've already had three people ask us if they can take her picture." His wedding ring is white gold. Without thinking Lucy thrusts her left hand into her coat pocket, feeling like a fraud for the first time since she started wearing her mother's.

THURSDAY, 18 OCTOBER 2007 ~ 1:48 A.M.
25 University Avenue ~ The Master Bedroom

LUCY RECLINES ON the unmade bed with her legs in the air, her hands bracing her calves. She points her toes toward the ceiling, lending a graceful air to an otherwise ridiculous position. Gray stands in the bathroom doorway watching her as she begins a round of slow breaths, deep and deliberate. The skirt of her sheer embroidered nightgown has fallen around her hips; the delicate fabric of the bodice strains with every breath she takes. She never fully undresses anymore; they may not be married, but she'd begun acting as though they were quite early on.

Even in the beginning she didn't wear any of his ratty old college T-shirts like all his other girlfriends. They'd put on one of those old shirts, light a cigarette, and wander around the bedroom poking through the bookshelves and CD case, every casual movement flaunting the fact that their panties were still crumpled in a ball at the foot of his bed. Lucy had been the first to buck this modern-dating morning-after routine, though she'd never had a chance to try it: they had stayed at her house that first night, and every night since.

Sweat beads in the space between her breasts; her cheeks are flushed with a postcoital glow. This is the time when Lucy looks almost beautiful.

"Does that actually help?" he asks.

She breathes in; she breathes out. "Gravity, Gray. Of course it does."

"How long are you going to do that?"

Lucy shrugs. As he drops a strand of dental floss into the wastebasket, she lowers her legs and turns onto her side, propping herself on an elbow. He uncaps the toothpaste and squeezes a dollop onto his brush. He doesn't look at her.

"What is it, Gray?"

"It shouldn't be like this. Look, Lu, it's not like—"

"Don't call me 'Loo.' "

"It's not like you're forty years old and just now trying to have a child. It doesn't have to be so methodical." She has informed him on more than one occasion that a woman's first fertility drop occurs at the age of twenty-seven. He needs no reminder that her twenty-eighth year commences in two weeks' time.

"You can tell me if you don't want to do this. It's not too late to change your mind."

"I'm not changing my mind. But you *did* say—"

"I'm prepared," she says, as though she hasn't yet convinced herself. "Your life doesn't have to change. Not if you don't want it to."

"Lucy." He shakes his head. "I can't be a father only when I feel like playing Frisbee."

"You can tell me," she says. "I won't resent you for it."

"I've told you I'll do it. I want it, all right? I may not share your fervor, but I can't help that."

She turns out the light on the night table. The springs creak beneath her as she settles into sleeping position—on her stomach, clutching her down pillow like some treasured childhood plaything, her toes curling over the end of the mattress. "You wouldn't believe it," she says. "This feeling. I see children in strollers on the street now and I feel this thrill, this urgency—"

"It's totally normal for you to feel that way. It's just how your brain's wired. But that toddler isn't quite so adorable when he's screaming because you haven't changed his diaper."

She turns her other cheek to the pillow so she's no longer facing him.

"Say it," he says tiredly. "Just say whatever it is you're going to say."

Still she hesitates. "I wasn't an only child, in the beginning."

He sits up in bed. "What?"

Lucy props herself on her elbows. "I was, and I wasn't. There were boys here. In the house. Two of them. They used to practice their magic tricks on me."

"I don't understand."

"I thought they were my brothers. If you'd asked me when I was five if I had any siblings, I would have said yes."

"But whose children were they?"

"Distant cousins. But they lived with us for a good long while, and after they left I never saw them again."

"That's weird," he says, because he doesn't know what else to say.

With a sigh she settles back onto her stomach. "Isn't it?"

He lies awake beside her, listening to the mice in the walls.

Chromosome X, NR0B1: *An excerpt*

1 *cgggcgccgcgggccatggcgggcgagaaccaccagtggcagggcagcatcctctacaacatgcttatgagcg*

74 *cgaagcaaacgcgcgcggctcctgaggctccagagacgcggctggtggatcagtgctggggctgttcgtgcggc*

148 *gatgagcccggggtgggcagagaggggctgctgggcgggcggaacgtggcgctcctgtaccgctgctgcttttgc*

223 *ggtaaagaccacccacggcagggcagcatcctctacagcatgctgacgagcgcaaagcaaacgtacgcggca*

295 *ccgaaggcgcccgaggcgacgctgggtccgtgctggggctgttcgtgcggctctgatcccggggtgggcagagcag*

370 *gggcttccgggtgggcggcccgtggcactcctgtaccgctgctgcttttgtggtgaagaccacccgcggcagggca*

446 *gcatcctctacagcttgctcactagctcaaagcaaacgcacgtggctccggcagcgcccgaggcacggccaggg*

520 *ggcgcgtggtgggaccgctcctacttcgcgcagaggccagggggtaaagaggcgctaccaggcgggcgggcca*

593 *cggcgcttctgtaccgctgctgcttttgcggtgaagaccacccgcagcagggcagcaccctctactgcgtgcccac*

669 *gagcacaaatcaagcgcaggcggctccggaggagcggccgagggcccccctggtgggacacctcctctggtgcgc*

743 *tgcggccggtggcgctcaagagtccacaggtggtctgcgaggcagcctcagcgggcctgttgaagacgctgcgctt*

819 *cgtcaagtacttgccctgcttccaggtgctgcccctggaccagcagctggtgctggtgcgcaactgctgggcgtccc*

896 *tgctcatgcttgagctggcccaggaccgcttgcagttcgagactgtggaagtctcggagcccagcatgctgcaga*

971 *agatcctcaccaccaggcggcgggagaccgggggcaacgagccactgcccgtgcccacgctgcagcaccatttg*

1045 *gcaccgccggcggaggccaggaaggtgccctccgcctcccaggtccaagccatcaagtgctttctttccaaatgc*

1120 *tggagtctgaacatcagtaccaaggagtacgcctacctcaaggggaccgtgctctttaacccgg* // gta . . .

II

THE SPOON GARDEN

She seemed to walk in an atmosphere of things about to happen.

—L. M. Montgomery, *Anne of Avonlea (1909)*

1925

25 University Avenue

THEIR FORTUNES IN the making, Joe and Jared now live in brownstones near Central Park in New York City with their wives and babies and their babies' nurses. It won't be too much longer before they stop coming home for Christmas, and their absences will reinforce their sister's half-formed belief that the Dearthing family's golden age has passed.

Shamelessly does Mary snatch at the last vestiges of her childhood. To halt that ceaseless march of generations from nursery to churchyard, to push each child back into the haven of the womb, and thus to recover her mother, who will not stir from beneath the grass at Saint Lucy's until the Day of Judgment: this is the sort of sentiment that colors her midnights.

Father and daughter have tacitly agreed that she will not marry until she's a B.A., even if she'll only spend her days baking pies and running the vacuum cleaner. No one will ever christen an ice shelf on the edge of the world with her name, but does that mean she should content herself with a secondary education? There are other things with which she must content herself, however: ice-skating on the pond behind the high school, Cadbury's Antarctic Explorer trading cards, and the published journals of Sir Ernest Shackleton. She must not dwell on thoughts of all those nameless white peaks and valleys, those hardy cartographers marking up their maps inch by frozen inch.

In the summertime Mary listens to the Boston Symphony Orchestra on the wireless in the conservatory, working on needlepoints for Red Cross fund-raisers while her father scours the financial pages with his pipe clenched between his teeth; she dominates the mahjong table at her aunt's Friday night gatherings until Cecelia's friends establish a new rule that all players must be at least thirty years of age; and she reads poets of whom her English teachers would scarcely approve.

MONDAY, 1 JUNE 1925 ~ 7:35 P.M.
The Garden

THE HONEYSUCKLE SMELLS like a dream, but if Mary doesn't pull it out, those bewitching vines will eventually smother the arborvitaes down the row from the rosebush that separates their yard from that of Mrs. Elizabeth Delaney. A widow of reduced circumstances, Mrs. Delaney provides her lone boarder with use of her husband's study while her son is away at Oxford. Yanking the vine out by the roots, Mary looks through the study window and spots Timothy Delaney seated at the desk. She sighs heavily. How can she find out if the boarder—a moody young biology student—will be living there again in the fall?

"I thought your father would have hired someone to care for the garden," comes a voice from behind Mrs. Delaney's rosebush.

"I—"

"Don't tell me," the boarder says, stepping into view. "The fresh air does you good." He throws a glance over his shoulder at the study window, then looks back at her with a mischievous smile.

"I don't believe we've been introduced," she says. Damn her timorous heart!

"You're Mary." He extends a hand and she quickly doffs her gardening gloves. "Edward Morrigan. Call me Teddy."

"Pleased to make your acquaintance."

"Likewise." He pauses. "I've been wondering about your labyrinth."

"My grandfather designed it."

"Yes, Mrs. Delaney told me. Every morning I've stood at my window looking down at it, trying to solve it with my eyes."

She plucks a honeysuckle blossom from the vine and presses it to her nose to steady herself. "How would you like to try it with your feet?"

Early fireflies flash above the narrow path between the hedges. "The labyrinth is approximately sixty feet in diameter," she says in her best museum-guide voice. "It is multicursal, which means—"

"I *know* what it means."

"Too clever by half. On with it, then. You lead and I'll follow."

"With pleasure, Miss Dearthing." Teddy takes her lightly by the hand and, through a succession of left turns, promptly leads them back to the entrance.

"As I was about to explain before I was interrupted"—she frees her fingers and suppresses a little smile of triumph—"once perceptive observers noted that a multicursal labyrinth could be solved by keeping exclusively to the right or left, new maze designs were developed in which this strategy would merely return the mouse to the point of entry."

Edward eyes her with appreciation. "You're very good at that, you know."

Aunt Cee calls her name through the kitchen window. "Time to mash the potatoes!"

"Thanks for the tip," he says softly. "Would you mind if I walked it one more time?"

"Not at all." She hurries across the lawn toward the house, head bowed low to hide the guilty flush.

SUMMER, 1925, TO AUTUMN, 1926

New Halcyon and Cape Eden, Massachusetts

TEDDY IS GOING to be a surgeon. His father was killed in a farming accident when Teddy was five, and now his uncle harvests the cranberry bog by himself. He lost his brother in the war, and his twin sisters, Maeve and Alice, are newly married and living within five miles of the family farm on Cape Eden.

He and Mary set the gramophone on the hall table and spend the weekend evenings dancing through the downstairs rooms, fox-trotting past the mahjong table where, once they've danced their way back into the foyer, Cecelia's friends reassure one another they need no longer harbor any guilt over Mary's expulsion.

IN THE SUMMER of 1926 his mother invites Mary's family to spend the weekend on the Cape. On the shore Dr. Dearthing does not let his daughter out of his sight, for she had nearly drowned on Cape Eden when she was seven. Teddy's sisters greet Mary warmly, and Aunt Cee tells her on the ride home that Mrs. Morrigan had proclaimed her "a perfect lady."

FRIDAY, 2 SEPTEMBER 1927 ~ 4:20 P.M.
25 University Avenue ~ The Backyard

MARY DROPS A POTATO sack over Teddy's head, binds his wrists with a bit of twine, and gives him a gentle shove as she clicks the button on her father's stopwatch. "You know what you remind me of?" she calls as he stumbles around a corner. "A homing pigeon!"

She follows him through the archway in the hedge, pressing the button on the timer as he falls on his knees in the gravel that surrounds the marble basin of the fishpond. As she pulls the burlap from his head he loses his balance and falls on his side against the pond's rim. "Untie me, will you?" he gasps as she smiles at the stopwatch. "This twine's hurting my wrists."

"Four minutes and forty-seven seconds. You look more like a monkey, actually. Poor little gibbon!"

Bending forward, he dunks his jaw into the cloudy green water and turns on her with a full mouth.

Her shrieks carry into the adjacent yard, where Mrs. Delaney is deflowering the rosebush for a dining-table centerpiece. Mary's neighbor drops the last bloom into her basket and turns back to her kitchen door, shaking her head at the regrettable absence of supervision beyond the picket fence.

SUNDAY, 18 NOVEMBER 1928
The Parlor

TEDDY BORROWS FOUR spotlights from the Drama Department, using fuchsia, blue, and gold filters to simulate the aurora australis on the parlor wall. Mary claps her hands with childish delight as he turns the lights on and off and on again from his cross-legged position on the floor behind the sofa, while the gramophone plays the university choir's particularly wistful rendition of "In dulci jubilo." Legend has it that the monk who composed the chorale heard it first from a host of heavenly visitors. The record ends, Teddy replaces the needle, and she revels in that quiet felicity at the end of a day well lived.

FRIDAY, 21 DECEMBER 1928 ~ 6:27 P.M.
Bender's Hill ~ Cape Eden

CHILDREN COME SPEEDING down the hill on either side of her, sled-blades glinting in the moonlight as they pass. The sky's a broad swath of velvet pinpricked in a thousand places, a smooth inverted surface from which the moon hangs like an alabaster Christmas ornament. Teddy, the flaps of his deerstalker cap tied tightly over his ears, stands beside her father on the crest of the hill. The young man pats his coat pocket every few moments to make sure the little black velvet box is still there.

Dr. Dearthing watches his daughter trudging up the hill, her cheeks red and her hair loose and disheveled beneath her knitted pom-pom cap. "This is it," he says to Teddy. "Go with God, my good man."

As she returns to them, her father says, "One more ride. After this we'd best be driving back to town."

So much of the child remains in the young woman who throws her arms around his neck. "Two more rides?"

"No," he says. "One more."

Teddy seats himself at the end of the sled, his legs spread wide so she can seat herself snugly between them, her red rubber boots sandwiched between his size-fourteens. Once she's settled he wraps his arms tight around her middle, and Mary holds on to the rope. They take off at a swift clip, the wind whistling in their ears. Above them, the good doctor takes his pipe from his mouth, and hearing his daughter's exhilarated laughter, closes his eyes.

Snowballs fly back and forth over their heads as they slow to a halt a full ten yards past the children's stopping-place. She sits up and looks over Teddy's shoulder, where her father is still puffing on his pipe. He is raising his arm in a wide arc over his head.

She shivers. "It's colder than Antarctica out here!"

"Sure seems like it," he replies.

"I can't feel my feet," she says.

"Me neither." As he tries to stand Teddy trips and falls on his face into the virgin snow. Mary giggles as she stands above him and takes his hand to pull him upright, a hopeless endeavor: in another moment she's tumbled into the drift beside him, her limbs tangled in the nine-foot striped scarf his grandmother knitted for him in crimson and yellow, the university colors.

"Wait a minute." Patting his pocket once more, he bends over with his hands braced on his knees, holding his breath to slow his pulse a little. "Be serious for a minute."

She laughs. "What for?"

They forget the sled, and he comes back for it in the morning.

JULY AND AUGUST, 1929
Various Locations Across the Continent

MARY LIGHTS A CANDLE for her mother inside cathedrals all over western Europe. She and Teddy fling themselves into the sea off the Côte d'Azur and spend their evenings over heaping plates of oysters on café terraces. They eat tortillas under the orange trees in the courtyard of the old mosque at Córdoba and purchase eight pounds of praline fudge from a Franciscan monastery outside Brussels. They take an express train through the Alps into Milan, where Mary weeps at the sight of *The Last Supper* on the refectory wall at the convent of Santa Maria delle Grazie.

They ride the milk train south through the Cinque Terre on the western coast of Italy, stopping half a dozen times for the goats or cows who've strayed onto the track from a nearby farm. They laugh to see these barnyard animals grazing on the weeds sprouting between the tracks, oblivious to the exasperated horn-blowings of the conductor. As the train proceeds, the two of them sit watching the sunshine glittering on the water as if it's the first time they've ever laid eyes on the ocean. In Florence, at the top of the Duomo, they meet a pair of honeymooners from Edinburgh and the husband takes their picture with Mary's Rolleiflex (while Mary teeters on an overturned egg crate). Mary reciprocates, and copies their address on the back of a dinner receipt.

Some days they don't leave their room until three in the afternoon, both of them blushing faintly at the decadence of it. He leads her down narrow, winding streets, laundry strung across the lane two stories above their heads, and she smiles unseeing at everything she passes, dogs and children and naked poultry hanging in the butcher's window. Mostly her thoughts return to that sublime soreness in the space between her legs.

They time their arrival in Siena for the Palio, the annual horse race, and they cheer for the Unicorn *contrada* because their pensione is located in that section of the city. Afterwards, in broken Italian, Mary begs the elderly proprietress of the Trattoria delle Due Stelle, in vain, for her ribollita recipe. In years to come Teddy will return home from the hospital every so often to find heaps of peeled potatoes and red cabbage and week-old Italian bread all over the kitchen counters, his wife smiling sheepishly above the cutting board. "Oh, rabbit," he'll sigh contentedly. "Not again!"

It will take her twenty-seven years of experimenting with quantities of herbs and vegetables and varieties of bread to make a stew that can even approximate the divine ribollita they'd had in that restaurant on that sunny August afternoon, at that little table by the window: flawless black-purple aubergines and ripe zucchini long as her arm spilling out of the grocery stalls across the cobblestone street, the steam rising off their bowls in delicate furls, a portrait of Victor Emmanuel II hanging askew on the wall above Teddy's head.

SEPTEMBER 1929
25 University Avenue

DESPITE THE OVERPROTECTIVE presence of a maiden aunt and self-proclaimed housekeeper, they are fortunate, these two—and they know it. In the evenings, when he returns from his late lecture, they go for an amble through the labyrinth while Aunt Cecelia is cooking supper. With an impish twirl of her heel Mary drops Teddy's hand and disappears through an archway in the hedge, and he finds her again only by the trail of smoke from her cigarette.

Her father insists upon moving into the corner room down the hall, and they transfer their clothing into the two wardrobes in the master bedroom. A few of her mother's dresses still hang in the wardrobe by the window, but Mary can't bring herself to take them down from the rack. Aunt Cecelia rocks herself to sleep at night in the third-floor turret, knitting pair after pair of baby booties.

Teddy's first cousin, having spent the better part of the decade on the fringes of the Parisian avant-garde, has created a fountain out of 379 spoons collected from estate sales all over Europe and New England, teaspoons and soup spoons and serving spoons, spoons made of silver and copper and tin: a wedding gift either appalling or ingenious, depending on one's taste. In most labyrinths the center is of little aesthetic interest, in keeping with the classical notion that the journey matters more than whatever may await one at the finish. Mary finds the spoon fountain to be a suitable reward.

Water travels up through a lead pipe at the center and, after a modest vertical display, cascades into the concave surfaces of the spoons at the highest tier, trickling down in ever more delicate rivulets, each descending spoon bent carefully to catch the small streams deflected from the spoons above it. Mary hooks the pipe into the marble pedestal above the old fishpond at the center of the labyrinth, turns on the water, and backs through the archway to watch: at a distance the spoon fountain is an amorphous mass, shiny and chaotic. Purple hydrangeas nod in the breeze as though in approval, but the goldfish slip through the murky green waters below, unimpressed.

In the kitchen, the scent of baking bread and the makings of the evening's repast, roast beef or vegetable stew; and on the pantry shelf, a tidy row of early peach and strawberry preserves from the Morrigan farm on the Cape. Aunt Cecelia reads in a ladies' magazine that burning dried herbs and spices brings good luck to the newly wed in a new home, and though the home may not be new it can do no harm to light a small fire in the great room. The scents of sage and clove permeate the ground floor. Two weeks later Mary will even catch a whiff of it while sorting boxes in the attic, where the housekeeper's wind chimes would ring if only someone could pry the windows open.

The second-floor turret room, her former bedroom, needs repapering. Mary chooses something cheerful, tiny pink rosettes on a pale yellow background—the right sort of wallpaper for a nursery. She picks the most sentimental record in her collection—what else but "My Blue

Heaven"?—and sets the gramophone on a night table at the center of the room, humming to herself as she lays the paper.

The needle skips as it reaches the end of the record. Distracted from cutting the final strip by a Painted Lady beating its wings against the window, Mary slices herself along the base of her thumb. Blood drips onto the hardwood floor and the razor falls at her feet.

"*Drat,*" she says, with all the fierceness of a barroom swear. She stumbles down the back stairs with her left hand swaddled in her apron, a sticky red line dribbling down her forearm.

Chromosome 2,
SLC1A4: *An excerpt*

1 *cccgcactctgcgcctctcctcgcctttctcgcacctgctcctgcgccaggccgcgagacccccggggcggcttcccag*

80 *aacctgcggagcacaactggccgaccgacccattcattgggaaccccgtcttttgccagagcccacgtcccctgcc*

156 *acctctagctcggagcggcgtgtagcgccatggagaagagcaacgagaccaacggctaccttgacagcgctca*

229 *ggcggggcctgcggccgggcccggagctccggggaccgcggcgggacgcgcacggcgttgcgcgggcttcctgcgg*

308 *cgccaagcgctggtgctgctcaccgtgtccggggtgctggcgggcgcgggcctgggcgcggcgttgcgcgggctcag*

385 *cctgagccgcacgcaggtcacctacctggccttccccggcgagatgctgctccgcatgctgcgcatgatcatcctgc*

462 *cgctggtggtctgcagcctggtgtcgggcgccgcctccctcgatgccagctgcctcgggcgtctgggcggcatcgctgt*

541 *cgcctactttggcctcaccacactgagtgcctcggcgctcgccgtggccttggcgttcatcatcaagccaggatccgg*

619 *tgcgcagacccttcagtccagcgacctggggctggaggactcggggcctcctcctgtccccaaagagacggtgga*

694 *ctctttcctcgacctggccagaaacctgtttccctccaatcttgtggttgcagctttccgtacgtatgcaaccgattat*

773 *aaagtcgtgacccagaacagcagctctggaaatgtaacccatgaaaagatccccataggcactgagatagaa*

845 *gggatgaacattttaggattggtcctgtttgctctggtgttaggagtggccttaaagaaactaggctccgaagga*

920 *gaagacctcatccgtttcttcaattccctcaacgaggcgacgatggtgctggtgtcctggattatgtggtacgtac*

996 *ctgtgggcatcatgttccttgttggaagcaagatcgtggaaatgaaagacatcatcgtgctggtgaccagcctg*

1070 *gggaaatacatcttcgcatctatattgggccatgttattcatggaggaattgttctgccacttatttattttgttttca*

1149 *cacgaaaaaacccattcagattcctcctgggcctcctcgccccatttgcgacagcatttgcgacagcatttgctac . . .*

III

PARTHENOGENESIS

Had I a right, for my own benefit, to inflict this curse upon everlasting generations?

—MARY SHELLEY,

Frankenstein (1818)

WEDNESDAY, 12 MARCH 2008 ~ 9:12 A.M.
Hasbro Fertility Clinic ~ New Halcyon

WELCOME TO THE DANCE of the gametes in a theater fit for the Age of Space, the stage a flat-screen monitor in an adjacent room attended by women in white lab coats. It's a relief, in a way, knowing that he will never be subjected to any greater humiliation than the one he is presently enduring.

Gray keeps his eyes down, on one of the little blue buttons on Lucy's blouse. "I can't believe I'm fornicating in a doctor's office . . . in front of an *audience.*"

"Thank you for doing this," she says.

He doesn't answer her.

"Please don't sulk, Gray. I didn't twist your arm."

But she knows how difficult it is for him to say no, to her or to anyone—she knows this, and she asked him anyway.

FRIDAY, 14 MARCH 2008 ~ 9:32 A.M.
Hasbro Fertility Clinic

IT'S NOT A YEAR'S WORTH of poor timing that's brought them here. That much is clear from the manner in which the doctor ushers them into his office.

"Your situation is quite rare," he begins.

"Whose?"

"Yours, Lucy. It's not the eggs, the eggs are perfectly viable. But your immune system is producing antisperm antibodies. Essentially your uterus treats all sperm as foreign i—"

"Yes," she says quietly. "I know what it means."

"Fortunately, we can remedy the situation with relative ease. There's intrauterine insemination, which is a fairly straightforward solution—"

The very last place she wants to be is in a doctor's consulting room discussing her "options." She thanks him, briskly, and leaves the office, Gray stuttering an apology in her wake.

"Defective," she murmurs as she hurries down the clinic steps, still struggling into her coat. "I'm defective."

SATURDAY, 15 MARCH 2008 ~ 2:48 P.M.
25 University Avenue

LUCY HIDES THE BEDROOM dresser mirror in the back of a hall closet. She loathes the sight of herself, and why shouldn't she? Her body cannot achieve the very thing for which it was designed.

She's been known to while away an hour or two in the attic, usually when she doesn't wish to be found. This occurs most often around the first of the month, when without fail at least two members of the Seventh Order will seek her out and inform her apologetically that their rent checks will be a few days late. The attic becomes her refuge whenever Gray mentions that his mother is planning another visit to New Halcyon.

Most attics are unpleasant places: cobwebs swaying in the breath of stale wind stirred up by the opening of the door, or perhaps a draft through a hole in the roof or a broken windowpane; the smells of mildew and dust and mothballs; the fear that any given thing you touch will fall to pieces in your hands. Even the natural oil on a clean fingertip leaves a stain on old wood. Why come here, why putter through all these material reminders of lives long since lived?

But there's more life in *this* attic than you'll find in most people's living rooms. Rocking horses and brightly painted toy chests bearing the names of their erstwhile owners across the broad convex lids; more wooden chests, lined with cedar and stacked to the lid with neatly folded sheets, towels, and undergarments; a large cardboard box labeled SCRAPS FOR QUILTMAKING on a set of shelves; below it, on the floor, the needles tucked through spools of thread in a small wicker basket; and above, on the top shelf, a row of paint, wallpaper, and fabric sample books; rusted film canisters; and leather diaries filled with the meticulous notes and diagrams of autodidactic naturalists, all the former heads of this household, their observations laid down on heavy paper in ink as black as it was then. Beside these shelves, a card catalog Ambrose had salvaged from the public library's technological overhaul some fifteen years ago, all the cards from A to Z still filed (though in the back of the drawers one might find the most curious additions: rocks from Tenochtitlán, Inis Mór, Maromokotro; a cachet of old love letters; or worry-stones of clear green glass). On top of the card catalog sit a Remington Rand typewriter case (Colin has appropriated the machine itself); a pewter spirit-kettle, circa 1850, for making tea *en transit;* and her mother's vintage camera collection.

Rusted wind chimes and baby mobiles made of pressed leaves and paper swallows hang from the rafters of the pitched roof. Far removed from the dust-laden sunlight that has found its way in, filtered through the oak trees outside the dormer windows (the sills lined with dead houseflies and empty perfume bottles), there are hulking masses of worn-out furniture, scuffed bureaus and tables and chairs with wobbly legs, all stacked carefully beneath the quilted dustcovers. It's all still here because someday someone is going to carry every stick of it downstairs and out to the backyard to reglue, strip, sand, and refinish. Surely someone will, one of these decades. Atop one of the hooded chests of drawers is a red-and-green metal Christmas tree stand she hasn't used since 2002. This corner smells of pine needles and turpentine.

She pulls the scrap box off the shelf and sorts through the crisply folded fabrics, leftovers from old projects and a few cotton sundresses.

Every dress bears a stain that never came out or a rip too conspicuous to mend—like the periwinkle one with the pearly buttons down the back and a torn crochet collar that Lucy imagines her grandmother wore when her grandfather took her to the pictures. Holding each garment up to her chest, she envisions how it looked when it was new and fashionable.

At the bottom of the box she finds a yellow calico apron with a bloodstain like a Rorschach blot on the skirt, the stain still vivid despite the good washing her grandmother must have given the apron.

Lucy sits in the armchair by the window for a good long while with the apron spread in her lap, idly fingering the waist-ties as she rides a very peculiar train of thought. Then with a sure step she descends the front staircase, pulling the basement door keys out of her side skirt pocket as she goes.

WEDNESDAY, 19 MARCH 2008 ~ 2:17 A.M.
The Basement

THE GEORGETTE NIGHT ROBE billows behind her as she skips down the steps. The delicate fabric flirts with her bare legs, a feeling so pleasurable that she will permit herself to wear it only on extraordinary occasions. It was part of Mary's trousseau.

She makes a pot of Fair Trade organic coffee and over the course of the night drinks half a dozen cups, settling herself into the leather armchair at the computer and propping her feet up on a small stool that has her name burned into the wood in capital letters beneath a three-banded rainbow, a babyhood relic.

She pours another dollop of cream into her cup, stirring as she watches the letters scrolling by the thousands down the computer screen, *aaaaaatgccgaaggcatgaacccgaatgctctctaccgcgaatgctctctaccgcgaatgctcgg-atctaccgggggggggagatattttgcccccgcgctctcaaaaaatgccgaaggcatgaacccgaatgctcgg,* mesmerized, as though she were scanning through another breaking piece of catastrophic world news. Even with a state-of-the-art processor the sequencing takes three full days, but she's enjoyed the wait. It's only a lark to her, a fine alternative to another night of fitful slumber, until the program chirps to signal the completion of the sequencing:

L. Morrigan *and* M. Morrigan,
99.99999729% MATCH.

Why spend this much time comparing her own DNA sequence with that of her grandmother? The differences between family members are infinitesimal, after all. Seeing as there are no surprises to be found here, it's the closest a bio-geek like Lucy comes to a thorough waste of time.

Tossing her head back, she drains the last cold cup of coffee, with granules of raw sugar left undissolved at the bottom, and as she toddles to the sink on stiff legs to wash out her cup, yawning widely, her thoughts begin to assemble themselves like little cardboard puzzle pieces falling onto a table in just the right arrangement. Standing in the center of the lab, in an unself-conscious fashion she places her hand on her satin-covered abdomen and considers: there are her mother's eggs still moldering in the back of the lab fridge; the complete DNA sample out of a speck at the bottom of a test tube there on the table, astonishing to her that it could have been preserved at all; the sleek steel contraption in the corner (the clear plastic casing filched from the Air Force junkyard in the dead of an autumn night in the early eighties), the plug on the floor beneath the wall socket, never once tested as far as she's aware.

Faced with all this, a crackpot like her father wouldn't hesitate a moment: replace the contents of the egg with the contents of the test tube, apply an electrical pulse to the new egg, and watch it divide. God only knows, he might've already attempted it in the simwomb. Would he have told Megan, if he had?

Megan's been down here dozens of times since Lucy's father's death, but only once has she ever made reference to the device beneath the dustcover. "Don't ever touch that piece of junk," she'd said. "You'll spend the rest of your life regretting it."

Lucy's pulse twitches wildly at her temples, her wrists, her throat, as if several someones were poking her gently with invisible fingertips, silently seeking her attention.

All right, Megan—she won't. Hand still pressed to her abdomen, Lucy knows she doesn't have to.

SATURDAY, 22 MARCH 2008 ~ 2:11 A.M.

The Third-Floor Turret Room

SICILY—TAORMINA, maybe—or some little town on the Amalfi coast? Of course, they can decide after they've purchased the tickets. Seeing as he's never known her to take a day off work, she ought to have a full two weeks' vacation. Gray leans back in his rolly-chair and imagines how her eyes will light up when he tells her where they're going.

Lucy knocks softly. "Are you almost ready for bed? There's something I want to talk to you about."

"Me, too." Gray bookmarks the musty volume in front of him, and she regards him with mild surprise. "I'll be right down."

"Okay," she says, turning on the threshold. "We'll talk."

Gray sits frowning at the empty doorway. Whatever it is she has to say, she knows he's not going to like it.

2:36 A.M.

Anteroom to the Master Bedroom

"NO, I WILL *NOT* hear you out. I just wish I had known two years ago you were clinically insane."

"Where are you going?"

"I'm going to sleep in the office."

"Where?" She laughs. "On the floor?"

"I'll drag a mattress out of the attic. Move aside, Lu."

"Just let me explain—"

"There's nothing to explain. You can't clone a dead person. It's impossible."

"So you're the expert now, are you?"

He folds his arms. "Twenty-five words or less. And then I'm going to bed."

She takes a breath to steady herself before she begins: "It's true that the membrane around a donor cell must be intact. A month ago I'd have said that cloning only the very recently deceased would be possible. But Gray—Gray, I've figured out how to reconstruct that membrane. I can make a baby girl who has a hundred percent of Mary's genes."

"You're the only person I know who's on a first-name basis with her own grandmother." He stares at her: she looks so fragile all of a sudden, like her skin is made of glass. The circles under her eyes make her look half-dead.

"What?" she says. "What are you looking at?"

"Normal people just adopt a child, you know that? What you want to do is pretty obscene, when you think of all those poor kids living in group homes!"

"It isn't a matter of infertility. This could be a massive breakthrough—something without precedent—if only I can . . ."

He summons all his willpower to keep from shaking her. So much for Taormina. "Listen to yourself," he says. "You're blinded by your own ego."

"Answer me this: What would you do, if you were me?"

A long and awkward silence follows. "You're going to harvest your own eggs?"

She shakes her head. "I'd use one of my mother's. For God's sake, Gray, don't look at me like I eat roadkill for breakfast."

"You've made all this progress?" he asks. "By yourself?"

"Well . . . no." The flush of discovery fades from her cheeks. "I found it." She pauses. "In his notes."

MONDAY, 28 APRIL 2008 ~ 1:22 P.M.
University of New Halcyon ~ The Quad

LUCY WILL NEVER comprehend the worldviews of those who condone needless wars and call themselves pro-life, who boycott deep-fried potato sticks and call it foreign policy, who believe evolution is no more than a crackpot theory. Heck, they'll believe any old hogwash spewed by their self-proclaimed "reverends." They're just a lot of jar-heads and Jesus freaks, recovering alkies in need of a new addiction.

In one swift glance Lucy surveys the scene on the quad, crossing her fingers that she doesn't spot Charles Harris Fuller among them. The most shameless and persistent reverend of all isn't here, thank goodness. "Stop stem cell research at NHU!" cries a young man in a suit and tie. The cobblestone avenue is carpeted with the flyers he's been pressing into the hands of students on their way to and from the library.

The Christian Union—better known, without affection, as "the God Squad"—is waging this particular campaign, though naturally it is winning few converts. None that Lucy can find, in fact—but failure only increases the venom in the members' rhetoric. She'd rather see the PETA kids out here with posters of monkeys under vivisection, and that's saying something. Adrenaline courses through her as she approaches the table, staffed by two girls who look frighteningly normal, aside from the Tiffany necklaces and open-toed high-heel shoes. Never trust a girl with a French pedicure.

"Excuse me," she calls to the boy in the suit. He turns to her, scowling, and she realizes with a start that he already knows who she is.

Lucy waves a hand at the paper-strewn walkway behind them. "I could have you shut down by the maintenance department for littering, you know."

"We have a permit from the Activities Office," he replies coldly. There it is, that tacky little flag pin stuck to his lapel. "It isn't my business if the students of this university are too lazy to dispose of their trash—"

"Oh, they've disposed of it! But perhaps if you gave them some propaganda worth reading—"

"You're wasting your time here," says one of the girls at the table.

"That's rich," Lucy says. "You're the people protesting what you clearly don't understand."

The boy in the suit crosses his arms as a gaggle of freshmen pass him by, a prime opportunity forfeited to a lost cause. "On the contrary, Miss Morrigan: *you* are the one in need of greater understanding."

Lucy stares at him coldly. "How do you know my name?" (And it's *Doctor* Morrigan, actually, but one must focus one's energies on the greater battle.)

"Everyone on campus knows your name, Miss Morrigan. We *want* them to know who you are—and what you do for a living."

"I'm working on a cure for Huntington's disease. What do *you* do for a living?"

"We're going to shut you down." He leans toward her, his rage shimmering beneath the placidly arrogant exterior. "Make no mistake about that. You won't be harvesting babies much longer. I suggest you start looking for a new job, Miss Morrigan."

Lucy makes no attempt at a dignified reply this time. "I hope you get Alzheimer's, you little shit! *ALZHEIMER'S*!"

For a few seconds the crowd on the quad watch in stunned silence as Lucy stomps away from the table. Then they begin to cheer.

LATE APRIL, 2008 ~ EARLY MORNING

25 University Avenue ~ The Basement

STRANGE THOUGHTS COME to the scientist's daughter in the witching hours. Lucy has spent half her life in this basement, but late at night she often pauses in her work, disoriented, having forgotten the whereabouts of equipment she's used two or three minutes earlier. She is passing her prime in this laboratory, yet she often feels like she doesn't belong here at all; and it isn't just her body craving the coolness of the bedsheets. It's still these rooms she belongs to, but part of her would rather be living here in a time well before the floor of the wine cellar was laid in cold white tile. The only time this baby will spend in the basement is the time before she's born.

What was it Megan said that afternoon at the veggie restaurant? *You ought to have been a poet!* Giggling fondly at the recollection, Lucy takes a sip of cold coffee before returning to her microscope.

THURSDAY, 1 MAY 2008 (DAY 1) ~ 9:46 P.M.
The Basement

THREE WEEKS AGO she had allowed him a peek at the contents of the culture dish beneath the stark white light of the electron microscope, what had seemed to him nothing more than an eerie pageant of swelling, shivering orbs.

Watching the slow and steady movements of Lucy's latexed hands, a hollow needle clasped between her thumb and forefinger, he assumed that he would play no integral part in this ludicrous scheme of hers. He was mistaken, of course.

So now it's his turn to don the latex. Reclining on a padded doctor's table she found in the junk pile behind the wine rack, her feet resting in a pair of stirrups, Lucy extends an arm behind her to tap the computer screen. "Here," she says. "Drop it here." The largest of these screens is hooked up to a fiber-optic camera the size of a needle point that is currently braving the murky recesses of her feminine terrain. Her uterine walls cover the length and breadth of the screen, the image pulsing with every heartbeat. He's stricken with claustrophobia just glancing at it from his miserable perch between her thighs.

"Gray . . . Gray? . . . I need you to pay attention here, darling."

"If I'm doing such a rotten job then you can ask one of the holy men upstairs to take over."

"Let's just do it, all right? We'll do it quickly and it'll be over and done with."

He shakes his head. "I take issue with your choice of phrase."

"Try not to make any unnecessary movements, all right? You'll lose the embryo."

Gray wants to hop up and down on the swivel chair just to spite her. But if he lost the embryo she'd only try again—though she'd give Megan the job this time. He'd asked Lucy more than once why she hadn't told Megan about this plan of hers, but she'd never given him a straight answer.

"Hey, Lu?"

"Yes?"

"Who's Skippy?"

"Who?"

"You were talking to 'Skippy' in your sleep one night. I thought he must have been an old pet of yours."

"Hmm," she says. "No idea. Dad was allergic to animals. That's what he *said,* anyway."

In silence he watches the tentative movements of his own instrument on the screen above her head. Lucy regards his face with affectionate amusement: such concentration! He looks like a five-year-old learning how to tie his shoes.

"I think I've done it," he says with a sigh. Gray has successfully impregnated his girlfriend.

SATURDAY, 17 MAY 2008 (DAY 17)
The Parlor

TO CELEBRATE THE result of the home pregnancy test they drink sparkling grape juice out of tulip glasses, though Lucy seems so deliriously happy she might as well be sloshed. The VCR offers a window into her fondest childhood memories: a special-edition leather-bound set of *The Chronicles of Narnia* unwrapped in a frenzy on Christmas morning, her grandmother placidly sipping her tea as Ambrose provides commentary from behind the camcorder; "playing" a red plastic ukulele as Mary sings some little ditty ("Gonna dance with a dolly with a hole in her stocking"); the two of them bent over a patchwork quilt, Lucy so thrilled to be helping that she doesn't notice her grandmother very discreetly ripping the seam she's just sewn; baking Christmas cookies with her father, red icing smeared all over her mouth, and when her father says "Lucy-bear, I believe the cookies are ready," Gray finally notices the irony of the oven alert; and the party for her eighth birthday, for which Ambrose borrowed a trio of Indonesian tortoises bigger than any of the children from a herpetologist who "owed" him "a favor." Gray shakes his head at footage of the poor creatures plodding through the labyrinth for the amusement of Lucy's classmates; one boy nudges the oldest, slowest turtle into a dead end and it falls asleep to avoid extricating itself. From off camera they can hear Mary telling Ambrose in a stern voice that "enough is enough" and suggesting, "Why don't I cut the cake while you phone your friend from the zoo?"

He sneaks a glance and finds her crying silently, the blue glare flashing on her face as images shift on the screen.

SATURDAY, 7 JUNE 2008 (DAY 38) ~ 11:10 A.M.
The Kitchen

PARTHENOGENESIS *(Par-thin-oh-JEN-uh-sis): Noun. The development of an unfertilized, usually female gamete, a phenomenon that occurs especially among the lower plants and invertebrate animals.* He watches her as she shuffles around the kitchen in her nightdress, making herself a cup of chamomile tea with a smile that might look serene or smug, depending on one's prior opinion of the girl herself. There is a photograph album on the table opened to a wedding portrait of Lucy's parents. Sipping his coffee with an air of domestic contentment unique to sunny weekend mornings, he turns the cellophaned pages and studies each photograph with keen interest.

"I can't get over it," he murmurs.

"What's that?"

"How much you look like your mother."

Lucy laughs as she stirs a spoonful of raw sugar into her cup. "I guess you never learned that's the number one most irritating thing you can say to a girl."

"Sorry." Gray frowns as he finishes his coffee. "You know, it only just occurred to me while I was trying to get to sleep last night that everyone is going to think you're cuckolding me."

"Hush," she says. "You keep forgetting the walls have ears."

"How are you going to explain it?"

Lucy slides into the chair beside him with a shrug. "I won't."

"Really?"

"Really."

He sighs. "The gossip in the department is going to be pretty nearly unbearable."

"Can't be helped, I'm afraid."

Gray turns another page. "You have so few baby photos."

"I was always in the hospital."

"Ah, yes," he says. "The rash that devoured your face."

She pulls a jumbo chocolate bar out of the junk food cabinet above the refrigerator and returns to the table with it. For such a sickly child she'd turned out hardy enough, all right—he marvels at the way her skin glistens with a hormonal radiance. Anyone could tell from half a mile that there's a little one on the way.

As she eats the candy she rolls her eyes heavenward with a sort of groan he's never heard from her before. Near swooning, she licks her fingertip and touches the crinkly foil wrapper to lift stray shards of chocolate; the finger returns to her mouth and a few moments later she seems to have remembered he's sitting beside her. "Have a piece?"

He breaks off a square and puts it in his mouth. It's cheap chocolate with a faintly plasticky consistency, but to her it's ambrosia. Will he become one of those partners guilt-tripped into driving forty miles in search of kumquat ice cream? He wouldn't put it past her to make such frivolous demands. Lucy may delight in her pencil skirts and seamed stockings, but there's no question of who wears the pants in this household.

Lucy crumples the candy wrapper and lobs it into the trash can. As she casts a glance at the kitchen doorway a brightness comes over her immediately, the classic we-have-company face. "Colin! And how are you this fine Saturday morning?"

With a spindly finger Colin flips the switch on the coffeemaker. "Not too bad, Miss M. I see the cravings are kicking in." She looks at him blankly. "There's a ring of chocolate all around your mouth."

Lucy laughs as Gray hands her a napkin. Since Lucy has become pregnant—impregnated herself, rather—her five boarders have been spending more time downstairs. They no longer haunt these rooms; they inhabit them. He supposes it's this new aura of hers that's the cause of it: two months ago she was a pallid slip of a thing, gimlet-eyed and mildly anemic, and now she looks like a poster girl for the dairy industry. The boys are drawn to her, whether by hormones or through some subliminal desire for maternal affection.

Thus their distinguishing features have emerged: Dewey shaves his head, and with his delicate features he looks disconcertingly like Sinéad O'Connor; Rob removes the pale red stubble on his chin only on Sundays (with an antique ivory-handled razor he'd found in the chest of drawers in his bedroom and that Lucy had allowed him to keep); poor Milo is so nearsighted that three rounds of Lasik surgery haven't enabled him to donate his eyeglasses to the Salvation Army; and Felix carries himself in such a way that if you dressed him in an expensive suit he could very nearly pass for an investment banker (albeit one who keeps the hours of the Japanese market).

Colin is the tallest member of the Seventh Order, and the thinnest. When Gray sees him it's almost always at the coffeemaker, and his idea of a square meal seems to be a lone slice of toasted unbuttered Wonder bread, on which he nibbles like a mouse, trailing crumbs out of the kitchen and up the rear staircase back to his room. Gray watches him as he loosens the twisty-tie on the polka-dot bread bag. "So tell me, Lucy," Colin says. "When are you due?"

"January," Lucy replies, and Gray notices how she bites her lip in self-reproach. She's already begun to show through her nightgown. He also notices with a pang of horror that her nipples are visible through the bodice. It's too warm for a robe, but couldn't she have gotten dressed before coming downstairs?

Of course not, he realizes as he's shifting his chair in what he hopes is a subtle attempt to obscure Colin's view of her chest. The Willendorf Venus wouldn't wear shorts and a T-shirt.

One might suppose that the members of the Seventh Order of Saint Agatha would respond to news of pregnancy outside the bonds of holy matrimony with some perceptible measure of disgust, but they seem more curious than anything else. Then again, "Order of Saint Agatha" has always been a misnomer: as any of them would tell you, their little fraternity is rooted in intellectual rather than moral dissent. Lucy is merely a product of her times, and besides, someone has to propagate this wretched species. She might as well do so with somebody as reliable as Gray.

Nevertheless, Colin regards her now with an air of forgiveness for sins it isn't his place to pardon, in the way an apostle might have looked upon Mary Magdalene. Lucy responds with an unspoken countercondescension. If she has fallen from the grace of some imaginary deity, she has descended on her own terms, and it is her long-held belief that men like Colin join cults of celibacy only because they've been resoundingly unsuccessful in the modern mating dance.

The toaster ejects one piece of toast as Colin pours himself a cup of coffee—black, no sugar—and a bowl of cornflakes. Why are those five always eating cornflakes at all hours of the day and night?

Colin nods to Gray as he ascends the back stairs with his toast balanced on the lip of his coffee cup. "You look lovely, Lucy," he calls when only his lower torso is visible. "You have my very best wishes." Gray wrinkles his nose as he returns to the photograph album.

2:15 P.M.
Third-Floor Turret Room

DISHEARTENED BY HIS book's rank on the Barnes & Noble website—it is just about the same as the population of Massachusetts—he backhands a Spanish orange into the air. *"Gallia est omnis divisa in partēs trēs . . . Gallia est omnis divisa in partēs trēs . . ."*

"Gray?" Colin's head appears in the doorway as Gray tosses the orange upward again. The fruit falls on the floor with a thump and he curses himself for leaving the door open.

"Sorry to bother you"—snide little bastard, isn't he?—"but Lucy wanted me to tell you there's something she needs your help with down in the basement." He follows Colin down the back stairs, suffering bravely through the awkward silence.

When she opens the door for him, her blouse and forearms are streaked with black dust. "There's a rocking chair behind the wine rack I want for the baby's room. I tried to pull it out on my own, but there's too much junk piled up in front of it. Would you mind giving me a hand?"

Later this afternoon she will feel it, the quickening—three months too soon—and after this she won't dare attend another Lamaze class.

MONDAY, 9 JUNE 2008 (DAY 40) ~ 10:30 A.M.
University of New Halcyon ~ Kellman Building,
East Wing Lab 61A

THE CHATTER AT THE LAB begins innocuously enough. Mrs. Bunce, the part-time technician, is the first to ask if she knows the sex of the baby.

Lucy smiles to herself. "It's a girl."

"A daughter, how lovely! Have you thought of a name yet?"

"I thought I might name her after my grandmother."

"Mrs. Morrigan?"

Lucy nods. "Though Gray thinks 'Mary' is too old-fashioned . . ." Called after the mother of a modern God, yet the name can't shake its air of mournful effigies crossed with polka-dot kitchen aprons. He'd argued in vain for another name—any other name at all—but not for the reason she's been telling people.

"Of course not, dear." Mrs. Bunce smoothes a lock of hair out of Lucy's eyes and Lucy flinches. Such offhand gestures of spurious affection always leave her feeling violated. "It's a good name, a good Christian name," says Mrs. Bunce.

Lucy turns back to the magnified image of a nerve cell cluster on her monitor. Still two hours 'til lunchtime! As her grandmother used to say, the hunger of the world is on her—hunger enough for two, anyway. The nerve cell cluster begins to resemble a portobello sandwich.

MONDAY, 23 JUNE 2008 (DAY 54) ~ 1:15 P.M.
Tepplethwaite Building, 4th Floor ~ Classics Department

HE'S NOT SURE how they found out about Lucy; someone must have run into her on campus someplace. Starved for gossip, the daytime inhabitants of these cramped and windowless offices gather at the coffeemaker to speak of The Baby, their vicarious excitement spreading down the hallway like an airborne disease. The head of the department hands him a cheap cigar wrapped in cellophane and his secretary orders two dozen vanilla cupcakes with rainbow sprinkles from the local bakery. The questions keep coming: "When did you find out?" "She must be thrilled!" "It was planned, wasn't it?" "Aren't you excited!" "Boy or girl?" "When's your baby due?"

His baby? This is weirding him out.

"Hey, Gray," says the new wunderkind, whose dissertation has recently won him a contract with a major New York publishing house—because his girlfriend is an editor there. "Congrats, man!" (Gray looks him over with a cold eye. What is all this "hey, man" stuff? He'll be up for tenure the year after next and this kid's still buying maximum-strength Oxy pads by the gross.) "I hear you're pregnant." Then he chuckles like a game show host—insolent little turd!

"Yes, well." Gray pats his abs without the slightest trace of a smile. "I won't begin to show for another month."

"Ha, ha! You're a real joker, Gray! Ha, ha, ha!"

The department secretary, a faded Southern belle who, Gray feels certain, dons her frilly white debutante gown on the second Sunday of every month to prove she has maintained her girlish figure, actually tells him that "mixed babies are just the cutest."

He can't even muster enough presence of mind to ask her for a clarification, which should rightfully take the form of a red-faced, sputtering attempt to pretend she hasn't actually said what he's just heard her say. The potted plants on the windowsill behind her desk are flourishing like worms on pavement in the middle of a heat wave and her parents donate a five-figure minimum to the Republican Party on an annual basis. "Do me a favor, Marla," he says.

She smiles indulgently. "Yeeees, Professor Poupon?"

"I'd appreciate it if you wouldn't speak to me unless it's absolutely necessary." He turns around and walks back to his office, picturing her staring at his back, dumbstruck, her mouth agape for so long that a thin line of slobber pools on the shelf of her pink chiffon blouse. Leave it to those godless bureaucrats to appoint such a twit to the organizational hub of the Classics and Medieval Studies Departments. (Budget cuts had forced the merger. There's now a dilapidated suit of armor, four feet tall and ugly as an armadillo, blocking the quickest route from his office to the watercooler.)

No sooner has he settled into his desk chair with the door closed than a troupe of freshmen are outside clamoring for entry. (Damn these office hours! He ought to post a notice on the door, something to the effect of "Available on prime-numbered Fridays between the times of 3:19 and 3:22 p.m." When the department head asks, he'll explain that the notice is only a gag.) It wouldn't be so intolerable if some of the more capable students ever stopped by, but for some reason it's only the skateboarding Kool-Aid huffers who show up week after week.

"Come in," he says tonelessly.

There are three of them leering in the doorway clutching half-eaten vanilla cupcakes, their mouths smeared with icing. "Hey, Doc! Congrats! We heard y—"

"Yes, yes—did you have a question for me?"

The boys trade glances. "Your eyebrow's twitching," one of them says tentatively. "You all right, Doc?"

SUNDAY, 27 JULY 2008 (DAY 88) ~ 8:05 P.M.
25 University Avenue ~ The Labyrinth

HER INITIAL FONDNESS for hand-holding hadn't bothered him; truth be told, when she'd stopped reaching for his hand on the evening walks home from campus he'd felt a twinge of disappointment. Now that she's hormonal she's started the reach-and-squeeze again in the privacy of her own hedge maze, but the way she rests her other hand on her middle only irritates him. She's swiped a pair of his running shoes, too, for her feet have swollen two and a half sizes.

He hesitates before a fork in the path. One way leads to a dead end, but he can't remember which. The heavy scent of honeysuckle makes his nose itch.

"Come on, Gray." She huffs. "You've walked this a hundred times if you've walked it once."

"Which is still a million fewer times than *you've* walked it," he mutters. He tries to drop her hand, but she renews her grip and pulls him to the right.

"There are five different ways to reach the center of this thing," she says. "Did you notice that?"

He doesn't answer her.

"I guess you've only ever walked it the easiest way."

"I didn't come out here to be ridiculed, you know."

Finally she drops his hand. "I'm sorry," she murmurs, pressing her palms to her eyelids. "I don't know what's wrong with me."

Gray pauses. "I think you should go to the doctor. What's-his-name at the clinic, your dad's old friend."

Lucy drops her hands and shakes her head, and a look of terror flashes beneath that mask of serenity. "I can't," she murmurs, turning away from him to finish the maze on her own.

MONDAY AND TUESDAY, 28 AND 29 JULY 2008
(DAYS 89 AND 90)
New Halcyon

PEOPLE'S JOKES IN THE LAB, the cafeteria, and even the ladies' lavatory become more insistent. Her skin is slick with a cold sweat and she shivers in the ninety-degree afternoons on the short walk home, which takes twice as long as it used to. Paranoia sets in like a slow-moving virus. The night passes, as most nights do, between a shallow and fragmentary slumber and trips to the toilet that seem to her like epic journeys.

The following morning, ten past nine: "*How* far along did you say you were?"

"Six . . . six and a half months." Lucy has always been a terrible liar, though for some blessed reason no one concerns himself with the arithmetic.

Twenty past eleven: "Jesus, you're the size of a house!"

A quarter to one: "So, Lu, when do you start calving?"

Four-thirty: "What's the verdict, then? Quintuplets?"

"No." She doesn't look up from the microscope. "Just one."

"Is he coming out fully grown, or what?"

"Ha, ha," she says flatly. "Guess I've been eating too much spinach." Is it a mistake, not telling them she's having more than one?

Any fewer than triplets becomes less plausible by the day. Quadruplets, she should have told them. She could have explained away the other three when the time came.

The following day the interrogations come to an abrupt halt. The guys in the lab stare at the floor when passing her in the hallway. Students eye her openly in the library elevators. Mrs. Bunce examines her whenever her back is turned; more than once Lucy has caught the woman's frowning reflection on her own computer screen.

Lucy rests her hands on this swelling mound of flesh—a casual gesture of feigned serenity. This is not normal; she isn't so obtuse, clearly she's made some sort of mistake. From a dusty corner of her memory, a snippet of audio surfaces, something she'd overheard her father saying to Megan in the sanctuary of the basement lab a very long time ago—Lucy had been so young, in fact, that she'd had no business being there at all, but Ambrose had always given her the run of the house. A brief string of words replays itself inside her inner ear twice, three times, until she can no longer ignore it.

What had her father said about the seemingly random coding between genes? *We shouldn't call it "junk DNA," Megan, because it isn't junk at all. It serves a very specific, absolutely crucial purpose . . .*

It's no use trying to recall what he'd said next. She'd been too busy poking about the very back of the laboratory, running her fingertips across the dusty steel surfaces of her great-great-grandfather's long-forgotten prototypes in hopes of finding something "new" to play with.

THURSDAY, 31 JULY 2008 (DAY 92) ~ 7:24 P.M.
25 University Avenue

EVEN IN HER OWN home she is the star of the sideshow. During an idle discussion of John Donne at the kitchen table—would she consider "A Nocturnal upon St. Lucy's Day" an antiepithalamion?—Dewey keeps sneaking fascinated glimpses at her abdomen, leading her to feign a bout of nausea so as to precipitate his departure.

The doorbell rings as she's on her way to the parlor. Through a clear pane in one of the seraphim panels, she sees that the young man on the doorstep is far too shaggy-looking to be a Jehovah's Witness.

"Hi, my name is Andy, and I'm volunteering with the Citizen Action Network. We're going door to door registering people to vote this Novem—wow," he breathes, staring at her middle. "When're your babies due?"

"Are you a Democrat?"

"We're meant to be nonpartisan—"

"You're not answering my question."

He clears his throat. "Yes, ma'am, dyed-in-the-wool."

"Then why aren't you in Ohio?" She slams the door in his face and informs him from the other side of it that she has been registered to vote at this address since the first of November, 1998.

The baby gives her a nudge of what feels like approval. She'll vote blue someday, no doubt about it. The thought gives Lucy a new sense of calm, which she enjoys just as long as it lasts.

9:58 P.M.
The Green Drawing Room

AGAIN THE DOORBELL echoes through the foyer. Lucy, sunk into a large armchair with a tattered copy of *What to Expect When You're Expecting* splayed over her knee (and an empty pint carton of Chunky Monkey on a coaster on the end table), turns her head to the doorway. "Can somebody get that?"

Another ring, longer and more insistent. "Somebody? Please?" The house is so dark and still that if she didn't know better she'd think herself alone. The bell rings a dozen times as Lucy eases herself out of the armchair with a groan. Whoever's waiting on the porch isn't about to budge.

"Do I have the word 'moron' tattooed on my forehead, or what?" Megan strides into the foyer, choosing a bunch of keys off her own ring as she approaches the basement door. As soon as they're on the stairs and Lucy's turned every bolt on the door, Megan begins:

"You've turned yourself into a real blue-ribbon experiment . . . Anyone with three brain cells to rub together can see that! . . . God only knows how little time we have left before you explode . . . I don't know what the hell I was thinking . . . I should have confronted you *weeks* ago . . ."

Clutching the railing, Lucy teeters on the top step as though she might faint. "Why didn't you?"

"I thought you knew what you were doing!"

"What makes you think now that I don't?"

Megan lets out a peal of hysterical laughter as Lucy lumbers down the stairs. Lucy reaches the floor and closes her eyes as the white tiles cool the soles of her feet. Megan is still gasping with derision. "Are you done?" Lucy says.

"Quite finished," Megan replies as she pulls the old doctor's table out from behind the wine rack. "There's not enough time to show you just how stupid you've been, is there?" Spotting the wooden footstool under the computer console, she places it beside the table to aid Lucy's clumsy ascent, then draws her a glass of water at the kitchenette sink.

"You need to tell me what you've done, Lu." Megan drops herself into the computer chair. "And make it quick."

Lucy perches herself on the doctor's table with her arms cradled under her middle as though the baby has already been born. "I used one of her eggs—"

"I *knew* it," Megan breathes. "You cloned your mother!"

"I didn't say I cloned her, I only said I—"

"Good Lord, what a disaster. You have no idea what you've done, do you?"

"Will you shut up and listen to me? I didn't clone my mother!"

"People start thinking that any old schmuck with a hundred thousand dollars' worth of lab equipment can spawn a whole new race of glow-in-the-dark mutants. People like you are precisely why what we're doing is illegal, you know."

"You call this trying to help?"

Megan takes a deep breath. "What they've been calling junk DNA is nothing of the kind. Your father knew this, of course. Our memories aren't recorded in the hippocampus." She pauses. "You see what I'm getting at here?"

Lucy shakes her head, her eyes roving over the soundproof ceiling panels. "Recorded . . . in every cell . . .?"

"It's like there's a QuickTime file inside every intron. And because the body remembers every detail of its physiological growth on a cellular level, any clone will be, and will consider itself, identical to the organism cloned, at the moment the DNA sample was taken."

Lucy hides her face in her hands. "I'm dead. I am utterly and thoroughly dead."

"No, you're not. We can fix this, but we have to do it tonight. It's imperative that you tell me exactly what you used."

Lucy points to the console. "Open the bottom drawer," she says wearily. "It's in there."

Megan retrieves the apron, folded and sealed in a Ziploc bag. "Leave it to you! You have no idea whose blood this was—"

"Actually, I do."

"I can't even believe you got a complete sample out of this."

"Dad left it in his notes."

"What?"

"A method for reconstructing the nucleus."

"What?"

"Don't look at me like that. He wasn't hiding anything from you." Lucy pauses. "It was just a theory he never had the chance to test."

"But *you* did." When Megan says this it sounds almost like a sneer. Lucy nods. "You know whose blood this is." Lucy nods again. "And it wasn't your mother's."

"It was my grandmother's."

"I see." Megan's pause seems interminable. "You'll have to have a cesarean."

"When?"

"Tonight—*now!*—when else?"

"Here?"

"We can hardly admit you to the university hospital."

"What about the . . ."

Megan laughs without mirth. "The 'baby'?"

"Yes," Lucy says with dignity. "The baby."

"I don't know."

"You don't know?"

"Jesus, it's not every day I clone a fully grown human! My best guess is she won't survive the birth. This was a ballsy experiment, but it failed. The only concern you should have now is for your own life."

"But we can't let her die!"

Megan doesn't answer this. She is thinking of the NYU professor spotted last April inside the butterfly conservatory at the Museum of Natural History one full month after his funeral. "I suppose it comes down to how efficiently we can handle the corpse of an unidentifiable child—"

"Megan!"

"Come on now, be reasonable. There's no way to fix this."

"But . . . but . . . isn't it possible she could live if she were born tonight?"

"I highly doubt it."

"Oh God, I'm going to vomit. Pass me that bucket over there."

Absentmindedly Megan hands her the bucket from under the kitchenette sink. "There's just one snowball's chance in hell . . ."

"Meeg?"

"That junk heap in the corner over there. I know you've been thinking of it all along, so don't bother looking so surprised."

"But I didn't think it worked!"

"Of *course* it works!" Megan throws her hands in the air. "Why did you think I warned you not to touch it?" They look at each other for several moments in silence. Megan clears her throat. "Like I said, it's a snowball's chance. And I meant what I said before, about your coming to regret it. You will."

"You'd do it, if you were me."

"That's true." Megan takes a deep breath. "But there might be all sorts of consequences you never could have anticipated. You said you used one of your mother's eggs. Did it ever occur to you that this so-called baby could retain a portion of your mother's memory?"

Mitochondrial DNA. "I never—"

"*You never.* Of course not. You still want to go through with this?"

"There's no alternative."

Megan nods. "From the look of you I'd say she's the size of a healthy toddler. I was going to suggest an ultrasound, but it hardly seems necessary at this point."

Lucy moans as Megan ventures toward the stairs. "Where are you going?" she calls.

"Crazy—want to come?" Megan replies. "We're going to need Gray's help. Is he home?"

"He's in his office," she says faintly. "Third-floor turret room."

"I'll be right back." Closing her eyes, Lucy listens to the unlocking and relocking of the dead bolts.

GRAY MURMURS HIS acknowledgment of the swift knock as Megan's head appears in the doorway.

"Gray, can I get your help with something downstairs for a moment?"

She hurries down the staircase ahead of him. "Is everything . . . ?" Turning on a step, Megan looks up at him and raises her finger to her lips. She produces her own basement keys, and once she's unlocked the door she ushers him through. He finds Lucy spread out once again on the doctor's table.

"Your luvvy here's in a bit of a fix," Megan says.

"Don't be flip, Meeg," Lucy says with a groan. "I can't handle it, not in this state."

Gray blanches. "Are you in labor?"

"We have to do a C-section."

"Here?"

Megan rolls her eyes. "*Yes,* here! How do you think the university doctors will react when they open her up to find what looks like a four-year-old child?"

Gray shakes his head. "Would you mind filling me in? Just the broad strokes will do."

"Good, 'cause that's all we have time for," Megan says. "Think of any cloning movie you've ever seen, where the clones look and act like and have all the memories of the cell donor. Nonsense in theory, but as it happens, the B-movie scenario is pretty damn near the truth. If Lucy had wanted a perfectly normal baby, she'd have had to clone at conception. So the point is—"

"I see where this is going."

"Ain't going nowhere, man. We're already there."

But Megan doesn't have an M.D.! "Are you . . .?"

"Qualified? Sure, I'm qualified. Aced the correspondence course." She laughs at his reaction. "Relax, Gray. My ex-husband was an ob-gyn, and believe me, I'm a hell of a lot more competent than he ever was.

"All right, here's what we do. Lucy rests here"—Megan hurries to the sink to refill the water glass—"while we pick up everything we need from the lab. There'll be a lot of heavy lifting, I'm afraid—but you're up for it?"

What can he do but gulp and nod?

Megan finds half a dozen sealed oxygen canisters stowed behind the wine rack; the rest they'll have to filch from the Biochemistry Department.

10:44 P.M.
University of New Halcyon ~ Franklin Center
for Biomedical Research

FIRST MEGAN "BORROWS" a surgical laser from a cabinet in the med school, Gray jumping at every small sound as he follows her out a back door. Then from a storage closet down the hall from Megan's office they remove three canisters each of carbon, hydrogen, and nitrogen, as well as two tall vials of calcium and phosphorus—along with the oxygen, ninety-nine percent of the human body's composition, in that very order. She pulls a dozen other "odds and ends" out of rigidly organized drawers and space-age steel refrigerators—"trace elements" and vitamins in liquid form—as if she's perusing the shelves of the baking aisle at the grocery store for ingredients in a recipe she knows by heart. "Praise the Gourd the security guard's gone back on the sauce. Try not to drop that on your foot, all right?" They stack the canisters in the hatch of her battery-powered Toyota station wagon.

"Are you going to . . . cut her?"

"There'll be a lot of blood, if that's what you're getting at. But with the laser there's an infinitesimal risk of infection, so try not to worry about it."

11:15 P.M.

25 University Avenue ~ The Basement

THEY STICK THE electrical plug in the wall and hook each canister to a spigot at the rear of the machine. "I'm going to need your help replacing these every so often," Megan tells him, and Gray is afraid to ask just how long all this is going to go on. Over the next thirty minutes the chamber fills with a cloudy liquid, rather gelatinous in consistency by the look of it.

Once she's assembled the surgical laser and various other instruments on a stainless-steel tray, Megan readies a general anesthetic. Splayed on the doctor's table, her skin suffused with an eerie radiance, Lucy looks like she's swallowed the moon whole.

He takes her hand. "Will you be all right?"

She looks up at him, smiling serenely. "Billions of women have done this, you know. I think I can handle it." Megan snorts as she runs a swab of iodine down the center of Lucy's abdomen.

FRIDAY, 1 AUGUST 2008 ~ 3:46 A.M.

The Basement

THE CREATURE BENEATH the machine's plastic casing resembles a four-year-old child. Her umbilical cord remains. So does the placenta, though it's been pricked with what can best be described as a translucent plastic meat prong, which now supplies all her nutrients. Were it not contracting and shuddering like some incarcerated animal, it would remind him of a poached egg.

For several moments he looks down at all of this—the bruises on her chest and limbs, her eyes swollen shut, the tight little mouth sealed in a grimace—and abruptly stumbles to the kitchenette sink to retch last night's Chinese takeout. Out of some preposterous sense of decency, Megan drapes the dustcover over the casing so that only the child's head is visible.

In the weeks to come he'll think of leaving; indeed, the thought will consume him in the wee hours, when he is alone in the narrow bed by the third-floor turret window. It has occurred to him, however, that if by some slim chance this child lives, she's going to need someone of sound mind to take care of her.

EARLY AUGUST, 2008

25 University Avenue

LUCY TAKES A SICK leave of two weeks after Megan informs the laboratory staff that she has suffered a miscarriage. She spends her days reading Victorian romance novels while looking almost as consumptive as their heroines. Gray sits useless by the bedside, surrounded by a sheaf of translations from his summer class that are in need of grading. He cringes at the sight of that ugly red line seared down the center of her belly, all too visible through her thin cotton nightgown.

Megan brings Lucy ayurveda tea in an old-fashioned teapot, with a delicate china cup barely bigger than a shot glass. "Most of the peons think you were harboring an alien pod," she says.

"If only that were so." Lucy sighs. "Last time I checked, that wasn't illegal."

An assortment of splashy floral arrangements and get-well-soon cards cover the dining room table. The Seventh Order prepare a spread of comfort foods, and when it's ready they form a procession up the back staircase, Colin at the head with a steaming bowl on an old lacquered breakfast tray, Milo bearing a tall glass of orange juice he squeezed himself, Rob and Dewey carrying flower arrangements (one a dozen white roses, the other an appalling array of yellow carnations and already-wilting baby's breath) that have just arrived today. Felix gives a curious backward look at Gray with all his lecture notes spread out before him on the kitchen table—Gray, The Boyfriend, who by rights should spearhead all cheerful get-well maneuvers.

Gray is sure they all think he's a callous bastard, but he distracts himself from this unpleasantness by asking himself how on earth these boys can remain so oblivious to all of Lucy's surreptitious activities.

A week later she declares herself fit as ever, and she drags a full-sized mattress down to the basement. Megan spends every evening at the house; the two women keep vigil over the poor godforsaken creature, drinking Fair Trade coffee by the gallon.

MID-AUGUST, 2008

25 University Avenue

OF COURSE HE'S afraid of what people would think of him if he were to leave his girlfriend right after her "miscarriage." This is only natural, though it certainly isn't reason enough to stay.

Two mornings in a row he passes through the master bedroom, the green-and-gold light spilling onto the rumpled sheets on the empty bed, and he enters the bathroom to find her in the shower. When she pushes aside the vinyl curtain to greet him, he spots that long red line running down the center of her stomach, and more of those mysterious little bruises all up and down her arms. "Come in," she says, and obediently he sheds his boxers and climbs into the old tub. He softens at the way she clings to him under the spray, how gently she glides the soap along his shoulder blades. When he takes the soap and runs his fingers down the scar, she begins to cry. Two mornings in a row he reaches for the towel thinking, *I can't leave. I can't.*

LATE SUMMER AND EARLY FALL, 2008

25 University Avenue

ONE NIGHT MEGAN intercepts him on a snack run in the kitchen. Clutching him lightly by the elbow, she whispers, "Lucy trusts you implicitly, Gray. It can't be easy for you, living with all this chaos, but I need to be sure you're in this for the long haul." Everything she hasn't said he can read in her face easily enough; he nods meekly. The point of no return is long past, and Megan, knowing this, speaks with a maddening air of self-assurance.

The day before Lucy returns to work, a man from Commonwealth Electric stands on the porch asking her if she knows why her energy usage has spiked in the last few weeks. "That's strange," Gray hears her saying. "I have no idea. But I have several boys renting rooms upstairs, so maybe they have something to do with it. I wonder if one of them picked up a fridge and brought it up to his room without my noticing . . . Well, yes, perhaps you're right, but I'm still going to have to get back to you later this week. Would that be all right?"

Every so often Megan will summon him to the basement, whenever she and Lucy are in the middle of discussing some logistical question that concerns him. They discuss the future of the girl in the steel-and-plastic coffin, speaking in hushed tones as though in awe of their incidental success—and they are, of *course* they are. Ten years ago it took the Scots how many tries to clone that sheep? Well over two hundred, at any rate. And if he remembers correctly, the poor thing got rheumy before the age of six.

Lucy speaks of restoring the upstairs rooms with their 1920s furnishings; she'll know what goes where from photographs in family albums. The old photographs in the foyer will be taken down and stored in the attic to ease the girl's confusion. The sooner they get her acclimated, the better. She must be made to understand as soon as possible that she is not the original Mary, and must therefore create a new life for herself. Megan admits, however, that the girl's memory may be fragmentary. She says so with a hopeful air—yes, hopeful, because a case of amnesia would make their task easier.

You're lunatics, he wants to shout. *Clinically insane, the both of you.* The two of them never discuss the possibility that should the girl survive—with memory intact—she will not suffer lightly the loss of her family. Whether or not they lived full lives in another time is entirely irrelevant.

Nearly seven months will pass in this way, Lucy with no better than a faint idea of the magnitude of Gray's discontent. It is just as well they spend their nights apart, for she would pale at the things he utters in his sleep.

Gray isn't even present during the most ominous of the two women's conversations, however. One night, a couple of days after Lucy's bed rest ends, Megan arrives at the house in an uncharacteristically flustered state. She informs Lucy that a friend of hers at the university hospital received a phone call from someone asking if Lucy Morrigan was still an inpatient in the neonatal unit. This friend of hers had replied that Lucy had not been admitted, requested the identity of the caller, and realized his mistake only when answered by the dial tone.

SATURDAY, 8 NOVEMBER 2008
New Halcyon

THUS IS THE Democratic Party relegated to the incinerator of history. Charles Harris Fuller—small-time embezzler (newly reformed), founder of the Church of Matthew, and brand-new daddy—throws a lavish party at his "stately" new home on Gwendolyn Drive in celebration of both the birth of his son and yet another presidential victory for the GOP. Born on election night, pudgy little Georgie is the toast of the evening.

Fuller has framed the birth announcement for display in the foyer. The half-page ad, which appeared in Wednesday's *Globe,* reveals to the world Georgie's precise birth weight (nine pounds, seven and a half ounces), along with a vivid description of his first bowel movement (a detail that will actually be published in *The Onion* the following week). Fuller's so proud you'd think he himself had given birth to the poor child.

There were, according to the write-up in Sunday's paper, $250 bottles of champagne flowing like holy water (though not so colorfully phrased), and a proto-Renaissance Madonna on the dining room wall, purportedly purchased in Assisi for twenty euros and recently appraised at more than half the cost of the house itself. The coatroom was still brimming with fine furs well past midnight (because the elephant is the greatest of all party animals). Such voyeuristic details might well enchant the booboisie, but the owner of 25 University Avenue scans the article with unadulterated contempt.

SUNDAY, 1 FEBRUARY 2009 ~ 6:56 P.M.
25 University Avenue

THE MEMBERS OF the Seventh Order of Saint Agatha have taken to cooking a grand dinner in Lucy's kitchen on the first of every month—perhaps to ingratiate themselves, seeing as at least two of the five of them are regularly late with the rent money. Whatever the motivation, the whole business assumes a vaguely ceremonial air. They stop just short of saying grace before the meal commences—to Gray's relief, as Lucy never once excuses him from the bread-breaking.

All five of them putter around the kitchen, each in charge of a particular dish—nearsighted Milo mashing the potatoes, his eyeglasses sliding down his nose; Rob and Felix chopping yellow squash and green peppers for ratatouille; Dewey tossing a cucumber salad; and Colin orchestrating the main dish, a leg of lamb marinated in a mysterious cream sauce, which he will only say is from a cherished recipe of his grandmother's. This statement startles Gray, as he has never once considered that these gaunt slips-of-boys have histories beyond the walls of the Morrigan house.

Colin keeps pulling a stained recipe card out of his back pocket, consulting it gravely, and hastily replacing it. Lucy sits on a high stool surveying them with fondness. "While you're all here," she says offhandedly, "I just want to let you know that my cousin Mary from Cape Eden is coming to stay with us for a few weeks. It's likely you won't see her much, since she's just getting over a long illness." The boys ask a few blandly polite questions, which Lucy answers in the same smooth tone, using ridiculous phrases like "convalescence" and "a change of scenery."

After dinner Gray follows Lucy to the basement. "Was that necessary?"

"Was what necessary?"

"All that elaboration."

"It sounds more plausible that way."

"But all those superfluous details . . ." Too much explaining makes the whole thing sound *less* plausible.

"It's all necessary. I can't allow for any suspicion."

"She'll be angry and disoriented. You have no idea what she might say if she's allowed to meet them."

"I'll explain all of it to her long before I've allowed her to meet anyone else. She'll be something of an anachronism, but we'll deal with these things as they come. Believe me, Gray, there's no cause for worry."

He folds his arms. "Of course there is. How much longer is she going to be in there, anyway?"

"It won't be more than a few days now."

"Won't it be upsetting for her, waking up in that thing?"

"Megan's gone out for a sedative. She says she might panic for a few seconds, but she won't be awake while we're removing her."

She might panic for a few seconds? Removing her!

Lucy makes them both a cup of coffee and they sit down in front of the machine, almost expectantly, as though they are spectators at some sporting event about to be broadcast on a television. This is the first time in six months he's looked at the device full-on; he'd always averted his eyes whenever he'd needed to be down here, though they have not moved the virtue-preserving dustcover by a single inch. Still, he can't bring himself to draw any closer, to see her face. He's afraid to.

The tapping sound begins softly at first, so that Gray believes he's only imagining it.

LUCY CAN'T DECIDE. Should they go up by way of the loop? That highboy won't be easy to move, that's for sure. If they go up the front stairs there's the risk of one of the boys coming out of his bedroom, but even if the key is still where it should be, the loop stairwell is so dark and narrow Gray might trip while carrying her. And then there's the matter of her lying to him when he'd asked about the windows. No, they'll just have to hazard the front stairs.

FRIDAY, 27 SEPTEMBER 1929 (?) ~ 2:05 A.M.
25 University Avenue ~ The Master Bedroom (?)

SAME BED IN a new season: her skin is filmed over with perspiration from some night in the middle of July. And yet there's a sickening chill coming through the open window, she can feel it, and it turns the dew on her skin to slime. Through closed eyelids she detects a puny sort of brightness, like sunlight in winter.

She lifts a hand in search of Teddy and finds a cold hard surface running down the length of her side. Then she moves to turn onto her stomach and finds she isn't able to.

She opens her eyes.

MONDAY, 2 FEBRUARY 2009 ~ 1:22 A.M.
The Basement

THE CARDIOMETER renders one beep indistinguishable from the one before it. The dustcover slides to the floor with the pounding of two white fists against the underside of the plastic casing; the screams are muffled by layers of steel and ersatz amniotic fluid.

"*Do* something, Lucy! For Christ's sake!"

With shaking fingers Lucy hits the key beneath an unlabeled indicator, and a mist rushes into the chamber. The girl thumps her open palms against the casing, her mouth forming words he can only wish he didn't understand, but in a few moments her eyes flutter closed and her long white hands fall limply to her chest. Megan arrives with an IV drip bag, two and a half minutes too late to be of any use. She presses a key he hadn't noticed before, and the casing pops open. The translucent meat prong releases its captive and the placenta bobs gently in the draining fluid like a forgotten bath toy.

Megan reaches in with both hands and clips the umbilical cord in one efficient stroke. Before they can ask, Gray lifts the body out of the coffin and the amniotic fluid soaks through his clothes. The flawless ivory skin, the dark hair pasted to her temples, the perfect breasts of a grown woman: the girl in his arms is a selkie in this godless age of technology, her sealskin coat irretrievably lost.

"I'll stay down here until you've gotten her into the bedroom," Lucy says, arranging a towel around Mary's hair to obscure her face. "If anyone sees you, tell them I fell asleep in my bathrobe again."

MONDAY, 2 FEBRUARY 2009 ~ 2:30 A.M. TO 7:00 A.M.
The Master Bedroom

IT TAKES MEGAN one solid hour to rinse all the slime from the girl's skin and hair in the claw-footed tub, and afterwards she trims the long fingernails. Lucy watches from her perch on the toilet lid, getting up to bring soap and towels as requested. Banished from the bathroom out of that same neo-Victorian prudishness, Gray lies on the bed, staring at the ceiling.

Megan dresses her in one of Lucy's nightgowns and asks Gray to carry her into the anteroom, the door to which she locks from the outside.

"What if she wakes up?" he asks.

"I gave her enough sedative to turn her into Sleeping Beauty."

"What if—"

"I'm going to catch a few hours' sleep on the couch," Megan says. "Trust me, I'll wake up long before she does."

After Lucy falls asleep in the bed, he unlocks the door and spends quite a while—he couldn't say how long—looking down at the girl from the black-and-white honeymoon portrait. Reluctantly he draws an afghan over her legs and leaves the anteroom. Relocking the door, he returns to his study—from which he was meant to be absent for "just a moment"—and falls heavily into his desk chair, nearly catatonic.

SHE COMES TO on the striped chaise lounge in the anteroom, an afghan cast over her legs as though someone had put her to bed there. Had she fallen asleep reading again? Good God, what a wretched dream! She shivers at the unseasonable draft. It's going to be a foul-weather day, judging by the feeble light coming through the curtain.

It isn't like Teddy to leave her on the lounge overnight. On any other evening he'd have picked her up and carried her into the bedroom the very moment the book slipped from her fingers. In moving she discovers a soreness in her wrists. The afghan is a violent shade of pink, brash, like something out of India. She's never seen it before. She looks over at her vanity table: her atomizer is there, and the lavender water Teddy bought for her in Paris, but what are all these things, these queer little bottles and tubes: "All-Over Shimmer"? "Anti-Aging Crème"? To whom do these belong?

And the Sacred Heart above the mirror—it's vanished, a discolored rectangle of wallpaper the only proof it had ever hung there. Her gaze drops to the mirror and she frowns at herself. *How has my hair grown four inches overnight?*

Panicking at the memory of this morning's nightmare, she runs to the hallway door and turns the handle: locked from the outside. Turning to her right, she eyes the door to the bedroom, slightly ajar.

Somehow she understands before she opens the door that she will not find Teddy asleep in their bed, though she would give anything to make it so. If only it were as simple a matter as the willing sacrifice of fingers, senses, the two decades of her life.

THERE ARE INSTANCES when even the most skeptical soul becomes distinctly aware she is not alone in the room, regardless of all appearances to the contrary. Jolted awake as though she'd dreamed of falling, Lucy lies motionless in bed for an interminable length of time. Fear touches her—but gently, very gently, like a fingertip tracing the down of her nape. Eventually she opens her eyes to face the apparition standing at the foot of her bed, whose slender white fingers grip the old brass rail like it's saving her from certain death.

The girl speaks with preternatural calm: "Who are you, and what in God's name are you doing in my bed?"

Chromosome 4:
Excerpt of a vernacular translation

1 *aagccaacctcgctcagcggacgactggccggatcccaacgcgctgccccttgcccagcctgcgagcgcgtggtac*
Exon #1. This is the start of *Homo sapiens* gene UGT8, encoding UDP glycosyl-

77 *gaaggcgcgtctgcatccatgccccagcccggggagctggaggcgctcgcagtcagaggcgagtgatgctaggct*
transferase 8. (UDP-galactose ceramide galactosyltransferase). UGT8 (also

152 *gagcgcgtggcggcccgtgtcgtgccccgctgagccaagtgcggaagggcagcggcgcgctccgactctgctcgccg*
known as CGT) participates in metabolic functions and aids in development

229 *cacgcagg*//gcggggcgcggctggggg // *gcggggggcctggccgcccgctgggagctgcggacg*
of both *loop=portal to afterlife?* the central and peripheral nervous sys-

291 *agcaggcgcgctgaggacccgagggaggacacggttaaagcattg* . . . // gtgagcggagggacac
tem. Also enables glycosphingolipid biosynthesis . . . *the fifth of May 1923.*

536 gccgttccagagggcggaagggggggcggtctgggtggaggagaggggcgttgtttgctccctgag
Ave Maria, gratia plena, Maria, gratia plena, Maria, gratia plena, ave, ave domi-

602 gtgagtgccgggcgaatggctgctgtccaggggcgggggggtgggaattagaaagcacagacag
nus, dominus tecum, benedicta tu in mulieribus, et benedictus, et benedictus fruc-

666 ggttgggctgaggaagttagaagtggttagtgggggttggcggggtagggagaaaggctagggg
tus ventris, ventris tuae, Jesus, ave Maria. Joe and Jared sit on either side of me,

731 ttgagggggtgtgaaggagatctttttaggctggcccctcatagcgcccgcgatcctgtttctgcc
their profiles etched in granite. Ave Maria, mater dei, ora pro nobis peccatoribus,

797 atatggcatccgttcgagggttctctcgcgtttgtgcgctcaaggcagagggagggtataacgggga
ora pro nobis, ora, ora pro nobis peccatoribus. Nunc et in hora mortis, et in

864 ggcgattcggccgaggaccttgtacttgacccctgaagggatgggcaccgcggagcccagaggccagag
hora mortis nostrae, et in hora mortis nostrae, et in hora mortis nostrae, ave Ma-

933 ccagctgccagggcagggatggaggtgggggaccaggaggagcttcgggacctcttcaactcccctt
ria. Father beside Joe in the pew; can't bring myself to look at him. Where was

1001 actccgtcttcccccctaaggaggaacaagagcgggatgtgttgggggtggggaatgtcttggggctgta . . .
I? Not even at home. Want of Mother, Mother, and the stink of blooming lilies . . .

IV

LIFE IN THE TWENTY-OHS:

A Handbook for the Chronologically Displaced

How I have loved this house in the morning before we are all awake and tangled together like badly cast fishing lines. Too many people have been born here, and have wept too much here, and have laughed too much, and have been too angry and outrageous with each other here. Too many have died in this bed already, there are far too many ancestral bones propped up on the mantelpieces . . . and oh, what accumulation of storied dust never allowed to settle in peace for one moment.

—Katherine Anne Porter,
"Pale Horse, Pale Rider" (1939)

MONDAY, 2 FEBRUARY 2009 ~ 7:00 A.M.

25 University Avenue ~ The Master Bedroom

WATERY LIGHT TRICKLES through the rosette window above the bed, a gift from her grandfather to her grandmother. Joseph Dearthing found the prospect of a young woman half-asleep in a pool of colored light as glorious as his great-great-granddaughter's boyfriend would one hundred and twenty-three years later; it was the inventor's daydream that had prompted the design in the first place. This is *her* bed, *her* rosette window, *her* green morning light—the nightmare may have bewildered her, but this much she knows for certain.

"No one's been hurt. Everything is going to be fine." Leave it to Lucy to come off sounding like one of those pathetic women who gibber at newborn babies. "I'm going to explain everything—"

Mary holds out her hands: her wedding and engagement rings are missing. "Who *are* you? Where is my husband?"

"I know it's difficult, but please try to calm down so I can explain—"

"Oh, you'll explain! But telling me to calm down when I've just come upon a stranger in my bed is rather audacious of you, wouldn't you say?"

"Mary, please—"

"I'm going to ring the police now, *if* you don't mind."

"Please—Mary—wait. I'll explain this as many times as you need me to, but you're going to have to get your head around it."

"What have you done with my husband?"

Lucy pounds her fists on the mattress. "Your husband was in the ground long before I was born!"

Mary laughs. "You're mad."

"I am your granddaughter." Lucy ignores Mary's snort of incredulity—Mary is incredulous, you see, that this girl not only has the nerve to wear her best satin nightgown, but that she has concocted such a ludicrous fantasy so as to lay claim to it. "But only in a manner of speaking. You are a . . . a facsimile."

"A facsimile?"

"In other words—"

"I *know* what 'facsimile' means."

"What I mean is, you are an identical copy of the woman who bore my mother." Lucy pauses. "Does that make sense?"

Mary renews her grip on the bed rail. Who *is* this woman, *and where in God's name is Teddy?* "Look, I don't know if this is an excessively complicated plot to swindle us or if you're just a run-of-the-mill lunatic, but if it's the former I'm sure we can work out some sort of an . . ." She snaps her fingers. "An arrangement."

"My name is Lucy Morrigan. I am a biogenetic researcher. And you are a human clone."

"You. Are. Stark. Raving. Mad."

There are footsteps from the hallway into the anteroom, and Mary's jaw drops as a tall colored man opens the bedroom door. "She's awake, I see," says the man, and he smiles at her tentatively.

"Gray, would you mind bringing Mary up a pot of tea—Darjeeling, am I right?—and a few breakfast-y things?"

"Excuse me, but whose help are you?"

Lucy hides her face in her hands. "Gray doesn't work for me, Mary. He's only bringing up your breakfast as a favor."

"So you're an accomplice, then, Mr. Gray."

"Gray is my first name."

"Are you aware that you are trespassing on private property?"

"I'll . . . I'd better get the tea."

"That won't be necessary, seeing as I don't drink arsenic for breakfast."

Gray glances at his girlfriend. "Maybe you'd better try a different approach."

Lucy pauses as he ducks out of the room. "I'm going to prove to you that I'm not a lunatic, and that this is not a hoax. Look on the dresser over there. Just look, will you?"

Mary glances over her shoulder and sees her copy of *Kinder- und Hausmärchen,* rather worse for wear, sitting on the dresser top beside a vase of dried roses.

"I've been reading it again," Lucy says. "Otherwise it would be located in the study on the third shelf from the top on the left side of the fireplace, between Margaret Hunt's English translation and Hargreaves's *Compendium of Irish Folklore.*"

This 1857 edition of *Grimm's Fairy Tales* has been handed down through three generations by the women of the household (whose proficiency in the German language ranged only from adequate to excellent). Five generations, actually: in small and meticulous scripts on the flyleaf are written the names of Mary's grandmother, her namesake; her aunt Cecelia; and herself, along with the dates bestowed. Beside Mary's name, *31 October 1915,* her eighth birthday. But Mary's name is not the last on this list as it had been yesterday. There are now two more entries penned in crisp black ink:

Lucinda Morrigan, 16 May 1941
To my only daughter. You are irreplaceable.—M.M.

Lucy Morrigan, 1 November 1980
Welcome to the world. Do with it what you like.

Mary looks into the mirror above the dresser. (The mirror has been restored to its rightful place in celebration of Lucy's pregnancy.) In the glass she holds the eye of the lunatic who's commandeered her bed, her house, her husband, and probably her bank account as well.

This daughter of hers—Lucinda—would be at least twice as old as this girl is. But that couldn't be right; if this girl in front of her is a Morrigan, then Lucinda is no blood relation. "This is a family heirloom. How *dare* you deface it."

"That book is now my possession. My grandmother left this house to my father and me when she passed away in 1989. I live here. This is my room. This is my bed. Gray lives here, too, and there are five young men who board here, all students at the university."

"Boarders? This house has never had boarders."

"Yes, well. I needed the money." Lucy realizes at once that this is the wrong thing to say. Most everything has been a mistake; she sees that now. The same furniture, the same wallpaper (Mary is too distraught to notice how it's peeling), the same worn wood flooring. This room is virtually the same as it was when Mary left it one September morning eighty years ago.

Mary gazes down at her with sympathy now. "We can arrange something for you, I promise. Just please tell me where Teddy is . . . and my father . . ."

"I'm sorry, but it's the truth, Mary. You are the product of a misguided experiment. Your memories have survived intact." She twists the corner of the bedsheet, wringing it between her fists as though it were sopping wet. "Which is why this is so difficult for you to understand."

"I'll ask you one more time: *Where is my husband?*"

Lucy swallows hard. "Cape Eden," she says. "Saint Jude's churchyard."

On her way out, Mary nearly upsets the lacquered breakfast tray in Gray's hands; on it he bears a plate of buttered white toast and three slices of greasy bacon he had gamely attempted to fry himself. He watches her fly down the hall to the corner bedroom—inhabited by Felix, if he remembers correctly—and cringes as she throws open the door.

The room is a pigsty, harboring every dish and coffee mug gone missing in the past three years. Tall, curtainless windows throw the morning light on a figure writhing, squinty-eyed, beneath the stained duvet. "Huh?" says Felix, his voice thick and toady. "What the—?"

The silverware rattling on the tray in his hands, Gray watches her in profile as she races down the far end of the hall toward the attic steps, her brow knotted in panic.

"Man," Lucy says, as a door across the landing slams. "Did I botch that, or what?"

He drops the tray on the vanity table and chooses a slice of bacon. "Yeah," he says. "Yeah, you did. Is—is something wrong?"

Stiff with alarm, she plucks a Kleenex from a box on the bedside table and brings it to her mouth. After a violent cough, she pulls the tissue away and stares at the blood, copious and bright red, like food coloring.

7:34 A.M.
The Attic

SHE PUSHES THE sticky old door closed with all her weight behind her shoulder. The stairs moan beneath her feet as the open garret comes into view, the sickly winter light casting every dusty object in shades of ever-darker gray. She gasps as she approaches the window:

Snow. Snow in September.

With unsteady hands she unshrouds the furniture, pokes through drawers, examines her own clothing hanging in the tall teak wardrobe that had belonged to her grandparents. She puts on last year's Thanksgiving dress, rolling a pair of silk stockings up her calves with trembling fingers. The holes in her slip, the brittle elastic on her garters—these signs she willfully ignores. In the backyard, the snow's piled high on the hedges, and she cannot see the spoon fountain.

Her eyes rove over every piece of circumstantial evidence: the blue-and-yellow nine-patch quilt, a wedding gift from Teddy's aunt Grace, the calico piecing faded almost beyond recognition; the tarnish on the Chatham silverware she polished a week ago; the small holes in the train of her wedding gown, the moths' doing. She runs her fingers over the delicate fabric, squinting, as though the veil is the postmark on a letter she'd mailed herself just for the fun of it. It makes no sense.

A full-sized mattress and box spring, draped in a dustcover, lean in one corner against the pitched roof. With an effort that leaves her gasping, she drags them onto the floor and makes the bed with flannel sheets from one of the cedar chests, piling it high with wool blankets. Sleep, that's how she'll pass the time until Teddy returns.

7:40 A.M.

The Parlor

GRAY SLAMS THE doors behind him. "So much for Sleeping Beauty."

Megan rubs her eyes. "She's awake?"

"And already at war."

"Shit. Where is she?"

"Hiding in the attic. And by the way, Lucy's coughing up blood."

Megan hides her face in her hands.

He folds his arms. "I'm taking her to the hospital."

Now fully awake, she jumps off the sofa, pointing her finger in a menacing fashion. "You'll do no such thing," she hisses. "I'll take care of it." As Megan jerks the doors open and runs up the stairs, Gray falls onto the couch and tries to steady his breathing.

7:46 A.M.

The Master Bedroom

"WHEN YOU'RE FEELING better, do me a favor and tell your boy toy it isn't my fault you're barfing blood."

"He knows it's not your fault, Megan."

"He's sure not acting like it." She takes the thermometer out of Lucy's mouth and reads it with relief. "So what are you going to do?"

"I think she's all right up there for the moment. After I get some sleep I'll go up and talk to her."

Megan shakes her head. "I think she's going to need more time than that."

4:47 P.M.
The Attic

THE KEROSENE LAMP swings from a rusty hook on the crossbeam as she reaches for it, clutching a box of matches in her free hand. In the top drawer of a certain bureau, which hasn't been moved since this house belonged to her, Mary finds a small velvet jewelry case containing an aquamarine ring, which she slips onto the finger where her wedding ring should be, and a rosary made of Connemara marble. She gets through two and a half decades on the rosary before flinging it across the room.

After a few deep breaths Mary starts to unwrap a china plate stored in the bottom drawer, and when she spots the date at the top of the newspaper page—January 25, 1978—the headlines beneath it slowly blur beyond legibility. The room is silent but for the tap, tap, tap of her tears dropping on the yellowed sheet of newsprint. There is a point, you see, at which a hoax becomes too elaborate to be anything other than the truth.

TUESDAY, 3 FEBRUARY 2009 ~ 2:15 A.M.
The Attic

THEY'VE BUILT A NEW roadway not far from here. Even under a mound of scratchy wool blankets she can hear the traffic roaring in the distance, hardly muted by the heavy snowfall.

8:35 A.M.

The Attic

HOW SIMPLE THIS IS—looking at nothing; feeling nothing. She doesn't even hear the footfalls on the attic steps.

"Mary, are you all right?"

Her own voice startles her, too; it sounds like a jigsaw on wood. "Go away!"

Lucy pauses. "I'm . . . I'm just going to leave a breakfast tray on the landing here."

When she returns from work in the afternoon Lucy will find the tray untouched.

9:07 A.M.

25 University Avenue

LUCY FLIPS UP THE collar on her old tweed coat as she locks the front door. Plodding through the snow en route to campus, she's so busy berating herself that she nearly runs into a telephone pole. What was meant to be the greatest accomplishment of her life has turned into the stupidest thing she's ever done. And it isn't just a stupid thing now that Mary's awake and angry as hell—it was a profoundly stupid thing all along. Gray was right; she'd been blinded by a preposterous combination of ambition and babylust. But why in God's name hadn't he stood up to her?

Lucy imagines how she would have reacted, had he delivered an ultimatum. Would she have given it up?

She won't answer that. It's unfair to blame him for going along with it, but she can't help thinking that perhaps she should turn her attention now to growing him a backbone.

MIDDAY
The Attic

THE FOUR-POSTER BED at the pensione in Siena was the size of a small house, all gilt mahogany and heavy tapestry curtains. The mattress sagged in the middle, but what did they care?

He stood at the foot of the bed so that the evening light fell on his back, and she could scarcely see his face. "You look like an effigy," he murmured. He was staring as though he'd never seen her before. "Like a figure in art."

And of course she had reached for the bedsheet then, but he'd torn it from her fingers.

Thus she passes the hours: bobbing in and out of consciousness, yearning for oblivion.

1:25 P.M.
Yobanashi Tea Room

IN ALL LIKELIHOOD Lucy will lunch alone this afternoon; Megan told her to order without her if she hasn't arrived by twenty past one. Lucy ought to be home right now, ensuring that the girl in the attic hasn't set the house afire, but why trudge all the way home only to talk to the attic door? Besides, she'd heaped enough food on that tray to keep the girl satisfied until dinnertime. With an exhausted sigh she opens her notebook after ordering a niçoise salad and a pot of white chrysanthemum tea. Occasionally she glances up at the door in hopes that Megan, or maybe Gray, will turn up.

Soon after her lunch arrives, a certain reverend invites himself into her booth. "Allow me to introduce myself," Charles Harris Fuller says. "I'm—"

"I *know* who you are. What do you think you're doing in my booth?"

"I'd just like a few minutes of your time, just a few minutes is all I'm asking." He might as well have declared himself the second Messiah. "Your father was a stubborn man," he begins. "A man of hubris."

"I was far better acquainted with my father's shortcomings than you could ever be, Mr. Fuller."

He wrinkles his nose at her failure to use his title. "That must have been something of an unfortunate experience for you," he retorts, and she is about to inform him that the conversation is well past finished when a change comes over his Silly Putty face—now his look is conciliatory, ingratiating even.

"I didn't drop by to spar with you, Miss Morrigan—"

"*Doctor* Morrigan," she says. "I have a Ph.D."

"Why, yes, of course." His smirk is that of a grade-school bully, one in possession of an unpleasant secret. "You may not believe it, but I'm well aware of your accomplishments."

She can't help responding like a neglected child. "Really?"

"Why else did you suspect I would seek you out?"

"For a featherbrained attempt to talk me out of my godless ways," she says. "I have a story for you, Mr. Fuller. It's about you, actually. Just a few months before my father died, he told me that you came to see him at the laboratory, though I still have no idea how you cleared security. He said you'd had some sort of project you wanted to discuss with him. He said he'd told you to 'stuff it'"—here Fuller laughs mirthlessly—"and that evening he informed me that if I ever even so much as entertained the notion of going born-again, he'd sit on me until I came to my senses."

"And you never called family services?" Fuller shakes his head. "Tut, tut."

"My point is made, Mr. Fuller. So, seeing as you will only leave this booth if I scream fire or rape, I suppose I'll just have to find myself a new one." With that, she picks up her salad plate and teacup and heads for the farthest table in the restaurant, a two-seater currently occupied by someone with whom she is well enough acquainted to impose herself upon.

10:45 P.M.

25 University Avenue ~ The Attic

A DARK, SLITHERING déjà vu wends its way out of the cobwebbed corners. It's as though she's already wept these tears for her husband and father—wept them with the eyes of someone else entirely.

Stacked in a wooden crate under the rolltop desk is a trove of family photographs in silver frames, carefully wrapped in linen napkins that will never again see the gleam of a polished mahogany dinner table. One by one she pulls them out of the box, choking as she unveils the honeymoon portrait taken on top of the Duomo. There are snapshots of her at every age, most of them with cherubs squirming in her lap, pulling at her earbobs and grinning as though they've just gotten away with something. These are her children, she realizes with a sinking feeling—her children, and her grandchildren.

The older photographs lie toward the bottom of the pile, and thus does Teddy reappear in black and white. With both hands she holds up the frame as if she were speaking to him in the flesh. "Teddy?" she whispers. "What in God's name are you doing in that uniform?" She props the frame against a piece of furniture and pulls out the next portrait—her father's.

At the bottom of the crate is an album from Lucinda's childhood, the kind with sticky cellophane page covers that yellow terribly after a decade or two. She opens the book to a family portrait taken circa 1950: Mary has aged gracefully, but these children are no longer young; the two boys are of marriageable age and sport rather dashing moustaches. The girl, etiolated but smiling almost bravely, wears her hair in braids. Edward is absent. It will be two more days before she discovers why.

Mary arranges the portraits of her family all around the bed, so that they seem to look upon her. Then she climbs onto the mattress and covers herself with her wedding quilt, sobbing quietly.

WEDNESDAY, 4 FEBRUARY 2009 ~ 3:40 A.M.
25 University Avenue

THE CALL OF NATURE has a way of weakening even one's most petulant resolves. The loop key isn't where it should be under the loose floorboard by the attic door (not that she could open either passage door anyway, with all the clutter), and she's loath to take the main stairs, but after half an hour tapping her stocking feet against the floorboards, she can hold out no longer.

Light shines in slivers under closed bedroom doors along the second-floor hallway—her brothers' old rooms. Strains of Martian-music seep through the walls—jazz? yes, jazz . . . no, it's not like jazz at all. The turret-room door is open wide enough for her to see that her carefully chosen wallpaper has been torn away in favor of pea-green paint. A floorboard groans beneath her.

"Hello?" The voice of a young man on the other side of the door momentarily confuses her; he sounds so much like her brother Jared that for an instant, the instant before she hears the creak of a desk chair relieved of its occupant, she believes she has finally roused herself from the nightmare. "Who's that?" comes the voice once more as Mary flees to the water closet at the far end of the hall. The tiny room is much changed: an electric light above the mirror, an odd assortment of men's toiletries, a new porcelain toilet with a lever instead of a pull chain, and an unfortunate proliferation of mold in the crevices. Dirty towels lie in heaps around the bathtub in the adjoining room.

Back in the hallway, avoiding the creaky boards, she peers at the yellowed news clippings and brightly colored notices tacked to the bedroom doors, though she can scarcely understand even those legible in the dim light. An editorial cartoon, "Mount Bushmore," features faces of the nation's not-so-illustrious leaders—Fillmore, Harding (*ha!*), Pierce, and a floppy-eared face labeled with nothing but a W. The idea of presidential portraits carved into a mountainside seems vaguely comical. On the next door, a *New Yorker* cover (February 9, 2004?—it's hard to see) depicts Cupid being interrogated by a pair of thuggish police officers, his bow and little red arrows the evidence on the table. On the third door is tacked a small blue banner proclaiming Jesus a liberal, along with a Jolly Roger scrawled in red ink on a scrap of notebook paper and an illustration of a black box with thin lines sprouting from the top of it like rabbit ears. "National TV Turnoff Week," it says. "April 20–26, 2008."

To her left, a face appears through the turret-room doorjamb, giving the impression that it has somehow been separated from its body. She gasps.

"Shh!" says the boy as he pulls her into the room by her elbow. "Don't let them hear you." His fingers are cold as a cadaver's. A pale slip of a boy he is, with legs like stilts. She follows him into the room, her old room, overwhelmed by his height and the smell of sandalwood.

A full bed sits directly opposite the doorway, hundreds of books stacked helter-skelter all over the floor on either side of it. To her right a long black desk is set against the curved wall, leaving an awkward crescent-shaped space out of which a queer metal floor lamp sprouts like an alien flower. On the desk, beside an unruly stack of paper, she spots her own Remington typewriter. "Where . . . where did you find that?"

He closes the door behind her. "The attic," he whispers. "You must be Mary." Nodding slowly, she accepts his hand. "I'm Colin. Nice to meet you." He drops like a rag doll into his desk chair and waves a hand at the unmade bed. "Have a seat. I've just made myself some peanut butter crackers. Care to partake?" She spots the cracker plate atop a stack of textbooks on a small night table, and she sees her picture of the Sacred Heart now hanging on the wall above the bed.

Colin glances at a small box, which displays glowing red numerals, on the edge of his desk. "You have insomnia, too, I take it." Outside, the wind whistles through the oak trees, and the high boughs tap at the window. "It's not always such a sty in here. Sometimes it's worse."

She looks over at him again to find him gazing at her expectantly. "Pardon?"

"I just asked if you were having trouble sleeping."

"I suppose I am."

"But you're feeling better, I hope?"

Is she meant to be returned from a sanatorium? "I am, thank you."

"Glad to hear it. You're very welcome here."

Smiling an ironic little smile, she examines a group of framed black-and-white photographs hanging above the desk, clasping her hands behind her back as though in a museum. "These are striking. Are they yours?"

He laughs. "How old do you think I am, anyway?"

"Oh, of course," Mary says, growing pink in the face. "I don't know what I was thinking."

"They were here when I moved in. I believe they were taken by a member of Lucy's family . . . her grandmother, maybe?" He points to a picture of a small boy with a dirty face guarding a crate of apples on a city street corner. APPLES, 2 FOR 5¢, OR A DOZ. 25¢, says the sign propped against the crate. "Look." Colin points to the bottom-right corner. "There are initials, 'M.M.', and the date—it looks like the first of September, 1931." He turns to her, smiling. "Would M.M. have been an ancestor of yours?"

"Yes," Mary whispers—then "yes," a little louder; she clears her throat. "I'm one of Lucy's Morrigan cousins."

"Ah," Colin says. He points to another photograph above the night table, a portrait of a rough-looking man sitting with his legs dangling out the back of a railroad cargo car, a banjo in his lap. "I like this one especially."

Mary could never have imagined just how much use she'd get out of that Rolleiflex.

"Colin, I was wondering . . . how did you come to live here?"

"Lucy advertised for boarders in the school paper. We were in need of a new place." He shrugs. "It was pure luck."

"How many of you are there?"

"Five in all. I must say, I'm quite offended she hasn't mentioned us."

"Yes . . . well . . . Lucy and I don't speak much."

"Is that so? She gave us the impression that you and she were pretty close."

Mary clears her throat. "I'm sure she would have mentioned you. It's just that she . . . she has so much on her mind these days."

"That's true. She's extraordinarily dedicated to her work, isn't she?" He pauses. "Ah, well. Never fear, we're a harmless lot." He flashes her a generous smile. "We might take a bit of getting used to, though."

"I was wondering, also . . . did you choose this room in particular?"

"We all wanted the turret room." Colin chuckles. "But the guys let me have it, since I was the one to find the ad."

"It used to be a nursery, you know." And before that, her own room; her bed was beneath the west window, her rocking chair where the bed is now, an ornate Tiffany lamp suspended from the plasterwork where there now hangs a flimsy beige shade with a proliferation of cobwebs. She suppresses a powerful urge to push him out the door and turn the key in the lock.

"Must've been a long time ago. Was it yours?" She nods. "Hey," he says. "Cheer up. We all have to grow up sometime." She freezes as he leans toward her, but he only pats her lightly on the shoulder.

"Yes," she murmurs. "I just didn't expect it would happen so quickly." Her eye catches on a solemn wooden figurine, the Madonna and Child, perched on the night table beside his snack plate. She hadn't noticed it before, with all the books around it.

"That was here before I was. Most of this stuff was—the pictures on the wall and all the furniture and things."

"But you kept it there." She nods at the figure before its incidental offering. Colin sits on his bed and places a cracker whole into his mouth.

"I kind of like it," he says as he chews. Crumbs dribble from his mouth, catching in the weft of his woolen sweater. "It's kitschy."

"Kitschy?" She pauses. "It belonged to my grandmother."

"I mean 'kitschy' in a fun way, you know. It's . . . it's an interesting piece."

So "kitschy" mustn't be the kindest of adjectives. She picks up the figurine and runs her finger lightly along the curve of the Virgin's cape. "There used to be a shop in town where you could buy all sorts of statuettes like this one," she says absently. "The owner was commissioned to carve the crucifix above the altar at Saint Lucy's."

"That must've been ages ago. Saint Lucy's closed, you know."

"Closed?"

Still chewing, he grins at her in mild amusement. "You've been out of town awhile, haven't you?"

"What is this?" She kneels on the floor beside the desk and lifts the receiver from a Bakelite rotary-dial telephone. "What an odd-looking thing. Is it a telephone?" She picks it up. "Gosh, it's heavy!"

"I found it in a box in the closet. So old it's cool again, eh?"

A chorus of knocks sounds at the door. Colin opens it to find his four comrades standing shoulder to shoulder with their fists still in the air. "We heard a voice," Felix says. All four gaze at her with painfully earnest expressions.

Milo eyes Mary through the bible-thick lenses in his spectacles. "And came to investigate."

"Now who's this?"

"You know you aren't permitted to bring girls up to your room, Colin—"

"*Especially* not at a quarter to four in the morning."

Milo sniffs. "Shame on Colin for keeping you all to himself."

"I wasn't hiding her." Colin huffs in mock exasperation as he returns to his desk chair. "Mary, these are my friends and fellow members of the Seventh Order of Saint Agatha: this is Milo, who has just given you the hairy eyeball—"

"Pardon me?"

"And from left to right are Rob, Felix, and Dewey—I mean, Dewey and Felix." Each of them is clad in black from neck to toe: they look like cat burglars, or revenants.

All four pile onto the bed, and the brass frame creaks ominously beneath them. "Hello, Mary," they say in unison.

This is beginning to feel like she's been invited to a cocktail party in her own bedroom. *Get out,* she wants to cry. *Get out, all of you, now!*

"You dress just like Lucy," one of them observes.

"I suppose I do," she retorts. "Those clothes were mine to begin with."

"Don't be bashful, now."

"Yes, yes, tell us all about yourself."

She folds her arms; her flesh creeps under their collective gaze. "But there's so little to tell."

"Hey, Colin, she knows about the Order?"

Mary cringes at the sight of the boys on the bed devouring the peanut butter crackers and scattering the crumbs. "This is the first I've heard of it. Are you some sort of confraternity?"

"Sort of," Colin says. "Think of us as a male purity movement for the twenty-first century."

"That's very admirable."

"We've taken a vow of celibacy," Milo announces.

"But that was ages ago," says one of the boys on the bed. "Long before Colin fell victim to love at first sight."

"Felix!" Colin hisses. "Don't embarrass her!"

She feels the heat radiating from her face. "I'm married, you know."

Colin starts. "But you're so *young*! How old are you, anyway?"

"A hundred and one."

"You're remarkably well-preserved," says Dewey, the bald one.

"Why, thank you."

"How old are you, really?"

"Twenty-two."

"You're even younger than I am!" cries Milo, the bespectacled boy. "You must be a Mormon."

Mary laughs nervously.

"Are you?"

"I'm Catholic."

The young men nod to one another. "Oh, good," Dewey says.

Felix eyes her appreciatively. "We didn't *really* think you were a Mormon."

"Is your husband still on Cape Eden?" asks the boy with the ginger beard.

"No," she says. The floor is in serious need of a waxing. "I mean, yes . . . he's . . . he's finishing his medical training there."

"On the Cape?"

"Yes, at a hospital there."

"Oh," says Colin.

Mary clasps and unclasps her hands as she fiddles with the aquamarine on her left ring finger. In an absurd attempt to banish the awkward silence, the bald boy blurts (several decibels higher than necessary, especially considering the time of night), "Are you one of the cyborgs Lucy's hiding in the basement?"

"I haven't been down to the basement," she says. "Not lately. It used to be a darkroom. And a wine cellar before that."

"Not anymore," Colin says.

The boy with the ginger beard stands up and gestures to his spot on the unmade bed. "Would you like to sit down?"

She looks down at the bed, the scratched brass frame, the sag of the old mattress visible beneath the disheveled sheets. Turning her head, she notices something that chills her: on the wall above Colin's desk is a framed print of Lorenzo Lippi's seventeenth-century portrait of Saint Agatha, who proffers her breasts to heaven on a silver platter. Teddy had cringed at the sight of it on their tour through the Pitti Palace.

"Mary?" Colin is saying. "Are you all right?"

She shrugs off his hand as he rests it lightly on her shoulder. "Sorry—yes—I'm quite well. But I had better retire for the evening. It was lovely to meet you all."

In the wake of her abrupt departure, the members of the Seventh Order look at one another in silence. Their lives have become decidedly more interesting over the course of these last five minutes.

4:34 A.M.
The Attic

MARY RETURNS TO HER bed on the floor, but sleep is out of the question. If she could only feel his breath, hot and even on the back of her neck . . .

Ten minutes later she ventures down the back stairs onto the second-floor landing, where her mother's finest needlepoint, a garden scene with a Watteauesque lady making merry on a tree swing, still hangs in a simple wooden frame. Down the back stairs, through the kitchen, the great room, the conservatory, the drawing rooms, the dining room, and the parlor: in every room what unnerves her is not how much has changed, but how so many things have remained, albeit far more scratched or threadbare than the last time she laid eyes on them. But the new icebox looks like a steel coffin set upright, and she gasps when she opens a cabinet door in the parlor to find a great black hulking box, on whose surface she sees her own startled reflection.

As she ventures into the front hall, the reason for the hidden photographs finally occurs to her. The walls of peeling paper are a palimpsest of vanished picture frames, their long-dead subjects personae non gratae through no fault of their own. The few frames still on the walls contain images in full color of people she's never laid eyes on, aside from the girl who calls herself her "granddaughter, but only in a manner of speaking."

Gone are the roses she'd put on the hall table the day before yesterday, nothing there now but a green ceramic ashtray filled with keys and a stack of unread mail. The candlestick telephone is missing, too.

Mary returns to the dining room, where by the light of early morning she spots the broken panes of glass in the dining room windows. As dawn gives way to the brightness of seven o'clock, sharp slivers of blue and green and crimson light cut through the dusty air, spilling sumptuously on the dining table. Mary sits in the chair at the head, the seat once reserved for her father. She places her hands, palms down, on the table's surface, so that her left hand assumes a bluish cast, her right viridian. Across the room, she spots those queerly tinted liquids in the crystal decanters and decides it must be a trick of the light.

Her grandfather had been both a classicist and a devout Catholic. The stained-glass windows he commissioned for this house depict angels of every rank above romantic Latin inscriptions. SIC TRANSIT GLORIA MUNDI, reads the banner beneath the feet of the angel of death, robed in scarlet and wearing an expression of sad inevitability.

5:05 A.M.
The Master Bedroom

THE SOUND BEGINS each time Lucy's nearly drifted off, but when she sits up, startled, there's no noise out of the ordinary—just the boys' shuffling footsteps and the settling of an old house. After a few moments holding her breath waiting to hear a baby's cries, she dismisses it as a stray cat starving for milk. Lucy presses the inhaler between her lips and breathes in gratefully.

7:12 A.M.
The Study

ON THE WINDOWSILL the amaryllis, a symbol of pride in the Victorian language of flowers, blooms toward the light. In eighty years no one has moved the photograph on the edge of the desk, an informal portrait of her mother, Aunt Cee, and herself. No one seems to have dusted it, either. The coal scuttle is empty and the logs on the fireplace aren't even made of wood. Her father's butterfly collection lies beneath a thick coat of dust on the mantelpiece; she can recall those summer afternoons he caught the butterflies, the gold and orange wings beating against the walls of a jam jar on the kitchen table.

Beside *Kinder- und Hausmärchen,* which that girl has replaced on the bookshelf beside the fireplace, Mary spots a book with a tattered green dust jacket and a most peculiar title: *Everyday Life in the Twenty-first Century: A Handbook for the Chronologically Displaced;* the author is one P. F. X. Godfry.

She opens the book to the table of contents, a dizzying list of unfamiliar topics. This is followed by a thorough introduction. A chart on the first page details which chapters are required reading, "depending on the decade from which you hail." (Should you be a displacement from the Clinton years, for example, you have no need for the chapters on the Internet, television, sexual mores, the civil rights movement, or the A-bomb, though you will want to absorb the passages on terrorism and bioterrorism, modern neoconservatism, and Botox.)

"Human anachronisms can detect one another with relative ease. It is not merely a matter of old-fashioned dress, archaic language, or antiquated habits, though these clues may prove helpful to the chronologically displaced individual in search of kindred spirits," Godfry writes.

The close of each chapter offers "coping strategies" for each unfamiliar aspect of "contempo-modern life," a term coined by Godfry that "is not a redundancy, but an adjective specifically referring to the time in which one finds oneself, as opposed to the time in which one 'belongs'—assuming, of course, that one's displacement is subsequent to one's natural chronolocation."

Mary turns to the back flap and then the back panel looking for a photograph of the author, but to no avail: the face of P. F. X. Godfry will remain a mystery, which is probably as he'd intended it. It's a load of tommyrot—after all, the man proclaims himself an "unabashed socialist" on the third page—but how can she close it now?

From the first chapter, entitled "For Travelers Belonging to the Decade of the Nineteen-twenties (Popularly Known, but only in Retrospect, as the 'Roaring Twenties')": "Your kind are extremely rare, comprising perhaps 0.02% of the chronologically displaced population, and because your delta is seventy years at the minimum (more likely eighty or more), you will do well to read this tome in its entirety." Readers from that era should employ an auxiliary source of historical information, however, as the material covered in the guide commences with the late 1950s. From a nearby shelf she pulls an American history textbook and a few outdated volumes on human genetics. These will do, for a start.

Desire for a cigarette overwhelms her, and not for the first time since this nightmare commenced. Clutching the book to her chest, Mary pushes one side of the sofa away from the fireplace and pulls back the corner of the oriental rug. From a shallow compartment beneath a floorboard she retrieves a weighty metal key with a bit pattern in the shape of a fleur-de-lis. This is the only key that opens the elfin door off the kitchen passageway, and the screech it gives turning the lock could wake the dead. Mary listens for footfalls above before she opens the door.

Two months before her wedding, she'd stashed half a dozen packs of Lucky Strike cigarettes in the old cookie tin in which she had always kept her Antarctic Explorer cards. No one has moved it even an inch from its place on a high shelf built into the narrow passageway—the dust covering the tin is thicker than a winter quilt.

Coughing, and with the book tucked under her arm, she pries off the lid, sighs as contentedly as is possible under the circumstances at the sight of those goodies still tucked inside, and climbs the staircase with nothing but a match to light her way.

CONTENTS, continued

INTRODUCTION

I begin with the boundless self-confidence that can arise only out of an unshakable faith in the precise order and nature of future events. I am fortunate to have the foreknowledge that the book you have just begun to read will be published the same year I receive my doctorate, and that my work will continue to spark philosophical debate decades after the university press has ceased to print it.

Some have asked, “Was Godfry a Kook or a Visionary?” Every man would like to consider himself the latter, but I hereby reject both characterizations. I am not a kook: my conclusions are based on carefully compiled statistics and scientific observations rather than any preconceived ideology, religious, political, or otherwise. Nor am I a visionary, for the historical and cultural illuminations contained within this volume are valid only because I witnessed the events firsthand.

But perhaps it would be wiser to begin at the beginning. I was born in 1933 in Peoria, Illinois, and I first visited the year 2008–one full decade after my death, incidentally–as a twenty-six-year-old graduate student in physics at the University of New Halcyon. This sojourn, which lasted approximately eighteen months, qualifies me to write of twenty-first-century politics, socioeconomics, and culture with unprecedented authority. I have done so not to allow those of my own era an extended glimpse, but to ease the transition of other chronologically displaced

7:32 A.M.
The Study

BLEARY-EYED FROM the worst bout of sleeplessness since the night of the laboratory fire, Lucy finds the door ajar but no one inside the room. She turns slowly on the oriental carpet in her stocking feet, acutely aware of every scent (talcum powder, mothballs), any small thing out of place (a long black hair clinging to the arm of the sofa, the position of which is four inches askew), or any book missing out of twelve thousand volumes (the slim, dark lacuna between *Kinder- und Hausmärchen* and Hargreaves's volume on Irish mythology where the first edition of a work by a local crackpot physicist ought to be; these days, said book sells for upward of eight hundred dollars on eBay). Chronic insomnia sharpens the senses.

Better to let her accustom herself in solitude, then. Lucy slides the ancient leather-bound *Grimm's* off the shelf and in her hands the book falls open to a woodcut illustration for "Die Sterntaler," "The Star Talers." "*Es war einmal ein kleines Mädchen,*" the story begins, "*dem war Vater und Mutter gestorben . . .*"

Through years of reading and rereading Lucy can recite this one more or less by heart. "Once upon a time there was a little girl whose father and mother were dead, and she was so poor that she no longer had a room to live in, or a bed to sleep in, and in the end she had nothing else but the clothes she was wearing and a crust of bread in her hand that some generous soul had given her. But she was a good and pious girl. Since she was forsaken by everyone in the world, she went forth into the open, trusting in God . . ."

A little girl, naked and shivering under a skyful of stars pointed sharp as oyster knives. Her grandmother had taped the pages of another illustration together to spare her mother, and eventually Lucy, an even more dreadful image. In that woodcut, another little girl, whose father has hacked off her hands, assumes the pose of Job, the blood squirting from her wrists in a manner reminiscent of a Flemish crucifixion scene.

A mess of inappropriate emotions has fogged her brain over the past two days. Who could understand this new hunger for sisterly intimacy? Last night, during a short and shallow slumber, she dreamed she'd fashioned a rag doll out of scraps of old dresses, sewn thick black strands of yarn to the crown of the head and shiny blue buttons where eyes should be, painted a thin red mouth and a coquettish set of eyelashes, and said to her creation: "You shall be my one true friend."

The rag doll blinked her blue-button eyes and jerked herself up to sit. She gazed at her creator with all the contempt her little plastic eyes could muster. *Never,* the golem replied.

Lucy replaces the book and slips through the kitchen passage, passing the loop entrance (the lock on which she's caught the Seventh Order trying to pick on more than one occasion), and takes the breakfast tray up the back stairs.

7:49 A.M.

The Attic

THE FIRST CIGARETTE disintegrates in her hands, as does the next one, and the one following it. The rusted cookie tin falls to the floor as Mary hides her face behind her tobacco–dusted fingers.

"Mary?" Lucy puts her ear to the door. "I've brought you some breakfast. You must be starving. You really ought to eat some—"

Mary's nostrils twitch at the scent of bacon. "*Don't* lecture me on my eating habits!"

"*What* eating habits?"

Stomping footfalls approach the door and Lucy backs away as she hears Mary fumbling violently with the latch.

There are a hundred things Mary could say once she finally pries the door open, but rage has silenced her. This girl who calls herself Mary's granddaughter has murdered Mary's husband, murdered her father, murdered her brothers and pushed their children out of the pram to the lip of their graves.

Lucy proffers the tray and Mary wills herself not to look at what's on it. When she finally opens her mouth, the words come out in a strangled whisper. "How do you . . . suppose it feels . . . to find your husband, your whole family—"

"I'm sorry, Mary. If I could undo what I've done, believe me, I—"

Mary takes the tray out of her hands, sets it on a pipe stand beside the door, and observes Lucy's pained expression as she slams the door in her face. She resets the latch and devours the bacon.

The rest of her perfume bottles line the windowsill, all of them empty. She opens one and brings it to her nose, but the scent has faded.

If she could undo what she's done . . . But could she do it again? Could there already be a third Mary? A fourth? Gooseflesh rises on her arms as she remembers the eerie green light in a hall of mirrors at the Cape Eden carnival. *You aren't you,* her reflection says, as she finds herself mouthing the words in tandem. *You are someone else entirely.*

If there's a third Mary, they must be keeping her in the basement.

FRIDAY, 6 FEBRUARY 2009 ~ 2:13 A.M.
The Garden

GRAY STANDS IN a snowbank over what used to be the kitchen garden, his hands shoved deep in his coat pockets. A dim light shines in the third-floor gable. What can she possibly be doing up there?

A lithe shadow passes back and forth across the window. He takes a few steps back, cranes his neck, and sees she isn't pacing the floor at all. It almost looks like she's dancing . . . with an invisible man.

8:27 A.M.
The Kitchen

"WHAT'S BECOME OF your cousin, Lucy?"

"Has she gone back to the Cape already?"

"Yeah, we were hoping to get to know her a little better."

Gray rolls his eyes. The way the Seventh Order communicates with outsiders reminds him of the three Graeae, sisters of the Gorgons. Better to share an eyeball than a brain, though.

"She's been through a rough time," Lucy says evenly. "I'm sure we'll see more of her once she's feeling better."

Dewey chews on a stick of beef jerky. "She looked all right to me."

The five of them take their coffee up the back stairs as Lucy pulls out a fountain pen and a sheet of Crane's stationery.

"Think she'll come down?" Gray says.

"I don't know."

"What about the conclave?"

"You seem to have forgotten," Lucy says teasingly, "that tonight is P.C. prayer group."

8:55 A.M.
The Attic

AN EMPTY ASHTRAY tops a stack of books by the bed. Throughout the night, every night, she slides her hand across the sheet to the far side of the mattress in search of him, finding no one.

She's awakened by a rustling from beneath the door, and when she ventures across the room she finds an envelope with her name written in an impeccable script. The note inside reads:

You are cordially invited to dinner.
Where: The dining room.

When: Tonight, 7:30 p.m.
R.S.V.P.: Regrets only.

4:47 P.M.
The Attic

WHEN FOOTSTEPS SOUND on the back stairs it isn't always that girl coming up with more food (and inane half apologies). There must be another boarder living in Aunt Cecelia's bedroom.

This afternoon, however, those same cautious footfalls approach the small stairs outside the attic door. Mary drops her book and tiptoes across the room, avoiding the creaky boards, and lifts the latch without making a sound. Yanking the door open in a single movement, she finds the colored fellow standing on the stairs with his hands in his pockets.

Gray hasn't felt fourteen in a long time, not since he asked Lucy out for coffee in the library lobby. "I was . . . I was just wondering if you were planning to come down to dinner."

"I am," she says. "But only because I could gnaw a leg off the kitchen table."

He laughs softly.

"I'm going mad," she says. "No, that can't be right—I've already gone mad, haven't I?"

Gray keeps his eyes on her feet. "I know I don't know you, but I can say with utter certainty you're the sanest person under this roof."

Mary attempts a smile. "I can't tell if that's a compliment or a warning."

"Both, I guess," he says, glancing at her face before turning away. "Well, I guess I'll see you downstairs, then."

Through the cracked-open door she watches him disappear down the gloomy hallway into the turret room. What is it about him—the way he speaks, the way he carries himself, the way he looks at her—that convinces her he's never told a lie in his life?

5:32 P.M.
Acme Supermarket

MEGAN WRINKLES HER NOSE as Lucy fondles a set of Saran-wrapped chicken breasts. Satisfied, Lucy places the styrofoam platter in her cart and glides past the frozen seafood section. Multitudes of jumbo shrimp, scrubbed pink for the occasion, languish on ice until the house-wives turn up with their Superbowl shopping lists. "You'd better crack a smile soon," Lucy calls over her shoulder. "Or your face might freeze that way."

Megan now fixes her withering eye upon a woman in fluorescent pink spandex leaning into a vertical freezer and poking through stacks of sugar-free ice cream. "If I were an anthropologist," she says, "I could do all my research without ever leaving the Acme. Too bad their whole-foods section is so pitiful."

"I'm going to have to run into town for the bread," Lucy murmurs as she consults her list.

"What was wrong with the baguettes?"

"Stale."

"They were baked this morning, Lu! This dinner doesn't have to be perfect, you know." Megan pauses for a response. "I meant to ask you—what about your little monk friends?"

"They'll be out of the house."

Megan looks at her.

"They've got some sort of regular meeting on Friday nights."

"Does it involve self-flagellation?"

"These jokes have gotten so *old,* Meeg. They've been living in my house for over three years and you're *still* making cracks like an adoles-cent boy."

7:39 P.M.

25 University Avenue ~ The Dining Room

"SHE'S NOT COMING," Lucy says glumly.

Gray taps his spoon on the table. "She's coming."

Megan looks at him pointedly. "And what makes *you* so certain?"

"I knocked on her door this afternoon. She told me she was."

They haven't heard her footsteps approaching through the parlor, so her appearance in the doorway makes all three of them jump. The lace cuffs on her black velvet dress are yellow as margarine; she has done her hair in a careful chignon. Her eyes rove hungrily over the serving platters. "It looks wonderful."

"Sit down, won't you?" Lucy points to the only vacant place set for dinner, beside a woman Mary can only hope is no relation to her. "Mary, I'd like you to meet Megan, my boss."

Megan extends a hand once Mary reluctantly seats herself. "In truth, you and I have already met."

"Megan!" Lucy cries.

"Just be glad you don't remember it. We won't bite, I promise. I'm starving. Oh, Lu, did you remember my—" Lucy hands her a plate with two breaded tofu cutlets. "Thanks, doll."

As Lucy leans over the table to pile her plate with green beans and mashed potatoes, Mary peers under her billowy silk sleeve at Gray seated across the table. "I meant to apologize to you earlier. You must have found it highly insulting, what I said the other—"

He doesn't look up from his chicken. "Don't worry about it."

"What's all this about?"

Lucy places her silverware neatly on her plate. "Mary thought Gray was a servant," she says, and Megan snorts loudly.

"I was disoriented," Mary snaps. "I wasn't thinking. There hasn't been a servant in this house since I was seven." The four of them eat in acutely awkward silence for several minutes before Mary helps herself to more potatoes. "What is it you do, Gray?"

"Classics. I teach introductory Latin and the religions of antiquity to a lot of bumbling, uninterested first-years."

She frowns. "But the university used to have such a fine reputation."

"Oh, it still does," he says. "But for some reason the student body doesn't usually reflect it."

Maybe he doesn't live in the turret; perhaps he just works there. Is it possible they're married? There is no other explanation, for Lucy wears a wedding ring.

Lucy hesitates, but Megan shoots her a go-on-already look, jerking her head in Mary's direction. "I—"

"Gray, I've noticed you don't wear your ring."

He chokes, bug-eyed, bringing his hand to his mouth before they can see the wine dribbling down his chin. Megan laughs and Mary shoots her a stern look. Who does this woman think she is, demanding special chicken and twittering like a hyena? "What's so hilarious?"

"This is my mother's ring," Lucy says calmly. "I've worn it since I was fifteen."

"I don't understand."

Gray lowers the napkin from his lips. "We're not married."

"So you *are* one of the boarders."

"He isn't a boarder, either, Mary. Gray is my boyfriend. We live together."

Stricken, Mary looks at Gray, who nods.

"Marriage is an archaic institution, Mary," Megan says. "These days most of them end in court anyway."

"But that's absurd!" Mary cries. "And what if . . . what if . . ."

Megan drops her fork and slouches back in her seat. "If you want to have a baby, you have a baby. There's just no piece of paper to sanctify the whole business."

"Rubbish."

"Nevertheless, that's the way it is now. You'll get used to it."

Mary looks back and forth at Lucy and Gray as though they've just informed her the meat on her plate is human flesh. "The two of you—you're living in sin, and you don't care a whit what anyone might think of you!" The chair scrapes against the parquet as she stands up.

Megan throws her napkin on her plate. "I knew this was a terrible idea."

"Please, Mary—please sit down. Let's be civil about this."

" 'Civil'? Are you *mad*?"

In the silence that follows Mary recalls Gray's comment on the attic steps, and she watches their frightened expressions as she begins to laugh. "Go ahead and have me committed, why don't you! You can all rest easily knowing no one will believe me!" She storms through the parlor doorway.

"On the contrary," Megan murmurs, "I'd be afraid they would."

Lucy rises from her chair to follow her out of the room. "Mary—please, don't leave yet—"

Mary opens the entertainment console doors and jerks a finger at the television. "What *is* this?"

Someone else's shadow darkens the foyer threshold. "Dewey!" Lucy makes a valiant attempt to hide her dismay. "I thought you were out at the meeting."

"I stayed home." His fists full of wadded tissues, Dewey shuffles into the room, pausing for a triple sneeze that showers his germs all over the parlor sofa. "It seems I have an upper respiratory infection." He turns to Mary at the open cabinet. "Did I hear you say you didn't know what a television was?"

"Don't mind her," Megan calls from the far end of the dining table. "She was raised in an ashram." Dewey peers through the doorway, squinting at her suspiciously before letting loose with another violent sneeze.

Lucy ushers him through the dining room and into the kitchen. "Let's just get you fixed up with some chicken soup, shall we? I have some in the freezer I can defrost in no time."

"That would be nice, but—"

"How about some o.j.? And have you been taking your vitamins?"

"Well, I—"

The kitchen door swings closed behind them and Megan turns to Mary. "We'll tell you all about the boob tube some other time. Come sit down and we'll have dessert."

"The *what*?"

"Let me ask you something," Megan says as Mary ventures back into the room. "What's the last day you remember?"

"Excuse me?"

"The last day you can recall. What day?"

"It was a Thursday . . . September . . . September twenty-sixth."

"Nineteen twenty-nine?"

"Yes, of course."

Megan laughs. "If you think *this* is misery, you should look in a history book. Start with the stock market crash."

"Megan, I know you like this tough-love way of doing things, but it isn't help—"

"Don't you shush me, Gray. She's in desperate need of a reality check."

"What I need," Mary says, "is to finish my meal in peace." They stare at her as she picks up her plate and walks out through the parlor door.

Mary trudges up the foyer staircase, weeping onto what remains of her dinner. A moment later, the front door opens and the other four members of the Seventh Order come tramping into the hall.

8:35 P.M.

The Dining Room

GRAY CLEARS THE TABLE, serves Megan a cup of her favorite Fair Trade organic brew, and disappears up the back stairs. The chicken soup thaws in the microwave and Lucy sends Dewey back to bed with a bowl on the breakfast tray. She falls into the chair beside her friend with a weary sigh.

"You through ministering to the invalid?"

"I should go up to the attic."

"Not yet. Give her a chance to calm down."

From the heating vent above their heads come the sounds of raucous male laughter. "Are they sacrificing a lamb up there, or what?"

Lucy gives her a glance of warning.

"Those dudes make me nervous."

"They're harmless, Meeg. It's a secular fraternity."

"Ha! That's what they tell *you*." As Megan sips her coffee a change comes over her face.

Lucy watches her in silence before speaking. "Whatever you're thinking about, it's aged you ten years in the last minute and a half."

"They're coming to the lab. The Feds. First thing Wednesday morning. Cheeky bastards," Megan growls. "They're so used to lying through their teeth that they can't even call it what it is—it's a search but they call it a tour. A *tour*! Like we work in a friggin' wax museum!"

Lucy feels the beginnings of another headache prompted by too many hours spent squinting in the glare of the computer screens. That, and the thought of yet another Bush in the Oval Office, which is quite enough to give a girl a perpetual migraine. "I should have left years ago. Scandinavia or someplace."

"We *all* should have," Megan says. "What are you going to do about it now?"

Lucy utters a cold little laugh. "Uh . . . *leave*?"

"You can't leave now, dear. The 'all-seeing Eye' has fixed its stare upon our shabby little laboratory." Megan takes off her glasses and rubs her eyes. "I know it's difficult, but things won't always be this way—"

"Won't they?"

"Don't worry about it too much. We've got private funding—there's only so much they can do to me."

Lucy sighs. "You want another cup?"

"No, thanks."

"There's something else, isn't there?"

Megan leans across the table. "Mark my words," she says. "She's going to want her husband back. You can't do it again, Lucy—you nearly killed yourself the first time."

"It wouldn't be like the first time."

"Listen to me, damn it! Think of your future, and Gray's, and mine." Mary's future is of scant concern. "Put it out of your head right now, because it's not going to happen."

"You aren't the one who's got to tell her that. What do I say?"

"Tell her it's impossible."

Lucy hesitates. "But it isn't."

9:00 P.M.
The Attic

"I THOUGHT YOU MIGHT need to see this." Lucy, avoiding the eyes of her ancestors perched in a semicircle around the bed, hands her a tattered manila envelope. "I'm sorry about the way things went earlier."

Mary opens the envelope and scans the first page in disgust. "So you're making it up to me by showing me a deed with your name on it?"

"I should have begun at the beginning."

"Always a wise place to start."

"My mother used to say that."

"Perhaps she got it from me."

"I'm sure she did—that is—"

"Don't let's dance around the pronouns, please. I simply will not refer to myself in the third person."

Lucy's decision to choose her battles doesn't make the awkward silence any easier to sit through. "I wanted to explain—"

"There's nothing to explain. I went through your bookshelves, I read some of your treatises on human cloning. For it, against it, ethical perspectives, reproductive technology, and all that rot. I understand now that you wouldn't fix it, even if you could. If I could go back to nineteen twenty-nine there would be two of me." She pauses. "The only thing I don't understand is why they all said it's impossible to clone the dead."

"Those books are all at least ten years old."

Mary cocks an eyebrow. "So the new ones provide instructions?"

9:19 P.M.
The Third-Floor Corridor

GRAY PRESSES HIS ear to the door.

9:20 P.M.
The Attic

"THIS ISN'T HELPING."

"You know, it just now occurred to me, Lucy. Perhaps I'm not dead at all. Have you locked your grandmother in the basement?"

"If that were the case you'd be a great deal older, wouldn't you?"

"Now, that's the other thing. In those books they say cloning a person only results in an infant with all the genes of the person cloned."

"Like I said, the books are wrong."

"And what of *this* book?" Mary taps the dust jacket of *Everyday Life.*

"It was published in nineteen fifty-nine—you noticed that, right?"

"Of *course* I noticed."

"People thought he was just a crackpot, but there were all these very specific things he'd written about which came to pass, the Kennedy assassinations and all sorts of things. He never mentioned them by name, but it was all laid out very clearly. By the time anyone noticed that he was too accurate to be making it up, nearly every copy of the book had dropped out of circulation."

"Along with the author, I suppose."

Lucy nods. "It's one of the greatest mysteries of the last century, except that most people haven't ever heard of it."

Another protracted silence. Mary breaks it. "You would go to prison if you were found out, I suppose."

"What makes you say that?"

"Common sense. Besides which, I've read this cover to cover twice already."

"So you've read it's illegal to use any type of government funding for stem cell research. Stem cells are—"

"I *know* what stem cells are."

Lucy stares at the double bed on the floor, lost in thought. Godfry does not mention this, but a cadre of neoconservative lawmakers—headed by men who compare Democrats to Nazis and deliver florid apologies for pro-life snipers on the Senate floor—are laboring assiduously on legislation to ban the use of private funding as well. But Mary doesn't need to know all this.

"What I don't understand is how it concerns you," Mary says.

"I'm a researcher at the university," Lucy replies. "And we *are* using government funds. They're being diverted from the vivisection labs." She laughs. "Makes you wonder what kind of scientist would take seventeen years to find a cure for lazy eye." The smile falls from her face as quickly as it appeared. "You can't discuss any of this with anyone, you understand? It isn't even safe to speak in private."

"Not even in this drafty old attic?"

"We'd be safer talking in a railway terminal. Don't *ever* let on you're not my cousin, not to anyone. Not even on pain of death."

That won't be a problem, seeing as she has nothing to live for. "That's why you put all our photographs away, isn't it? And the family tree?"

"You are a copy of someone who passed away twenty years ago. Leaving all those pictures lying around is practically inviting someone to turn me in."

"But those boys—"

"I couldn't trust them even if I wanted to."

"Colin seems like a nice fellow."

"I heard you were introduced."

"I met him on the way to the W.C."

"And all the rest, I take it?"

Mary nods.

"I wasn't expecting you'd meet them so soon. Otherwise I would have prepared you."

"Colin asked me if I was feeling better. I guessed you had told them I was a cousin of yours passing my convalescence here."

"What else did you talk about?"

"I can't remember much more. They said I dressed like you . . . and I told them I was married— "

"Did you tell them where your husband was? Did you?"

"Yes," Mary says, after several moments' pause, "I said he was studying medicine on the Cape."

"There *is* no med school on the Cape, Mary. For God's sake, there isn't even a hospital!"

"Of course there is!"

"It closed twenty years ago, all right?" Mary looks at her, stunned into silence. "Don't tell them anything from now on. Not even what seems like the most inconsequential bit of information—not even what you had for breakfast."

"Then what *am* I supposed to talk about?"

Lucy cringes to feel that familiar trickle starting in her nose again. "The weather. It's as reliable a topic as ever." She puts her hand to her face and rises from the chair. "Well, I'm glad we were able to sort a few things out."

"But you've said nothing of Teddy," Mary ventures. "I know he's dead. But I need to know— "

"You don't need to know anything," Lucy says as the blood trickles down her lip. "It's better if you don't."

"Better for whom?" Mary cries as Lucy hurries to the door and slams it behind her.

conservative social critics assert that the brassiere-burning freedom mavens of the nineteen-sixties catalyzed the general collapse of feminine modesty in Western civilization. It is a sad truth that most young women of the "twenty-ohs" prefer raiment which serves as an overt showcase for those physical attributes most commonly scrutinized for evidence of sexual fitness. To utilize a phrase they will no doubt find rather antiquated in these times, precious little is left to the imagination, whether on television, the silver screen, or the streets of Smallville.

You will also discover that these inhabitants of the future usually exhibit laissez-faire sexual attitudes, behavior which is epitomized by the phenomenon commonly known as the "one-night stand," most often an unfortunate byproduct of overindulgence in alcohol, narcotics, or both. Other manifestations of severe moral turpitude include, but are by no means limited to, orgies, particularly in urban nightclubs rife with glittering diablerie; necrophilia; liaisons arranged through a technology known as the "Internet" (for a comprehensive explanation, please see Chapter 46); brazen homosexuality; and cohabitation outside the bonds of holy matrimony, which is widely condoned due to practical economic concerns.

Should you find yourself as appalled at these circumstances as I did, I am happy to report the existence of a dim ray of hope: a widespread renewal of the secular male purity movement, which began in America in the early decades of the

9:32 P.M.
The Attic

SHE HAS JUST BEGUN, again, the chapter in Godfry's book that distinguishes time-travelers from other "chronologically displaced persons" when someone knocks on the attic door, a soft tapping too tentative to be Lucy returning to apologize. She tugs the door open.

"I just wanted to make sure you were all right." Over her shoulder Gray notices a battered washstand wedged between two bulkier pieces of furniture. A fresh bar of soap lies glistening on a porcelain dish; cloudy water fills the bowl.

She steps aside. "Would you like to come in and sit down?"

Staring at the picture frames arranged on the floor around her pillow, he seats himself in the chair by the rolltop desk. She steps across the neatly made bed and sits in the armchair by the window, watching him as he eyes the tidy row of relics on the desk's top surface. "Was that your camera?"

She nods.

"May I?"

She nods again.

He handles it carefully, adjusting the recalcitrant shutter-speed dial between his thumb and forefinger, watching her through the viewfinder as she smoothes her skirt over her knees. "It's in very good shape."

"I suppose it is, after eighty years." She pauses. "May I ask you something?"

"Shoot."

"Pardon?"

"Go ahead and ask."

"Why haven't you married her?"

He should have expected this. Gently, he places the Rolleiflex back on the desk. "Lucy doesn't want to get married."

"So you've asked?"

He doesn't answer.

"Then how do you know she doesn't want to?"

"You don't know Lucy," he says, with a hard little laugh.

"Nor do I care to."

"I know you're angry, but this wasn't supposed to happen. She loved you—her grandmother, I mean."

"If she loved me that much she ought to have named a child after me. A real child, a normal child. That's what ordinary women do."

"Lucy isn't an ordinary woman."

For a few moments she stares at the floor, absorbed in thought. Then she looks up as though something has just occurred to her. "She couldn't have a child of her own . . . could she?"

He shakes his head. "Not without help."

"I don't wish to know what it is you mean by that. Dear God," she murmurs, "what's happened to the world?"

Gray pauses. "She gave birth to you. Did you know that?"

"I won't hear any more about any of that," she says quickly. "I can't begin to imagine all the fiendish things she must have growing down there in the basement."

He laughs. "If I took you down there I think you'd be pretty disappointed."

"Why?"

"It looks like a doctor's office," he says. "Well . . . there are a few odd things here and there . . ."

"Such as?"

"Lucy's father owned a skeleton. It's still down there."

"You see—I knew it!" She leans back in her chair and folds her arms over her chest. "You haven't answered my question, you know."

"Which question is that?"

"You know perfectly well which question."

He squirms in his chair.

"I see," she says quietly.

"What do you see?"

"You don't love her."

He pauses. "It's not that I don't. It's just—"

"There is no 'it's just this' or 'just that.' Either you love her or you don't."

"It's not that simple."

"I think it *is*."

"Listen," he says, "it wasn't at all complicated for you—you and Edward and your little storybook romance. I'm sorry"—this is in response to the expression on her face—"I don't mean to be condescending. What I'm trying to say is that it doesn't come so easily for most people nowadays. Most of us have to flail around for years until we find something that fits."

"You try on girls like you would dress shirts?"

"Things are different now," he says weakly. "There was this thing they called the 'sexual revolution,' during the sixties—"

Mary shakes her head.

At last he says, "She doesn't love me, either."

She looks away. Then she clears her throat. "I want to know what happened to him."

"To Teddy?"

She nods. "Will you tell me?"

"I . . . I really shouldn't."

"I found a picture of him in uniform."

"You know he's dead, Mary. He's been dead for more than sixty years. What good can come of knowing the details?"

She closes her eyes. "Did she tell you to say that?"

"She hasn't told me to say anything."

"There was another Great War, wasn't there?"

"They had to start numbering them," he says softly. "World War Two."

"Please—please tell me what happened." She begins to cry, and he looks at her helplessly. "Do you have any idea what it's like to . . . to wake up one morning . . . and find you're completely alone in the world?"

"Believe me, if only it were in my power to help somehow,, I—"

"Your father . . . your brothers . . . your husband . . . all dead." She stares at the floor, her eyes wide but vacant. "Of course you don't. How could you?"

"He was in the Medical Corps. He was stationed in Normandy—I don't know when, exactly. It must have been after the invasion."

"What invasion?"

"France was occupied. The Allies launched an invasion in June of nineteen forty-four. They called it D-day."

"Go on."

"I don't know how he died." He pauses. "I'm sorry."

She sinks to the floor, trembling, and he crawls over the bed. "Gibbon," she whispers. "My poor gibbon."

Tentatively he touches her elbow and she responds gratefully, throwing her arms around his neck and sobbing into his chest.

AN HOUR LATER they sit side by side on the old mattress heaped with scratchy wool blankets. His chest is cold and clammy from her tears, which have soaked through his oxford shirt. Mary is serene, accepting—like a virgin martyr. "It's funny you called him gibbon," he murmurs.

"I liked the ring of it," she says defensively. "He used to call me rabbit."

"It's funny because gibbons mate for life."

"It seems," Mary says, after a long pause, "they're the only primates who do."

SATURDAY, 7 FEBRUARY 2009
The Attic

SHE COMES UPON the framed family tree tucked behind the rolltop desk and sits for what feels like hours rereading the dates and years of all their deaths: Teddy's, Aunt Cee's, her brothers', her father's. And hers.

She winds up the gramophone and puts on the university choir's recording of "In dulci jubilo," but after a few moments she lifts the needle again with a trembling hand. Is there something new in the cabinet, some band that shouldn't exist yet?

KOOKABURRA, says one record label. BORN IN A TRUNK (MEDLEY), says another. TROUBLE IN MIND catches her eye and she drops it on the turntable. It isn't at all the kind of music she would listen to on an ordinary evening, but as she listens she slings her legs over the arm of the old chair by the window, hankering for a cigarette, or a hot buttered rum—either would do.

I'm gonna lay my head on some lonesome railroad line . . .

Her head is in her hands, for she understands what Nina Simone is singing now in a way she never could have before.

let the two-nineteen train ease my troubled mind.

10:00 P.M.
The Master Bathroom

NO MATTER HOW hot Mary runs the water, every bath she takes reminds her of that summer at Cape Eden, the summer she was seven. As she slides into the tub she recalls the force with which the undertow dragged her beneath the surface, and how when she came up briefly, gasping and flailing, she could see her father sprinting across the sand, pumping his arms like an Olympian.

Afterwards they clung to her, all of them wanting to stroke her hair and kiss her cheek, but it was her father who clung to her the hardest. Her mother was crying; so was he.

She lies still in the water, straining to place the sounds coming from other parts of the house. Every so often her heart leaps into her throat at what sounds at first like an old familiar voice.

MONDAY, 9 FEBRUARY 2009 ~ 2:55 P.M.

The Third-Floor Turret Room

"WHAT DOES THIS MEAN?"

He jumps in his chair.

"I'm sorry," Mary says. "I didn't mean to frighten you."

"It just gets so quiet in the afternoons." He drops his red pen on a stack of uncorrected translations and leans back in his chair. "Before they come home, I mean."

She points to the window decal taped to the door.

"It's a peace symbol," he says. "Have you read about Vietnam yet?"

"I can't keep them straight," she says. "All these wars, there are so many of them."

"Yeah," he says stupidly.

Now she points to his laptop, where the screen saver gives the illusion of hurtling through space. "What is that?"

"It's a computer."

"Computer," she murmurs. "What does it do?"

"A lot of things. You can use it as a typewriter, except you can make changes without retyping a whole page. You can use it to play games—"

"What sort of games?" She watches as he opens the solitaire program. "Those are meant to be cards?"

"Yup."

"Why wouldn't you just play with a deck?"

He shrugs. "If you don't have a pack handy—"

"Can you play mahjong?"

"I don't know. Maybe you could download it."

"Down load it?"

"Never mind."

"What else does it do?"

"You can send messages to people all over the world—it's called electronic mail. E-mail for short."

"May I see?"

"Sure." He opens his school e-mail account and, ignoring the half-dozen messages from the more earnest among his students, clicks the "compose" button.

"Where do you put the stamp?"

He laughs. "You don't need a stamp. You just click 'send' and off it goes."

"It doesn't cost anything?"

"Well, you have to pay for Internet access every month. It's not too expensive, though. I think ours costs about forty."

"Forty cents?"

"Dollars."

"But that's outrageous! It costs two cents to mail a letter!"

"That's inflation for you."

"I'll say."

"It's forty-six cents now, by the way."

"But that's absurd!"

"Tell me about it. And the delivery's more unreliable than ever. Sometimes when you send a message over the Internet it doesn't work—we say it's 'lost in cyberspace'—but on the whole it's much more reliable."

"What's the Internet? And cyber . . . space?"

"It's the way we share information. There are these pages called websites, where you can find anything from cookie recipes to encyclopedia entries to political propaganda and God only knows what else."

"So there's a library inside that little machine?"

"Sort of. But if you printed everything out it would fill a whole lot more than a single library."

"How can you possibly fit all that information into such a small contraption?"

"Well, it isn't all stored on one computer. There are networks, and servers—"

"What?"

"You have a record collection, don't you?" She nods. "It's sort of like that, except the record is much smaller and has a much larger capacity."

"I see. How do you use it, then?"

He double-clicks on the Web browser icon on his desktop and his home page loads instantly.

"The *Globe*! " she cries. "You can read the papers on this thing, too?"

"You want to try it?" He stands behind the chair as she seats herself.

"This looks like a typewriter."

"It's basically the same."

She peers eagerly into the screen. An earthquake in Nepal yesterday morning has caused the loss of at least two thousand lives, and counting. An unrepentant Klansman is sentenced today for the murders of two civil rights workers in 1966. A statement signed by a mere eight senators condemns the forty-fourth president's nominee for attorney general, who was convicted of drunk driving in 1982. And as for local news, last night a Marblehead man was struck by an ambulance while walking his collie.

"I don't want to read any more of these headlines," she says. "Is it just today's news, or . . . ?"

He points to an icon on the top right. "There's an archive."

"How do I get to it?"

"Oh, sorry. You see that thing down there, below the keyboard? It's called a mouse."

She laughs. "Is it, really?"

"You use it to navigate. Here, watch this." Leaning over her shoulder, he flicks his fingertip over the trackpad and on the screen a little black arrow responds. He clicks the mouse and a new page loads: BOSTON GLOBE NEWS ARCHIVES.

"How do I do this?"

"What are you looking for?"

She hesitates. "His obituary."

"I don't think that's wise."

"Are you going to help me or not?"

"All right," he says. "Click here, on the advanced search engine link."

Search word(s)?

"Morrigan," she types.

Search category?

Waving him away when he offers to take over the mouse, she chooses "obituary" from a drop-down list.

Search dates?

"*09/26/1929 to present.*"

"That isn't necessary," he says quickly. "Besides, the search will take a lot longer."

She turns to him as she clicks the "search" button. "Methinks the gentleman doth protest too much."

"The gentleman doth protest because he wisheth to preserve the lady from that which might alarmeth her."

Seven items appear on the search list. She returns her attention to the screen and he sighs in defeat.

MORRIGAN, EDWARD	1944
MORRIGAN, JANE	1947
MORRIGAN, EDWARD, JR.	1953
MORRIGAN, JOSEPH	1953
MORRIGAN, LUCINDA	1986
MORRIGAN, MARY	1989

"You see why I—" He frowns at her. "Why aren't you . . . ?"

"I found the genealogy behind the desk. All up to date, except for one," she says calmly, tapping one of the names on the screen. "All but Teddy Junior. Strange! You knew it already, didn't you?"

"I knew about Lucy's mother, but Lucy never told me anything about her uncles." He points to the bottom of the screen. "It says here, the text of entries before nineteen ninety-five aren't in the database. We can go downtown to the library, look them up on microfilm."

Mary had imagined a dozen scenarios to explain their absence, but in truth her children never became explorers of sea or space, and will never return to great fanfare. "No," she says quietly. "No, there's no need." She enters the surnames of all her closest friends, finding their parents and brothers but none of them. "All married, of course," she says to herself. "Damn it."

D-e-a-r-t-h-i—

"Haven't you seen enough?"

n-g. Same search parameters.

"Mary, please don't."

"You're right," she says softly as he leans over her shoulder again to close the browser window. "There's no point. I already know my father died in nineteen sixty-two."

GLOBALIZATION: The spread of capitalism like an airborne virus (see section on INFECTIOUS DISEASES, Chapter 54) from first- to third-world nations, and the burgeoning economic interdependence (and detestable cultural homogeneity) which inevitably results.

GROUND ZERO: Generally, the point at which a nuclear explosion occurs; thrown about with irritating frequency regarding the early-autumn, early-century tragedy. See A-BOMB, Chapter 5.

HAZMATS: Shorthand for "hazardous materials." See ANTHRAX, BIOTERRORISM, NUCLEAR WASTE.

IDENTITY THEFT: The act of impersonating another by using that person's social security and credit card numbers. A serious problem at the turn of the century.

INDIE: Short for "independent," as in music and low-budget films. Also, as of late, a cliché for weepy adolescent songwriters.

JESUS FREAK: A Christian zealot, often but not always possessed of a hypocritical and judgmental nature. A cabal of outspoken "Jesus freaks" currently pull the strings of the Grand Old Party (see Chapters 53 and 55).

KICKS: Slang for tennis shoes.

KLEPTO: A serial shoplifter, often a wealthy, easily bored whippersnapper with no productive pastimes; an abbreviation of "kleptomaniac."

MC- [PREFIX]: Used to mock the ubiquitous fast-food chain McDonald's, not the Irish race. Examples include, but are by no means limited to, McJob (i.e., a peonage), McMansion (see SUBURBAN SPRAWL), McWorld (see GLOBALIZATION), et cetera.

TUESDAY, 10 FEBRUARY 2009 ~ 1:31 P.M.
Yobanashi Tea Room

"AWW, YOU WERE EARLY!" Lucy says brightly, shrugging off her coat. "I've been looking forward to this all—"

She raises her eyes to the flat-screen television above the bar, and Gray watches the smile fall from her face. "Half a dozen people have asked the manager to change the channel in the last five minutes," he explains.

"Why hasn't she?"

"She says they have to keep it tuned to the campus station."

"Bullshit," she mutters.

"I was thinking we could go somewhere else."

"I don't have time to go off campus, Gray. I have to be back at quarter past two." Lucy scowls up at the face of Charles Harris Fuller, who is addressing the God Squad as part of a lunchtime lecture series in an auditorium across campus. Or rather, he is addressing the TV cameras, since those in the room need little persuading.

"Now, I know what you're thinking," Fuller says.

"Just one of his many talents," Lucy scoffs.

"You're thinking it just isn't right to deny your grandmothers a cure for their ailments," Fuller goes on, "and believe me, I *laud* your devotion—"

Lucy flags down the hostess and asks if they might move to another table across the room, away from the television. The hostess glances at the far side of the restaurant, where the only empty chair is opposite one of the ubiquitous pasty-faced grad students with his notes spread out all over the table. "Sorry," she says, "but it'll probably be at least twenty minutes before a table opens up." Lucy slides into the booth with another sour glance at the TV.

"It won't be so bad," Gray says. "We'll ignore him."

"—but you and I both know there's a serious moral ambiguity we simply must address. Is this not our obli*ga*tion, as a sentient race?"

Grimly she opens her menu and looks it up and down as if she hasn't already memorized the tea and sandwich lists through years of frequenting the place.

"Hey, Gray! Hey, Lu!" someone calls from behind them, and Gray ducks behind his menu.

"—and of course we as Christians believe that just because we *possess* these technological capabilities"—gesturing excessively, his gold pinkie ring flashing under the sickly fluorescent lights—"does not necessarily mean we should *use* them."

Felix gives him a playful punch to the shoulder. "What's up, guys?"

"Mind if we join you?" Colin begins to slide into the booth beside her.

"We do, actually," Gray replies, and Lucy stares at him in awe. "This is a date."

"Oh—oh, right—of course, of course—"

"Sorry about that," Felix says, turning to the television. "Hey, what's this joker doing live on NHU-TV?"

"I thought you'd be there yourself," Lucy says, teasing. "He's speaking in the Schimmel Auditorium."

"Nah, no way," Felix says. "I know how uncharitable it is for me to say so, but I really wish that guy would chug some bleach."

Gray laughs. "After he's done brushing with it?"

Felix slaps him on the back. "Yeah, yeah! Exactly!"

Colin shakes his head. "Was that really necessary, Felix?"

Felix rolls his eyes. "Go down to Schimmel, why don't you?"

"You know what?" Lucy says, grabbing her coat and sliding out of the booth. "I'd rather eat in the cafeteria." Gray hesitates before following her out, and the boys promptly snag their booth.

Fuller's finally coming to the end of his tirade. "You, the students, have every right to protest what goes on in the windowless laboratories of this university. It is your prerogative to call into question the moral validity of these projects; indeed, it is your *duty.*"

"Good thing she left when she did." Felix yawns.

"Yeah." Colin stares up at the screen for a close-up of Charles Harris Fuller's ear-to-ear grin. The God Squad has given him a standing ovation. "She'd've *really* blown a gasket at that one."

11:37 P.M.

25 University Avenue ~ The Labyrinth

THE SNOW-CLOUDS have drifted off to other parts, leaving a crisp edge around the near-full moon. The hedges are so overgrown she'd need to walk sideways to keep the snow off her collar. Instead she walks with her shoulders squared, and only back in the attic will she notice how damp ermine stinks.

A succession of left turns will only return the mouse to the point of entry.

She steps through the archway, still hankering for a cigarette. No spoons atop the fountain now, and the drifts have covered the wrought-iron benches where her mother used to read to her in the afternoons.

You're very good at that, you know.

11:37 P.M.

The Third-Floor Turret Room

"WHAT ARE YOU LOOKING AT?"

He glances over his shoulder, casually, as though she hadn't startled him. No sense telling her he'd been looking at nothing. "She's gone out for a walk."

Her breath fogs the windowpane and she wipes the glass with the sleeve of her cardigan. "She's left the house? Where is she?"

"In the maze. See that hedge rustling near the center?" She nods, slowly. "How did it go earlier?" he asks.

"How did what go?"

"Didn't you go up and talk to her?"

Lucy doesn't answer.

"Not so well?"

"I don't know." She drops onto the bed and her hair fans out just so over his pillow. "Let's just—let's not talk about her again tonight."

He returns to his desk chair. "I've got a dozen translations left to grade, so . . ."

She extends a long slender hand to choose a bit of light reading—Ovid or Juvenal?—from the stack on his night table, for the interim.

WEDNESDAY, 11 FEBRUARY 2009 ~ 8:44 A.M.
The Kitchen

LUCY IS CHANGING the coffee filter when Mary comes down the back stairs in an old chenille night robe, poking her head around the corner first to be sure no men are present. "I need to go into town today," Mary says.

"What for?"

Mary pulls an empty pack of Lucky Strikes out of her pocket and drops it on the counter.

The used coffee filter falls into the trash can with a wet thud. "How did you get those?"

"Tucked it away last summer. The tobacco's gone bad."

Lucy sighs. "They're coffin nails," she says. "It was proven fifty years ago."

"What?"

"Smoking causes cancer."

"Cancer?"

"Now would be a good time to quit."

"I don't want to quit."

"Didn't you hear what I said?"

"I heard what you said, and I'm telling you I'd die to smoke one. I'm going into town."

"I'm not sure that's a good idea."

"You'd rather I stay here and rot?"

"It's a different world outside this house. You're not prepared for it."

"Why am I even asking you for permission?"

"Because you need a ride, that's why. And I couldn't give you one even if I wanted to. I have to go to work."

Mary turns back to the stairs. "I'll ask Gray."

"Don't," Lucy snaps. "I'll take you. Just give me a few minutes to finish making breakfast."

8:52 A.M.
The Basement

LUCY DIALS MEGAN'S number at the lab. "Is it all right if I don't come in today?"

"Is everything okay?"

"She's run out of cigarettes."

"How did she get a*hold* of any cigarettes? Can't you just buy her some on the way home from work?"

"I think she's ready to leave the house. I didn't want to discourage her."

Megan sighs.

"Damn, I forgot all about the Feds. I'm sorry Meeg, I can—"

"No, no, it's all right," she says wearily. "It's just as well you won't be there."

8:52 A.M.
The Second Floor

AS SHE WOULD PREFER not to meet any members of the Seventh Order before she's bathed and dressed, she pulls a fresh towel and washcloth from the second-floor linen closet and gives herself a quick scrubbing in Lucy's bathroom. She reclaims her French dressing-robe and heads for the stairs to the third floor, but there will be no tip-toeing past the turret room: Colin sits facing his open doorway as though expecting her, a mug of black coffee steaming between his spindly fingers. Mortification glues her to the spot.

He takes a sip of his coffee. "Good morning, Mary."

"Good morning, Colin," she mutters, just before she disappears up the stairs in a flash of white calf and virgin-blue satin.

She finds a leather handbag of her mother's in someone else's wedding trunk. Inside are a cigarette case of tarnished silver and an ivory holder. Under the lid of the same trunk is stapled a warranty card stamped with an expiration date of December 31, 1947. After donning her favorite velveteen dress, her Donegal tweed coat, and a blue cloche she'd found still hanging on a hat rack—though her hair is now too long for it—she descends the attic stairs, her heart in her throat at the prospect of meeting the distant future head-on.

9:55 A.M.
The Kitchen

"I HEAR YOU'RE going to have an adventure today." Gray's eyes sparkle over his coffee mug. "I wish I could come with you."

"Why don't you?" Mary asks.

"Meetings," he says gloomily as he wipes the bacon grease from his fingers with a paper napkin. "And a lecture, and office hours."

"I studied Latin at the high school, you know."

"Did you?"

"I might like to sit in on a lecture of yours sometime—if you wouldn't mind."

Dear God, what a terrifying thought. "I wouldn't mind at all."

Lucy appears in the doorway in her black wool peacoat, jingling the car keys as though they're late for a doctor's appointment.

10:26 A.M.
Hilary Road, Eastbound

HILARY ROAD links the university to downtown New Halcyon, where the grid is laid with similarly feminine names. Between the years of 1893 and 1904 a Boston pharmaceutical magnate bought up half the town, and in 1905 he had its principal streets rechristened after each of his seven daughters.

Dirty snow piles line the street. "These motorcars are so strange-looking," Mary had said at first sight of the Prius, and she murmurs this again, several times, once she and Lucy are on the road—they pass mostly SUVs with entertainment systems mounted to the ceilings to pacify their diminutive backseat occupants. Dun-colored houses loom tall and uninviting along the side of the road, their driveways occupied by more of those clumsy automobiles—or military tanks, what's the distinction? Billboard advertisements for "custom luxury homes from the mid-$900,000s," encrusted with icicles, mark what few fallow corn and potato fields remain.

" 'Luxury' is something of an understatement, is it not?"

"Our house is worth nearly three million."

Mary gasps.

"Inflation," Lucy offers.

This revelation stuns Mary to silence for another mile. "What's happened to the farms along this road?"

"Sold before I was born." Lucy brakes at a red light and turns to look at her. "Are you sure you want to do this?"

Mary looks at her as she would at a sister who'd stolen her beau; it is a placid sort of resentment.

10:45 A.M.

297 Lavinia Street ~ New Halcyon

THANKFULLY THE family-owned tobacco shop is still open for business. The same wooden sign in fresh crimson and yellow paint hangs above the doorway: E. M. HIGGINS, TOBACCONIST. EST. 1904. Inside, too, things are much as she remembers them: the heavy wooden tables; the low stools topped in red velvet where old men can savor their stogies, free of their nagging wives if only for an hour; the display cases lined with pipes and cigar cutters with exquisitely sharp blades; the shelves of imported cigarettes, jars of loose tobacco, pouches of pipe tobacco from all over the world (Troost Special Cavendish was her father's favorite), and flavored rolling papers behind the counter; the dim glass-fronted humidor in the back. The elderly Higgins standing behind the register is familiar, too, though he's not the Higgins she remembers. This Higgins was still learning his multiplication tables when Mary was here last.

Sinatra sings from a radio on a high shelf. Their entrance rouses a pair of middling-to-elderly men out of their smoke-laden indolence at the corner table. "Now, aren't these two a picture!" says one.

"You said it," says the other. "Like they just stepped out of a time machine."

"Maybe they're shooting another period piece down the road there. What was the name of that film they did a few years ago?"

"Oh, hell, how should I remember? It was terrible!"

"That's putting it too nice." The other man nods emphatically. "I only went to see it because my house is in the first scene."

Mary smiles indulgently as Lucy launches into a coughing fit.

"Good morning, ladies," Higgins says. "How may I assist you?"

"I'd like a pack of Lucky Strikes, please."

"Certainly." He plucks a pack from a high shelf and places it on the counter.

"I'd like more than one, actually."

"We don't carry them by the carton, I'm afraid."

"I'll take a dozen, then."

"Make that four packs, please."

"Are you planning to bring me into town again in another two days?" Mary hisses. "I need a dozen."

"I'm not paying for a dozen packs of cigarettes."

"Half a dozen?"

Behind the counter the old man smiles faintly in amusement. Lucy sighs. "Sorry for the confusion. Half a dozen, please."

Higgins presents Mary with another five packs and she stares at the stark black-and-white message on the label: *Smoking causes cancer, emphysema, and impotence.*

"Didn't believe me, did you?"

"I didn't want to," Mary replies.

"Seems to be the case with most enjoyable things in life," Higgins says. "Would you still like them?"

Mary hesitates, not because she's thinking of forgoing the cigarettes but because she wants to ask Higgins if she can just sniff that jar of Troost. "Yes, please."

"You can quit tomorrow, eh?" The cash register, which looks old enough to have been in the shop the last time Mary was here, gives a cheerful jingle. "Or perhaps the week after next. That'll be forty-eight dollars and sixty-three cents, please." Lucy hands him a fifty before she exits the shop, still coughing, and Mary receives her change. Every dime lying heads-up in her open palm is stamped with the face of a future president.

11:00 A.M.
Lavinia Street

"LOOKS LIKE IT'S going to snow again."

"My God. Forty-eight dollars could feed an African nation."

"Not anymore." Lucy follows her down to the end of the block, past a horde of teenage boys off from the prep school because of the snow. One of them pops his head into Higgins's shop, and Mary laughs as the old man shouts, "Come back when you're eighteen, boy—not a day before!"

"Where are you going?" Lucy calls after her.

"The Italian bakery—is it still here? They made the most delicious rum cakes." As she reaches the corner of Lavinia and Third she sees the Italian bakery is gone.

"There's another bakery on Leonora Avenue."

"Carmella's?"

Lucy shakes her head. "I forget what it's called, but it's not Carmella's. Their cupcakes taste like styrofoam."

Another anomaly in her peripheral vision—Mary jerks her head to the opposite corner to find that Chester's, the drugstore, is no longer there. Staring up at the sleek pink logo above the old brick doorway, she waits for a car to pass before striding into the street. "What's a *lingerie* store doing here?"

Lucy pulls her to the curb by her elbow as another motorist taps his horn. "It's called Luscious. Cheap women's clothing."

What Mary sees in the boutique window saps the color from her cheeks. Lucy has not considered the effect her own clothing has had. It isn't so much a matter of Mary's seeing someone she doesn't know wearing her clothes; it's that the absence of these trappings of modernity—including the sort of clothing one sees in all the shopwindows these days, which bear no resemblance to the fashions of eighty years past—has prevented Mary from acknowledging the reality of her strange new time.

Now, as Mary stares agape at the white plastic mannequins in the boutique window, their absurdly pointed nipples poking through sheer shimmery tunics and spandex minidresses, Lucy realizes that she should have prepared her for sights like this.

Mary watches Lucy's reflection in the shopwindow cross the street and come up beside her. "They don't wear this sort of thing *out of doors,* do they?"

"I'm afraid they do."

"But I wouldn't wear that in front of my own husband!" Mary presses her palms to her eyelids and Lucy catches sight of the aquamarine ring on her left hand. The shopgirl on the other side of the glass stares at them as she makes a pretense of dusting the display window.

"I used to eat ice cream here." Mary's voice is low and thick, a note of hysteria all too clear.

"Look, I'm not the first crackpot to do something outrageous in the name of science, and I certainly won't be the last. We don't have any other choice but to get you acclimated as best we can."

"Acclimated for what?"

"For a new life. There's no choice."

"There's always a choice," Mary says darkly.

"Go ahead then, Jane Doe. I'm walking back to the car now, all right?"

Mary stomps through the snow behind her. "I'd bet all I've got they voted you Ice Princess at the winter ball."

Had such a dubious honor been bestowed at a New Halcyon High social function, Lucy knows she would have taken it. "You think she's nice?" she once overheard one of her former friends saying of her in the second-floor girls' bathroom. "Just get to know her better."

The irony of it burns her cheeks even now. She stops suddenly and turns to face Mary. "I don't want things to be like this. I know you hate me, and you have every right to, but I can't take back what I've done. I . . ."

Mary reaches into her shopping bag and tears the cellophane from the first pack. "Yes?"

10:50 A.M.

Kellman Building ~ East Wing, Lab 61A

MEGAN WILL NEVER forget the morning Charles Harris Fuller moseyed into the lab like he'd founded the place. That was how long ago now? She accused him of selling indulgences to the security guards—they were a load of meatheads, they'd fall for practically anything—but Ambrose had raised his eyes from the microscope without a trace of surprise. It was almost like he'd been *expecting* him.

Now she eyes with unadulterated disdain the man rifling through her filing cabinet. *Kluxer! Gargoyle! Flying monkey!*

"I'm sure you're aware of the Miller-Santorum Bill, and how its passage will affect your work here?" the agent asks.

"Sure am. You guys are real diligent with the reminders."

He frowns. "What's that supposed to mean?"

Spook! Troll! Nazi fiend! "It means that your boss's boss's *boss's* boss calls *my* boss on a daily basis to remind us of how we'll all be imminently unemployed. But seeing as the bill hasn't actually passed yet, the only thugs I currently answer to are those on the grant committee. Now, are we done here, boyo?"

Who cares how hard they laugh when one of them declares she's in desperate need of a good lay? Or, horror of horrors, if they start spreading rumors she's a *lesbo*?

She doesn't care if they don't take her seriously, so long as they leave her alone.

"You need to account for these numbers." He tosses a copy of last year's budget on her desk. "We expect to hear from you by the end of the day Monday. Somehow I don't think it'll come quite so easily to you as slinging insults, *doctor.*"

11:25 A.M.
The Happy Flapper, "Vintage Clothes, Accessories & Other Delights" ~ 116 Leonora Avenue ~ New Halcyon

A BELL ABOVE THE door announces their arrival in the empty shop—empty of other customers, that is. This place, which had been a bookstore not one week ago, or so it seems to Mary, now reminds her of a shop she and Teddy had been to in London that sold old costumes used in Shakespeare productions. (In the mid-nineties Austen & Brontë, New Halcyon's last independent bookstore, closed its doors here five months after a Barnes & Noble opened just off the interstate.) In keeping with the name, bright feather boas hang from the ceiling. A girl in an Atari T-shirt sits behind a defunct antique cash register, playing solitaire on a glass counter displaying fine costume jewelry, opals and pearls and sterling silver. The walls are covered in prints of paintings by Mucha and Parrish, their heroines lush and melancholy, along with posters advertising candy, cosmetics, cough drops, and cigarettes.

Lucy strides to the counter. "We're here for a new wardrobe."

The shopgirl looks up from her cards. "Bad break-up?"

"I'd rather not get into it."

"Which of you is it for?"

"I'm looking for pieces from the nineteen-twenties, please."

"We don't keep those things out front," says the girl. "Too delicate . . . and expensive. Just follow me." The shopgirl bounces down the center aisle, past racks of halter tops, embroidered bell-bottoms and punk-rock T-shirts with the collars torn off. Mary gapes at a black KISS shirt hanging at the end of the rack that looks as if it was shredded by a wild animal.

The aisles in the back room are neatly labeled by decade from the 1880s (VICTORIAN) to the 1940s (SWING!), with men's and women's clothes of each period on adjacent racks. Mary ambles down her aisle, running her hand down the sleeves of tailored gabardine jackets, evening gowns of heavy moss- and claret-colored velvet, crêpe-de-chine slips and beaded dresses in sherbety hues with dropped waists and layers of diaphanous tulle, herringbone suits and cable-knit angora pullovers softer than goose-down, and coats like her own made of blue or green Donegal tweed. Sequined dancing slippers and scuffed leather heels line the shelf above the rack. Here it is again, the inescapable odor of dust and mothballs.

Mary tugs on Lucy's coat sleeve. "Why did you bring me here?" she whispers. "These clothes are already worn."

"You can go to Luscious if you want new clothing," Lucy hisses.

"I think we'll be able to find you a few things," the girl calls out, flipping through the racks with a practiced hand. "What are you, a size six?"

"She is," Lucy says, as the salesgirl pulls a tape measure from a hook beneath the light switch. Mary raises her arms and the girl deftly measures her bust, waist, and hips.

"Perfect!"

"What about this?" Mary fingers the collar of a lavender chiffon blouse with a pleated bodice and bishop sleeves. She gasps as she reads the price tag. "This blouse would have cost five dollars in nineteen twenty-nine!"

The girl in the Atari T-shirt gives a hearty chuckle. "Inflation's a bitch, huh?"

"Pardon me?"

The girl smiles absently as she pulls another two dresses from the rack, both of which are too similar to ones Mary already owns. Over the next half hour Mary chooses two dozen pieces to try on, all the while unnerved by the shopgirl's apparent belief in the quaintness of what she considers pretty and fashionable (if not exactly new). The shopgirl carries each garment back to a dressing room behind a worn velvet curtain. Once she's slipped each dress over her head, Mary is required to venture out of the dressing room for judgments from both Lucy and the shopgirl.

"That looks totally amazing on you," says the shopgirl to a form-fitting sweater of black wool with a white trompe l'oeil bow on the collar, an early Schiaparelli design.

Lucy shakes her head. "Dear *God,* no."

Mary puts her hands on her hips. "Why not?"

Lucy turns over the price tag so Mary can read it, and Mary's hand flies to her open mouth. "I'd have to take out a home equity loan," Lucy says.

Regarding the final item, a yellow-and-white georgette day dress with cap sleeves and a hem embroidered in a cheery spring green Mary had discovered on the 1930s rack, Lucy says, "You look like a daffodil."

The skirt flounces delightfully as Mary turns to face herself in the mirror. "I believe that's the idea," she says to Lucy's reflection.

"You look like a doll," says the shopgirl.

"Is that meant to be a compliment?"

"Take it," Lucy says.

"The dress or the compliment?"

"I agree," says the shopgirl. "And now that we've got you squared away, why don't I take care of your sister?"

"But we—"

"We didn't come here for me," Lucy says quickly. "Mary was just in need of a little retail therapy."

> RETAIL THERAPY: *A neologism coined in the late 1990s which refers to the temporarily salubrious effect an extravagant shopping excursion can have on one's disposition or self-regard; used all too often without ironic intention. See also entries for* OVERCONSUMPTION *and* CONSUMER WHORE.

Mary frowns as she straightens her stocking seams. That glossary is coming in handy.

"Still," says the shopgirl to Lucy, "I'm thinking of a swing dress we just got in last week that would look just divine on you. You're also a six, I'm guessing."

"You guess correctly." As Lucy follows the shopgirl down another aisle, Mary spots a tweed jacket on the men's rack (beside the neckties and bowler hats) and raises the sleeve to her face. It smells like pipe smoke—some other brand, not her father's, but it reminds her nevertheless. She dips her hand into the left-hand pocket and closes her fingers around a box of matches. The script on the box cover reads *The Dragon Volant, 373 Aurelia Avenue, New Halcyon,* and there is a whimsical little graphic. Gently she shakes the box (less than half full) and slips it into her mother's leather handbag. Meanwhile, two aisles over, Lucy is conversing with a cheerful falseness that makes Mary cringe.

"It's an investment, really," the shopgirl is saying. "Now clothing's not made to last more than a season, two at most. It's disgraceful. I'm still wearing my dad's Adidas T-shirts from the seventies and my brother buys one today and it falls apart in the wash."

Lucy shakes her head. "Awful, isn't it? That's why I only wear vintage."

"I'd love to know where you usually shop." The girl in the Atari T-shirt eyes the gray wool skirt and creamy satin blouse purchased by Lucy's grandmother in a Boston boutique in November of 1928. "Your outfit is totally fabulous."

"Oh—what a sweet little footstool!"

"Embroidered by hand, too. Not cheap, eh?" says the girl, as Lucy whistles at the price.

"Do you sell much furniture?"

"We get loads of random things from estate sales. My boss just picked up a solid oak wedding chest from the late nineteenth century, if you're interested," she says to Lucy, who laughs.

"I don't think so. You should see my attic."

"TAKING YOUR LITTLE sister on a shopping spree," says the shopgirl later, merrily. Mary stares at the calculator on which the girl is tallying the bill. "I just think that's so cute."

1:05 P.M.
The Dragon Volant ~ 373 Aurelia Avenue ~
New Halcyon

HER FATHER'S OFFICE had been three doors down, on the second floor. Mary turns her face from the second-story windows at 379 Aurelia—it's a law office now—and eyes the illuminated menu posted by the front door. "They ended Prohibition, I take it."

"Nineteen thirty-three. Are you hungry?"

The Dragon Volant is a thirties-style lounge, authentic because it opened the day after the demise of the Twenty-first Amendment. In the front, a long polished bar before a gilt mirror, flanked by sturdy bronze deco nymphs Colin would no doubt judge "kitschy," were he ever to enter the place. These statuettes were imported from Paris along with a circular stained-glass ceiling panel featuring the eponymous flying dragon, its multicolored wingspan backed by artificial illumination. Beneath this centerpiece, plush snugs with tall mahogany dividers line the walls under sconces of Tiffany-style glass. Votive candles, already lit, dot the circular tables in the center of the restaurant. As one would expect in a place like this, the stereo system hums with the likes of Bing Crosby and Edith Piaf. Through the kitchen door drifts the scent and sizzle of frying onions.

A young man in a tweed jacket at the far end of the bar looks up from his notebook as they choose their stools. He smiles at Mary briefly before returning to his notes, and she fancies he's a distinguished novelist hard at work on his new magnum opus. "Don't try to smoke in here," Lucy says, seating herself to Mary's left. "It's illegal."

Mary points to a portrait of F.D.R. on the wall above the mirror. "Isn't he the governor of New York?"

"He *was,* yes." Lucy is recalling a certain pinnacle of Morrigan family history: her grandmother's invitation to tea at the White House in the spring of 1937, where Eleanor Roosevelt had provided her with a recipe for pumpkin bread. "He was also President. Thirty-second or thirty-third, I forget which."

The bartender approaches, a young woman dressed in dungarees and a white butcher's apron. "How're you doing?" she says. "F.D.R. was number thirty-two. Sorry, couldn't help overhearing. Would you like the lunch menu?" Lucy nods and the girl slides photocopies of a handwritten menu across the counter. "Anything to drink?"

"Just a glass of water for me, please," Lucy says. "Mary?"

Mary scans the glass shelves. The mirror behind them makes the bar look doubly loaded. "I'll have a G and T."

"Mary!"

"Yes?"

"It's one o'clock in the afternoon!" Chuckling to herself, the barmaid reaches for a bottle of Bombay Sapphire from a high shelf. "I had no idea you were such a . . ."

Mary looks at her pointedly. "Don't you have me confused with someone else?"

Lucy clears her throat and turns to her menu.

"What are you having?" Mary asks.

"The tuna melt."

"What's a tuna melt?"

"Broiled tunafish with cheese on top," Lucy says.

Mary wrinkles her nose. "Why would you eat that of your own free will?"

Lucy rolls her eyes as the barmaid presents their drinks, each garnished with a slice of lime. "Have you decided?" the young woman asks.

Mary hands her the photocopied menu. "I'd like the goat cheese salad, please."

The barmaid nods and looks at Lucy.

"I'll have the same."

The food comes quickly, along with a basket of freshly baked French bread from the bakery with the inferior cupcakes. Their plates are almost clean when Lucy heads for the ladies' room, and Mary spends the next few moments sipping her gin and tonic and gazing with unfocused eyes at the portrait above the mirror. Teddy had always called Hoover a "bumbling ninny," which Mary had pointed out to be redundant.

A voice from two stools to her right startles her out of her reverie: "You're starting early."

She turns to find a bespectacled man of perhaps forty, attired in a black wool turtleneck under a suit jacket with a small enamel pin of the American flag affixed to the lapel. There's something not quite right about his looks; it's as though someone has taken hold of his ears and pulled them back from his face, tightening the flesh over his cheekbones. She hadn't noticed his entrance, but he's already clutching a tall glass of what looks like tomato juice. "Excuse me?"

"It's not yet one-thirty in the afternoon," he says. "You're starting early."

"I'm not sure why that should concern you, sir."

"Well," he smirks—his laughter has a forced quality that chills her even further—"for all I know that could be seltzer you're drinking, but somehow I doubt it." He proffers his other hand. "I'm—"

"Hey, Fred!"

The man looks over his shoulder at the fellow at the far end of the bar, who has been eyeing this scene over his open notebook. "Excuse me?" says the man in the black turtleneck, for there are no other customers at the bar besides these three.

"Yeah, you. Can't you see the girl doesn't want to talk to you?"

"What business is it of yours?"

"It's my business as a gentleman, that's what."

The man's face looks even odder when he's angry. "You're asking for a pummeling, Howdy Doody," he snarls.

"You're even older than I took you for!" the young man cries gaily, and Mary gazes at him in puzzled admiration. Cloaked in a miasma of ill-feeling, the man in the black turtleneck quits the bar for a booth in the back.

"Must be the Botox," says the bartender to no one in particular.

"D'you know what Botox is short for, Wendy?" The young man in the tweed jacket leans in toward the bartender, wrinkling his nose. "*Bovine toxins!* Just think of all the fun Thackeray would have, if he were writing today."

"God damn it," Wendy mutters as she takes the young man's glass and refills it with ginger ale. "I have to dole out at least two free drinks whenever that joker comes in here."

"Damage control," the young man says soberly. "Must've had a rough night, eh?"

"Yeah. He usually orders a double bourbon." The bartender garnishes his ginger ale with a slice of lime, delivers it on a fresh napkin, and turns to Mary. "D'you want another gin and tonic?"

Mary hesitates.

"It's on the house."

"Thank you very much," she says. "But I was wondering . . . What was it that man was drinking?"

"What, a Bloody Mary?"

"Is that really what it's called?" She laughs. "What's in it?"

"Tomato juice, vodka, pepper, and a dash of hot sauce. Good for nursing a hangover. Want one?" Mary nods, and Wendy turns and opens the fridge beneath the cash register.

"Pardon me," Mary calls across the bar, and the young man looks up from his notebook. "I'd just like to thank you for your . . ."

"Intervention?" He laughs. "You're most welcome." He pauses for a moment, then snaps his notebook shut, hops off his stool, and rounds the bar with his hand outstretched. "I'm Patrick." He smiles widely, revealing a gap between his two front teeth that lends him a mischievous air.

"Mary."

"Pleased to make your acquaintance, Mary." He points to the small brown shopping bag, stamped with the Higgins label, on the empty seat beside her. "Mind if I sit here?"

She whisks the bag off the stool and drops it on the floor as Wendy shakes her drink. "Oh, please do!"

"They're coffin nails, you know. Just quit two weeks ago, myself."

"Yes," she says ruefully. "I've heard."

Wendy delivers the Bloody Mary. Lucy climbs back onto her stool, looks at Mary's drink, then at Mary, and rolls her eyes.

"Lucy, this is Patrick. He's just rescued me from a very awkward encounter."

Lucy accepts his hand over Mary's plate. "What kind of awkward encounter?"

"Ah, not worth mentioning." Patrick takes a sip of his ginger ale. "I'll be watching my back from now on, though. Religious dissidents are the new pinkos, even in true-blue Massa-choo."

Mary gazes at him, mystified.

"I can see I'm only going to bore your sister here," Patrick says. "Sometimes I forget to climb down off my soapbox."

"Oh, no," Lucy says faintly, nudging half a cherry tomato with her fork across her otherwise empty plate.

"I ought to be on my way anyhow." He takes one more slurp of his ginger ale and slides the glass across the bar. "Can't sit here *all* day people-watching. So long, Wendy, and thanks for the pop."

"I thought you were taking notes for your book," Mary says.

"I was."

"What kind of book is it?"

He leans in. "You really want to know?"

Eagerly she nods. "Is it a novel?"

"Naw," he says. "It's . . . well, let's just say it's self-help." Mary frowns at this. "You take care, all right?" He tucks his notebook under his arm. "I'd hate to see a girl like you getting mixed up with the wrong crowd."

"A girl like me, eh?"

"Yes, a girl like you," he says as he dons his fedora. "A girl with sense." He reaches into his breast pocket and hands her a package of what look like Chiclets. "Miraculous invention. You'll never hanker for another cigarette."

2:45 P.M.
Saint Lucy's Church ~ 761 Aurelia Avenue

THE REREDOS BEHIND the altar has retained little of its neo-Gothic glory. Vandals have plucked and pocketed the heads of the Madonna and Child of the central panel, and their scattered fingerprints reveal the dark, dull wood beneath a thick patina of dust. A couple of moving men from a Boston auction house arrive tomorrow morning to disassemble the piece.

Frescoes of the life of Lucy, patron saint of the blind, have disappeared beneath a layer of chalky white interior paint. The portraits of the apostles high above the nave won't be effaced so easily, but the hour is at hand: the commotion from within comes from a troupe of housepainters erecting the scaffold. In an interview for the local newspaper, Reverend Charles Harris Fuller had explained to a timorous young reporter that Catholic effigies are nothing more than holdovers from a pagan era.

Mary and Lucy see as much through a small window in the locked front door. Outside, Mary pulls at the door handle, stomping her foot in frustration, and Lucy shakes her head at a white banner strung above the entrance:

Saint Lucy's will reopen on Sunday, March 1, 2009, as the first New Halcyon ***Church of Matthew*** *under the auspices of the Reverend Charles Harris Fuller. ALL ARE WELCOME in this house of worship!*

Done in splashy electric-blue lettering, the sign would be more appropriate for a pizza joint under new management. "I saw him at the bar earlier," Lucy murmurs.

"Who?"

"Fuller. He was sitting in one of the booths in the back by himself."

"Preachers don't belong in pubs," Mary says, tugging at the door handle one last time. "Unless they're preaching to the tipplers." She sniffs in disgust.

"The reverend *is* a tippler," Lucy says. "I want to tell you something very important. A word of advice. Beware of men with two first names, pinkie rings, and Cloroxed teeth."

"Is that supposed to be funny?"

"Am I laughing?" She pauses. "I'm sorry about your church."

"*My* church?"

Lucy shrugs.

"Do you mean to tell me you haven't even set foot inside?"

"Not lately, I haven't." Lucy has a foggy recollection of going to Mass with her mother, but she has not been inside since Lucinda's funeral on November 4, 1986. Both her parents had been cremated, their ashes sprinkled in the perennial garden behind the labyrinth.

"Where are you going?"

"The churchyard," Mary replies. "I am going to hop the gate."

Lucy follows her around the corner and down the snowy alleyway leading to the padlocked entrance to the graveyard. Mary overturns a rusty tin pail on the sidewalk and steps up to swing her boot over the gate. Beyond, the drifts are dazzlingly white, reminding Lucy of a verse by a certain morbid poet—she can't recall which—who had remarked that the snow remains purest within the cemetery gates. Her mother had loved that line; she'd underlined it three times in her tattered paperback copy of the poet's collected work. Lucy hops over the gate and follows Mary at a respectful distance, past all the somber stone angels flanking the walkway.

How queer this must look, a young girl sobbing over a row of weatherbeaten headstones. Thank goodness the passersby are too concerned with getting home to notice her.

Mary has fallen on her knees in the snow, her shopping bag forgotten atop a neighboring marker. *My father's name was Ambrose, too,* Lucy wants to say, but her tongue has turned to ash.

An old Toyota station wagon pulls up to the curb beyond the far gate on Pamela Lane, the horn honking gaily. Megan rolls down the window on the driver's side. "This is the very last place on earth I'd ever expect to find you two."

Swinging her shopping bag, Lucy turns up her coat collar with her other hand as she wends her way between the snowcapped headstones. "Give me a hand, would you? I don't want to ruin the bag." Rolling her eyes, Megan opens the door and catches the shopping bag as Lucy passes it over the back gate. Then Lucy climbs over the gate and joins her.

"You going to answer me, or what?"

"We were just walking back to the car and Mary wanted to stop." Her hand on the hood, Lucy leans in to the open driver-side window. "This was her parish."

"Oh, Lu." Megan shakes her head. "For God's sake, don't encourage her."

"Believe me, I'm not. How'd it go today?"

Megan shrugs. "You parked far from here?"

"Behind the dentist's office."

"On Lavinia? That's a-ways away. Come on, I'll give you a ride."

With effort Mary gets up off her knees. Every part of her feels frostbitten. Though she has never been one to believe the dead are more likely to hear us if we speak at their mortal resting-places, she mutters a few words anyway as she wipes the snow off her father's stone with her mitten. *Able and compassionate physician,* it says. *Devoted brother, husband, father and grandfather.* To his left is his wife; to his right, his sister, who survived him by two years. No one has been interred in this plot since 1964.

From the sidewalk, Lucy calls to her.

"Hop in," Megan cries. "Or catch your death!"

This time Mary hops the gate with the ease of a tomboy despite her frozen limbs. "Pardon me?"

"You'll come down with pneumonia. Get in, I'll drive you to your car."

"How did you know we were here?" Lucy asks.

"I didn't. I was just driving by on my way back from the gynie."

"Gynie?"

"Just *get in,* would you, Mary?"

Mary slides into the backseat and pulls the door closed behind her.

Megan eyes her through the rearview mirror. "Could you close your door again? It's still open."

"Oh." She slams the door this time. "Sorry."

"No matter. So what were you ladies up to this afternoon? Besides the purchase of tobaccky sticks, that is."

"We went to the Happy Flapper."

"Find anything?"

"I think we maxed out my credit card."

Megan rolls her eyes. "So," she calls over her shoulder to the girl huddled in the backseat, "how are you getting on?"

"Getting on?"

"Do you really not understand me, or is this just your defense mechanism?"

"Megan!"

"You're right. I do apologize. And I'm sorry if I was a bit hard on you the other night, Mary. As you now know, I'm a gal who speaks her mind." She steers the hatchback into the driveway at the dentist's office and Lucy opens the passenger's-side door.

"Care to follow us home for dinner?" Lucy asks.

"You sure that's a wise idea?"

Lucy smiles. "Probably not."

"How about I come by later on this evening?"

Mary smiles stiffly as she slams the rear door. Megan is far too brash, too loose for Mary's comfort. A respectable woman would never drive an automobile like this, with dented fenders and dog hair all over the backseat.

8:00 P.M.

25 University Avenue

LUCY TAKES HER dinner to the basement. After Mary and Gray have eaten, Mary lights the lantern and the two of them wander through the attic, thumbing through the younger Ambrose's notebooks and anything else they come across. But Mary soon stumbles upon a passage on Ambrose's vision of the "afterlife" (*The body harbors all manner of microscopic beings, all fulfilling their evolutionary destiny, and in this respect the corpse is as alive as it ever was*), and she snaps the book shut and stuffs it back on the shelf feeling both nausea and pity.

Mary pulls a metal film canister off the shelf and holds it to the lantern so she can read the label. "What's this?"

"A very old home movie."

"You mean pictures of our own family?"

He nods.

"Can we watch it?"

"Sure, if we can find the projector." They spend several minutes rooting through a pile of miscellaneous junk in the corner of the room, though she is of little help. "I think that's it," he says, pointing at a black case on the floor at her feet.

The film spans the years 1950 to 1961, grainy footage of two young men and a teenage girl in the beginning, at picnics and graduations. At the start of each segment there's someone, Lucinda usually, holding up a cue card with the date and place written in bold capitals. One son grows a beard and is celebrating a new child with each successive scene. His wife is beautiful, crisply dressed, exuding an air of capability. To Gray she looks like Donna Reed. The other son appears, smiling, in military uniform. After 1953 most of them cease to appear in these scenes: no more children, no more sons, so it's just the girl alone; for years and years she's surrounded by no one but her elderly relatives and neighbors. Mary's father, his hair grown thin and white, never smiles for the camera; he lurks at the periphery of every scene, smoking his pipe and reading the newspaper.

It seems Mary is usually the one operating the camera, but in a few segments they spot her in the background conversing with some other matron.

"I wish I could hear what they're saying."

"There was no sound in home movies until the early eighties. Hey," he says, "I have an idea." He drops the phonograph needle on the edge of a record already on the turntable, and she laughs as Charleston music begins to play. "The music may not match, but it's better than silence," he says.

"Say," Mary says. "Now *I* have an idea." She stands in the path of the projector and the edge of the picnic table wraps itself around her waist. The Mary of the movie looks up from her conversation, now smiling into the camera; her face superimposed, this Mary smiles with her.

"Don't do that," he says. "You're giving me the heebie-jeebies."

"My life is a heebie-jeebie," she replies, darting to the side to watch a close-up of her father. During the film's last few minutes she stares at all the faces of people dead and buried still laughing on the celluloid. Moving pictures were a marvel to her once, but this is too much.

Mary shields her eyes from the bright white light as the filmstrip reaches its end, smacking the other spool as it continues to wind. Gray turns off the projector.

Her hair tousled over the pillow, she lies on the mattress with her arm cradling her head. She raises the ivory cigarette holder to her lips in one long languid movement as if she's an old film star, a femme fatale.

"You shouldn't smoke in bed."

"You're quite right." But she takes another puff, and another. "Oh dear, where are my manners? Would you like one?"

"No, thanks. I don't smoke."

"Because smoking causes cancer, emphysema, and impotence?"

"Impotence?"

She laughs. "Open the window, if you like."

"Nah. I'm fine."

"May I ask you something?"

"Sure."

"Why are you here?"

"This is where I got a job."

"You know what I mean."

"Why am I living with Lucy?"

"Why are you *still* living with Lucy."

"I don't know," he says. "I guess we both keep putting off talking seriously about our relationship until things settle down."

"What '*things*'?"

"You, for instance."

"*Me!* I've got nothing to do with it!"

He shrugs. "You have pretty much everything to do with it."

LETTERS. HE MUST have written letters while he was away, but if they were tucked in some drawer in this attic surely she'd have found them by now. Where, then?

Their first night in Paris is the one she returns to in that purgatory between stillness and sleep. The memory is more than eighty years old, but she's every inch as lithe as she was the night they were making it. The smallest sensation sets her off, like a lace brassiere-strap falling down the curve of her bare shoulder, or a spill of talcum powder down her back. Sometimes, while half asleep, she runs a fingertip lightly up and down the inside of her arm just to simulate his touch.

Teddy's never touched this skin.

She puts out the cigarette and turns down the lantern, watching the paper swallows glide through the drafty air overhead.

THURSDAY, 12 FEBRUARY 2009 ~ 1:26 A.M.
25 University Avenue

THE LOOP KEY heavy in her pocket, Mary opens the attic door and listens for any sound coming from the far side of the turret-room door. His desk lamp throws a dim light through the crack; either Gray is working intently or he has nodded off over another stack of ungraded papers.

The key turns in the lock with little noise this time. With one hand on the railing and the other holding the lantern, she takes slow, probing steps down to the first floor, where she hesitates. If the basement is truly without interest, as Gray says it is, this is her chance to find out; so she continues down one more flight to a landing so tight and dark her brother once likened being inside it at night to being buried alive.

But the door will not give, not even an inch, not even when she turns the key in the lock. Sighing, she ventures up the stairs to resume her original mission, looking back over her shoulder at the utter darkness lapping at her heels just as she did when she was small.

INSIDE THE LOOP on the first floor, she slides her hand along the wall in search of the drawer handle. "Papa keeps all his most important things here," her father had said to her once, only that had been in the daytime. "No one knows of this place but you and I, your brothers, and Mama and Aunty Cee." And every son and daughter between then and now.

The drawer howls as she pulls the handle. She half-expects to find a family of mice nesting at the bottom, but there isn't so much as a cobweb. At the front of the drawer is a stack of accordion folders bulging with papers, but as she pulls the compartment out of the wall she finds a small metal strongbox and a heavy book, both wrapped in clear plastic.

She sits on the steps and pulls the strongbox out of its wrapping in the weak lantern light, fumbling with the rusty latch for several moments before she pries it open: airmail envelopes. The letter at the top of the pile bears a faint postmark—she squints—from 1942.

Whatever the book is, it must be of some interest, so she carries it back to the attic along with the strongbox.

2:28 A.M.
The Attic

LONG ROAD HOME: *The Great Depression Through the Lens of Mary Morrigan,* a book of photographs put out by the University Press in 1989 to coincide with the dedication of a wing of the university's art gallery in honor of the photographer. The jacket flap proclaims that she has won half a dozen prizes for her photographs documenting the Depression and its effects on the lives of everyday Americans from Plymouth to Redwood City. Several of them even graced the cover of *Life* magazine in its first year. Slowly Mary turns the pages, poring over snapshots of train-hopping, banjo-playing hobos; barefoot children gathering dandelions on a grassy slope in Appalachia; the queues outside urban soup kitchens on Thanksgiving Day; seven-year-old boys hawking apples or newspapers on street corners; a boy of no more than four bent over on a railroad track, his fingers black with soot, coal tumbling out of his coat pockets; families who purchased two-dollar yearly passes to Yellowstone for extended "vacations" (this captions the photograph of a young girl posing shyly beside a Model A roadster above a valley dotted with buffalo); shantytowns, called Hoovervilles, on the margins of floundering industrial cities. Some of the pictures she remembers from Colin's wall; others hang above the sideboard in the dining room.

"I don't believe it," she murmurs. "I just don't believe it." She'd had three small children. She can't imagine she left them with a nurse—or even Aunt Cee. But she reads in the introduction that Joe, her younger son, wasn't born until 1934, and Lucinda not 'til 1941. A paragraph at the bottom of the page explains that Teddy served as a physician in the Civilian Conservation Corps for nearly two years. There was no want of opportunity for the taking of such pictures. There's another photo someone took of her while she was working, looking down through the viewfinder of her Rolly while her infant son yawned in a sling on her back. She gasps at a snapshot of herself having tea with the president's wife in 1937.

The final chapter includes a few dozen photographs taken in the decades afterwards, small-town homecoming parades at the ends of other wars, and civil rights marches, and a handful of family photographs. Her favorite is one of Teddy and their two sons posing beside a great hulking lion they fashioned out of snow with fangs made of icicles. The caption tells her that her husband departed for Europe not long after it was taken.

She slides a shaking finger under the flap of the first envelope.

He'd volunteered for the Army Medical Corps and he was stationed in a veterans' hospital in London and later "somewhere in France" after the Allied invasion. In his letters he'd told her all about the Medical Field Service School he'd attended before leaving for Europe, the field hospitals and his patients, the men who needed straitjackets more than morphine. He even told her about the psychiatrist who became hysterical himself after going five full days without sleep. "These," he wrote, "are stories you will never hear on the wireless or in the papers. And would you believe they're still treating soldiers from Dunkirk?"

Dunkirk. She isn't sure where that is.

Unfailingly, in every last paragraph he wrote of home, evoking the smells of kitchen, garden, and wife as if he'd been writing for his own benefit. "Kiss the little ones for me," he wrote. "And keep lighting those candles."

She frowns at that. It wasn't like Teddy to ask for prayers, especially since he must have known she'd have been lighting candles beneath the statue of the Virgin at Saint Lucy's even if he'd asked her not to.

Other passages are cheerful, even whimsical. He muses in a letter from June of 1942 that while he is currently engaged in writing to the Mary of the present—"or near future, to be more accurate"—is he not also speaking to all the Marys who will reread this letter over the years?

She falls asleep at some point, but when she wakes up in the early afternoon she resumes her reading; soon there are only two letters left in the stack. She opens the first, the last airmail letter.

> *You won't believe this, rabbit. I don't really believe it myself, but I have to explain what I've enclosed in this envelope* some-*how . . .*

MONDAY, 28 AUGUST 1944 ~ 10:15 A.M.
Carentan, Basse-Normandie

TWENTY-FOUR ON, twenty-four off. A line from Shakespeare surfaces in his memory and he appropriates it with eagerness, blameless though he may be: *What, will these hands ne'er be clean?*

He can't go back to the dank crypt beneath the hospital, not yet. On a curve of the road out of the village he passes a whitewashed cottage where an elderly woman sits on a low stool shelling peas. "Hair the color of virgin snow and hands gnarled with acute arthritis" is how he will describe her in a letter to his wife. The old woman eyes him carefully as he greets her. After a moment of uneasy silence she asks him inside for a glass of water. One kindness inspires another, and after a generous helping of yesterday's stew she insists he allow himself time for a bath.

A large copper tub sits on the floor by the back window, through which he can see her laundry drying on a line strung between two low boughs. After half a dozen trips to the well and four kettlefuls of hot water, he pulls off his uniform and sinks gratefully into the basin. The old woman whisks his clothes from the floor and disappears through the back door before he can protest.

He lies in the tub until the water feels colder than the air, and when he steps out of it and goes to the window he sees his uniform pinned to the clothesline. The lady of the house emerges from a copse of fir trees at the far end of the yard, carrying his underclothes in a basket, having taken them down to a brook behind the trees and cleaned them with almond soap on a wooden washboard. The gooseflesh rises on his arms as she pins his undershirt to the line. On a chair beside the tub he notices a folded stack of clothing she has laid out for him, a cotton shirt and a pair of rough wool trousers; they are cut for a smaller, shorter man, but he manages to get them on.

The Frenchwoman returns with a basketful of clean laundry. *"J'ai besoin d'un frison."*

"Excusez-moi?"

"Cheveux." She reaches up and tugs gently on a lock of his hair. *"Tes cheveux."*

"Pourquoi?"

"Un bracelet. Pour ta femme. Comprenez-vous?"

Dazed, he nods as she pulls a pair of sewing scissors from the pocket of her apron.

TUESDAY, 29 AUGUST 1944 ~ 12:07 A.M.
The Crypt of Église Saint-Fiacre ~ Carentan, Basse-Normandie

. . . THEY TALK BLITHELY *of their postwar plans, resuming their practices, continuing their families. Now more than ever I find myself unable to join in those conversations. Believe me,* I am *trying my best to keep my thoughts from superstition, and it may be after all that my snow-haired benefactress merely wished to spook me, out of a misplaced resentment for the ruined state of her lifelong home. You see, here I am now, trying to comfort you, to convince you that it means nothing!*

Keep it or burn it—do as you like—I'll say no more of it.

I love you, rabbit. Kiss the children for me.

HE SIGNS HIS NAME beneath an infinity symbol, which he has looped with less brio than usual. The candle on the table flickers as he sits with the airmail envelope in one hand and the bracelet in the other. This will surely upset her, but wouldn't she rather have it than not?

He slips the bracelet into the envelope and licks the seal.

THURSDAY, 12 FEBRUARY 2009 ~ 3:34 P.M.
25 University Avenue ~ The Attic

WHAT BRACELET? There is no bracelet enclosed.

The final envelope contains a condolence letter from the State Department. She scans it over and over, making sense of nothing but each word on its own. Why would the Germans bomb an aid station twenty miles from the nearest front?

4:08 P.M.
The Third-Floor Turret Room

GRAY LOOKS UP from his notebook. "Come in, Mary—hey, are you all right?"

She clutches the last airmail envelope. "I guess I shouldn't have read these all in one go," she says with a rueful smile.

"You want to talk about it?"

She shakes her head. "I was actually wondering if this room was empty when you arrived."

"There's the usual bric-a-brac in the closet. Why do you ask?"

"I'm looking for something." She takes a step toward the closet door. "Do you mind if I . . . ?"

Fortunately he cleared all the dirty gym socks off his closet floor this morning. "Not at all. Here, let me help you. There's a box of things on the top shelf—everything else is mine."

"I don't know why I thought it would be here," she says sadly once they've sorted through the bric-a-brac, none of which dates further back than Lucinda's school days (an illuminated vanity mirror made of mustard-yellow plastic and a slew of spiral-bound notebooks, some blank, some half used). "This was Aunt Cecelia's room." Then she pauses, looking thoughtfully at the ceiling.

"What is it?"

She points to a trapdoor above his desk he'd never noticed before. "The crawl space," she says. "Weren't you aware of it?"

He shakes his head.

"She never tells you anything, does she?" Mary sniffs. "Clear your desk, if you please. I'll need to stand on it to reach the door."

It had never occurred to him that the conical space at the turret's pinnacle could be used for anything, but when he follows her up through the trapdoor he gasps at all the light coming through the three small windows in the roof. Mary kneels at the edge of the space with the crown of her head pressed against the cobwebbed ceiling, riffling through another box of Lucinda's notebooks. Aside from a threadbare footstool, the room is empty. As Mary pushes the box across the dirty floor in frustration, Gray looks up through the windows at the cumulus clouds floating by. "The house must be full of secret places like this," he murmurs.

What can she do but smile like the Sphinx? "Now you can come up here whenever you don't want to be found," she says, and he smiles back.

FRIDAY, 13 FEBRUARY 2009 ~ 3:45 A.M.

The Study

THE BOTTOM DRAWER'S locked, but Mary rummages through the others: Scotch tape, paper clips, a sheaf of year-old to-do lists. She pulls the top drawer out of the desk and dumps its contents onto the blotter.

Colin leans in the doorway, his arms folded across his chest, smiling as though pleased he's startled her. "What are you doing?"

"I'm looking for something that belongs to me."

"You'd better be more careful," he says. "You don't want the LGB finding you in here."

"LGB?"

"You know . . . like the KGB, but with Lucy in charge? Oh, relax, it's just a joke." He pauses. "I came down for a cup of tea. Care to join me?"

"Thank you, Colin, but I'd better go back to bed."

"Suit yourself." He shrugs. "Good night, Mary."

Unless it's in the bottom drawer, the mourning bracelet is not to be found in the desk.

4:19 A.M.

The Sewing Room ~ Second Floor

MARY HOLDS HER BREATH as she opens the door to guard against the lingering stink of death. Her grandfather's heart had failed him in the study, but she had never felt this way entering it afterwards. As it happens, the smell in the dark-papered little room isn't at all peculiar, though raising the sash would ease the stuffiness. She flips the light switch and stands in the middle of the room, shaking her head. In the corner is the door to the loop, but her private superstition prevents her from considering it as an alternate route to the basement.

Even now this is the room where people leave the things they no longer want, but don't have the heart to discard: a hideous little armchair covered in nubby orange tweed; a box of old books on no-longer-popular topics (astrology, celebrity trials of the twentieth century, hydroponic gardening); a tattered dog pallet labeled SCIPIO in red machine embroidery. The highboy in the corner is still stocked with sewing notions and neatly folded fabric scraps, but by the time she reaches the bottom drawer it's clear to her the bracelet wouldn't be here, either.

In that bottom drawer is another item of interest, however: a half-finished quilt done in purple calicos, one of which catches her eye. Bringing the fronting to her face to study it in the dim light, she finds a pattern of little silver skulls on a plum-hued background. (It is a novelty fabric left over from Halloween 1987.) When she spreads the quilt on the floor to study the design she realizes who it was who never finished it.

10:47 P.M.

The Attic

GRAY PORES OVER the book of photographs, uttering a "wow" here and there at the pictures his mother would call "heartstring-tuggers," as Mary sews a seam on the quilt spread over her legs. "Holy cow, Eleanor Roosevelt! Did you see this one?"

"Yes," she says through a mouthful of pins.

"What's with all the eights?"

Mary pulls the pins from her mouth. "It's meant to be an infinity symbol."

"You designed it yourself?"

She holds up a sheet of graph paper, the pencil lines crisp and carefully drawn. "I must have. This is dated nineteen eighty-eight. Do you like it?"

Now he realizes where he's seen this quilt before: on the home video, the night Lucy got silly on sparkling grape juice. "It's funky—not at all the kind of thing I'd expect from an old lady."

She rolls her eyes and returns her attention to the seam, wearing a faint smile as she works.

"Do you think you'll start taking pictures again?"

"Maybe—if I ever leave the house. And if I can get my Rolly fixed."

"There's a camera shop on Hilary Road. I bet they can fix it."

"Did you know there's a wing of the university art gallery named after me?"

In his six years at NHU, he has never once set foot inside the art gallery. "I didn't," he says. "Congratulations."

"I know," she begins, her needle poised above the cloth. "I know it isn't right for me to say things like that. I didn't design this; they didn't name the gallery after me."

"You know the difference," he says. "It's just a flaw in the language." He turns another page and alights upon the snow lion. "Was Teddy much older than you?"

"What makes you ask?"

"Just wondering."

She clears her throat. "He was thirteen months older."

"You went to school together?"

"We met when he moved here to go to the university. He was boarding next door."

"At the Delaneys'?"

"How did you know?"

"You're kidding! That house still belongs to the Delaneys. Mrs. Delaney just turned ninety-four." He pauses. "I guess she'd be the daughter-in-law of the Mrs. Delaney you remember. Nicest lady you'll ever meet. I should take you over sometime."

"Yes," she says. "I'd like that."

"It says here you wanted to go to Antarctica."

"I still do."

"I guess you never went." He pauses. "Why?"

"How should I know?"

"I mean, why Antarctica?"

"It was always a preoccupation of mine," she murmurs. "I collected the Explorer cards; they used to come with cigarettes and chocolate bars . . ."

"Is that how you got addicted?"

"To chocolate?"

He laughs.

"If I ever leave New Halcyon, that's where I'd like to go."

"Antarctica?"

She shoots him a sly glance. "It still exists, doesn't it?"

Gray turns to the last page in the book, a candid portrait of Lucinda in bell-bottoms, and snaps the book shut with a shiver. The way she's smiling in that picture, she might as well be Lucy.

SATURDAY, 14 FEBRUARY 2009 ~ 1:32 A.M.
The Third-Floor Turret Room

LUCY LEANS IN the doorway, her arms folded across the sheer bodice of a nightdress he's never seen before. "How's it coming?"

"It's not," he says, bookmarking another musty volume and pushing his rolly-chair away from the desk. "Time to call it a night."

"You always say that," she says as she seats herself on the narrow bed by the window. "You must be getting *some*thing done."

Standing in the center of the circular room, he pulls off his shirt and corduroys and drops them in a laundry basket at the foot of the bed.

"We haven't gone running in months," she says. "We should start running again."

"Maybe when it gets warmer."

"The snow's melting. We could go tomorrow."

"Let me see how much I can get done in the morning, all right?"

She nods, picking the lint off his duvet. "Why don't you come back to bed?" she asks. "*My* bed."

"I don't know. That bedroom just gives me the creeps."

"You slept in that bedroom for three years, Gray."

"Fine, I'll sleep there if it means so much to you. Come on, get up."

"I didn't mean to pick a fight over it. Just forget I said anything." She turns off the lamp on the night table and pulls back the bedclothes for him. Dutifully—for there is no finer word for it—he slips into bed beside her, winds his arms around her waist, and delivers the sort of long, languorous kiss that is never an end in itself.

Half an hour later he wants nothing more than to sleep, but in this pregnant silence he can't nod off until she's said what's on her mind. She lies on her side facing the wall, but he can hear her nibbling on her thumbnail.

"What is it, Lu?"

"I've decided something," she says slowly. "But I know you'll think it's a bad idea. In fact, I'm sure you'll be utterly opposed to it."

He rolls his eyes at the back of her head. "Then why are you bringing it up?"

"Because it's important." She turns over to face him, her long white hand resting on the pillow between them. "I'm going to clone him."

Gray reacts as though he's been electrocuted.

She sighs. "I knew you'd think it was crazy."

" 'Crazy' doesn't quite capture the essence of it, Lucy." He puts his undershirt and boxers back on and jumps out of bed. "You nearly killed yourself the first time doing something that was completely unethical, and now you want to do it *again*? No, you've far transcended 'crazy.' And has it occurred to you that you could enable an entire race of clones?"

"The chances of that happening are nonexistent—but if it did, they'd be blank slates, products of a man and a woman, like normal babies. They'd be as human as everyone else."

"You don't know that."

"You *see* how miserable she is. I just . . . I feel I owe it to her. To put things right."

"You *can't* put things right. What's done is done and bringing another person back from the dead is not going to absolve you."

She eyes him calmly. "You're even more upset than I thought you would be."

"When does it end? That's what I want to know. Are you going to resurrect your entire family tree?"

"I made a mistake. I just want to correct it, insofar as that's possible."

Doesn't she understand it's this attitude that leads people to squander their pensions at the blackjack table? "Where are you going?"

"Back to bed," she calls from the hallway. "*My* bed."

His protests have only cemented her resolve.

9:25 P.M.

The Attic

LUCY CROUCHES beside the cabinet under the gramophone, sifting through old records in their friable paper sleeves. Mary stands at the wardrobe door, rearranging one of her new dresses on a hanger. It doesn't sit well with her, this silent companionship; Lucy has conjured a phony sense of ease through a roast beef dinner and an expensive shopping excursion. *Look at all I've done for you—you can't possibly despise me now.* "You remember that portrait of Roosevelt above the bar at the Dragon Volant?"

"What about it?"

"Why didn't you mention I'd had tea with the First Lady?"

"You didn't. My grandmother did." She flips through a handful of albums—ancient university orchestra recordings, Judy Garland, Jelly Roll Morton, the Boswell Sisters. "You could have told me you wanted to read the letters."

"Would you have let me, if I had?"

Lucy pulls another record out of the cabinet and smiles to herself as she reads the label. "She used to play this record for me all the time."

"Put it on."

"You won't remember it," Lucy says as she drops the needle on the record. "It was written in the thirties."

Laugh, Kookaburra! Laugh, Kookaburra!
Gay your life must be.

"What a darling little song." Mary speaks quietly, and with little enthusiasm.

The lilting voice begins the second verse; Lucy replaces the rest of the records and closes the cabinet. Surely Mary wouldn't have told the boys about the secret passage . . . but what if she's told Gray? If she's told him, Lucy will never hear the end of it. "No one but you and I know about the loop, Mary. I'd like to keep it that way."

Mary sniffs. "We were keeping that secret long before your parents ever laid eyes on each other." She sinks into the chair beside the rolltop desk and eyes Lucy for a long moment. "I need you to bring him back. I don't mean to sound melodramatic, but I really can't live without him."

"You're doing fine so far."

"My life isn't worth living without him." With a heavy sigh, Lucy drops into the armchair beside the gramophone. Mary waits a few moments for a response. "Of course, I can't expect you to understand that, now, can I?"

These words couldn't be more effective if they'd been delivered with a slap to the face. "For what it's worth," Lucy says coldly, rising from the chair, "I'm already working on it."

Mary clings to the desk chair with white knuckles. Lucy pauses for a moment, taking a bit of grim enjoyment from the look on her face.

"There's just one more thing," Mary calls after her.

"Yes?"

"I'd like my rings back."

"Which rings?"

"You *know* which rings. My wedding band. My engagement ring."

"The engagement ring is with my mother's jewelry," Lucy says. "But the wedding band . . ."

"Where is it?"

The song ends and the needle begins to skip. Lucy hesitates. "They left it on your finger."

Chromosome 8:
Excerpt of a vernacular translation

1 *ggagtttattcataacgcgctctccaagtatacgtggcaatgcgttgctgggttattttaatcattctaggcatcgttttc*
This is a variant of *Homo sapiens* gene MYC (or MYC.c), which encodes

82 *ctccttatgcctctatcattcctccctatctacactaacatcccacgctctgaacgcgcgcccattaatacccttctttcctc*
v-myc myelocytomatosis viral oncogene. Oncogenes are those that encourage

165 *cactctccctgggactcttgatcaaagcgcggccctttccccagccttagcgaggcgccctgcagcctggtacgcgcgtggc*
cell growth and proliferation; several oncogenes, such as MYC, have an addi-

247 *gtggcggtgggcgcgcagtgcgttctcggtgtggagggcagctgttccgcctgcgatgatttatactcacaggacaagga*
tional function: to trigger the death of the cell should it begin to prolifer-

327 *tgcggtttgtcaaacagtactgctacggaggagcagcagagaaagggagagggtttgagagggagcaaaagaa*
ate abnormally. Cellular suicide (apoptosis) is the body's last line of defense

400 *aatg* // gtaggcgcgcgtagttaattcatgcggctctcttactctgtttacatcctagagctagagtgctcg
a—*pipesmoke, July 1925, two fireflies find their way into the conservatory.*

470 gctgcccggctgagtctcctccccaccttccccaccctccccaccctccccataagcgcccctcccgggtt
A Few Figs from Thistles. *Cee knows she never makes the fig cake as well*

541 cccaaagcagagggcgtgggggaaaagaaaaaagatcctctctcgctaatctccgcccaccggccc
as Mother did—it's the way she smiled when I told her it was delicious.

607 tttataatgcgagggtctggacggctgaggacccccgagctgtgctgctcgcggccgccaccgccgggcccc
Darting here and there among the flowerpots, I imagine those languid green-

679 ggccgtccctggctcccctcctgcctcgagaagggcagggcttctcagaggcttggcgggaaaaaga
gold flashes are professions of love. Father turns out the lamp so we can watch them

746 acggagggagggatcgcgctgagtataaaagccggttttcggggctttatctaactcgctgtagtaa
dancing in the dark. We sit like that for awhile, in a perfect silence apart

813 ttccagcgagaggcagagggagcgagcgggcggccggctagggtggaagagccgggcgagca
from the crickets. I look up to find them both gone, back through the open

875 gagctgcgctgcgggcgtcctgggaagggagatccggagcgaatagggggcttcgcctctggcccagc . . .
window above our heads . . . "I would indeed that love were longer-lived," . . .

V

THE WASHER AT THE FORD

For I am every dead thing,
In whom Love wrought new alchemy.

—John Donne,
"A Nocturnal upon St. Lucy's Day, Being the Shortest Day" (1617)

Chapter 51

The Rise of American Neoconservatism

"On some great and glorious day," wrote H. L. Mencken in 1920, "the plain folks of the land will reach their heart's desire at last and the White House will be adorned by a downright moron." In the first eight years of the new century this first prediction is still fodder for debate, but the second is not.

The proponents of the "neoconservative" movement, the origin of which predates the now-fabled "right-wing conspiracy" to depose the president in the late 1990s (see Chapter 52), are a misbegotten breed, stirring patriotic sentiment to serve as smoke screens for dubious political and military maneuvers (all of which line their pockets one way or another, it need hardly be said). Continual and widespread attempts to discredit dissenters at times border on the fascistic. Due to the sheer length of such a list, I must abridge countless more examples, politicians and pundits alike whose words and deeds display greater immorality than those they so vitriolically denounce, and whose secular crusades remain obfuscated in the language of Christian righteousness. I am unable to divulge the names of such phonies, however, for twenty-first-century American society is litigious to an absurd degree. I therefore wish to spare my future self the aggravation and expense of an (albeit groundless) libel suit. Suffice it to say that there is precious little Christlike about these people . . .

SUNDAY, 15 FEBRUARY 2009 ~ 4:32 A.M.

25 University Avenue ~ The Attic

IN THE FIRST PART of the dream she is passing down a dark corridor with vaulted ceilings, frescoes of a unicorn hunt crumbling off the walls.

A door appears in a recess to her left, and as she raises her hand to the knob she finds she's already on the far side of it, inside the loop. But the entrance on every floor is locked and she has forgotten the key, and she pounds on the door outside the study, shouting and screaming. No one hears her.

9:05 A.M.

25 University Avenue

IT TAKES HER HALF an hour to find her rosary, which had wound up behind the card catalog when she'd thrown them in despair. She shakes the beads and the dust bunnies fall back to the floor.

Gray tells her the Boston-bound public bus stops at the university gate at fifteen and forty-five minutes after the hour from 6:00 a.m. to 11:00 p.m. She missed Mass last Sunday, but she suspects she'll be forgiven. After all, she didn't know what day of the week it was.

NOON

Saint Gregory's Catholic Church ~ Mount Ivy, Massachusetts

NEEDLESS TO SAY, Pius XI is no longer pope. The priest faces the congregation, speaking in English. The liturgy sounds rather graceless to her now, but the sibilant sound of prayers spoken aloud still calms her. *Ab omni perturbatione securi:* that had always been her favorite line. *Protect us from all anxiety.*

No one, not even the oldest among them, receives the Eucharist on the tongue. She walks up the aisle at communion with her hands clasped in front of her, terrified that she'll drop the Host. Miracle of miracles, she does not, and she returns to her pew weak with relief.

1:45 P.M.
Aboard Bus No. 8

THE BUS CRAWLS DOWN avenues of new houses with all the architectural virtue of a stack of cigar boxes. Her fellow riders are mostly elderly women on their way home with small sacks of groceries. The bus turns an unfamiliar bend, and in another few moments her own house comes into view.

TUESDAY, 17 MARCH 2009 ~ 11:22 A.M.
University of New Halcyon ~ Kennedy Building,
Lecture Room 212 ~ Elementary Latin

"I WAS DISAPPOINTED with these midterm results," he is saying as one of the rear doors opens and Mary takes a seat in the back row of the small auditorium. "It appears—" He gives her a feeble smile of acknowledgment, and the three girls in the front row turn around to scowl at the newcomer. "It appears that some of you have invented entirely new declensions." Several students laugh. Why hadn't she said anything at breakfast this morning about visiting his class?

"I was planning to go over the exam answers, but seeing as ninety percent of your mistakes were made out of sheer carelessness, it hardly seems like a productive use of class time." He sneaks a glance and finds her listening attentively. "Now open your *Ecce Romani* and let's do a sight translation of the Catullus poem on page one hundred eighty-six." As his students open their textbooks he strides up the stairs to the back row and hands Mary his spare copy, and the smile she gives him could obliterate every unpleasant memory of the last ten years.

2:02 P.M.

"I'm so sorry I interrupted you. It took me ages to find the right building."

Half a dozen students are milling about behind her, clutching their exam papers.

"How—"

"I went to the Classics Department," she says. "Your schedule was posted on the bulletin board."

"Ah. Well . . . I'm glad you came."

"You don't look so pleased. Are you feeling all right?"

"Listen, I have to stay for a bit to answer questions."

Mary looks over her shoulder. "Oh, yes, of course."

"So I'll see you at home?"

2:07 P.M.

The Quad

A FAMILIAR FIGURE approaches on a rusty three-speeder. "I thought that was you!" Colin says gaily as he slows to a stop. A wave of students parts to let him through, and among them he seems even taller and skinnier than usual. "What are you up to?"

"Hello, Colin. I was just attending one of Gray's classes."

"Oh? And what did you think of him—er, it?"

"I found out just how rusty my Latin is."

He laughs. "Where are you headed now?"

"Home, I suppose. You ride a bicycle to campus," she says. "As though it isn't only a ten-minute walk." The Sacred Heart prayer card taped to the crossbar catches her eye.

"Find it amusing, do you? Actually, I don't usually ride it," he says. "Only when I'm late for class."

"Oh, don't let me keep you—"

"Come with me," he says, wheeling his bike toward the Kennedy Building, and she follows him. "You have to sit in on *my* class now. I've got a T.A. gig, you know. Bioethics, it's a great course."

"Well . . ."

He leans the bicycle against a lamppost and fastens the lock. "Hey, and afterwards we can head over to the Yoba Room. My treat."

"The what room?"

"Yoba Room. It's the postgrad and faculty restaurant. You're a big tea drinker, aren't you? You'll love it."

3:26 P.M.
Yobanashi Tea Room

"HOW DID YOU enjoy your introduction to bioethics?"

"It was fascinating. What that girl said about how the generations dilute one's genes, but that memes survive intact—"

"Yeah, that's Dawkins. Pompous Brit."

"Just fascinating. I'd like to read his book."

"I'll lend you my copy," he says as he holds the door open for her. "Couldn't get past chapter two, myself."

Reproductions of centuries-old nautical maps line the dark red walls, and the ceilings are strung with Chinese lanterns. "What kind of music is playing?" she asks as she eyes the glass pastry case beside the cash register. A smattering of grad students slouch over their notebooks at nearby tables, the tea in their cups apparently forgotten.

"I don't know, some self-indulgent indie hack. All that music sounds the same, don't you think? Come on," Colin says, grasping her hand at the fingertips and leading her to a table by the front window.

A menu of fancy-schmancy teas from all seven continents was compiled chiefly to impress visiting scholars of every discipline. (The Antarctic option, the menu states, was concocted from dried colobanthus blossoms by a couple of stir-crazy meteorologists wintering at Rothera, a British base. The menu does not mention this particular tidbit, but the NHU postgrad tearoom is only one of five venues in North America offering this tea that's brewed, essentially, from penguin poop.)

"Why do you live in the attic?"

"I'd really like to try this colobanthus tea," Mary says. "But it's twenty-two dollars a pot!"

"Don't worry about it. Rob works here, you know."

"I didn't."

"Now you do. The tea is free."

"Your treat, indeed!"

He grins. "So why do you live in the attic?"

"I heard you," she says. "I was just hoping I didn't have to answer."

"Heeeey, guys! Fancy meeting *you* here, Colin. He's only in here every afternoon," Rob says to Mary. "Just using me for my freebies."

Colin points to the plate of goat cheese tartlets on Rob's tray.

"Are those for us?"

Rob rolls his eyes as he sets the plate on the table. "They are now, I guess. What'll you have to drink?"

"A pot of colobanthus for the lady, and I'll have the Rooibos Provence, if you please." Colin chooses a tartlet and stuffs it into his mouth.

"Excellent choice, sir. You must be aware of red tea's antioxidant properties."

"Why d'you think I ordered it, fool?"

The goofy grin vanishes from Rob's face. "Bolshy little turd!"

They watch him swagger off to attend to actual customers and Mary shakes her head. "'Bolshy?'"

"It's slang. Comes from—"

"Bolsheviks. What do you take me for?"

Colin shakes his head. "I don't know, Mary—sometimes you act like you've been living under a rock for the last two decades."

"Only two?"

He pushes the plate across the table. "You should try one of these. They're positively scrumptious." He pauses. "There's a spare room between Felix's room and the bathroom, you know."

"I know."

"Why don't you take it? I can help you move all the junk out of it. We'd have it clean in no time."

"That room—it makes me uneasy."

"Yeah," he says. "Who could blame you?"

"Then you . . . you know what happened?"

"What?"

"Oh . . ."

"What happened?"

"Nothing. I mean—we just had a relative . . . die in there."

"That'll do it. Then again, you've prob'ly had relatives die in practically every room in the house." She shivers. "Think about it. D'you know of any others?"

Grandfather in the study; Grandmother in the parlor; Great-uncle Henry in what was formerly the blue bedroom. Father? Aunt Cee? Lucinda? Herself? "No."

Rob returns with a couple of ceramic teapots and matching cups. "You might want to let the colobanthus steep for a few more minutes."

"Thank you, Rob."

"Just holler if you need anything else."

Colin pours his tea and pops another tartlet, chewing thoughtfully.

"Hey, you could requisition Gray's office, couldn't you? I can tell you for a fact he never does any work there."

"And how do you know that?"

"I see him goofing off, juggling oranges and staring out the window and whatnot."

"When do you ever have cause to be on the third floor?"

He shrugs. "Lucy's employed me as a messenger on more than one occasion."

"But if he's living in that room, you can't expect him to be working *all* the time."

"He's living there?"

"He sleeps there every night. Didn't you notice the bed?"

"I thought it was just another procrastination tool." Colin chuckles. "So there's trouble in Blissville, eh?"

Mary sighs. "I doubt there ever was such a place for those two."

"You're wrong," he says as he picks up the last tartlet. "They were definitely happy once, in the beginning. That first summer." He pauses. "Everything's perfect in the beginning, isn't it?"

Someone taps on the window and Mary turns, startled.

"Well, speak of the devil!" Colin says, as Gray gives her a confused half smile that communicates his thoughts with utter clarity: *What the hell are you doing with that guy?*

"Come in," she mouths.

"Can't," he mouths back. "I have a meeting." He taps his watch.

"You and your meetings," she says, and he waves before hurrying back to the Tepplethwaite Building. (He'd been so gleeful upon reading a nasty review of the wunderkind's new book that actually enumerated the factual errors therein—a bronze shield identified as a relic of the First Punic War? Even a child could see through that one!—and he had resolved to celebrate with a tall chai latte. Seeing those two laughing like old friends dampened his elation, however. *Speak of the devil, ha, ha, ha?*)

"How do you like your tea?"

"Not quite what I expected," she says. "It tastes like swamp water."

4:33 P.M.
Kennedy Building

After tea she walks Colin back for his evening class, and when she enters the ladies' room off the lobby she becomes a most unwilling eavesdropper.

"I'm telling you, Liza: if you sleep with him tonight, he'll only ever see you as a walking vagina"—the girl emerges from her stall—"a vagina on a pretty pair of legs." She glances at Mary as she strides to the sink, and Mary averts her eyes as she ducks into a stall.

"Liza? Are you listening to me?"

Liza flushes the toilet. "I've been trying not to," she says, and Mary can tell she is making a strained attempt at playfulness.

"Then don't come crying to me the next time you get screwed over," says Liza's friend over the drone of the hand-dryer. Mary can't hear what Liza has to say to this, and in another moment the two girls have quit the ladies' room. After fumbling with the lock on the stall door, Mary stands at the sink for much longer than necessary, her hands trembling beneath the running faucet.

4:45 P.M.
University Avenue

On the short walk home she has time to mull over all the things she'd have written down had she brought a notebook to that lecture room. "That's Jung you're talking now," Colin had said to one student. "The awareness of one's place among the generations, like one in a set of matryoshka dolls." A woman's unborn daughter already has a lifetime's worth of eggs, which means the mother-to-be also carries the eggs that will become her granddaughters. Understanding settles upon her, languidly, like the urge for a catnap: this is a succession to which she does not belong.

She walks University Avenue slowly, looking through windows just as she used to. It was always easier at nighttime, of course. Mary stands at the little white gate watching Mrs. Delaney watching television in her parlor. The old woman hunches forward, slowly, and is startled awake again by something Mary cannot hear or see.

If you sleep with him tonight, he'll only ever see you as a vagina . . . on a pretty pair of legs. Mary sighs as she turns away from the gate at 23 University Avenue. *Seems they're the only primates who do.* With the way things are today, it's a wonder people fall in love at all.

Or do they?

WEDNESDAY, 18 MARCH 2009 ~ 2:05 A.M.
25 University Avenue ~ Upstairs

SHE DREAMS ABOUT Teddy again, but this time they are interrupted in their lovemaking by an ocean rushing out from between her legs. His fingers turn to starfish and in another moment there's nothing left of him but sea foam. She sits up in bed, tasting salt on her lips, and when she pulls the top sheet away she sighs heavily at the gracelessness of her subconscious mind, its utter deficiency of metaphor. Blood coats her thighs and stains the sheet beneath her, and the dull ache in her abdomen makes her dizzy.

Rummaging through the back of the wardrobe's bottom drawers, she finds a sanitary belt, stretched-out but still wearable, and a near-empty box of Kotex. She strips the bed, chooses a new nightdress, drapes her robe around her shoulders, and tiptoes down the steps. Lucy's door is locked, so she scurries into the hall bathroom to wash herself and rinse the sheet. When she's finished she opens the bathroom door, and Felix leaps forward to cover her mouth before she can shriek.

"Felix! You frightened me."

"I'm sorry, I didn't mean to. I just have to go."

"Go?"

"Yeah, *go.*"

"Oh."

"You don't look so hot."

"Oh—no—I'm quite well."

"Dysmenorrhea?"

Mary just stares at him.

"You got cramps, right?"

"I—"

"My sis gets 'em all the time. Explains why you're washing your sheets in the bathtub and why you're all pasty-faced. Jesus, you look like a corpse! Why don't you use the machine?"

"Which machine?"

"The washing machine, silly girl."

"I don't know how it works."

"C'mon downstairs and I'll show you. While we're waiting for your sheets to dry I'll whip you up a Felixir."

Dewey pops his head out his bedroom door. "That's one of the top five worst puns of all time. You ought to be shot."

Felix ignores him. "When we were younger I used to make this drink for my sis that always got her feeling better in no time at all. Here," he says, pulling the wet sheets down from the shower-curtain rod and dropping them into her arms before closing the door in her face. "Just let me pee and I'll be right down."

2:15 A.M.
The Kitchen

WHEN HE SET UP the laboratory in 1977 Ambrose moved the washer and dryer from the basement to the walk-in pantry. At the time

Lucinda was lying upstairs in the fetal position, suffering from a particularly nasty case of dysmenorrhea herself. Megan helped him position long wood planks on the wrought-iron stairs so they could inch the machines up to the first floor on a rusty old dolly, one at a time. On occasion Megan still complains about how many glasses of sherry it took to banish the soreness from her quads the next day.

"It's easy as pie," Felix says, as Dewey bangs the cupboard doors in search of the Lorna Doone shortbread cookies Milo polished off earlier in the day. "Just throw your dirty laundry in, add some detergent, and choose your setting. You should always use cold water, you know—hot sets the stains."

"I did know that."

"Sure you did." He closes the washer lid and adjusts the other two dials—"Low, because it's such a small load, and we'll just set this to normal wash, like so"—and when he pops the last dial she hears the water rush into the chamber. Felix clucks his tongue as the machine begins to shake. "This thing is on its last legs, I'm afraid."

"The last washer I used didn't work quite the same way," she says. "Thank you for the demonstration."

Felix bows. "Most welcome, my lady. Now for the Felixir!"

He fills a small saucepan with water and turns on the stove. "Do we have any raspberry tea?"

Dewey shrugs. "How should I know?"

"Well, you *might* have a peep inside the tea tin over there by the coffeemaker."

Dewey pries the lid off the Horniman's tea tin and empties the contents onto the counter. "There's plenty of *green* tea—"

"Is that what I asked you for?"

"—and a coupl'a bags of peppermint—"

"No raspberry?"

"No raspberry."

"How about chamomile?"

"I don't see any."

"Then peppermint will have to do. What kind of milk do we have?"

Dewey opens the refrigerator and peers inside. "Skim," he says definitively.

"That's no good. How about creamer?"

"There's a carton of half-and-half in here. Expired two days ago, though."

Felix pops the carton open and takes a sniff. "It's still good." He turns back to the refrigerator door and alights upon a small glass jar of aloe vera gel.

Over his shoulder Dewey pulls out a plate with half the chocolate cake Mary baked three days ago. "I thought that stuff was for sunburns."

"It's also a laxative."

"It's yours, then, I take it?"

"Zip it, Winky."

"But I don't need a laxative," Mary says.

"It cools you off. You know what I mean?"

She shakes her head, looking doubtful.

"Hey, don't close the fridge yet—do we have any more ginger?"

"Fresh ginger?"

"Yeah, from the stir-fry last time." The dish to which Felix refers was part of the belated-rent-apology dinner of two months before.

Dewey pulls a slime-coated produce bag out of the cheese drawer. "Aww, yuck!"

"Guess we'll have to use the dried stuff," Felix says. "Don't shut it yet." He plucks a jar of horseradish from the door.

Dewey frowns. "Why horseradish?"

"Clears you out." Felix dunks the peppermint tea bag into the boiling water in the saucepan and adds a dollop of horseradish, three tablespoons of aloe vera, and a generous pinch of dried ginger.

"I wouldn't drink this, if I were you," Dewey says. "You'll be on the pot for three days straight."

Milo shuffles down the back stairs wearing a pair of bedroom slippers so ratty they could pass for induction into some back-alley museum of germ-ridden curiosities. "What is it?" He yawns. "And can I have some?"

"Do you have cramps, too?"

"I just want to see what it tastes like."

With a triumphant flourish Felix places the mug on the table. Mary raises it to her mouth and wrinkles her nose as she takes the first sip. "Trust me," she says. "You'd rather not know."

"What does it taste like?"

"Well, what do you *suppose* a concoction of peppermint tea, aloe vera, cream, and horseradish would taste like?"

"I never *said* it was going to taste good," Felix whines.

"You're quite right," Mary says. "But it was very kind of you to make this for me. Thank you, Felix."

"Aren't you going to drink the rest of it?"

"Must I?"

He folds his arms. "Yes."

Now Colin and Rob come shuffling down the steps.

"You scamps woke us up," Colin says.

"You're never asleep at a quarter to three," Dewey replies.

"I was making Mary my infamous Felixir."

"That's the worst pun I've ever heard in my life," Rob says, scratching the growth of a new gingerbeard.

"Yeah," Milo pipes in. "You oughta be shot."

Felix claps her on the shoulder. "Drink up, girly." Dutifully she takes another sip, and another, though she is beginning to feel as though she is imbibing her own vomit.

"Hey, ask Mary," Milo cries. "Maybe Mary knows."

"What is it I might know?"

"The broom closets."

"If all they've got is brooms in 'em, then why're they always locked?"

"Look at her! Look at how she's smiling. She *definitely* knows."

"Must be a family secret."

"It is, actually. The brooms all have golden handles."

"Those brooms must fly," Dewey says. "That's my theory. Otherwise why would she lock them up?"

Mary laughs. "Are you calling Lucy a witch?"

Milo pokes her on the shoulder. "You want to hear *my* theory?"

"Sure."

"It's where she keeps her skeletons," he says in a stage whisper.

The table erupts into laughter.

"Come on, Mary—why the long face?"

"Your sense of humor stretches the margins of good taste, my friend."

"Nonsense, it's not in poor taste at all. In truth, I have to wonder if Milo here has struck a nerve."

"What is it you're implying?" she asks, still half playful.

"Everyone has secrets," Colin replies. "But Lucy seems to have more of them than the average Jane."

"What makes you say so?"

The five of them are staring at her now, the smiles fading from their faces. "What about the bodies she keeps in the basement?" Milo asks.

"There *are* no bodies in the basement," she cries in exasperation. "What is it you call this, a conspiracy theory? Don't you boys have anything *important* to think about?"

"Relax, Mary."

"Yeah, sheesh!"

"I'm not saying she even has any real secrets," Colin says. "I'm just saying she's always carrying on as though she did."

"Yeah, and it's *weird.*"

"I think she does have secrets," Milo says. "And I think it would do her good to let it all hang out for a change."

"Milo, if you're referring to that other theory of yours, I think you should stop it right now."

Mary rolls her eyes. "Why air them out, when keeping them doesn't hurt anyone?"

"Yes, but who decides?"

"Who decides what?"

"Who decides what's harmless and what isn't?"

"The keeper of the secret, I suppose."

"Now that doesn't make any sense at all, Mary. It ought to be the potential victims of the secret-keeping."

"Sir, that is patently illogical."

Colin smiles indulgently. "You went to college, didn't you, Mary?"

"I did."

"Where?"

"Here."

"Here? When did you graduate?"

"Last year."

"Last year! How is it that we've only just met you?"

Mary stares at him, suddenly queasy. "It's no secret Lucy and I don't get along too well. We . . . we didn't speak for quite some time."

"But I never even passed you on the quad!"

"We . . . we must have crossed paths at some point."

"NHU is the third-largest public university in Massachusetts," Dewey pipes up.

"Nah." Colin looks at her, shaking his head. "I would have remembered you from someplace."

"So you met your husband here?"

She nods.

"You haven't been married long, I take it."

She shakes her head.

"Why haven't we seen your husband?"

"He's still on the Cape." This is not a falsehood.

"It's only three hours away."

"Don't pry, Felix."

"Oh ho, *now* who's the stinky hypocrite?"

"Funny thing," Mary says. "You boys hardly talk like you belong to a Christian fraternity."

For several moments they fidget like kindergarteners. "We always make up for it in the morning," Milo says in a small voice.

"We're . . . we're not divorced," she says quietly. "I suppose that's what you've all been wondering."

"We thought it might have been a starter marriage," Felix says. Thanks again to P. F. X. Godfry, this phrase requires no explanation.

"Mary?"

"Yes, Dewey?"

"How did you know your husband was the one you wanted . . . you know . . ."

Felix speaks with a look of mild distaste: "For the rest of your life?"

Her stomach has now joined her womb in this state of revolt, and it makes the prickling behind her eyes too much to bear. "It isn't a voluntary death sentence, Felix," she says, rising out of her seat.

Voluntary death sentence—now, when had she used those words before?

SUNDAY, 22 MARCH 2009 ~ 9:30 P.M.

The Study

THERE IS A VAGUE AIR of expectancy in the evenings, as though her descendants are going to be late arrivals at a dinner party. Yet her children are dead, all three of them.

She isn't—*wasn't*—their mother. She'll never be anyone's mother now, despite the mess she made of the bedsheets.

Mary rips the first few pages out of a diary she began the summer before last, and titles the new page *Confessions.* Confessions of whom? A "justified sinner"? Indeed!

"Mary?" Lucy stands facing the sofa, an empty Kotex bag hooked on her index finger. "Are you menstruating?" Then, remembering herself, she hurries to opposite ends of the room to close the doors. "Well? Are you?"

Mary snaps the journal shut. "Why *else* would I need the napkins?"

Lucy sits on the sofa arm, crumples the Kotex wrapper, and tosses it into the can behind the desk. "There's something I should tell you," she says in a low voice. "The bleeding, it . . . it doesn't mean you'll be able to have children."

Mary stares at her. "Are you saying . . . ?"

"It isn't possible." She pauses. "I'm sorry. I . . . I'll buy you more pads."

As Lucy closes the door behind her, Mary stares at the amaryllis wilting in the window. Then she opens the diary and writes as if her pen were possessed.

TUESDAY, 24 MARCH 2009 ~ 8:05 P.M.

The Third-Floor Turret Room

"I'M SORRY TO BOTHER YOU, but I need to look for something in here." Lucy caresses his shoulder briefly as she strides toward the closet. "I won't be long."

"What is it you're looking for?"

"Oh . . . ," she says faintly, rummaging through the same box Mary had checked.

"*You're* being evasive, too," he says.

She looks at him sharply. "Who else is being evasive?"

"Mary. She's been looking for something." He pauses. "I'm starting to think you two are looking for the same thing."

She turns from the closet and flops down on his bed. "Just before my grandfather was killed, he met this old Frenchwoman who made him a mourning bracelet."

"A mourning bracelet?"

"Out of his own hair. For her."

"For Mary?"

She nods.

"And you're looking for it now . . . for his DNA."

She nods again.

“It’s not with her other jewelry?”

“No.”

“Have you ever seen it?”

“I remember her wearing it when I was a child.”

“She was still wearing it forty years afterwards?” He wrinkles his nose. “That’s downright creepy.”

“Be that as it may, I know the damned thing’s around here someplace.” She rises from the bed with an air of renewed purpose. “And I need it.”

SUNDAY, 5 APRIL 2009 ~ 10:40 P.M.

The Basement

“WHAT?!”

“Please don’t try to talk me out of it. I—”

“You’re *loco.*” Megan chucks the contents of her mug down the sink, splattering coffee all over the cabinets. “You belong in a straitjacket!”

“Can we talk about this calmly?”

“Oh, ho, look who it is—the goddess of reason! How dare you? How *dare* you jeopardize my—”

“This has nothing to do with you, Megan.”

“What if you get caught this time, huh? Think it’ll have nothing to do with me then? I can’t believe you, Lucy. I can’t believe how un*grate*ful you are.”

“I don’t owe you a goddamned thing,” Lucy says frostily. “Let’s get that straight. I owe you nothing.”

“You owe me your life, you little monster!”

“Go ahead and fire me!” she cries as Megan stomps up the steps.

Megan won’t fire her, of course, but by lunchtime tomorrow Lucy will sure wish she had.

MONDAY, 6 APRIL 2009 ~ 9:17 A.M.
The Backyard

MARY TAKES A WALK in her Wellingtons down the wooded path at the back of the garden with one hand in her coat pocket, fingering the pack of chewing gum Patrick had given her. She's not ready to use the gum—not yet.

The diffident sunshine and the smells of wet earth and new foliage have got her humming bits of "Rhapsody in Blue." In the early summer, just before the wedding, Teddy had carved her name on an oak tree where a wooden swing once hung from a high branch, and beneath her name, what looked like a rough sideways eight. It's still here, the carvings filled in with lichen.

Someone calls her from inside the labyrinth, and for one moment Mary forgets herself entirely; for it sounds like the voice of her mother.

"Mary?" No, it's Lucy. Sighing, Mary returns to the maze entrance, choosing each turn sans thought.

Lucy is waiting for her at the center. "I thought I'd find you out here."

"And right you were."

Lucy gestures toward the bench beside the old fountain, and they sit facing each other. "I've figured it out," she says quietly. "But there's a catch. More than one, actually."

"Well?" Mary says. "Out with it."

"The first thing is that Teddy died in nineteen forty-four, which means he was thirty-eight."

(How would Teddy have looked at thirty-eight? A few silver hairs at his temples, maybe a couple of faint lines on his brow—but still boyish, surely.)

"Now," Lucy goes on, "you remember why you're twenty-two, and why your last memories were of wallpapering the second-floor turret room?"

Mary nods with motherly patience.

"So if I clone Teddy, he'll be fifteen years older than you remember him. He'll have retained many more memories than you. He'll remember the Depression, he'll remember your children . . . and he'll know a lot of things that might unsettle you."

"Memories from the war—is that what you mean?"

"He won't be the same man you remember."

"I understand that." She pauses. "Have you found the bracelet, then?"

Lucy shakes her head. "I can't find it anywhere. And I haven't been able to find a complete sample in any of his old clothes, or anywhere else—"

"How can that be? You found one of mine easily enough!" It's as though he never lived here at all.

"I don't know why." Lucy pauses. "But it leaves me with only one other option."

"Your hands are shaking."

Lucy thrusts her fists into her jacket pockets.

"What is it?"

"We're . . . we're going to have to exhume him."

Mary looks away.

"So what I'm trying to say is . . . Are you sure you want to do this?"

"Yes."

"You wouldn't have to come along, if you—"

"I'll come. I'm coming."

"We'd have no way of . . . I mean, it's only possible because you had him buried at Cape Eden. Veterans are usually taken to Arlington. Saint Jude's was closed in the eighties, so with due caution we'll be able to—"

"Saint Jude's, too?"

"Yes, Saint Jude's, too." Lucy pauses. "There's one more thing. He . . . he might not be normal, Mary."

"Speak plainly."

"War veterans often suffer from post-traumatic stress disorder, but he—there's a good chance he'll remember his own death. There's no way to predict how those memories will affect him."

"I see."

"What do you see?"

"You're afraid of creating a monster."

Lucy can't look at her.

"But you've already created one, you know. What's the harm in giving life to another?"

Lucy clears her throat. "You're ready to go ahead with it, then?"

Mary nods.

"I knew I wouldn't change your mind, but I needed to warn you. We'll just have to hope for the best. It may not work at all."

"If it doesn't work, you'll try again."

Lucy closes her eyes. "I should have known you'd say that."

SATURDAY, 18 APRIL 2009 ~ 6:58 P.M.

Saint Jude's Churchyard ~ Cape Eden

THE SUN THROWS its last light across the fallow green fields as Mary fidgets in the backseat, chest tight and stomach fluttering at the thought of what tonight will bring. The place is much as she remembers it, though all the back roads have been paved and new brick bungalows dot the hillsides. While they're here she'd like to drive by Teddy's old house, but something keeps her from asking. Better to remember it as it was; better to imagine some other family repainting the shutters and tending the kitchen garden, some other local crew harvesting the cranberries the second weekend in October. When they reach the crossroads by the dairy—still here!—Gray wrinkles his nose at the smell of manure, but Mary breathes it in happily.

A winding road takes them into the woods, the sea visible here and there through the evergreens. The church sits in a small clearing, where what feels like six months ago their two families had assembled for a wedding portrait. As Lucy gets out of the driver's seat to wrestle with the rusted gate, Mary looks up at a gaping hole in the roof.

Saint Jude's has fallen into a state of picturesque decline in the twenty years since the parish was folded into Our Lady of Perpetual Sorrow nearly thirty miles away. For a brief time afterwards a caretaker kept the grounds just tidy enough for the handful of weddings held here each summer, but no one has been married in this town since 1996. A maintenance worker from the township comes out here with a Weed-whacker twice a year, but otherwise the church and cemetery wear their neglect in a most romantic fashion. Those who knew the Catholics of Cape Eden buried here before the Second World War have long since joined them.

Mary does not enter the church, not yet. The grass has grown so high that she lifts her knees like a drum majorette as she walks, her eyes roving over the headstones. Why feel such pity for these forgotten dead? Wouldn't she rather be surrounded in heaven than remembered on earth?

Lucy looks up at the wisp of a moon hanging above the fir trees. "We'll have just enough light," she says. Gray approaches the entrance to the church, where a heavy chain and lock hang from one of the wooden handles on the double doors, useless since the other handle came off. He opens the door.

The pews beneath the holes in the roof are stained with rainwater and pigeon shit; the wretched birds flutter and coo along the eaves. Even in the failing light he can see there are panes of colored glass missing in the pointed arch windows on either side. The modest rosette above the choir loft must have been a source of pride in such a small-town parish.

An elaborately carved confessional stands to the right of the entrance. He peeks inside to find a velvet kneeler, a metal screen, and a nest of newborn mice; he shuts the door again quickly. In the corner beside the confessional he discovers a water-stained prayer book on a low wooden table. The last entry, a supplication for the soul of a dying aunt, is dated April 1983.

A small marble statue of the Virgin remains in a niche beside the altar; a bouquet of dried roses, drained of color, hangs upside down from a bit of thread fastened to the wall beneath her feet. Before her stands a wrought-iron candleholder, covered in wax drippings, and an empty wicker offering basket on the floor beneath it.

The floorboards creak under his feet as he examines each of the Stations of the Cross, carved in oak, the paint worn off except in the crevices. From the trees outside a mourning dove sounds its plaintive cry over and over.

Lucy is perched on the hood of the car when he comes out of the church.

"So is this what's known as 'casing the joint'?" he says.

"Har, har," she says.

"What are we going to do until it's late enough to come back?"

"There's a bar a few miles down the road. We'll play pinball."

"Har, har," he says.

"Come on," she says. "We'd better check on her."

SOMEONE CUT THE grass on the Morrigan plot quite recently, but Mary gives only a passing thought to who it might have been. When she spots his father's stone her heart begins to pound. To the right of it:

JANE MORRIGAN
dear mother
1881–1947
"Who can find a virtuous woman?
for her worth is far above rubies."

"A perfect lady." What would her mother-in-law think of her now, in these grass-stained dungarees?

And there it is, another simple stone slab, broad enough for two inscriptions side by side. Their bodies rest six feet beneath the grassy place where she kneels now, her face buried in her hands.

EDWARD MORRIGAN

1906–1944

Gave his life for his country on the French front.

Loving son, husband, father, and friend.

It had been so much easier to think of him being away these last two months, off at some long and tedious medical conference in London or Brussels. To the right of this inscription is: *HIS WIFE, MARY, 1907–1989,* the two years hewn more than four decades apart.

From behind her come the sounds of two pairs of sneakers threading through the grass.

"LOOK." GRAY POINTS to the base of Teddy's and Mary's headstones. A small basket of fresh yellow chrysanthemums is nestled in the grass beneath Mary's name. "Who put them there?"

"Some distant relative," Lucy says. "We have a lot of them out here. Mary? Are you all right?"

But Mary can't bear their company right now, let alone any more of these inane questions.

THE SOMBER REDS and blues fade from the rosette window, leaving the two of them in darkness on the dirty floor on either side of it.

Mary looks at her, sitting cross-legged across the loft with such a smug look on her face (though it's Lucy's attempt at sympathy), and she can only wish that Lucy felt what she feels: coming back here to her husband's parish church, where she came for Mass on so many Sundays, and where they were so recently married, to confront all the proof that her life is truly over. Lucy should rightfully shoulder this pain; Lucy deserves it.

"Why can't you leave me in peace for once?"

Lucy clears her throat. "I'm not trying to hound you."

"Why did you follow me up here then?"

"I just . . . I just wanted to be sure you were all right."

"You see now that I haven't flung myself over the loft railing, so why are you still here?" The blank look on Lucy's face only fuels that placid rage. "I have to wonder, Lucy—what sort of granddaughter *were* you? Did you love your grandmother for who she was, or did you love her for what she could do for you?"

"That isn't fair," Lucy says quietly.

" 'Fair'!" Mary laughs. "I'm not being fair? Let me tell you something: You may know the details of my life—and you may own what once belonged to me—but you know *nothing* about me."

Lucy stands and opens the door to the loft with a creak that echoes through the church. "It must have relieved you to say that."

"Not in the least," she replies.

So Lucy, shaking from the encounter, ventures down the steps in the darkness to wait for her in the car.

7:45 P.M.

Interstate Route 588 ~ Tommy Dolan's Bar & Restaurant

SOMETHING'S GONE on between the two of them; Lucy can see it in the way Gray's been carrying himself this evening. He doesn't look at either of them when he speaks, and his words are suffused with an anxiety that—in Lucy's mind—can't be entirely due to the prospect of this nocturnal adventure. How has it escaped her notice? It's because this is the first time in months they've spent more than half an hour in each other's company. Then again, her own absences may be the very thing fueling her paranoia.

At the bar off the highway he orders the beef goulash and eats it with a relish disproportionate to the quality of the food, shoveling each lumpy forkful into his mouth with his nose nearly in his plate. As her own food grows cold, Lucy watches Mary paring her chicken cutlet into pieces small enough for a four-year-old. Clearly her thoughts are elsewhere.

After they've eaten, Gray approaches the pool table, Corona in hand, and joins the next game (much to Lucy's surprise). Mary spends a long time flipping through the selections on the jukebox by the door, choosing songs by Bing Crosby and Dexy's Midnight Runners (the name has piqued her curiosity). At the table, Lucy opens her notebook and reviews her father's notes, which she has painstakingly copied so she'd only have to decipher them once. Mary returns to the table and opens a Henry James novel. All three are oblivious to the elderly bartender's stares. Who reads a book in a bar run by and for "working stiffs"?

Mary approaches the bar to order a ginger ale and a gin and tonic. She leans over the bar as Tommy Dolan pours the Gordon's—he doesn't have any Bombay Sapphire. "I like your taste in music, young lady." ("Come On, Eileen" won't play for another two and a half minutes.)

"I'll bet you I'm older than you are," she tells him.

"For that, sweetheart," says the highly amused bartender, "your drinks are on the house."

11:05 P.M.
Saint Jude's Churchyard

MARY HAS NEVER dabbled in Gothic literature. The few ghost stories she read as a child featured no corpses, no nocturnal winged rodents, no peculiar fogs or odors. Nevertheless, the romance inherent in an abandoned churchyard in the moonlight has not eluded her in these few moments before she recalls their purpose. One by one they hop the rusted wrought-iron gate and plod single file through the tall grass, their flashlight beams swinging to and fro among the headstones. Mary carries a green electric lantern in her other hand. The woods around the little churchyard shiver with the breeze coming in off the ocean half a mile away, and she gulps the air, greedily, hoping in vain to steady herself.

She wears one of Gray's old Villanova T-shirts with the collar cut off and a pair of dungarees rolled up to the top of her Wellingtons. She's pulled her hair back in a loose chignon, and her arms and face and neck are so milk-white that she shimmers like an opal under the faint crescent moon. Lucy watches Gray pretending not to watch Mary. When Lucy isn't looking Gray is looking at her instead, for her weariness has begun to show. There are those bruises on her arms—more than the marks of a chronic sleepwalker—and her sallow skin, her painful thinness.

Gray suggests they slice through the turf and attempt to roll it up like a carpet, something he saw once on a home improvement show, and in this they are surprisingly successful. Lucy sets the plastic laboratory case on top of the headstone and flips the latch. The earth is cold and hard beneath their feet, and the digging will not be easy. They proceed in silence, stopping every few minutes to cock an ear for passing cars.

When they're about three feet down he stops digging and turns to Mary. "Do you think maybe you'd be better off waiting in the car?"

"They're just bones, Gray."

"You didn't seem to think so a few hours ago."

"It was a shock." She tosses another shovelful. "That's all."

Another hour passes before Gray's shovel strikes the coffin lid. Lucy flips the switch on the electric lantern, leaving it perched on the lip of the grave. Feverishly they remove the last shovelfuls of dirt, digging themselves a narrow trench around the sides, hitting the edge of Mary's own coffin in the process. "Don't look at it," Lucy tells her. "Don't think about it."

So Mary stands at the foot of the coffin with her eyes fixed on the dull brass nameplate. Lucy places the lab case on the lid and Gray stands opposite her.

"Here." Lucy pulls three surgeon's masks out of the case, handing one to Gray, who dons it obediently. But Mary shakes her head.

"Please take it."

"It won't smell," Mary says. "He's been here too long."

Lucy puts her hands on her hips. "And how would you know that?"

"My father told me."

"If it isn't going to smell, then why do we need to wear them?" Gray says through his mask.

For a moment Lucy wants to rip the mask off his face, but she thinks better of it. "Wear it or don't wear it," she mutters as she fits one over her nose and mouth. She pulls out a crowbar and offers it to Gray. "You want to do the honors?"

"Not particularly," he says as he takes it. He turns to Mary. "Are you sure you want to be here?" She nods, impassive.

The two of them brace themselves for a shriek and a swoon. With her case under her arm, Lucy inches toward the foot of the coffin, standing close to Mary so that Gray can raise the lid. It pries open easily. Mary breathes.

"Last chance," Lucy whispers.

He glances at them before he raises the lid.

THERE IT IS, that yawning chasm of eternal oblivion visible through his gaping jaw—as though they'd buried him alive, and he died midscream. How in God's name did she *ever* think she was prepared for this?

Lucy shudders. As he looks over the corpse in the military uniform (mostly eaten through), Gray feels like an asshole for having looked at this man's photograph with such continual scorn.

Bending at the waist as if to join him, Mary balances herself with her left hand on the wooden rim and reaches for his left hand with her right. Slipping her fingers under his—what's left of his skin pulled taut around his knuckles—she twists his wedding ring around his finger and slides it off.

Standing up, she pulls a handkerchief out of her back pocket and runs it through the center of the ring, polishing it with exaggerated care. Dumbstruck, Gray and Lucy stand watching her across the open coffin. Mary slips the ring onto her middle finger and, turning, she digs the toe of her boot deep into the wall of earth behind them, climbing out of the hole in a matter of four or five seconds. She hoists herself onto the grass so her legs are still dangling into the void.

"I'd like to go inside and sit down for a moment, if you don't mind."

Lucy and Gray exchange a look over what is left of Lucy's grandfather, and when they look up again Mary is gone.

Lucy dons a pair of latex gloves and braces herself for the distasteful business at hand. Mary, coming around the crumbling stone façade, is certain she is losing her mind at last: through one of the windows a small light flickers. As she opens the front door she sees it: a votive candle lit beneath the shrine of the Virgin. If she thought to look, she'd find a strange fifty-cent piece in the offering basket. Mary stands still in the doorway, listening for movement, but there is none save the pigeons cooing in their sleep.

WHAT DO YOU need me to do now?"

"I don't need your help until we're ready to fill it in."

"So, should I—"

"Yes," she says curtly as she bends over the coffin with an instrument he can't identify. "Go and see if she's all right."

THE DOOR CREAKS open again behind her. "Mary?" The outlines of columns and pews are barely discernible in the moonlight coming through the holes in the roof. He sees the votive candle burning beside the altar and assumes she's the one who lit it. As he ventures up the aisle he can see her in the first seat, her head bent, her shoulders heaving silently, and he slips into a seat several rows behind her.

After what seems like half an hour, during which time Gray convinces himself of the nonexistence of God, he approaches her pew and sits down beside her. Even in the dark he can see that her face is tear-stained; her fingers shake as she removes the silver chain from her neck and the ring from her middle finger, loops the one through the other, and refastens the clasp.

"Lucy will be finished by now."

Nodding, she follows him out.

"HANG BACK," HE says as they approach, in case Lucy hasn't yet lowered the coffin lid.

"Let's get this closed and get the hell out of here," she hisses from the grave. Gray lowers himself into the hole and they refit the lid on the coffin. Lucy hands Mary the lab case, and the two of them scramble out again. It takes longer than they expected to fill in the grave, the still night air punctuated by the sound of their shovelfuls landing on the lid.

SUNDAY, 19 APRIL 2009 ~ 4:58 A.M.

The North Sea Road ~ Cape Eden

THE PRIUS SLOWS to a crawl, gravel crunching beneath the tires. Slouched over a balled-up sweater of Gray's in the backseat, she half-opens her eyes to find herself bathed in the warm yellow glow of a porch lamp. (She would recognize the house were she fully awake.) There are whisperings in the front seat, but she can't make out the words.

"I never knew you had an uncle here," Gray whispers.

Lucy shrugs. "It never came up."

"So *he* was the one who put those flowers on the grave."

"Nice work, Sherlock."

"Why didn't you tell her the truth?"

"Why would I?"

He pauses. "Don't you ever speak to him?"

"I haven't seen him since my grandmother's funeral."

"But that was twenty years ago!"

"They never really got along, anyway. Dad said Mother called him gauche for turning the family house into a B and B."

Gray turns away from the passenger's-side window. "Well, we're here now. I'll wait in the car and you can go in and say hello."

"Don't be daft, Gray. It's five o'clock in the morning."

"The light's on. I just saw someone walk by the window there."

"I'm not ringing the doorbell at five in the morning to say hello to an uncle I haven't seen since I was nine years old."

"Why not?"

"Because it's absurd, that's why. We're going home."

"Whatever you say. You're driving."

Jerking the steering wheel to the left, she pulls out of the driveway as a shower of gravel rains against the wooden sign stuck between the tidy flower beds. Through the rearview mirror he sees someone pulling back the curtain in the front room.

"'World's End,'" she mutters. "What a stupid name."

MONDAY, 20 APRIL 2009 ~ 2:25 A.M.
25 University Avenue ~ The Third-Floor Turret Room

A SLICE OF MOONLIGHT illuminates her face and shoulders; the straps of her nightgown have slid down around her elbows. What right has she to look so satisfied?

He reaches over and pulls the delicate pink straps up over her shoulders. "How exactly are you going to pull this off?"

Lucy opens her eyes. "You mean Teddy? I'm using another egg of my mother's."

"But you can't carry him. How, then?"

"Remember the first night I brought you down there? I told you: that thing can build from scratch."

"I remember, all right." Gray shudders briefly. "And I hate that phrase."

"It doesn't seem to bother you when Mary uses it."

In the narrow bed he turns away from her to face the wall. "That's because she's talking about pie crusts."

SPRING, 2009

The Basement

THUS IS TEDDY conceived on the last night in April in the year of their eightieth wedding anniversary. As expected, Lucy is rarely seen, and when they do see her she's testy from too much late-night coffee. Gray aids in the installation of a generator to avoid any further visits from representatives of the electric company, and she dons her headphones cheerfully. Two or three nights a week she reappears to ask for his help refilling the element canisters, and two or three nights a week he thinks of pulling and quickly replacing the plug while her back is turned.

FRIDAY, 8 MAY 2009 ~ 6:30 P.M.

The Woods Behind the House

MARY GOES FOR LONG walks at dusk down a path behind the house, between the backyards of University Avenue and the woods beyond them (still untouched, but for how much longer?). Three nights out of seven Gray accompanies her, though they never talk much. Blooming forsythia and rhododendron bushes reach over wooden fences, and she raises her hand to touch their branches as she passes. She ambles down the lane all but wearing the twilight, jauntily, like a brand-new dress.

Sometimes she'll ask him if he's been down to the basement, and he'll tell her he has, but only to help Lucy. "I haven't . . . I haven't seen him," he says. To this she makes no reply.

On this particular evening a small figure greets them at the fence just beyond the Morrigan property.

"Professor!" comes a faint voice. "It's been too long, my friend!" Wise and amiable nonagenarian that she is, Mrs. Delaney seldom wants for visitors, but Gray still feels a pang of guilt as he approaches her back gate.

"Mrs. Delaney," he says, "I would like you to meet Mary. She's a cousin of Lucy's."

"How do you do, Mrs. Delaney?"

"I'm quite well, all things considered." She laughs. "Why don't you come up to the house for a little snack?"

6:55 P.M.

23 University Avenue

MRS. DELANEY puts an old-fashioned kettle on the stove and proffers a plate of chocolate-chip cookies. "My granddaughter made these," she says as Mary picks a cookie. "I must say, I have a weakness for them. You'd do me a favor to have another. Here, take a third!"

Obediently Mary chooses two more cookies. "When did you move here, Mrs. Delaney?"

"Nineteen thirty-six. My husband grew up in this house, did I tell you that, Gray? We moved back here because he'd secured a professorship in the Classics Department." Mrs. Delaney slips into a chair across the table from them, shakes her head, and presses her palm to her temple. "Dear God, sometimes I wonder where all the time's gone." She pauses, knowing that kind of thinking is a waste of the time that remains. "So you're visiting your cousin Lucy, eh?"

"I've sort of . . . moved in, indefinitely, actually. I'm at a bit of a crossroads, you might say."

"Ah." Mrs. Delaney nods sagely. "And how are you keeping busy?"

"Reading, mostly. I go for long walks whenever the weather holds. And I've been doing a bit of gardening."

"Lucy's grandmother had a lovely garden, you know. We used to trade whatever the other was lacking, and she always gave me the nicest cabbages in the patch. Was Mary your grandmother as well?"

Mary nods.

"Strange our paths haven't crossed before, isn't it?"

"It is," Mary says. "Though I've been away for quite a while."

"Well, if you ever manage to revive that old garden, you let me know. I haven't had anyone to trade with in twenty years now." Mrs. Delaney turns her head and eyes her sharply. "Whose daughter did you say you were? Teddy Junior's?"

Mary swallows before she nods.

"You tell him I said hello, next time you go home to the Cape."

How is it that no one ever told her what happened to Teddy Junior? Perhaps her memory is spotty—poor woman! "I will," Mary says quietly.

FRIDAY, 15 MAY 2009 ~ 7:00 A.M.
25 University Avenue ~ The Master Bedroom

SHE STEALS INTO the room as Lucy's alarm clock goes off. "When can I see him?"

Lucy groans, pulling at the tangled bedsheets. "This is why I usually lock the door, you know."

"Well?"

"You can't."

"Why not?"

"Too traumatic for you."

Mary laughs incredulously.

"It doesn't matter, anyway. He's just a bundle of cells at this point. It's not like you can go down there and have a conversation with him."

"It's only that I—"

"Everything's going well so far. You're going to have to trust me."

Gripping the old brass bed rail, Mary looks out the window at the labyrinth, which in its current state begs for an army of pruning shears. Then she turns and leaves the room without another word.

"Oh, and don't bother asking Gray," Lucy calls after her. "He doesn't have a key."

SUNDAY, 17 MAY 2009 ~ 8:50 P.M.

The Foyer

LUCY ANSWERS THE DOOR and sighs in relief as Megan strides into the hall. "I'll help you," Megan says as Lucy unlocks the basement door. "But on two conditions."

"This is the last time." Lucy closes the door behind them.

"It sure is, because you're going to dismantle the simwomb as soon as he's out of it, even if—"

"Yes," Lucy says. "Even if."

Megan flips the switch on the space-age coffeemaker. "And once it's over you have to get her—or them—out of here, out of the country. ASAP."

"Yes," Lucy says slowly. "Yes, I suppose we'll have to."

"I'll call my friend at the Bureau tomorrow so we'll have all the IDs ready. Meanwhile you two can head to the bookstore—make a beeline for the travel section." She chooses a mug from the cabinet above the sink. "Have you told her yet?"

"Told her what?"

"How long she can expect to live."

"But I don't *know* how long she can expect to live."

"You have to warn her, at least."

"I can't. It's like handing down a death sentence."

"She has a death sentence whether or not you choose to inform her of it," Megan says. "Though I suspect she'll have a pretty clear idea soon enough."

"What's that supposed to mean?"

"You want me to tell her for you?"

"Yeah," Lucy snorts. "Right."

MAY 2009

25 University Avenue

SPECIALTY COOKBOOKS on sea vegetables and chocolate-making, hitherto unused, rouse her to new and exciting culinary experiments most afternoons. A chocolate fig cake also makes an appearance on the kitchen table every so often, *Help yourselves!* written on a yellowed index card tucked under the plate. It's gone within half an hour. Lucy never samples anything Mary makes; when she comes home in the evening she rarely even ventures into the kitchen to greet Mary before retreating down the cellar steps.

Mrs. Delaney's talk of cabbages prompts a search through the pantry for Aunt Cecelia's old recipe box, and when Mary finds it she whoops in triumph: the last card in the box bears the title *After 109 Attempts, the Perfect Ribollita!* in her own prim handwriting.

Colin and the rest of the Seventh Order eat better than they have in their lives, and she fancies her cooking is putting flesh on their skeletal forms at last. Milo pulls a bay leaf out of his mouth, giggling like a small girl. Behind his study door Gray eats with just as much relish.

The pruning shears make their overdue appearance. By Memorial Day the labyrinth, along with all the other shrubbery in the Morrigan demesne, has been trimmed to perfection. Gray watches Mary from his study window, following her swift and competent movements, her hands in white gardening gloves. Dressed in a flowered apron and a cheerful straw hat, she plants young lemon mint and other herbs from the Mediterranean market downtown in the old kitchen garden, slipping off her glove to finger the fragrant, furry leaves. The overgrown boys on the second floor look down from their bedroom windows and sigh at her quaintness; she brings to mind some quondam golden age they were born seven decades too late to experience.

MONDAY TO SUNDAY, 1–7 JUNE 2009
The Backyard

IN THE MORNING she rises before the sun burns the dew off the grass. For the last four decades the spoon fountain has lain tarnished beyond recognition under a dusty sheet in the old toolshed behind the labyrinth. On a picnic table outside the labyrinth, Mary spends a full week restoring it with pink polish, spoon by spoon, to its refulgent glory.

One by one the members of the Seventh Order trickle downstairs and out-of-doors to watch her as she works, their pasty-white faces starved for sunshine. "It's the most peculiar thing I've ever seen," says Dewey.

"And that's saying something," Felix replies.

Mary laughs as she squirts more polish on her rag.

"Where'd you get it, Mary?"

"It was a wedding gift from my husband's cousin. He moved to Paris to become a sculptor."

"Oh, yes, it's very avant-garde."

She steps back to appraise her progress. "You'd still say so?"

Felix frowns. "What do you mean?"

Late Sunday morning, a gurgling tintinnabulation through the open window distracts Gray from his reading. With a knee on the narrow bed, he looks out the window to find the old fountain functioning once again at the center of the labyrinth, the water cascading down a strange contraption of silver eating utensils, all of it flashing in the sun like a chandelier. Intuition alerting her to his presence by the third-floor turret window, Mary turns and looks up at him, her smile as radiant as the wedding gift.

SUNDAY, 5 JULY 2009
25 University Avenue

MARY TUCKS *Long Road Home* away on a shelf of coffee-table books behind the sofa. On rainy afternoons she pores over another shelf stuffed with softbound volumes of poetry that had belonged to Lucinda, reading all the marginalia scribbled in pencil, and by the middle of July she has become engrossed in a handful of works on yoga and vegetarianism, books Lucy's father had purchased with the best of intentions over several consecutive Januarys. "Did you know that Leonardo da Vinci was a vegetarian?" she says to the members of the Seventh Order as they nosh on sticks of beef jerky late one night on Colin's bed.

"Yeah," Rob says. "We tried it, actually. The purists among us believe a vegetarian lifestyle is essential, but—"

"Purists?"

"The founders of the Order."

"Why?"

"Beef is an aphrodisiac."

"Like everything *else* in the fridge," Felix grumbles.

"So you weren't vegetarians for very long, I suppose?"

Milo shakes his head sadly. "I just couldn't give up chicken nuggets."

SATURDAY, 18 JULY 2009
25 University Avenue

WHILE SHE SEWS the pieces of her purple "eights" quilt, Gray is looking up the values of her Antarctic Explorer trading cards on the

Internet. Only the Amundsen would sell for less than four hundred dollars.

He finds a sticky mat and an old yoga DVD for her to watch on the small television in the parlor; though she is little more than amused at first, Mary becomes ever more intent on balancing herself on one leg with her hands pressed together at her chest, a pose whose simplicity she discovers is deceptive.

He surprises her with *March of the Penguins* on DVD and they watch it in the parlor over egg-and-horseradish sandwiches. Being in this room reminds her of the night—the month before they were engaged, wasn't it?—when Teddy projected her own private aurora from behind the davenport (where Gray is now polishing off his sandwich) with "In dulci jubilo" playing on the gramophone. When she begins to cry Gray assumes it's the sight of an expectant mother penguin carried off in the jaws of a sea lion that has upset her.

11:34 P.M.

The Attic

SHE SETS DOWN the needle on the university choir recording—*In dulci jubilo, nun singet und seid froh!*—and tells him about the night she saw the aurora australis on the parlor wall.

"That's why you were crying, before."

Mary looks out the gable window at the nimbus around the full moon. There isn't a star in the sky.

"Give me a translation," he says. "For the German, I mean."

"Yes, Professor, you ought to know the rest of it." She pauses to listen to the next line:

Und leuchtet als die Sonne . . .

"'And he shines bright like the sun . . .'"

Matris in gremio . . .

"'On his mother's lap,'" he says.

Nach Dir ist mir so weh!

"'My heart aches for you,'" she murmurs, and for one blessed moment he loses the context.

Tröst mir mein Gemüte . . .

"'Console me,'" she says. "'I beg you.'"

The rest of the lyrics pass without translation as she sustains his gaze.

LATE JULY, 2009
25 University Avenue

THE BABY GRAND in the great room is next. She finds her old songbooks under the lid of the piano seat, though it soon becomes apparent that the instrument is in dire need of a tuner if she's to brush up on her Bach. One of Gray's students does it for free, and she invites him to stay for ribollita.

After dinner Gray turns to his books, skimming whole passages without understanding amid the ceaseless drone of the cicadas through the open windows. He redoubles his focus, reminding himself that her company is his reward.

Later on in the evenings she borrows a few more of his CDs, everything from John Coltrane to Norah Jones, and listens to them on an old stereo in the attic. More often than not he joins her. Lounging in the semidarkness, she chews the Nicorette that Patrick gave her, popping one piece after another out of the crinkly foil wrapper. She rediscovers Nina Simone, now digitally remastered, and replays "My Baby Just

Cares for Me" until Gray says seven times is enough. She tells him it reminds her of Teddy—not that she needed any reminding.

Once she's read the *Globe* in the early mornings (and finished the crossword), she often returns to her most compelling reads. Shackleton, in his densely worded accounts of survival at the edge of the world, never fails to lift her spirits.

During her fourth reading of *Everyday Life in the Twenty-first Century,* the author's "chronolocation" in the present year suddenly hits her. P. F. X. Godfry could be walking around New Halcyon at this very moment! Perhaps she's even passed him on the quad at NHU.

Something is nagging at her. That snowy February afternoon, her first day out of the house: lunch at the Dragon Volant, the putty-faced preacher, Patrick slurping his ginger ale and scribbling in his black-and-white composition notebook. *Howdy Doody. You're even older than I took you for!*

She drops the book, hurries down the attic stairs, and knocks on Gray's office door. "I'm sorry to bother you, but I have to know something. What's Howdy Doody?"

Gray chuckles at the non sequitur. Then he answers her question.

How obtuse she's been all these months, reading that book over and again and never once thinking of the boy at the bar! His fondness for the old-fashioned speakeasy, his disdain for modern vanities, the tweed jacket and fedora she's seen the like of only at The Happy Flapper:

P is for Patrick. And if she ever sees him again, she's going to ferret out his secret.

MONDAY, 3 AUGUST 2009

25 University Avenue

MARY FILLS EVERY vase in the house with purple hydrangeas from the garden, which has blossomed forth once again under her care.

There aren't enough vegetables to "trade" with, but Mary offers them to Mrs. Delaney as though there were plenty to spare. She gets her cabbages from the Mediterranean market.

"Happy anniversary," she murmurs as she sets another vase on the dining room table. "Did you ever imagine we'd live to see eighty years?"

SHE DREAMS OF Teddy nearly every night. Most of the time he's just as he was, but once in a while, if it's been a day heavy with melancholy, it's what was left of the man in the coffin who comes to her, his bones sliding silently between the bedsheets.

bleeding-heart kiddies in antiwar T-shirts are ushered out the door at school assemblies. Military recruiters resort to harassment and bald prevarication to achieve their monthly goals: *id est*, "body counts." All members of the White House press corps must behave like lapdogs. These "journalists" might as well be stenographers. Only the foreign press takes note of the protest demonstrations and flag-draped coffins returning from the Middle East.

The President (whose family, it is well known, conducted business with the Nazis) has never been compelled to answer a question out of which he could not easily squirm his way. Dissenters are accused of every crime, real or imagined, from unpatriotism to terrorism, and thus the party defuses any and all opposition. Uncle Sam Moneybags answers only to his corporate cronies. In the year 2009, which many hoped would bring with it the end of a very dark age, the G.O.P.–party of bigots, hypocrites, zealots, the obscenely, insanely wealthy, and all those duped by their thinly veiled falsehoods–exerted an increasingly tight stranglehold. The terrorist bugaboo ensures their supremacy. AND YOU THOUGHT McCARTHY WAS A MENACE?

This fascism breeds on the fear and paranoia of those citizens whose capacities for critical thought have sadly atrophied. You may disapprove of my use of the word "fascist" to describe their operations, especially if you belong to a post-World War II era. But I have witnessed amiable middle-aged men vanish into black unmarked vans, their permanent disappearance greeted with

SATURDAY, 31 OCTOBER 2009 ~ 10:15 A.M.
University Avenue

ON THE MORNING of her birthday Mary rides the bus into town to buy a couple of pumpkins at the market, one to carve and one to give to Mrs. Delaney.

When she gets off the bus at her stop, she walks directly to the house next door and takes the side path around to the back door. After knocking once, twice, pausing and knocking again, she opens the door and sets the pumpkin on the kitchen table. "Hello?" she calls. "Mrs. Delaney?"

When Mary ventures into the parlor she finds Mrs. Delaney in a rocking chair, an afghan and an open book in her lap. Her eyes are open and a stiff blue thumb marks the page.

Mary stumbles through the back gate and up the conservatory steps, forgetting to knock before she opens the door to Gray's office. Rubbing his eyes as he sits up in bed, he listens patiently as she tells him what she found, all the while keeping her eyes on the floor because he isn't wearing an undershirt.

"I'll call her granddaughter," Gray says. "I know Lucy has her number around somewhere."

"I'm sorry," she says. "I know it isn't right to carry on like this. I just—"

"She was a sweet old lady and I'm sorry she's gone," he says. "But she *was* nearly ninety-five."

Mary presses her handkerchief to her eyes. "Now *I* don't have anyone to trade with."

6:15 P.M.
25 University Avenue ~ The Kitchen

IN SILENCE MARY carves a toothy grin on the pumpkin face. Milo sits across the kitchen table with his hand in the candy bowl, plucking the peanut butter cups from the mix.

She turns the jack-o'-lantern so he can see it. "What do you think?"

Milo nods with conviction. "It looks just like him."

"Like *who*?"

Carefully he opens a wrapper, removes the paper cup, and savors the first bite. "Whoever you were aiming for."

7:09 P.M.

The Attic

NO NEW MUSIC on the stereo tonight. "Black and Tan Fantasy" spins on the gramophone as Mary sprays herself with her refilled atomizer and secures the clasp on her mother's favorite necklace. From the wardrobe she chooses a black shift and an evening dress of violet silk chiffon with blue and green iridescent glass beading in scrolling nouveau patterns, slit up the sides, with a bateau neckline and a scalloped hem. Even now she feels an echo of the thrill that had rippled down her bare arms at the sight of it draped on a papier-mâché dress form in the window of the boutique on the rue de la Paix.

She'd clutched Teddy's arm like a child in the glow of a toy-store window at Christmastime. His eyes were already fixed upon the dress, imagining how it would suit her curves; he'd resolved to purchase it before they even crossed the threshold, let alone discovered the price.

She raises her arms and the chiffon falls onto her like a sheet of water. Peering into the mirror to powder her nose, she realizes that she no longer has that small scar above her eyebrow, a souvenir from the day she'd nearly drowned. What startles her is not that the mark has vanished, but that she'd failed to notice until now.

7:09 P.M.

The Kitchen

MILO IS STILL SITTING at the kitchen table, methodically consuming each and every peanut butter cup before proceeding to the miniature dark-chocolate bars.

Lucy looks up from the chopping board at Gray. "You're going to botch the damned thing unless you let me—look! *Look!* You dropped a bit of shell in with the egg!"

Gray peers down into the mixing bowl. "I was just about to fish it out."

"You've used too much flour."

"I'm following the recipe."

"You're going to ruin it."

Blithely he whisks the batter, which has the color and texture of wet cement. "You sound like a Harpy."

She slams her paring knife on the counter. "Watch the roast for me, would you, Monsieur Pépin?" Then she notices Milo and the telltale pile of Reese's wrappers. "Last time I checked, I was your landlady, not your babysitter. Stop eating that candy, or there won't be any left for the children."

Lucy stomps out of the room and bangs the basement door behind her. A few seconds later they can hear the turning of half a dozen dead bolts. Milo opens another peanut butter cup.

7:39 P.M.

25 University Avenue

THE BANISTERS GLEAM beneath the light from the wall sconces, and the second-floor landing smells faintly of lemon polish. Dinner smells of roasting beef, sautéed garlic and onions, and freshly baked bread evoke an era bygone even for her, a time when her mother donned the apron. Mary fingers the pendant around her neck as she comes down the stairs, stroking the amethyst to reassure herself it's still in its setting.

She finds the study door wide open and a fire burning in the grate. Gray is stretched out on the sofa, his eyes focused on a book in his lap. The doorbell rings and he looks up to see her pick up the half-empty candy bowl and open the door.

On the doorstep are two children, a boy of about seven and a girl of twelve or so. The boy wears a miniature suit and tie and the girl looks, for want of a better word, like a harlot—dirty lace gloves with the fingers cut off, ripped fishnets, and enough eyeliner to rival any pint-sized Cleopatra who might be traversing the neighborhood at this very moment.

"Trick or treat," the harlot says briskly.

The boy looks up at her, awestruck. "Are you a goddess?"

Mary laughs. "Oh, I'm not—"

"Don't be a stooge, Brian. She's obviously supposed to be a flapper."

Mary turns to the girl. "And who are you?"

"I'm Madonna, of course."

Mary's hand flies to her throat.

"'Like a Virgin'? Hel-*lo*!"

The little boy leans in and tugs gently on the hem of her dress. "Don't you want to know who I am?"

"Oh, yes . . . yes, of course. Who are you?"

"I'm Tom DeLay!" he cries. "I wanted handcuffs but my mom wouldn't let me use hers."

"Tom DeLay?"

"The congressman," sniffs the harlot. "He's headed for the slammer now, though. You don't get out much, do you?"

Mary gives her a tight-lipped smile as she holds out the candy bowl. The boy chooses two pieces and the girl takes as many as she can grasp in one hand. "Good night, children."

"Ugh," says the girl as Mary closes the door. "How patronizing."

"I like her," the boy says plaintively. Mary turns the knob, shaking her head in disbelief.

Gray leans in the study doorway. "I'd better get the door from now on." He pauses. "I never did get a chance to wish you a happy birthday."

"Thank you."

"You look . . ."

"Dreadfully old-fashioned?"

He shakes his head.

"Quaint?"

He shakes his head. "Radiant."

"You're too kind. I'm looking rather consumptive, I think."

"What's this?" He reaches for the pendant on the necklace she's wearing, his fingertips hovering an inch above an amethyst in an elaborate gold setting studded with pearls. Glowing blue in the dim light, each pearl is tiny as a grain of sand.

"It was my mother's."

"It's beautiful."

She looks away, regarding her image above the mantel without satisfaction. "One of the pearls is missing."

"I didn't notice."

"I see it at once whenever I look in the mirror."

8:05 P.M.

The Dining Room

LUCY'S DINNER TASTES just as good as it smelled from the second-floor landing. True to prophecy, however, the cake is ghastly. Mary finds it difficult to swallow. "Mmm," she says. "It tastes a bit like . . . pound cake . . . actually." She steels herself before taking another forkful. "It's very toothsome, Gray."

When Lucy speaks, Mary and Gray can barely make out what she is saying, but it sounds like, "My tongue is glued to the roof of my mouth."

The dining room doors swing open, and lo, the Seventh Order have materialized. "We smelled there was cake down here," Colin says.

Gray makes a sweeping gesture toward the lumpy thing all done up in purple frosting, as if it were a three-tier wedding cake. "Help yourselves."

"Believe me," says Lucy, "you'll live to regret it."

"It honestly isn't *that* bad," Mary says.

The boys serve themselves and nod in approval as they stuff their faces. "This tastes just like the cake my grandma used to make," Dewey says.

Gray grins. "Thanks."

Dewey chews thoughtfully. "Nobody ever ate much of it. The pigs loved it, though."

Lucy drains her glass of Pinot Grigio to rid herself of the taste. "I didn't know you lived on a farm, Dewey."

"I didn't."

Milo pats his stomach. "You guys should make cake every night."

"Too bad it can't be Halloween every night, too, huh, Milo?" Lucy says. "I'm giving you a bill for all the candy you ate. It's only eight-thirty and we have five pieces left."

"No worries," says Milo. "Just give them some cake."

"And be sued by every mother on University Avenue? I don't think so."

Colin looks around at the dinner. "So, what's the occasion?"

"It's my birthday," Mary announces.

"Why didn't you tell us?"

"I don't believe in fussing over birthdays. They happen every year, you know."

"It's a shame your husband couldn't be here," Colin says. "Is he still tied up on the Cape?"

"Yes . . . well . . . it couldn't be helped, I'm afraid. He's in the middle of exams and we decided it would be best if . . ." Mary glances across the table, where Lucy and Gray are staring at her with their mouths open.

Rob reaches for the knife. "Mind if I have another piece?"

"Me, too?"

Gray clears his throat. "Take as much as you like."

Colin turns to Mary. "What were you saying?"

"I was . . . oh, oh yes, we keep in touch daily by e-mail. A marvelous innovation, isn't it?"

Gray closes his eyes.

"I wouldn't know. I haven't used a computer since 1988." Colin cuts himself another slice of cake, runs his finger up and down both sides of the knife, and inserts his finger into his mouth. Lucy glares at him in disgust, and he laughs. "It's not my fault," he tells her. "I got my table manners from the troll who raised me."

"You should show your mother more respect," Lucy says.

"Is that another one of your purist principles?" Mary asks Colin.

"Nah," he says. "I just try to limit my time in front of electronic devices. Someday scientists will discover they've been zapping our brain cells all along."

So that's why he commandeered her typewriter. "We're going out," Mary says. "Would you like to come?"

"Out?" Milo cries through a mouthful of cake. "Where?"

"Boston," Gray says flatly.

"We don't really *do* 'out,'" says Felix.

"Why not?"

"'Out' is a place men customarily go in search of sexual conquests. So you see—"

"We're just celebrating her birthday, for Christ's sake!" Gray huffs.

Colin frowns thoughtfully. "No . . . no, we'd really better not. Thanks for the offer, though."

"And thanks for the cake," says Rob.

The boys rise from their chairs and begin to clear the table (tomorrow is rent day, after all). Milo tries to remove Gray's plate even though he's still eating from it.

AS GRAY PULLS his coat from the hall closet Mary eyes his rumpled oxford shirt and corduroys. "You're going dressed . . . like that?"

He shrugs. "I don't have anything else to wear. Besides, at the place we're going to you can be as formal or informal as you like."

"But *I'm* dressed. Don't you think you ought to be, too?" She snaps her fingers. "I've got an idea!" She takes his hand and leads him upstairs.

9:26 P.M.

The Master Bedroom

GRAY STANDS IN FRONT of the full-length mirror dressed in a very old tuxedo, the white dress shirt still stiff with starch. He fingers the bow tie.

"You're exactly his size. Isn't that extraordinary?"

He looks at her over the shoulder of his reflection. "I don't know how I feel about this."

She frowns. "Doesn't it fit as well as it looks?"

"It isn't that." He turns to her, hesitating. Would she understand if he told her how wrong it feels to be wearing his clothes?

She would, but it would disappoint her. "Do you mind . . . if I skip the bow tie?"

Smiling, Mary snips the stem off a red carnation and tucks the flower in his buttonhole.

9:38 P.M.

The Driveway

HER JACK-O'-LANTERN leers from the top step on the front porch, the candle inside still burning brightly. A dozen children, some of them wearing gaudy rubber Dubya masks with large flappy ears, swarm around the Prius en route to the door.

"There won't be enough candy for all of them!"

"She's in the basement," he says. "She won't answer the door."

"Should we ask her just once more if she'd like to come?"

Come to think of it, he and Lucy have never gone out together, not once in four years. "Nah," he says. "She's working."

He turns the ignition and pops a CD in the player, and as Nina Simone begins to sing Mary sighs happily, her breath-cloud visible in the still-warming car. "It'll get you in the mood," he says as he pulls out of the driveway. "We're going to hear her live."

10:47 P.M.
The Violet Hour Dinner/Dance
Boston, Massachusetts

A COLORED GIRL—no, an *African-American* girl—in a white chiffon dress sits at a baby grand piano at the center of the stage, and as they enter she's singing "I Put a Spell on You." The lightly tinkling piano makes Mary think of melting icicles.

On the dance floor, half a dozen couples (all formally dressed) dance cheek to cheek. It's easy to pretend they've just entered the Midtown Bar and Grill, Atlantic City, in 1955—so much so that the myriad girls in their brightly colored minidresses, frosted lipstick, and spidery eyelashes seem acutely out of place. So does Mary, of course. Most of the women here, with their pink pumps and bare shoulders, aspire to resemble the likes of Grace Kelly, a bit too thin and a tad too blond.

Gray puts his lips to her ear as he takes her coat. "Are you dazzled?"

"Oh, yes," she says happily. "It's just that when you said we were going to see her, I thought you meant . . ."

"Oh," he says. "No, Nina Simone's been dead for years. This woman says she's her granddaughter, but she can't be. Sure sounds enough like her, though."

"She's lovely," Mary murmurs, watching the girl's slender arms and her fingers tumbling blithely over the keys as though she'd been born on the piano bench. Gray watches the girl onstage, too, reflecting on the irony of the singer who belted "Mississippi Goddam" playing dance tunes at a dinner club. Half the songs in "Nina's" Violet Hour repertoire were never played again outside the Midtown Bar and Grill.

The hostess takes their coats, hands them a ticket, and shows them to a table for two along the mezzanine wall, which is covered in a faded wine-colored velvet. From here they can see a small band in the pit below the stage. A waitress delivers a pair of dinner menus.

Gray takes the menu out of her hands. "Don't look at it. You'll have a heart attack when you see the prices. I know you will because *I* did the last time I was here, and I'm already accustomed to the evils of inflation."

"I know how much things cost these days, Gray. I haven't been living under a rock for the last nine months."

"We're not having dinner, anyway."

"Let me see the menu."

Ignoring her outstretched hand, he peruses the menu's last page. "Maybe we'll order some dessert to make up for your suffering my 'toothsome' little concoction, eh? Apple pie . . . banana-almond-mocha cream, mmm! . . . double chocolate . . . caramel-chocolate fudge . . ."

"I'd like the banana-almond-mocha, please."

The waitress appears. "We'll have two slices of banana-almond-mocha, a glass of Shiraz for me, and . . ."

"An amaretto and cranberry for me, please."

The waitress nods and disappears again.

"Oh!" Mary exclaims as a girl in a beehive teeters past the table in white vinyl go-go boots. "Have you ever seen such an odd-looking outfit?"

Indeed he has—much odder, in fact—at any number of the frat parties, raves, and nightclubs he occasionally attended as an undergraduate, and now wishes he had not. But the sense in which those girls had been "odd" was altogether different. "I've always thought this restaurant was built on some sort of temporal vortex. Everyone here looks like they belong in a different decade."

"Nina" finishes her song and takes a long drink from a glass of water. "I'm going to sing another song," she says, "and it's a song you've heard a lot of times before. But I'm going to sing it again for you now, and I want you to try to listen to it like it's the first time. How's about it?"

The crowd begins to clap and the couples on the floor take one another by the hand, shoulder, and hip again.

"Come on." Mary pushes back her chair and stands up. "How would you like to dance?"

"Sure, if you don't mind looking like a fool by association."

She grins. "I don't."

He looks up at her, hoping the drinks will arrive and she'll put off the dance for a while. Gray hasn't danced since his cousin Sylvia's wedding. It was 1992; he had attempted a moonwalk. Why hadn't he considered this before he decided to bring her here?

"Come *on,* Gray."

He shrugs off the heavy tuxedo jacket and follows her down the mezzanine steps and onto the floor as Nina sings, "My baby don't care for shows, my baby don't care for clothes . . ."

Mary takes his hand and rests her other arm lightly on his; he puts his other hand on the small of her back and she feels his tension. "Lighten up," she whispers. "If you come out onto the floor acting like you've got two left feet, then you can only prove yourself right." She raises their arms into an arch and twirls herself through it, and as her hair brushes his cheek he notices that the song's nearly halfway through already. If this tux only belonged to him, he could—

"Stop thinking," she says. "Just dance with me."

But Mary herself is thinking as he spins her again. *I am dancing with a colored man,* she says to herself. *And no one thinks anything of it.*

The chandelier overhead and the candles on the tables spin and flicker as he gives her a full turn about the floor, and other men regard him with transparent envy. She looks up at him, flushed and smiling, and he puts his cheek to hers just because he can. That familiar scent!

The song ends. "Thank you for humoring me," she says.

"No," he says. "Thank you for making me."

"Ready for a slow number?" Nina murmurs into the mic as Mary's hand falls from his shoulder. She looks up at him, her head cocked.

"I . . . thought you didn't want to dance."

He casts a cursory glance over her shoulder. "Your birthday cake hasn't arrived yet."

"What . . . what song is this?" she asks, but she knows.

Paying no mind to the new resistance in her arms, he replaces his hand on the small of her back and pulls her in. Yeah, she smells just like Lucy—no, Lucy smells like *her.* When he looks at her face now he realizes two things: first, that he has already seen her naked—

I want a little sugar in my bowl

—and second, that he knows exactly how she's going to age.

I want a little sweetness down in my soul . . .

Mary clears her throat. "Is something wrong?"

"What?"

She glances away. "You're looking at me oddly."

"We can sit, if you want."

"Have they brought the cake?"

"No."

I want a little steam on my clothes . . .

"Right," she says, with a barely perceptible shiver. "We'll keep dancing."

"You've heard this one before, haven't you?"

"Yes," she whispers. "I didn't remember it at first."

You been acting different, I've been told . . .

Mary eyes the girl behind the piano. "I wish I'd practiced more diligently."

"Hmm?"

"I'm barely proficient."

Whatsa matter daddy, come on, save my soul . . .

"Oh," he says. "The piano."

Where is her relief as the song ends?

He follows her back to the table, spread with their drinks and two generous slabs of banana-almond-mocha, garnished with a leaning tower of alternating banana slices and chocolate squares. She prods this silly flourish with her fork, frowning, and Gray laughs. "Much better than mine," he says as he eats, and laughs again when she breaks into a guilty smile. Through four more songs they eat and sip in a half-contented, half-uneasy silence, making only an occasional remark on the music.

Eventually the spotlight falls on the emcee. "Though our live entertainment has ended for the evening," he booms, "I'm pleased to announce that Miss Nina will remain in the corner booth to display yet another of her many talents." What's left of the crowd begins to clap. "Have you guessed what it is? Yes, that's right—only twenty dollars for a glimpse of your future, ladies and gentlemen!"

"Oh, Gray! I've always wanted to have my palm read!"

"I thought you didn't believe in that sort of thing."

"Oh, I don't, not really . . . but . . ." Her face falls as half a dozen people surround the plush corner booth at the far edge of the dance floor.

"You look like you've just discovered Santa doesn't exist."

"The line's so long . . . and I don't have any money . . ."

"It's your birthday. My treat." Gray signals to the waitress. "We'd better order another round." He pulls a twenty out of his wallet and slides it across the table, and she thanks him shyly.

Half an hour later the last girl in line, one of those with the platinum hair and frosted lipstick, slides out of the corner booth with a smug little smile. Clutching her beaded purse, Mary approaches the girl in the white chiffon dress.

"Took you long enough." Nina sips her drink and discreetly slips another twenty into the black checkholder by her elbow.

"Pardon me?"

"Oh, I saw you over there on the mezzanine." Nina laughs. "You want to have a seat?"

"Yes, thank you." Mary slides into the booth.

"Don't be so timid. Life's too short, you know what I mean?" Nina is older than she looks onstage. With those fine lines around her eyes and mouth, she must be nearing forty.

"I certainly do."

Nina waits for a moment. "Well?"

Mary places both her hands palms-up on the table. "Which one?"

"Which do you write with?" She offers her right hand across the table, but Nina is scrutinizing her face. "I see a trip. Definitely. A long trip, a vacation. Someplace cold?"

"I . . . I hadn't thought of going anywhere . . ."

"Yes, you have. Don't worry, it's a good idea. It will make you happy."

"You see that on my palm?"

"I haven't gotten to your palm yet. You just look like a cold-weather kind of girl. You from around here?"

Mary nods.

"See? I was right. These goddamned New England winters, though, let me tell you. I'm taking the act to California the first chance I get."

"You're very good."

Nina smiles wryly. "I'll keep practicing."

"I was wondering . . . if you see anything . . . in the way of . . ."

"Romance?"

"How did you know?"

Nina laughs. "Honey, that's what *every*one wants to know." She nods her head at the table by the mezzanine railing, where Gray is sipping his wine and pretending he isn't watching them intently. "You're not with him."

Mary shakes her head.

"Too bad," Nina says. "He's built like Adonis. So there's someone else, is there?"

"I'm waiting for him."

"And how long have you been waiting?"

"It's hard to say." She pauses. "The better part of a year. It seems like longer."

"It always does. And tell me, how much longer do you expect to wait?"

"Two months . . . I hope."

"And you have had no communication with this gentleman in the meantime?" Mary shakes her head as Nina examines her hand, squinting, alternately probing and smoothing the base of her palm with a fingertip that feels like fine sandpaper. "Sorry, honey. I wish I could tell you I see it, but it doesn't look like it's in the cards."

"What . . . what is it that makes you say so?"

"I hope for your sake that I'm wrong," Nina says. "Lord knows I misread a line from time to time."

That's all she's going to get, apparently. The sibyl takes a sip of her watered-down Fuzzy Navel and Mary fumbles with the clasp on her little beaded purse.

Nina holds up her free hand as she finishes her drink. "Keep it, doll."

"But—"

"You need it more than I do."

"But, how—"

Nina leans in across the table, laying her warm hand over Mary's one more time. "I can smell it on you," she whispers. "The mothballs."

BACK IN THE vestibule, Gray helps her into her coat. "What did she say?"

"Nothing I wanted to hear."

He follows her out the door. "Are you ready to go home, then?"

A group of college kids troop down the street in full costume, a Chinese dragon with a huge blue-and-green head, more boys in floppy-eared Dubya masks, green-suited leprechauns in top hats, and a gaggle of red-nosed clowns: one on stilts tips his hat to her as they pass. Mary smiles up at him. "If we go home now," she says, "I'll spend the rest of the night moping in the attic."

At the corner up ahead, the clowns are filing into an all-night diner. The manager comes out onto the sidewalk and brandishes his dishrag at the clown on stilts, who is refusing to take them off. "You mean to tell me you discriminate against incredibly tall people?" the clown says. "I don't think the Boston chapter of the ACLU would be too pleased to hear of this!"

"Take them off, wise guy! Take them off or I call the cops!"

She points to the door of the club on the opposite corner, flanked by well-heeled girls lighting their cigarettes with a Zippo. "Do you know that place?"

Perhaps in the daylight she would notice the building itself—in 1929 the site of the Halo nightclub was an Elliot Brothers department store. "It's a nightclub. Not the kind you're used to, either. You sure you don't want to go home?"

"So you've been there!"

"It was a long time ago."

"Isn't it a nice club?"

"Trust me, it's not your kind of place." Immediately he sees he ought not to have said this, for she takes his hand and leads him briskly across the street.

"Let me be the judge of that," she tells him.

HALO IS A glittering seven-story cesspool of ear-numbing techno and not-so-clandestine coke deals. The elevators with their mirrored walls were already infamous when Gray spent one unhappy evening here during his freshman year of college. In the erstwhile jewelry department, small-time heiresses sip fifteen-dollar cocktails at the blacklit bars (the original glass counters), and the second-floor menswear department now offers a pair of thirty-foot screens showing eighties cartoons (and the occasional Japanimation porno) on continuous loop.

Far better nightclubs have opened their doors in the two decades since the building's grand reopening, but the cover is cheap and the old-fashioned atrium and Corinthian columns lend an air of respectability.

At first Mary is just as dazzled by all this as a child entering the "North Pole" display in the fourth-floor toy department would have been three generations ago.

She puts her lips to his ear. "They call this music, do they?"

"Most people wouldn't."

A group of college kids are gyrating to some Top 40 remix. "And that's dancing?"

She doesn't seem to notice that people are staring at their clothes. He touches her elbow and steers her toward one of the bars, where he has just spotted two vacant stools. "Why don't we get a drink?"

"I'd just like a glass of water, please."

After ten minutes of trying, he catches the bartender's attention and orders a glass of Shiraz and a bottled water. Mary grabs his arm and points to the dance floor. "Did you see that?" she cries. "That girl vomited all over the floor and went right back to dancing!"

As Gray hands her the water and a glass of ice a boy of no more than fourteen approaches the fuschia-hued mess on the floor with a mop and bucket. "Whatever they're paying him, it isn't nearly enough," he says.

"She's not the only one." Mary shakes her head as she eyes the dancers. "They're *all* blotto, every one of them."

Gray drinks half his wine in one go, seeing as she's nearly had enough of the place. "Will you be all right here for a minute? I just have to go to the men's room." She nods, still mesmerized by the debauchery on the floor, and Gray lays his suit jacket over the back of his stool and nudges his way through the crowd. A few seconds later a slick-looking fellow in a white T-shirt hops onto the stool without so much as a do-you-mind.

"Sir? Sir, that seat is taken."

"Relax," he says with an insolent grin. "I'll be gone by the time he gets back."

She shoots him a look of disgust, drains her water glass, and turns back to the dance floor.

"You look like you could use a pick-me-up," he says.

She turns her head. "Excuse me?"

He opens his hand, and she sees an aspirin tablet in his open palm. "Go on, try it. First one's free."

It mustn't be aspirin, then, but she doesn't care to know what it is.

"Please give up your seat," she says coldly. "My friend will return momentarily."

The man mutters something under his breath that leaves her red with indignation. She watches his back as he disappears into the crowd, wondering at how his shirt glows purple in the darkness. At once she becomes aware of herself, alone and more than a little disoriented, amid a vast crowd of people with masks for faces. Closing her eyes against a swell of panic, she wills Gray back through the throng.

"Did anything happen?" Gray asks. "You look like something happened."

"A man offered me an aspirin tablet, and insulted me when I refused it."

Gray rolls his eyes. "It's not aspirin. That stuff fries your brain."

"Then why would anyone take it?"

He picks up the suit jacket from the back of the stool. "*Now* are we done with our little anthropological survey?"

"Yes," she replies. "Quite finished."

AT THE ALL-NIGHT diner across the street the clown troupe is still playing cards in one of the window booths. A pair of stilts is propped against the doorjamb.

"I'd love some breakfast."

"And I'm going to need a few cups of coffee for the drive home," he yawns.

WATCHING THE CLOWNS' raucous game of Spit lifts her spirits, but she turns away with a tight-lipped smile when one of them compliments her on her "costume." She finishes her orange juice and eyes him as he mops up his egg yolk with a piece of rye toast. "Can you hold out for six o'clock?"

"Why six?"

"I was hoping we could go to Mass at the cathedral."

"I highly doubt you'll find a church in this town that still has a six a.m. service."

"Why?"

He shrugs. "Same reason Saint Lucy's closed."

SUNDAY, 1 NOVEMBER 2009 ~ 4:35 A.M.
The Violet Hour Parking Lot

SOMEONE HAS SCRAWLED *BOO!* on the back window of the Prius in red Magic Marker. He grumbles as he unlocks the door.

"Would you like to know what she told me?"

"Yes."

"It's just a lot of hocus-pocus anyway. I don't know why I was so set on going."

"What did she tell you?"

She presses her handkerchief to the frosted side window before applying it to her eyelids. It seems the night has caught up with her at last. "She said I was . . . that I was waiting for someone who wasn't coming back."

His eyes on the road, Gray shakes his head at the irony. Miss Nina told her future, all right—her future from seventy years ago. She has the same hands, doesn't she?

"Why are you frowning?"

"I don't believe in any of that stuff," he says. "And you shouldn't, either. It nearly ruined your birthday."

SHE WEARS THE hallmarks of a sleepless night—hair fallen out of its careful arrangement, the stale breath, the stocking runs—and when she shivers in her sleep he turns the dial up on the heater. The dark-roast coffee-to-go keeps him alert enough to drive, but he grows increasingly delirious all the same—he imagines that they are together, married, and that he is driving them home to a bed they share.

This time the man in her dream has skin that changes colors, like a chameleon that cannot choose between earth and sand. She opens her eyes. "Will you wake me up in time for Mass?"

"Yeah," he says. "I'll drive you."

5:45 A.M.

25 University Avenue ~ The Third-Floor Turret Room

GRAY FINDS LUCY asleep in his bed. As he kicks off his dress shoes she stirs, and he fumbles with the button-fly on Teddy's trousers. "I didn't think you'd be out so late," she murmurs.

"Tell you about it in the morning," he says, sliding into the narrow bed beside her.

"It *is* morning," she yawns.

"Happy birthday, Lu."

She gives him a sleepy smile and drifts off again.

TUESDAY, 3 NOVEMBER 2009

Wm. Grace & Son ~ 11 Lavinia Street

MRS. EUGENIA DELANEY'S funeral service befits a very practical, very old lady: it is held at a small family-run home on the quiet end of Lavinia Street, so no "Ave Maria" in the lugubrious drone of the church organ driving everyone to tears; and if the number of mourners seems rather small, it is only because Mrs. Delaney outlived all her friends and most of her family. Gray and Mary attend, but Lucy claims she can't take the afternoon off.

The next Monday a For Sale sign will appear on the lawn at 23 University Avenue.

THURSDAY, 5 NOVEMBER 2009 ~ 10:30 P.M.

25 University Avenue ~ The Attic

WARDROBE OR RELIQUARY? Her clothes are falling to pieces: the crumbling lace; the cracked leather and elastic; the crêpe-de-chine like a garment made of spiderwebs. How utterly shameful that a stranger should notice the odor before she did!

Gray finds her standing in the middle of a pile of old clothing, hair disheveled and eyes fierce, and he understands the source of her frustration. Momentarily he returns with a J. Crew catalog, and she thumbs through it with a look of distaste. "You could keep shopping at that vintage store downtown," he says, "but the smell is going to follow you."

"You noticed it, too, then?" She frowns. "And you never said anything."

How can he tell her he likes that smell of mothballs and talcum powder, that he finds it comforting? "You're taking this too much to heart. If you want new clothes, why don't you make some?"

She drops herself into an armchair by the open wardrobe, shaking her head. "I'm not skilled enough. Making a quilt isn't so difficult."

Comforting, as in grandmotherly. He shouldn't like the smell, not on her, anyway—she's nobody's grandmother, and she never will be.

"Let's go downstairs for a bit. I have a hankering for a turkey sandwich," he says, bending to retrieve the catalog from where she'd tossed it on the neatly made bed. "You might end up changing your mind about this."

"I don't think so," she replies as she pulls an old cardigan off a hanger and dons it with a shiver. "I couldn't sleep at night knowing I'd spent two hundred and fifty dollars on a party dress."

SATURDAY, 14 NOVEMBER 2009 ~ 9:15 P.M.
The Attic

GRAY BRINGS THE digital camera up to the attic. She isn't there, which means she's probably in the labyrinth. But before he goes down to find her he lowers himself into her armchair by the window and turns on the Tiffany lamp on the table beside it. The little leather diary he's seen her writing in from time to time sits on a pile of books at his elbow. Give in to curiosity, or adhere to conscience? Having no sisters, he's never faced this age-old test before, and he promptly fails it.

Several pages have been torn out of the front of the book. *I have never kept a serious record of my life before,* she has written on the first remaining page, *so I cannot say why I feel compelled to do so now.*

She could come up at any moment and catch him red-handed. He snaps the book shut and goes down to the hall closet for his coat, leaving the camera on the study sofa.

9:22 P.M.
The Labyrinth

THE SPOON FOUNTAIN glitters in the moonlight. She is thinking of that Christmas Eve, the Christmas of the engagement, when her father had driven all night to bring her home from the Morrigans' dinner party. She'd laughed when he told her it was to be her "last Christmas"—"So now the truth comes out: marriage is a death sentence!"—but he had not laughed in return, and after a long pause she had said, in the small voice of a child, "I'll always be with you at Christmas, Father." Had she kept that promise?

The memory vanishes with the sound of footsteps on the gravel. "Mary?"

"Hello, Gray," she calls through the hedge. "I'm in the center."

His chuckle materializes in the air. "That doesn't help much."

"Follow the sound of my voice," she says. "Wooooooooooooo!" It sounds like she's in good spirits. And why shouldn't she be?

"You must be frozen solid by now," he calls. "How long have you been out here?"

"Not long. It gets so stuffy up in the attic."

He pokes his head through the archway. "You don't have to spend every night up there, you know. Hey, we should go out more often. What do you say to Boston this weekend? Tonight?"

"Not tonight," she says. "I'm not feeling up to it."

He brushes the leaves off a bench and sits down. "You coming down with something?"

"I'm not ill," she says. "It's just been a difficult day."

"Oh," he says, feeling stupid.

"I'm thinking too much."

"What are you thinking about?" *Stupid, stupid.*

"My old life. How it will be, having my life back."

"But this *is* your life," he says, as gently as he can.

"Don't let's talk about this again. I won't consider any more of your 'worst-case scenarios.' "

He bends over the gravel path with his elbows on his knees and his hands clasped together. He is as much a part of her life now as she is of his, and any reminder that she doesn't prefer it that way stings.

"I keep thinking about my family, and sometimes I imagine that Lucy can bring my father back, too, and Jared and Joe and—"

"That's not going to happen," he says. "If she keeps up her private research for too much longer we'll be visiting her in prison."

Slowly she seats herself on the rim of the fishpond, looking anywhere but at him.

"I'm sorry," he says.

"Don't be." She attempts a smile. "The truth should hurt once in a while. Keeps one honest."

After a brief but violent rustling in the hedge on the far side of the fountain, a bat shoots out of the laurel and flies over their heads.

"I have these little moments of utter panic," she says slowly. "I feel sure I'm going to lose him all over again, and I have to bite my tongue to keep from asking you if you've been down to the basement, because I know you've told me a hundred times you haven't seen him . . ."

Widowed at thirty-six, she lived another forty-odd years taking pictures, raising children, doting on grandchildren. But she never remarried—and not for a lack of opportunity. She was, and is, as faithful as they come.

He clears his throat. "Is there anything I can do to make things easier?"

"Just one thing: Don't mention my 'contingency plan.' "

"Let's go inside," he says. "There's something I want to give you."

9:46 P.M.
The Study

IN MARY'S HANDS the digital camera—a sleek, newish model—still somehow looks to him like a prop from a black-and-white sci-fi show, one of those cheesy melodramas with every surface on the set covered in crinkly aluminum foil. "I saw one of these when I was on campus," she says. "I figured it must be a camera from the way the girl was using it."

"It's yours."

"Oh, Gray, I couldn't . . ."

"My mother gave it to me, but I haven't used it once. No sense leaving it to gather dust." He pauses. "What is it?"

"It just feels like . . . like I'm trying to be somebody else."

"Of course not," he replies. "How is it wrong to indulge in your own hobby?"

"But I'll never be the photographer . . . she . . . oh." She shakes her head. "You know what it is I'm trying to say."

"Don't look so grim. Just take the camera, and if you get some use out of it, then it's more than I've done."

She nods. "You'll have to show me how to use it."

Clumsily he takes the camera out of her hands and depresses the power button, and the LCD screen flashes images of their feet side by side on the oriental rug. She watches as he presses the zoom lever in, out, and in again, and indicates the button she should press to take a picture.

He should have known this was a bad idea. Here he's given her something she clearly does not want and will probably never use, all so he can comfort himself remembering that she has something that belonged to him. He ought to have given her a fountain pen.

10:09 P.M.
The Basement

SOMEBODY'S old-fashioned Catholic guilt sure has worn off on him. Balancing the breakfast tray on his hip, he knocks on the basement door.

She doesn't move from her chair. "Yes?"

"It's me," he calls.

Her feet fall heavily on the stairs. A few more moments while she unbolts the door, and there she is, standing beneath him on the stairs with a strangely defiant look on her face.

"I thought you might like a snack," he says, smiling a plastic smile.

She turns around and stomps back to the computer chair. "If I wanted tea I could make it down here myself."

He lays the tray on the counter. "What's your problem?"

"I can't do this anymore."

He can hardly hear her over the roar of the generator. "'This'?"

"What exactly were you talking about up there?"

"What do you mean?"

"Don't play dumb, Gray. You're hopeless at it." She pauses. "I came up to go to the bathroom. Obviously you didn't hear me."

"But I didn't say anything you could have possibly misconstrued."

Her words come etched in frost: "It wasn't anything you said."

"What are you so jealous of, anyway? Since when do you even notice whether or not I'm around, let alone who I'm looking at?"

"I hate you."

"Well, good. I'm glad we finally got that out of the way."

"I mean it."

"I don't doubt you. I think this would be a good time for me to leave the room."

"You're a bastard."

"That's not actually true."

"You're making it worse."

"You're bringing it on yourself, Lu. You're so obsessed with this"—he jerks his finger at the simwomb—"that you're imagining things. Ask Megan—maybe it's just a vitamin deficiency."

"You're in love with my grandmother!"

"You've been saying for months that she isn't your grandmother, and now that calling her your grandmother makes me sound like a pervert, you have no problem fudging the distinction."

"Just tell me," she whispers. "Do you . . . do you want to . . . ?"

"I've had enough, Lu. I hope we can discuss this calmly in the morning—not that there's anything to discuss. Good night." With knees as firm as Jell-O, he ascends the basement steps. As he closes the door he hears her storming up behind him to secure the dead bolts.

SUNDAY, 15 NOVEMBER 2009 ~ 2:20 P.M.
The Kitchen

Slowly Mary stirs the batter, staring sightlessly into the fragrant golden-brown concoction.

"Lost in thought?"

Mary remembers herself, glances at Lucy, and sighs. "You might have left me there."

"Sorry."

She pours the batter into the bundt pan as she waits for Lucy to go on. "Was there something you wanted?" Mary asks.

"I was just wondering how you liked your birthday night out."

Mary frowns as she dons an oven mitt, slides the pan into the oven, and winds the timer. "It was two weeks ago, Lucy."

"I keep forgetting to ask you."

When they look at each other now Lucy knows Mary's not buying it. Mary hesitates. "Did Gray tell you . . ."

"Tell me what?"

"Why are you looking at me that way?"

"Did . . . did something happen?"

"I suppose he didn't tell you, then—what the palm reader said."

"When the heck did you go to a palm reader?"

"At the dinner club. She sang and played, too."

"Isn't that something. What did you ask her?"

Mary averts her eyes.

"I guess she told you he wasn't coming back."

Mary looks up at her sharply. "How did you know?"

I could have told you she'd tell you that, Lucy thinks. *I could have told you the same thing for free.*

"Tell me, Lucy! Has something gone wrong?"

Because junk DNA manifests itself on the fingertips! Lucy utters a strangled little laugh, a laugh of relief. "My grandmother used to tell me that palm readers were frauds and hucksters," she says. "And anyone who paid good money for one was—"

"Answer my question, Lucy."

"—and yet here you are, staking your future happiness on a lounge singer who reads palms on the side. No, there's nothing wrong with Teddy."

Her cake won't be done for another thirty-five minutes. "Perhaps you should try spending a bit of time with him once in a while," Mary says coldly as she unties her apron strings.

"You aren't talking about Teddy, are you?"

"You know, for a girl with a doctorate you can be remarkably dim." She drops her apron over the back of a kitchen chair and disappears up the back stairs before Lucy can get a word out.

SUNDAY, 6 DECEMBER 2009 ~ 1:55 P.M.
The Kitchen

ITS SOUNDS ARE often graceless, it is true, but the German language has much to recommend it. In German one can distill a complicated concept—one that would necessitate a string of words in English—into a solitary noun that rolls off the tongue with a tingle of satisfaction. There is, of course, *Schadenfreude,* the ghoulish pleasure one takes in the misfortunes of others; and *Gemütlichkeit,* a state of cozy, cheerful, tranquil belonging. And there is *Backpfeifengesicht,* a face deserving of a good hard smack. In this instance, however, it is *Hintergedanke* that marks her: a nagging thought on the margins of her consciousness, a vague unease.

Colin sits across the table, fingering her rosary beads. "They're so smooth," he says, rolling a Hail Mary between his thumb and forefinger. "What are they made of?"

"Connemara marble," she says. "They belonged to my mother."

"Did they come so polished, or was she that devout?"

She smiles. "A bit of both, I suppose."

"So you take the bus to Saint Greg's, huh?"

"Sometimes Gray drives me."

"That's nice of him. I guess it's all decked out now for Advent?"

She nods. "Red and white poinsettias. They had a little girl from the congregation light the candle on the wreath."

"I love poinsettias," he says. "They always remind me of my grandma."

"Where do you go to Mass, Colin?"

"The campus chapel," he says. "It's nondenominational."

"What does that mean?"

"It means it isn't devoted to any sort of Christian church in particular. A Unitarian minister does most of the services now. Have you ever been?"

She shakes her head.

"They used to have Catholic Masses, but that ended with Saint Lucy's. It's a shame you have to go so far out of your way."

She shrugs. "It isn't as though I have much else to do."

Colin looks as if he wants to ask her another probing question, perhaps about her future this time, but eventually he says, "You said something a while back, something I keep thinking about. Remember, at this table, when you said we didn't sound like boys who belonged to a religious fraternity?"

She nods.

"Well, I know it's true, and I know it's something we need to work on—and we have been—"

"You mean you're trying to sound more pious?" She laughs. "I didn't mean anything by it, Colin. You're just a lot of colorful characters, there's nothing sinful about that."

"Sometimes there is," he says, smiling slyly. "It's not that I want to sound more pious to other people. I just feel like I've got to do less talking, you know?"

She nods.

"I don't believe in proselytizing," Colin says. "I believe that every one of us has to find our own faith in God, on our own terms. And I believe a person who doesn't set foot in a church all his life can still be a better Christian than many people who do. Ritual means little without the noble conviction behind it. Like lighting a candle without the intention." He pauses. "Don't you agree?"

"I do." Her smile is warm, almost motherly. The *Hintergedanke* is gone for the present. "Very much. But there are many people who'd find that talk just a teensy bit blasphemous."

"Don't I know it," he murmurs. "Mary . . ."

"Yes, Colin?"

He gets up from the table, fills the coffeemaker with tap water, and flicks the switch. "I was wondering . . . if I might ask you for a bit of advice."

She looks up at him in mild surprise. "Of course."

"I have a choice to make. Probably the hardest choice I'll ever face in my life, come to think of it."

"And you've prayed for guidance."

"I have . . . but I still haven't come to an answer." The trickling sound of percolating coffee fills the momentary silence. "What do you think of Machiavelli, Mary?"

"The end justifies the means, and all that?"

He nods.

"I don't know. Are you planning a war?"

Colin laughs as he pours himself a cup. "You want some?"

"No, thank you."

"That's what I want to know, though." She wrinkles her nose as he drains his mug without putting any milk or sugar in first. "Does the end justify the means?"

"It all depends."

"On?"

"What means, and to what end?" Mary pauses. "Ultimately I don't see the trouble, so long as you're following your conscience. I won't ask you what this is about, but . . ."

Colin chuckles. "Didn't you just ask without asking?"

"Touché."

"Let's just say it's girl trouble."

She shoots him a sly sideways glance. "You're thinking of leaving the Order, are you?"

"It's not that kind of girl trouble."

"What other kind is there?"

He rinses out his mug and leaves it on the drain board. "I'll let you know how it all works out. Thanks for listening, Mary."

those games of Risk, Diplomacy, or any variants thereof, in which schoolchildren maneuver the armies of all the imperial nations across a pastel map of the Continent. If only the unscrupulous leaders of the world could be set to rights as easily as a set of brightly colored pawns fashioned out of plastic.

Finally, over the course of reading *Everyday Life in the Twenty-first Century* you have probably wondered more than once if I plagiarized myself. For the record, I did not.

P.F.X. Godfry,
New Halcyon, Massachusetts
December 1958

TUESDAY, 22 DECEMBER 2009 ~ 12:46 P.M.

25 University Avenue

GRAY'S MOTHER offers to come to New Halcyon for the holiday, but Lucy won't hear of it. "Make an excuse for me," she tells him. "Any old excuse. There's entirely too much going on here."

2:55 P.M.

The Woods Behind the House

SAW IN HAND, Gray follows Mary through the evergreens, pausing here and there beside a tree to assess its fullness, gauge its height, and sniff the branches. A hundred yards from the back gate she finds the perfect tree and turns to him with an impish smile.

"I'm not sure this is actually legal," he says.

"We found our Christmas trees out here every year."

"But somebody must own all this."

"Tell me, how much does a tree cost at the hardware store these days?"

Eighty-five dollars. "You're right," he says. "I think we've found our tree."

"I used to love this. My father and I, it was our ritual the weekend before Christmas. Do you think we should ask Lucy's opinion before we cut it down?"

"Nah," Gray says. "Lucy hasn't put up a tree in years." He flicks a dead branch off his boot with the tip of the butcher saw, shifting his weight from foot to foot. "How do you feel?"

"I like it." She leans in and takes a sniff. "Balsam fir. It won't last as long as a Douglas, but I don't care, it smells lovely." She pauses. "You weren't talking about the tree, though, were you?"

"I was talking about your leaving." He has two weeks left with her—two weeks at most.

"I go on forgetting I can't ever come back. If it weren't for that, well . . . it would be a relief, to be going away."

"Will you miss the house that much?"

"Of course I will," she says, giving weight to each word.

"But have you thought about what you'll do, if . . ."

"I've promised to leave regardless, haven't I?"

"Will you be . . . will you still go south?"

"Like a goose for the winter." She laughs. "Although it will be summertime there."

"You'll have to wait to see the aurora then."

"I shall have to wait regardless. I've been reading up on New Zealand—"

"I hear it's gorgeous down there," he says softly.

"That's what I've been reading. There's this town that's something of a way station for scientists coming and going. I think we should spend some time there, maybe wait for next winter."

"Summer?"

"Did I say winter?" She just stands there for a moment or two, admiring the tree. "Now what if I take it by the trunk and hold it steady while you cut?"

Mounting the tree in the red-and-green metal stand takes longer than he expected. It's well past dark before he begins the drive to his mother's house in Connecticut, the wipers working furiously against the snow.

THURSDAY, 24 DECEMBER 2009 ~ 5:30 P.M.
The Kitchen

"WHERE ARE YOU GOING?"

"Mass," she says simply.

"Are you planning to walk? The bus isn't running tonight."

Mary sinks into a kitchen chair and covers her face with her mittens. "How am I going to get to Saint Gregory's?"

Lucy shrugs.

"But it's Christmas Eve! I have to go to church!"

Lucy bites her lower lip. "Well . . . I guess I could drive you—"

"But Gray took the car!"

"—only into town though, I'm not driving to Saint Greg's in this weather."

"Saint Lucy's?"

"The Church of Matthew," Lucy replies. "But you've got to promise me you'll sit in the back pew and leave *right* after the service."

"I promise." Mary frowns. "But do you mean to tell me you have another car?" It would explain why they never park the Prius in the carriage house.

"It was my dad's," Lucy says. "I haven't driven it since he died."

8:04 P.M.

The Church of Matthew ~ 761 Aurelia Avenue

AFTER THE SERVICE the congregation gathers around the crèche to snap pictures of their children. Chatter of home-sewn Wise Men costumes and elaborate Christmas-dinner menus recedes as Mary slips into the shrine of the Virgin, where white poinsettias with pots covered in red and green foil are arranged at her feet. She kneels and, clasping the railing, launches into a silent prayer for a reasonably happy ending.

"Spending a little alone time with our namesake, are we?"

She turns from the statue, staring at the preacher who has just delivered the most hysterical sermon she's heard in her life. And he's eyeing her now with that same calculating air that made her flesh creep at the Dragon Volant ten months ago.

"I deliberated on whether or not I should keep this shrine as it was," he says. "I see now that I made the right choice."

"How do you know my name?"

Fuller kneels beside her at the railing with a sigh too heavy for a man of forty-three, assuming a pose of prayer to avoid the curiosity of his parishioners. "I know a great deal more than that, my dear. Please—don't get up. All I ask is a few minutes of your time—"

"I'm sorry, sir," she says, "but you must have me confused with someone else."

He leans closer, and in the midst of her revulsion she notices how the vein in his temple throbs. "Not if you're Mary Morrigan."

She stiffens, crosses herself quickly and puts her palms to the railing to raise herself from the kneeler, but he grabs her firmly by the elbow. "I'm only asking for five minutes. You can spare five minutes, can't you?"

She nods, now terrified, and he relaxes his grip. "Thank you. I'm sure you've heard some rather unpleasant things about me, Mrs. Morrigan, and I must admit there's more than a grain of truth to them. But if nothing else I am a man of reason, and I'll hazard a guess it's a virtue you appreciate."

Mary raises her eyes to the painted marble statue above them, and this time the Virgin's expression seems sadly sympathetic. "What is it you want from me, Reverend?"

"You've misunderstood me. I only wanted to take this opportunity to inform you that I'm aware of your present circumstances. You see, I've been following your—now, how *would* you refer to her? I suppose I'll just have to use her Christian name—I've been following Lucy's scientific exploits for quite some time now."

"This has nothing to do with me, Reverend Fuller. If you wish to discuss Lucy's work, then you must speak to her directly."

"Perhaps I should be more blunt," he says in a tone of exaggerated patience, as though he were speaking to a wayward child in the Nativity pageant. "You and I are well past the point of bluffing. I've seen you in the churchyard out back, weeping your poor little heart out above a man who died long before you say you were born." He pauses. "Do I make myself clear?"

She nods, taking shallow breaths now, fumbling through her coat pockets in search of her handkerchief.

"As I was about to say, I am about to embark on a certain project of great importance, and I believe Lucy's expertise would prove truly invaluable. So, in that sense, you might say I'd like to offer her a sort of . . . *freelance* position. You will simply have to trust me when I tell you that this project would be a tremendous opportunity for her. Now, I'm well aware that Lucy would be completely unreceptive should I make her this offer without any sort of stipulation, but I believe in always working toward the greater good—don't you, Mrs. Morrigan?"

Mary presses the worn-soft cotton fabric to her eyelids. "That would depend, Reverend."

"On?"

She looks at him. "Your notion of what's good."

"I'm not interested in philosophizing with you, Mrs. Morrigan. The fact of the matter is that your very existence could serve as proof in court of Lucy's illicit activities." He pauses. "I doubt you'd like to see her go to prison for them."

Mary averts her eyes, but for Fuller this is answer enough. "You and I have more in common than you care to admit," he says gently. "I believe we could help one another. By all means, mull it over for a few days."

"Are you finished, now, Reverend?"

He nods.

She rises swiftly from the kneeler. "Merry Christmas."

8:25 P.M.
Aurelia Avenue

LUCY FIDDLES WITH the radio dial in search of a station that isn't playing Christmas carols. "Took you long enough."

"I'm sorry." Mary slams the passenger's-side door. "He spoke for nearly an hour."

"Narcissistic freak. I *told* you it'd be a waste of time."

"It wasn't a waste. They had a lovely Nativity scene," Mary says. "The little girl who played Mary held a baby-doll."

Lucy turns the dial up on the heater. "Have they changed it much?"

One month from now, with any luck, Fuller's only fodder for blackmail will be having afternoon tea in some quiet café in Christchurch. Why tell her?

"Yes," Mary says vaguely. "Yes, they've changed it quite a bit."

CHRISTMAS DAY, 2009 ~ 10:30 A.M.
25 University Avenue

MEGAN HAS GONE to her brother's in New Hampshire, but she'll be back tomorrow evening to resume her basement vigil. Gray, of course, is in Connecticut, trying his best to seem enthusiastic about the umpteenth oatmeal-colored scarf his mother has knit for him, this year with matching socks (along with a Yankee candle gift set to bring home to Lucy). The day after tomorrow the Seventh Order will return from their parents' homes, which are located along the eastern seaboard from Bangor to Burlington (New Jersey, not Vermont).

There are no gifts beneath the tree, which Mary has decorated with the old ornaments—just a small white envelope with her name on it. "What's this?"

"Open it."

It's a two-hundred-dollar gift certificate to a sporting goods store in town. "It's for your trip. I thought we might go down there once Gray gets back. Stock up on snowboots and things."

"How did you know?"

Lucy frowns. "About Antarctica?"

"Did Gray tell you?"

Did Gray tell her! She closes her eyes. "I spent half my childhood listening to y—her talk about the aurora australis." Lucy clears her throat. "Megan's working on getting you a passport and all that sort of thing."

"Thank you, Lucy."

"Come on." Lucy rises out of her chair. "We'll make a nice breakfast."

Mary's body hums electric whenever she thinks of Teddy lying one floor beneath her, dreaming, waiting to be born. Once Lucy returns to the basement she goes for a long, brisk walk in the woods, and in the evening she seats herself by the fireplace to sew the borders on the infinity quilt.

Still, there is nothing quite so eerie as Nat King Cole's version of "The Christmas Song" on the central sound system, echoing through an empty house.

Tomorrow Lucy will call Gray at his mother's. "I'm expecting him within the next day or two," she'll say, as though Teddy will appear on the front step with a bottle of Barbera d'Asti and a dozen red roses instead of opening his eyes in a coffinful of goop. "Do you mind coming home tonight?"

"Gray, honey," she'll hear his mother whine in the background. "Why do you have to leave so soon?"

THURSDAY, 31 DECEMBER 2009 ~ 11:45 A.M.
The Basement

THE GENERATOR makes an awful din. Wearing Lucy's headphones, Megan camps out beside the simwomb with a dog-eared copy of Carl Sagan's *Billions & Billions,* bopping her feet to whatever's playing on the central sound system. Gray wears a pair of insulated plastic earmuffs Ambrose used when cutting the lawn. A padded card table beside the old leather armchair holds a cordial glass, a monk-shaped bottle of Frangelico, and a plate of gingerbread cookies Mary baked this morning. Over a stack of exam papers Gray watches Megan read as she sips, nibbles, and pours again, smiling contentedly like a young housewife whose husband is out of town on a weeklong business trip, like a woman with no responsibility for any life besides her own.

"I've got to pee." Megan jumps up from her chair and bounds up the steps. "Keep an eye on Sleeping Handsome."

Gray rises from his seat, where he places the stack of exam papers, and approaches the machine to have a look at Teddy's face. As he eyes the electrical outlet, plugged into the generator on the floor in the far corner, he must remind himself that to pull the plug is tantamount to murder. It *is* murder.

It doesn't matter, he tells himself. Edward Morrigan has already lived his life. This dubious logic sees him on his knees in front of the generator. He lays a heavy hand on the plug, grips it with thumb and forefinger. With steely clarity Gray realizes this moment will define him for the rest of his life.

Megan opens the door and he springs from the corner, picking up the papers and hastily seating himself. The exams flutter in his hands as she brushes the crumbs from the seat of the armchair before resuming her ritual of fine liqueur and Carl Sagan.

He clears his throat. "How much longer, do you think . . . ?"

From the simwomb, a very faint tapping begins.

11:45 A.M.
Downtown New Halcyon

FOUR NIGHTS AGO Gray pulled the Prius into the driveway with two flat tires. Megan may need to use her hatchback, and none of them is feeling industrious enough to change two tires in one go, so Mary and Lucy take the bus into town to spend the gift certificate. Reveling in her anticipation, Mary barely notices the mingled odors of gasoline and unwashed underarms, or the cold, humid air inside the bus due to a broken heating system and the collective breath of three dozen passengers.

They buy for two in the appropriate sizes: polypropylene snow pants, thermal long johns (with and without willy-slits), parkas (his is dark green and hers is a pretty powder blue), and a couple of backpacks. Mary picks out a sturdy new pair of boots. The bill comes to well over two hundred dollars, but Lucy foots the balance.

12:11 P.M.

25 University Avenue ~ The Basement

MEGAN CLIPS THE cord before Teddy can regain consciousness, and then there is the awkward, slimy business of removing him from the simwomb. "I am *not* doing this *ever* again," Megan says through gritted teeth as she grips him by the underarms to lift him out. "Twice is more than enough."

With a garden hose Gray fills a large copper tub, which Lucy had found amid the junkpiles last week and scoured specially for the occasion, and he adds a few bucketfuls of hot water from the kitchenette sink. After he helps Megan lay Teddy in the tub, he reads the old movie-ticket stubs tacked to the corkboard—*The Age of Innocence, The Last Temptation of Christ, The Gangs of New York;* he never knew Ambrose had been such a Scorsese fan—while she bathes Mary's husband, lathering between his fingers before trimming his fingernails with a clipper she produces from her handbag. "Don't look at me that way," she says to Gray. "He looks like Nosferatu."

"You going to cut his hair, too?"

"Not 'til he's awake."

Teddy lifts his head, opens his eyes, and regards her calmly, without surprise. "Is this it, then?"

The soap slips from her fingers into the murky water. "Is this what?"

He shrugs. "Heaven, I suppose."

"I'm terribly flattered, Dr. Morrigan. But no, this is not heaven."

Teddy retrieves the soap and begins to wash himself. "You've been reborn," says Gray from the computer chair. "More or less."

"Pardon me for asking, but who are you both, and where exactly am I?"

"Just relax." Megan dries her hands. "We'll tell you everything."

And they do, which means he spends the following half hour becoming a human prune in the cooling bathwater. As promised, Megan cuts his hair with a pair of sewing scissors as she talks. "We'll turn our heads when you want to get out," she says, as though she hasn't seen plenty of him up to now. She points to the stack of Gray's clean clothing waiting for him on a chair. All this provokes in him a terrible feeling of déjà vu, and at first he suspects that Megan and the old Frenchwoman share a preternatural identity. This is the last day of the year 2009; Mary is alive, but a younger Mary than the woman he left in 1942. How is this possible?

"You're looking at it," Megan says ruefully. She gives the base of the simwomb a swift kick, leaving a small dent in the chrome. "Your granddaughter-who-is-not-your-granddaughter wanted a baby."

"Say that again?" He shakes his head. "Where's Mary? Can I see her?"

"They're not home yet," Gray says tonelessly. "They've gone out to buy you clothes for your trip."

"What trip?"

"To Antarctica. Well, New Zealand first, but that's where she wants to end up. Frolicking with the Emperor penguins."

That first-team all-American smile spreads across his face. "Well, I'll be damned."

The cellar has changed so much in the intervening years that he doesn't even realize he's in his own home until Megan says, "Once you're dressed we can help you upstairs to bed. You must be exhausted."

Teddy nods. The doorbell rings and Gray rises from his chair, but Megan holds up her hand. "Don't answer it."

1:00 P.M.

The Foyer

THE DOORBELL RINGS on the hour, as if the caller is both expected and all too punctual. Colin hurries down the stairs to answer it.

"You're right on time, sir."

Charles Fuller sashays into the foyer carrying a monogrammed leather briefcase. "I make a point of it, my dear boy." He pauses. "No one's home?"

"They're in the basement."

"Perfect." Fuller strides to the basement door and jiggles the knob. "Have you figured out how to pick the lock?"

"There're half a dozen dead bolts, Reverend—"

"You mean to tell me you've never actually been down there?"

Colin shakes his head.

Fuller sniffs. "I see."

"If you'd like to come upstairs, I can show you some of the—"

"Yes. Yes, we'll do that first."

Colin follows him up the stairs, calling his attention to all the squares of unfaded wallpaper. "Lucy took down all the old family photos," he says. "After her miscarriage and before Mary arrived. It was my first clue, you might say."

IN THE ATTIC, Fuller throws one of Mary's dresses on the floor in disgust. "This is just a lot of moth-eaten crap, Colin."

"She is who I say she is, Reverend. I swear."

"I *know* she is—she all but admitted it to me herself! But we need access to the basement in order to prove it, don't we?"

1:09 P.M.

The Basement

"WELL, *SOME*ONE ANSWERED THE DOOR."

Teddy sits upright in the tub, with an earnest look on his face. "Are they back?"

"Lucy doesn't ring her own doorbell, and she certainly wouldn't be puttering around up there knowing we're down here." Megan turns to Gray. "Are any of the monks back yet?"

"Colin's the only one home so far."

All three of them jump at the knock on the basement door. "Hello?" Colin calls. "Is anyone down there?"

Megan motions for Gray to speak. "Yes, Colin. What is it?"

"There's a leak in the upstairs bathroom. I . . . I just thought I should tell someone."

Shaking her head, Megan pinches her nose as she gestures to the door.

"Is the toilet overflowing?" he calls.

"No . . . I mean . . . I don't think so . . . but maybe I'd better check again . . . um . . . I'll be right back."

She puts her finger to her lips as Colin retreats. "Just what I thought," she says. "Two pairs of footsteps."

"I think all this paranoia is eating away at your brain."

"Gray?" Colin knocks on the door. Megan shakes her head. "Gray?"

1:14 P.M.

The Study

FULLER SITS AT Lucy's desk, drops his briefcase onto the ink blotter, and begins rifling through her drawers. "They're on to us." He jerks at the handle on the bottom drawer—locked. "You have the key for this one?"

"I didn't think to—"

"You mean you haven't even picked it?"

"No, sir, I—"

Fuller slams the top drawer, which has nothing in it but stationery and a box of paper clips. "What have you been doing here these last two years, if all you could do for me was unlock the front door?"

1:14 P.M.
Aboard Bus No. 8

LUCY SLIDES THE shopping bags under their seat. "I can't believe we just spent two hundred dollars on long underwear."

"You can say that again," Mary murmurs. A little boy of five or six, with tousled blond hair and a miniature pair of railroad overalls, keeps turning around in the seat in front of them. Mary smiles but he just stares at her, lethargically, and she wonders if he's right in the head.

She rests her hand on the back of his seat and gazes out the window, and the little boy pokes her with a sticky wet finger. His lower lip glistens with drool. "Are you sisters?"

"No," says Mary. "I'm her grandmother."

The child's mother turns around and scowls at her as Lucy delivers a sharp elbow to the ribs. "There's no need to be sarcastic!"

"I'm not b—"

"I apologize for my sister's rudeness," Lucy says. "She's having a bad day." (*My sister:* how that phrase makes her tremble as it passes her lips!)

The mother sniffs as she pries her son's hands off the back of his seat and wrestles him into a seated position, turning his head to face forward as though he's a life-sized doll. "Now, Avery," she says. "What did I tell you about talking to strangers?"

"But you're right here, Mommy—"

"That's not the *point,* sweetie," says Mommy through her teeth.

Avery and his mother disembark at the next stop, and an elderly woman carrying a bunch of lilies in a cellophane wrapper gets on and takes their seat. Mary leans forward to drink in their scent.

Then someone else taps her on the shoulder, and she lets out a gasp when she recognizes him: P. F. X. Godfry, notebook in hand.

"Pardon me, but I believe we've met before." He leans toward her from across the aisle to offer his hand. "Mary, right?"

"That's right," she says, her heart beating quickly as she marvels at her luck. "And you're . . . Patrick."

"I was thinking I might see you down at the Dragon again. I hope that evangelizing miscreant didn't frighten you away."

"It's not that," Mary says, glancing behind her to find Lucy pretending not to eavesdrop. "I like the Dragon Volant. I've been thinking about going back. But the business district isn't what it used to be—*you* know what I mean, Patrick—it got me so glum I just haven't returned. Except for the market on Hilary Road, I mean."

"The Mediterranean market? Love that place. Have you tried the fresh dates?"

She shakes her head.

"Ah!" He gives a little shiver of delight. "They're worth dying for."

"I'm surprised to hear you say such a thing," she whispers, leaning so close their noses are nearly touching. Lucy can't possibly overhear her as she says, "Seeing as all those farm workers are still making subsistence wages."

Now he hesitates, and she can tell he's trying to remember exactly what they talked about at the bar that day. Then she gives him a smile that can leave no doubt.

"So you've read my book, have you?"

"And I know you haven't written it yet."

He laughs softly; there is garlic on his breath. "Clever girl."

"Will you tell me how you did it?"

"Did what?"

"Came here—from *then.*"

He leans back in his seat and looks over her shoulder. "I don't understand you, Mary," he says, no longer whispering. "And I'm afraid we're approaching my stop." Not knowing what to say to stop him, she watches in panic as he picks up his notebook, tucks the pencil in the breast pocket of his overcoat, and puts on his hat. The bus slows as he grips the pole and puts his lips to her ear. "Tell you what," he says softly. "If I ever see you a third time, I promise I'll tell you."

Mary smiles up at him in resignation. "I quit smoking," she says softly. "Thank you for the gum."

"Glad to hear it, and you're welcome."

"Happy New Year, Patrick," she calls as he shuffles up the aisle.

As the bus pulls away she turns to the window and he waves his fedora over his head. "See you in the funnies!"

Several minutes pass in silence before Lucy gives in to her curiosity. "How do you know that guy?"

"From the Dragon Volant. You remember."

"You know him from someplace else, though."

"How could I?"

"You tell me." Lucy stands and picks up their shopping bags as the bus turns onto University Avenue. "After all, you're getting out now far more than you used to."

1:22 P.M.

25 University Avenue ~ The Dining Room

FULLER EYES THE ROW of decanters on the sideboard. "This scotch looks like it's been tampered with." He picks up the bottle and pulls off the cap, grimacing at the thick glob of mold on the tip of the stopper. "Hey, Colin. Find me something *potable,* would you please?"

"I don't know if we have anything," he calls through the open dumbwaiter.

"What *do* you have, then?"

Colin opens the press above the refrigerator. "Vodka."

"What kind?"

"Stoli."

Fuller heaves a disapproving sigh. "There's nothing else?"

"No, sir."

"I trust you have orange juice?" Colin nods and moves away from the dumbwaiter. "Tropicana?" Fuller calls out. "I can't stomach that crap from concentrate."

"Yes, sir, we have some."

Fuller's cell phone rings, and Colin can hear his wife asking where he is as he rinses out a highball glass that probably hasn't been used in three or four decades.

"Yes, sweetheart, I *know* we have company coming. I won't be too much longer . . . Cherie, honey, that's what I pay the housekeepers for . . . Yes, well, I *know* it's New Year's Eve, but I don't remember giving them the day off . . ."

Colin delivers the screwdriver as Fuller snaps his phone shut. "Thank you, my boy." Colin lingers uncertainly as Fuller wanders back into the foyer, examining the few pictures left on the walls while sipping daintily on his drink.

"You make a mean screwdriver," he says, eyeing the photograph of Lucy's parents taken at the family reunion more than thirty years before. It's too bad, what happened to Ambrose, but in a way he had it coming to him, didn't he? "Go on, Colin. Mix one for yourself so we can have a toast."

"I don't drink, sir."

Fuller steps backward, taking in the grand sweep of the staircase and the cathedral ceiling, the plasterwork and the chandelier swathed in dust. Such splendid details, all gone to waste!

Someday (God willing), when the NHU chapel is under his sole supervision, this house will be his campus rectory. Before that it must be purged of its history, of course: first the Dumpster, then the exorcism.

That dining room, those magnificent windows . . . All those bedrooms could be turned into administrative offices, the pert young ladies going up those stairs every morning in their pointy high-heeled shoes and gold cross pendants, ever cheerful to be coming to work for a great and noble cause. It's a bit distant, to be sure, but with the university expanding at its current rate all the houses on this street will be fraternities and admin offices in another five years. They've already purchased the house next door.

Fuller happens upon a small print of a Raphael Madonna hanging above the hall table and smiles, nodding to himself as if he's just made some important decision. The wallpaper will have to go.

"They should be home any minute," Colin ventures.

"Yes, yes, of course. We'll wait for them in the study. Come on, Colin, and bring your drink."

1:22 P.M.

The Basement

"I'M SORRY IF I'M being too informal," Gray says. "It's just that Mary always calls you that. I can call you Edward . . ."

"Teddy's just fine," he says blithely. "I've never been one for formality."

"Edward?" Clearly Megan's thoughts have been elsewhere these last few minutes. "There's something you should know. Lucy's been putting off telling Mary about it, but I guess it's just as well I'm telling you first."

He sits in the water with his knees pressed to his chest, patiently waiting for her to begin.

"Our cloning technology still has its shortcomings. Let me put it this way—you're like a mimeograph, you see?"

"I see," Teddy replies. "How long do we have?"

Megan blinks.

"That *is* what you mean, isn't it?"

"Yeah," she says. "But I honestly can't tell you. My best guess is four to six years before—"

"What?" Gray hollers.

"Shut *up,* Gray." She turns back to Teddy. "Four to six years before you begin to see signs of advanced aging. Then again, I could be completely wrong. You could live for thirty years or more." She pauses. "But I don't think so."

"Could you please pass me the hose?" Teddy asks her. "I'm ready to get out now."

Gray sits fuming by the chalkboard in the corner. Couldn't she at least have waited to drop a bomb like that 'til the poor man put some clothes on? And why is he so goddamned nonchalant about all of it?

Megan hands Teddy the hose and turns around as he emerges from the tub. He gives Gray a sympathetic smile as he towels himself dry. Gray stares at the dark curling hair on Teddy's pasty-white calves.

"Wow," Teddy says as he holds Gray's old slacks against his waist. "These look like they'll fit me perfectly."

"They will," Gray says.

"You said they've been gone a couple of hours now, didn't you?"

"Yes, but we can't go up there yet," Megan says. "There's definitely something fishy going on upstairs. I'd bet a year's salary Colin's let one of those Jesus freaks into the house."

"These zealots you were talking about—they're more or less harmless, aren't they?"

"No," Megan says. "Not harmless. And if we unlock the door we compromise the safety of this laboratory."

"That doesn't solve the problem of what happens when Lucy and Mary get home," Gray says. "I think we should go upstairs."

She flashes him an arch smile. "To fix that leak on the second floor, eh?"

Teddy puts on Gray's white athletic socks and a pair of his old running shoes. He ties the laces. No one speaks again for several minutes.

"What did it feel like?" Gray blurts. "Knowing you were going to die?"

"I never thought I was going to die," Teddy says. "There wasn't time for that."

"You don't remember any of it?"

Teddy shakes his head, staring thoughtfully at the floor tiles. "Did you know that during the French Revolution, the heads of guillotine victims showed unmistakable signs of life? They couldn't speak, of course, but there were plenty of doctors who swore they communicated for up to thirty minutes by blinking their eyes, one for yes or two for no, that sort of thing."

"I've read about it, yes."

"I don't remember dying," Teddy says. "But I remember being dead."

"Long tunnel?" Megan asks. "Blinding white light?"

"No." His voice has a distant quality, like it's coming through a tin can. "No, there wasn't any light . . ."

This can't be the man Mary's in love with. Rather, this is not the man Gray's imagination has fashioned out of those old photographs and all her wistful anecdotes. This is not the all-American football hero, nor the incorrigible romantic who proposed to her a week before Christmas at the end of an exhilarating round of night-sledding, nor the young physician who wondered if growing a moustache would make him appear more authoritative to the most crotchety of his elderly patients.

"On second thought," Gray says, "I'm not sure I want to hear any more."

1:32 P.M.
The Front Porch

LUCY PULLS HER KEYS from her coat pocket. "That was Godfry, wasn't it?"

"Who?"

"You know who. That guy on the bus." Lucy turns the key in the lock, then frowns as she realizes she's just bolted the door. "It was unlocked," she murmurs. "Son of a bitch."

"What's the matter?"

"This door is never unlocked."

"One of the boys must have forgotten—"

"No one's back yet," Lucy says, her hand heavy on the knob. "Except for Colin."

"Let's get ourselves inside, anyway," Mary says, pushing the door open and dropping her shopping bags by the hall table. Lucy follows her reluctantly, closing the door behind her and pulling off her coat.

The study door is a few inches ajar. Lucy stomps across the hallway, ready to tear into Colin for both leaving the front door open and using the study without her permission, and Mary follows her.

Looking haggard and resigned, Colin stands in the far corner of the room by the drawing room passageway, his arms folded tightly across his chest.

Standing in the center of the room is Charles Harris Fuller. "How nice to see you again. I trust you had a pleasant holiday?"

Lucy's fingers close into fists at her sides. "Get the fuck out of my house."

Fuller clucks his tongue. "Such language!"

"I'm calling the cops."

"So I can point them to the basement?" He laughs. "You'll do no such thing."

"You've got nothing on me. Haven't you ever heard of a warrant?"

"That can be arranged. Sit down, Miss Morrigan."

"That's *Doctor* Morrigan, you big—"

"According to university records, you never resubmitted your dissertation after revisions were requested by your advisory panel, *Miss* Morrigan." He pauses to gloat for a moment. "Now, then, shall we get down to the purpose of my visit?"

Mary sits on the sofa and tightly folds her arms. Lucy turns to Colin. "You let this scum into my house?" He doesn't answer. "You were spying on me all along, weren't you?"

"I wouldn't put it quite that way, but yes, I guess I was."

"All five of you?"

"No," he says. "Just me."

"From day one?"

He shakes his head. "Reverend Fuller approached me after a meeting of the Christian Union two years ago. He knew I boarded with you. And I . . . I knew you were up to something in the basement, but it never occurred to me . . . that it could be something you could go to jail for."

Lucy snorts. "Look, kids, it's Ronald McConscience! Do you have any idea how unethical *you've* been?"

"I know it must seem that way to you now, but it's all for the greater good."

She is shaking her head. "They've brainwashed you. And here I thought all this hooey about Saint Agatha was just a way to make yourselves feel better about not getting laid."

Colin takes a deep breath. "Even if I hadn't been talking to Reverend Fuller and the other members of the Church of Matthew—"

" 'Talking to,' eh? So that's your euphemism?"

"My faith is not a substitute for a lack of anything else in my life. And even a simpleton living under your roof could have put two and two together—"

"As you did."

"Please listen to me, Lucy. I'm not your adversary."

She laughs. "If you think I'm going to roll over for you Jesus freaks, you've got another think coming."

Mary holds out her hands to him. "Why are you doing this, Colin? What did we ever do to you?"

"You haven't done anything wrong, Mary," he says gently. "But Reverend Fuller is right when he says you're a lost soul. Through no fault of your own, you have been condemned to—"

"Oh, for God's sake, Colin, cut the bullshit!" Lucy cuts in.

"Treating us with hostility isn't going to get him out of your house any sooner." He turns back to Mary. "Please hear me out. The point we are trying to make here is that a human being must only be born from the union of a man and his wife."

"But I was!" she cries. "I had a father, and a mother—"

"No, Mary." Colin shakes his head sadly. "No you didn't."

1:40 P.M.

The Basement

GRAY HAS HIS EAR pressed to the inside of the basement door. "It sounded like she said 'Get the fuck out of my house,'" he calls down to them.

"Chucky Fuller," Megan says. "I should have known."

"I don't mean to be curt," Teddy says, "but aren't we wasting time?"

"You're right." Gray turns the first bolt. "We've got to get that lunatic out of the house."

"Don't touch that door, Gray." Megan dodges past Teddy and takes the stairs two at a time. "If you open it now, everything we've worked for goes to shit."

"Mary's life is more important than your career, Megan," Teddy says.

"It isn't my career I'm thinking of," Megan says fiercely. "And the fact of the matter is, Mary has already lived her life—as you have yours."

Teddy folds his arms. "You bring me back and then tell me to drop dead, is that it?"

Gray comes back down the stairs, shaking his head. "We've got to call the police."

"We are *not* calling the police," Megan says.

Teddy stares at her. "You suggest we do *nothing*?"

"You've never seen her as a real human being, Megan," Gray says. "You've treated her like a science experiment, and you don't care if she lives or dies."

"That's not fair, Gray—"

"Oh, yes it is. Come on, Teddy. There must be a couple of baseball bats in this junkpile somewhere."

Megan laughs. "What's with this machismo crap?"

"Don't you care that Lucy's in danger?"

"Of course I do. It isn't Lucy you're bent on saving, though, is it?"

"There's no time for this innuendo. I've got a better idea, Gray." Teddy pushes at one end of the highboy dresser on the wall by the wine rack. "Help me move this?"

"What for?"

"Trust me," he says. The highboy budges only an inch at a time; now Gray knows where Ambrose kept his dumbbell collection.

Behind the highboy is another one of those strange little doors. "What the . . . ?"

Teddy kneels and pries at the molded baseboard with his fingernails (the task would be easier had Megan not trimmed them, Gray thinks). "I just hope it's still here . . ."

"What?"

"The key, of course." Teddy looks up and finds Gray staring at him. "The key to the loop."

1:40 P.M.
The Study

"I BELIEVE YOU PLANNED THIS. Oh"—he laughs—"not the Mary Morrigan sitting here in front of us—the *first* Mary. Lucy's grandmother."

The notion of her nine-year-old self conspiring with her ailing grandmother to resurrect her sends Lucy into hysterics.

"Did anyone ever tell you that you have a most irritating laugh?" Fuller pops his briefcase open and lays its contents out on the blotter as if the desk belonged to him: a thick manila file, and a sealed plastic bag containing some dark and as-yet-unidentifiable object. He opens the folder, pulls out a small, yellowed newspaper clipping, rounds the desk, and offers it to her.

Now giggling to herself, Lucy accepts it, careful not to touch him. "'Are You Troubled by Insomnia?'"

"The *other* side."

She turns over the clipping, and gasps. MORRIGAN, LUCINDA. The obituary.

"My mother?" she cries. "*My mother?* What could you possibly want with my mother?"

Mary looks down and catches sight of something queer along the backs of her hands. The voices in the room fade as she stares at her hands in her lap.

Fuller snatches the clipping from Lucy's fingers. "Just how stupid do you think I am?"

"Pretty damn stupid," she replies. "But I still don't know why you saved this."

This can't be happening; these marks on her hands just can't be what they look like.

"I can't believe you've been keeping a file on me," Lucy says, flipping through the rest of the papers in the folder. "And that it's so *thick*! Who are you, the bogeyman?"

They may be faint yet, but they're unmistakable: *liver spots.* "Jesus," Mary murmurs, her hands spread trembling above her lap. "Oh, Jesus . . ."

"What is it?" Lucy kneels in front of her and takes Mary's hands in hers. "Oh, *shit.*"

"What's happening to me?"

"It's fine. You're going to be fine. It's just—"

"Tell me the truth for once, would you?"

Lucy just looks at her.

"These spots—do they mean what I think they mean?"

"I don't know."

"You don't know?"

"Is there any sense in swearing to a God I don't believe in?"

"You can't mean that."

Lucy gazes at her sadly. "I don't know, and that's the truth."

Fuller comes around the back of the sofa, eyeing her hands over her shoulder. "They sure look like liver spots to me. Poor thing! You see what happens when you tamper with nature?"

1:45 P.M.
The Basement

"YOU MEAN THERE'S a secret passage?" He turns to Megan as Teddy pulls a neat section of molding from the wall and produces a Victorian key, heavy and ornate. "Did you know about it?"

She shrugs. "Ambrose mentioned it once. Oh, please, don't look so betrayed—it's not as if anyone ever uses it! You'd better spray the lock with WD-40 first, Edward. Wait a sec, I think there's some under the sink."

"First let's find something to knock him out with, if it comes to that," Teddy says over his shoulder as he replaces the molding. "I don't know if we have any bats, Gray."

"Don't go up just yet," Megan says, handing him the spray can and walking back to the simwomb. "Just give me a few minutes to make this thing unrecognizable. A few more minutes aren't going to matter."

1:47 P.M.
The Study

FULLER HOLDS THE plastic bag up to the light, and the object inside looks like nothing more than a gnarled scrap of metal. "The world is a terrible place, and it needs our Lord's message now more than ever. And in this little piece of metal we have discovered a means of providing it to people all over the world, even to those heathen anarchists, such as yourself, who continue to deny his divinity. Can you guess what this is?"

"I'd rather watch you shove it up your ass."

"Now you listen here, you little bitch. I could leave you to rot in your basement, and I know for a fact that no one would give a shit. Isn't that right, Mrs. M.?"

"Please don't call me that." Mary glances at Lucy's face, at first seeing more curiosity than suspicion.

"Why not?" Fuller says archly. "It's your name, isn't it?"

"You have no right to address me so familiarly. Nor to speak to Lucy in such an undignified manner." But when she looks at Lucy now, there's no mistaking her expression. Mary can't bear to sustain her gaze.

"I've been called worse," Lucy murmurs.

In misery Mary stares at the blemishes on her hands. She should never have gone to that church on Christmas Eve.

"Somehow you feel safer thinking I'm your enemy," Fuller says to Lucy. "But you know what? I'm *not.* You must know that other groups believe you should die a slow, agonizing death right along with the abortionists. We, on the other hand, recognize how valuable you are."

Lucy snorts.

"Some of my colleagues aren't yet convinced, but I am. God gave us this technology for a greater purpose—not to prolong our own physical existences by replacing our failing organs, but to convince us of our true immortality, to restore our rightful place in the Kingdom of Heaven."

"I do *not* like where this is going," Lucy mutters.

Fuller holds out the plastic bag. "Don't you see? We have every reason to believe that this was one of the nails with which the Romans nailed Jesus to the cross!"

Mary looks up at him in astonishment.

Lucy moans as she drops her head on her knees. "No. No, no, *no.* I do *not* like where this is going."

"We believe that this technology—which Lucy appears to have perfected—is the key to the Second Coming."

Mary gasps. "You mean . . . you want to clone *Jesus*?"

Lucy begins to laugh again. "You're just a bunch of lunatics," she gasps, clutching her sides.

Colin's face darkens. "Stop it. Stop laughing."

"Ha. Ha, ha, ha. This is the funniest thing I've heard in years. Ha, ha, h—"

"This is not a joke!" he shouts. "*Look* at me, Lucy." Colin holds out his emaciated arms like a repentant heroin addict. "Do you think I'd throw everything I have into some harebrained fundamentalist crusade?"

"I've never been one to tell people how to live their lives, but now that you mention it—"

"Please don't mock me," Colin says, now eerily calm. "I have nothing—I mean nothing—without this project."

"I'm sorry you feel that way," Mary says quietly.

"It isn't a matter of feeling," he replies. "It's the truth."

1:48 P.M.

The Basement

MEGAN BEGINS TO dismantle the simwomb, scattering the parts under the dustcovers in the dark recesses behind the wine rack. No one can go to prison for being a pack rat, nor can they arrest a dead man for stealing lab equipment from the university. She will return what she herself has filched.

Brow in a knot, Gray stands beside the computer chair staring sightlessly at the old copper tub still half full of cloudy water. Lucy had never told him. There is a secret passage in this house—there are *two* secret passages! And she never thought to mention their existence? Mary had known of them, too, of course, but it's Lucy's secret-keeping that rankles him.

Teddy examines the flat-screen monitor hooked up to the central sound system. "How does this thing work? Ah, I see. Almost like a real typewriter, eh? You said there are thousands of songs stored in here?"

Gray nods. "But don't you think we should be—"

"Not *yet,* Gray!" Megan shouts from the gloom.

"I need something to play so she'll know I'm down here—"

"She already knows you're down here."

"—and that I'll be up there soon."

Gray points the mouse to the search field at the top right of the iTunes screen. "Go ahead and type."

I-n d-u-l-c-i j-u-b-i-l-o, he types, and then asks, "Now what?"

Gray reaches over and hits "enter." One song found: it's a different recording by a choir of prepubescent Britons, but it will suffice.

"Now, how do I play it?"

"Enter" again, and angelic sounds fill the room.

In dulci jubilo, nun singet und seid froh!

THIS IS THE SORT of music that makes Gray feel sad and inadequate, like he's attending his own requiem.

Teddy frowns. "I thought it was supposed to play upstairs."

"It's the central sound system. It's playing in every room on the first floor, plus the basement."

1:53 P.M.

The Study

"THIS IS THE OFFER, LUCY. Sequence the DNA and I won't tell the authorities Mary is a clone."

"You can't prove it."

"Yes, we can," Colin says gently.

"Look, you two are wasting your time. There's no way you're going to get me to do this. I'd much rather go to prison."

"I was afraid you'd say that." Fuller pulls a pistol the size of a chew toy out of his pocket. "That's why I brought this along."

Lucy laughs. "Now you *really* look like a gangster!" He points the gun at her chest. "Oh, come off it, Fuller," she says tiredly. "I know as well as you do that thing's not loaded."

He stands above her and presses the barrel to her temple. "You girls think you can bluff me, huh?"

Lucy looks up at him, unfazed, and this time there is no bluff; she feels suffused with fearsome serenity. "Go ahead," she says softly.

Fuller laughs as he pockets the gun. "I won't indulge your little death wish."

"Like I said," she replies. "It isn't loaded."

Static crackles from the speakers above the drawing room doorway. Then:

In dulci jubilo, nun singet und seid froh!

Mary cocks her head. Gold and fuchsia lights flash against the wallpaper in a darkened room in her mind.

"What's that?" Fuller snaps. "Where's that music coming from?"

"Teddy," she murmurs, and all at once she's lost for breath. "Teddy . . ."

Lucy grins triumphantly. "What was it you said earlier, about nobody missing me if I rotted away in the basement?"

Mary rises unsteadily from the sofa, brushing the folds from her skirt and hastily wiping the tears from her face with her palms. Fuller and Colin gape at her like lobotomy patients. A steady thumping begins in the cellar, heavy footsteps, more than one set, and a moment later it sounds as if it's coming from the blue drawing room—no, the passageway—

"The broom closet!" Colin cries. "I *knew* it!"

Nach Dir ist mir so weh.

Fuller freezes in front of the fireplace as they hear the key turn in the lock. Lucy laughs to see him cowering there under the mantel like a frightened child. "You were right, Colin," she says. "It's where I keep all the bones."

The door creaks open and a face appears in the doorway, a face all save Mary have seen only in black-and-white photographs.

Trahe me post te, trahe me post te.

Over Teddy's shoulder, Gray watches Mary's face transfigured at the sight of her husband. For all that matters now, they are the only two people in the room.

Mary goes to him, reaching trembling hands to his face. "My God!" Teddy murmurs, stroking her hair. "You're so *young*!"

"Who the hell are you?" Fuller demands, but Colin stares at Teddy in horrified understanding. Fuller glances at his minion and the stranger's identity finally dawns on him.

Megan seizes this opportunity, striding into the room to kick him hard in the shin. "Hiya, Chuck!" she cries gleefully, as Fuller crumples howling to the floor.

Coelorum gaudia. Quanta gracia! Quanta gracia!

The song ends and an awkward silence descends on the study. Fuller's cell phone plays Pachelbel's Canon from his inside breast pocket, but he's too busy whimpering to answer it. And in a vast white kitchen on Gwendolyn Drive, Georgie drooling on her new blouse, Cheryl Ann Fuller slams the cordless back on its cradle and screams in frustration. Georgie begins to bawl.

"I have to go home," Fuller announces from the floor, as though he'd been invited into the house as a guest. Lucy laughs at this.

He rises to his feet, smoothes his lapels, and thrusts his finger at her. "We are *not* done here."

"Oh, yes we are," Lucy replies, as Teddy and Gray pick him up by the armpits and drag him out the study door. Megan rounds the desk, returns the nail in the bag—but not the file folder—to Fuller's briefcase, lifts the sash, and chucks the briefcase out into the snow.

"They'll be here with a warrant!" Fuller screams over his shoulder. "First thing Monday morning!"

"I'll bake a coffee cake," Lucy calls through the window as they push him out the front door and turn the dead bolt behind him.

"I'll make sure the back door is locked," Gray mumbles, avoiding Mary's eyes as she appears shyly in the study doorway.

"Oh, gibbon," he hears as he trudges down the hallway. "Oh, rabbit." He can't imagine feeling what she's feeling now for some woman he has yet to meet. She may very well be delightful, but she will not be Mary.

Lucy turns to Colin, who has seated himself on the study sofa with his head in his hands. "You'd better start packing."

Chromosome 16:
Excerpt of a vernacular translation

1 *ctccacaggatgcttatggg* // cccgctagtccttcagcgtttagccagcgccctgcaccatgctgag
APRT encodes a *bluebells up and down the avenue. Mother and Aunty wear*

67 taccagggacgctgctaggcacaggcagacgagacccccccacggcccccagttaggggctccaggaca
their best dresses (Mother in her chocolate-brown silk; Aunt Cee's new dress re-

136 caggcagacaaggcccctcacggccgcagtcaggggctccaggacacgggcagacgaggcccctcac
minds me of the curtains in Katherine's parlor). We climb the hall steps two at a

203 ggccgcaggtcaggggctccaggacacaccttccctcttctcattgggcagaacgtttcaggggtcac
time, even Aunty, who always says it isn't ladylike. A man takes Mother's picture

271 aactcacaatctggaagaccacacgaagctgcccctgatcttccagcagggcattgatttctgccc
as she drops her ballot into the box; used too much wax on his moustache; smells

337 tcctgggacgggacccaggggagaggttcccctcaggtgagtcggtgcagggcctcctggctgct
of peppermints and shoe polish. Half past 3, hot fudge sundae at Chester's, I save

403 gaggcagtgccagccggactcccccaaatgcaggctccacagggacagagccctctgcaccctgccc
the cherry for Mother. Mother's chocolate fig cake recipe—a dozen figs (stems

470 gccgcctccccttgcctgcatctgctgttgctattcatacccacacgtgcttggtggcctgccctcctccc
trimmed); 7 ounces coarsely-chopped chocolate; 8 tablespoons butter (cut into

541 agggtgcctgctgctgcccaccctggtggtctccccacttctgccccttctgggccaccatccacctggcc
bits); 2 tablespoons Cognac; 6 eggs (separated); a third of a cup plus 3 tablespoons

612 cccagtgatgtatcccctactctgagctgcatttggggatggctgaggccagaggggaggggtccaggccc
sugar; a pinch salt; 2 cups fresh berries (Father prefers half raspberries/half blue-

683 tggggcaagtaggaggtacaaggacacaggtcagctagcaggaggaatggcagaaagccaccagcc
berries). Custard topping: two dozen figs (stems trimmed, coarsely chopped); one

748 ccagctccaccctctgctctctgggccttgtcctcaccccaccgaggatgccggagtcttcctgggaagggag
and three-quarters cups milk (more if necessary); half a cup heavy cream; 4

821 atccggagcgaatagggggcttcgcctctggcccagccctcccgctgatcccccagccagcggtccgca . . .
egg yolks; one half cup sugar; one teaspoon vanilla. The oven should be set to . . .

VI

MARY MODERN

Our first night at the whaling station was blissful. Crean and I shared a beautiful room in Mr. Sorlle's house, with electric light and two beds, warm and soft. We were so comfortable that we were unable to sleep.

—Sir Ernest Shackleton (*c.* 1919)

THURSDAY, 31 DECEMBER 2009 ~ 3:39 P.M.

25 University Avenue ~ The Third-Floor Turret Room

SUNLIGHT GLITTERS on the snowdrifts, as if tomorrow's arrival were an utter certainty.

In these last few hours he has no choice but to share her company. He could revel in her presence as she packs her suitcase, waiting starved like an orphan for any casual gesture of affection; or he could remain here, in his office chair before a stack of exam papers, as the sound of their easy laughter taunts him through the walls.

Even with Teddy gone, for an hour or for good, no amount of time alone with her could satisfy him. Every ramble they took through the woods behind the house, every midnight confessional over turkey sandwiches slathered in mayo, every companionable silence:

It is not enough. It will never be enough.

Suggested Reading

Author's note: I have endeavored to compile a list of the most germane and current books available in the year 2009. If you are reading this book before that year, I hope you will accept my apologies for the unavailability (however temporary) of any of these works.

Dillman, Jonathan. *Quagmire in the Fertile Crescent: Dispatches from Baghdad.* London: Random House, 2006.

Ehrenreich, Barbara. *Nickel and Dimed: On (Not) Getting By in America.* New York: Henry Holt, 2001.

Farmer, Paul. *Pathologies of Power: Health, Human Rights, and the New War on the Poor.* Berkeley: University of California Press, 2003.

Franken, Al. *Lies (and the Lying Liars Who Tell Them): A Fair and Balanced Look at the Right.* New York: Dutton, 2003.

Gosher, Johnny. *"I've Got Jesus to Keep Me Warm": Poverty and Morality in the New Bible Belt.* Minneapolis: Sojourner Press, 2005.

Mandelbruck, Oliver. *On the Manipulation of Time and Space.* Cambridge: Harvard University Press, 2001.

Palast, Greg. *The Best Democracy Money Can Buy,* revised edition. New York: The Penguin Group, 2003.

Pelton, Robert Young. *The World's Most Dangerous Places,* 8th edition. New York: HarperCollins, 2009.

Watson, Robert K. *Looking for Oil in All the Wrong Places.* Washington, D.C.: The George Washington University Press, 2004.

3:39 P.M.

The Attic

"CLEVER, ISN'T IT?" He turns to the back jacket flap for a glimpse of the author.

"There's no picture of him." She watches how his wedding ring, newly restored to him, flashes in the dusty light.

"I suppose I'd better have a look at this," he says, pulling a history textbook out from under the pile on the table. "Let's pack Godfry, too." Then he notices the little leather diary on the top of the stack. "And what's *this,* pray tell?"

"I've been writing in it."

"You never kept a diary before."

"I did. I rarely wrote in it."

He brandishes the diary, grinning, holding it out of her reach as she snatches for it. "Don't be silly, rabbit. It's only a record of how you passed the days. 'First of December. Oatmeal for breakfast again, raisins this time—' "

"I do *not* write twaddle!"

"What is it, then?"

"It's . . . well, you could say I've been inspired."

He opens the book to the first page. " 'Confessions'?" He laughs. "What can you possibly have to confess?"

She folds her arms. "You think I just sat around waiting for you to come back—that I did nothing but eat and sleep and use the toilet for a year—is that it?"

He reaches up and runs his fingers through her hair. "It's grown so long," he murmurs.

"Don't try to distract me. For all you know I could have *plenty* to confess."

He takes her face in his hands. "Do you?"

Mary looks aside at her open suitcase. "No."

Suddenly he frowns.

"What is it?"

"How queer." He runs his thumb across her eyebrow. "Your scar is gone."

3:39 P.M.

The Study

MEGAN HAS ANOTHER friend at the Social Security Administration—a very old, very dear friend to expedite two sets of identification on a day's notice. An elderly couple of Laurel Hill, Massachusetts, have provided their surname and social security numbers, as they have no further need for them. Mary dissolves into laughter. "Teddy, look! I was born in nineteen eighty-seven!"

Frowning over bank documents spread out on the blotter, Megan and Lucy scrape together the funds for a one-way trip to New Zealand for Mary and Teddy. Lucy purchases the plane tickets on the Internet. They will depart Logan International Airport a day and a half from now, and the number of layovers in between will make it feel like a game of global hopscotch. Three days from now Megan will retrieve Ambrose's car from the short-term airport parking lot. Once they've arrived in Christchurch, the couple formerly known as the Morrigans are on their own.

While Mary is in the shower Teddy asks Lucy about the fates of his and Mary's children. "I know they aren't *ours,*" he says. "But I'd still like to know."

The presence of her long-dead grandfather, in full color and smelling of Gray's aftershave, prompts a flutter in her stomach. He's not quite as tall as she'd pictured. "I understand," she murmurs, looking out the study window as she tells him the plain truth—something else she isn't used to.

In the second-floor turret room, a stack of unwanted paperbacks, the print of Saint Agatha on the wall, and an unmade bed are the only reminders that Colin ever lived here. When the remaining members of the Seventh Order must venture out of their rooms, they do so under a miasma of apprehension. Lucy has informed them that they have only the weekend to find new lodgings.

Another tornado has ripped through the master bedroom. Men's oxford shirts, still buttoned and starched, on wire hangers from the dry cleaner, lie in a pile on the unmade bed; the floor is heaped with New Balance running shoes, white cotton undergarments, and colorful acrylic sweaters from the eighties and nineties.

A fuchsia pullover flies across the room and lands on the vanity table with a clatter of delicate glass bottles. "I don't want to wear these clothes!"

"Come now, dear." Teddy smoothes his necktie beneath his argyle sweater vest. "They're not so bad."

"I don't even wear these dungarees for gardening." Fingering the Saint Christopher medal around her neck, she looks him up and down. "You don't know what people are dressing like these days," she says. "You look terribly old-fashioned."

Half an hour is wasted wandering through the house so Teddy can see how things have changed, and how things have not. Mary tells him about Ashtanga yoga and macrobiotics and her triumphant shortcut to the recipe for the perfect ribollita. They fondle one another in hallway alcoves and resurrect old jokes. Occasionally he murmurs something that makes her feel as though he has her confused with someone else.

"Forgive me, rabbit," he says. "I *do* have you confused. I left a few months after your thirty-fifth birthday, you know." After this their conversation returns to lighter and less complicated territory, and they decide to spend their last night in America somewhere on Cape Eden. When she asks him where, he'll only say it's a surprise.

"How will we do it?" Mary asks him as he kisses her on the forehead where her scar should be. "How do I condense more than a lifetime into a single piece of luggage?"

"You don't," he says. "All we need are the clothes on our backs."

As she sorts through her chosen belongings she finds a certain book tucked between her bright and ugly sweaters. *New Year's Day, 2010.*

Keep it, Lucy has written on the fly leaf. *I won't have anyone to pass this on to but you.*

Teddy glances over her shoulder. "What's that?" She hands him the book. "Ah," he says. "Are you going to keep it?"

Remembering the first time her mother read her "The Star Talers," she runs her hand across the leather-bound cover. "It wouldn't be right."

How does the story end? *The little girl has just given the shirt off her back when the stars begin to fall at her feet, not stars now but hard smooth coins. Suddenly she finds herself clothed in a new shirt of fine linen. She gathers the silver from the ground, and is rich all the days of her life.*

He hands her a fountain pen from the desk and she sits on the bed, her hand hovering above the page. Then she closes the book and replaces it on the night table. "I don't know," she says. "I just don't know what to say."

Later they open the hall closet to find his old deerstalker cap still hanging on the door hook. "My hat!" Teddy cries happily, only to see the flannel fall to pieces in his hands.

4:45 P.M.

The Third-Floor Turret Room

"*EA FĒMINA NŪLLUM timōrem sēnsit sed, propter virtūtem, sē necāvit.*" For several terrifying seconds he loses his carefully acquired vocabulary, and the words mean nothing to him. A snowball hits the window with startling force. "Gray!" Lucy calls. "Can you come down here, please? I need your help with the car."

What car?

Lucy unlocks the carriage-house doors as he steps through the snow in his sneakers. "Christ!" she sputters, hiding her nose in the crook of her elbow. "Something must have crawled in and died here." Many moons ago, by the smell of it.

As he comes up behind her he sees an automobile enshrouded in the darkness. She pulls the tarp away to reveal a black Beamer, maybe twelve years old. "Whose car is that?" he asks.

"My father's."

He approaches the car, blinking in disbelief. There had been that conference in New Jersey when the Prius was in the shop, that hellish six-hour bus ride sitting beside a man whose corpulence rivaled that of William Howard Taft. She had never once thought to lend it to him? "You had a working car in this garage," he says slowly. "And you never told me."

She shrugs. "I drove Mary to church while you were away. But until then, I'd forgotten about it."

Sure she did. The secret passages, the BMW—it makes him wonder how much else she never thought worth mentioning, all the other pointless little secrets he won't be around long enough to discover. "Why didn't you ever tell me about the loop?"

Lucy opens the door and plops down in the driver's seat. "It's called a secret passage for a reason, Gray."

Now Teddy and Mary are trudging down the driveway, suitcases in hand, his arm tight around her waist. Gray looks away, toward the junk in the corner of the garage, as Lucy starts the engine and backs the car out of the carriage house. "Meet your new wheels," she calls to them as she rolls down the driver's-side window.

Squinting in the dark, he approaches another hulking mass in the far corner and lifts the tarp. A Ford Model A, squatting on the filthy cement floor for want of its tires.

"Oh," he hears Mary gasp behind him. "That's . . . that was my car."

"It will never run again," he says, as if this is some prophecy of profound importance.

"Not without wheels, it won't." His back is still turned, so her attempt at a smile is lost. She comes up beside him and rests her hand on his elbow. "I left your camera on your desk. I'm sorry, Gray. I just couldn't get the hang of it."

Motionless, he stares at a stack of empty paint cans in the corner. "Don't worry about it."

But I left you something else, she wants to say. *Something to remember me by. I left it on your bed.* She opens her mouth, but she can't summon any sound.

It happens far too quickly, as permanent farewells always do. Teddy shakes Gray's hand. Lucy pulls the ring from her finger and slides it onto Mary's. "I've been meaning to give this to you. I know you miss having your own."

"Thank you. It looks very much like mine."

"Mother had hers made after yours." Lucy pauses. "I'm sorry, Mary. For everything."

"You've apologized enough." Mary hugs her. "And I never thanked you—for Teddy."

Leaning against the front-porch railing with her arms folded, Megan watches it all like a stoic.

Teddy waits in the passenger's seat as Mary kisses Gray on the cheek, and he embraces her. *Come on,* he says to himself. *Life is too short for subtlety.* In the end, of course, he tells her nothing. He'll need a few weeks to decide whether or not this decision is one he should regret.

5:25 P.M.
Interstate Route 588, Eastbound

SHE DRIVES FIRST. He sits in the passenger's seat with the paper open to the international news in his lap. He's already read the entire newspaper, even the fluff in the arts section. "It seems so strange to think that I'll never see either of them again," Mary says.

"Do you want to go back?"

She hesitates. "No."

5:37 P.M.

"GOD," HE SAYS. "I'd love a cigarette."

"They cause lung cancer," she replies. "They discovered that in the sixties. So I made up my mind to quit."

"And have you?"

"I have. And I think you should, too."

"Why does it have to be everything enjoyable in life?"

"That's what I said, too."

For several moments she watches him in silence out of the corner of her eye, wondering at the sense in phrases like "my grave" and "the night we exhumed you."

"Tell me, Teddy: What were our children like?"

"Lucinda was just learning to walk when I left. And the boys . . ." He laughs. "There was this one time they made a snow lion for you in the front yard; it was sitting on its haunches and facing the house. We took two stepladders out of the toolshed and they made this unbelievable sculpture out of fresh snow, just like one of those stone lions at the New York Public Library, except it was seven feet tall—that's no exaggeration—with icicles for fangs. You came to the parlor window and you . . ."

"Teddy?"

"You started to cry." He looks out the window. "That was the Sunday before I left."

"I took a photograph that day. I saw it in the—damn, I forgot all about the book!"

"What book?"

"It doesn't matter now," she sighs. "They're dead, you know. All three of them."

"Who told you that?"

"I saw the obituary listings. On the Internet. Another war . . . in Korea . . . and Lucinda . . ."

"I know about Lucy. Joe must have been killed in Korea, but Teddy didn't go. He already had a family of his own, by that time."

"But I looked up the articles afterwards—"

"The newspapers must have confused their names. Teddy lives on the Cape now, in our old house—didn't you know that?"

Of course she did—she has known since that night in April when they drove up the North Sea Road with her half-asleep in the backseat. She nods, slowly. "It's a bed-and-breakfast now, isn't it?"

Teddy nods.

"The same bed-and-breakfast we're driving to now, isn't it?"

He nods again. "I called to make a reservation while you were in the W.C."

"What will we say to him? How will we act? Do you think he'll know it's us?"

"Gray said Lucy hadn't seen him since she was a child, so I doubt he's aware of all the goings-on down in the old wine cellar. And if he remarks on our uncanny resemblance to his own parents, we'll just laugh and say—"

"Teddy . . . you mean we won't *say* anything? We won't tell him?"

"What for? What good can come of it?"

"But he's our—"

"Mary, dear." He squeezes her knee. "You've had far more time than I have to grow accustomed to the idea. He's not our son."

"I know," she says. "I know. It's just so hard to . . ."

Teddy slides his hand around her shoulder, tracing the nape of her neck with his thumb. "Try to smile for me, rabbit. We had a great life together, didn't we?"

"It's not over yet."

"Yes," he says, dropping his hand again. "Yes, it is."

Slowly she turns to him, squinting in disbelief.

"Mary," he says sharply, as she swerves into the right lane. She pulls onto the shoulder, her heart in her throat.

"What's wrong?"

"What did you say?" She can't bear to look at him. Can it be that after all she's been through, he . . . ?

"I said that that life is over, Mary. We have no children, we have no home. We don't belong to the people we thought were our families—oh no, Mary, did you think I was . . ." He winds his arms around her and pulls her to him above the parking brake. "How could you *ever* think I would—stop crying, rabbit, please don't cry. I'm not going to leave you again."

"Lucy said you'd be . . . you'd be different . . ."

"I *am* different. It's like part of me belongs somewhere else . . . and I've only just borrowed it back for the time being."

"Don't say things like that. You're frightening me."

"All right, all right. We're starting a new life now—today." He pauses. "Albeit a short one."

She clears her throat. "We'll keep driving." She shifts into gear and drives in silence for several minutes, until they pass a road sign indicating a "scenic view" a hundred yards ahead. "Pull over there," he says. "Let's take a break."

"I'm fine to keep going."

That look on his face—how she's missed it. "That's not what I meant," he says.

A dirt path through the woods leads them to a clearing dotted with battered wooden picnic benches covered in graffiti, and beyond this a metal railing from which one may enjoy the scenic view: a brook now mostly frozen over beneath a canopy of skeletal maple trees. The air is rank with the smell of burning rubbish; a wisp of smoke rises from the treetops on the far side of the creek. Mary turns off the engine and Teddy opens the passenger door and stretches his legs. She follows, only to find him smiling at her over the roof of the car as he opens the back door. He climbs back in and she follows. He unbuttons her coat, pulls the scratchy pink sweater over her head, and lays her down on the cold leather seat in her long-sleeved undershirt. He drapes his wool overcoat over his head to conceal them from any onlookers, making faces at her as he unbuttons the fly on her dungarees and pulls her underclothes down to her knees with fingers to chill the devil. She stares at his swollen navel, a wide bump under the hem of his argyle sweater.

"I missed you." His breath is hot on her ear. "God, I missed you."

She cries out like it's the first time.

6:30 P.M.

25 University Avenue ~ The Study

THERE EXISTS ONLY one photograph of all three of them, a formal family portrait Ambrose had arranged to be taken in the library. The reason it isn't hanging on the foyer wall would be clear enough to anyone who looked at it: Lucinda doesn't just look mortally ill—she's far beyond that point. That he dragged her from her deathbed to pose for this photograph is nothing short of horrifying. Six-year-old Lucy, on her mother's lap, is the very picture of health. Now Lucy wishes she'd torn it out of that family album years ago.

She locks the study door and takes even breaths to slow her pulse, seating herself and placing Fuller's file before her on the blotter in slow, deliberate movements. She opens the folder.

6:22 P.M.

Interstate Route 588, Eastbound

"WHAT ARE YOU thinking about, rabbit?"

"Oh, nothing."

Tapping cheerfully on the dashboard, he gives her one of those sly sideways glances you only give someone you're in love with.

"Godfry," she murmurs. "I'm still thinking about Godfry."

"It's just one of life's ineffable mysteries. Don't torture yourself wondering over it."

"I met him, you know."

"You *met* him?"

"Twice, in fact. I asked him outright, but he was coy with me." She sighs. "By then we'd reached his stop."

"You met him on the bus?"

"Yes, and before that at a restaurant downtown—you know liquor is legal again, dear?"

"I did, yes, dear," Teddy says, smiling in amusement. "Which restaurant?"

"The Dragon Volant."

"Ah," he says. "We had our last anniversary dinner at the Dragon Volant. You had an excellent roast duck, as I recall."

"Don't you think it was horribly irresponsible of him not to tell his readers how he did it?"

"Who, Godfry? He could have been one of us. Did you consider that?"

"Don't say 'one of us.' You make us sound like Martians."

Teddy smiles. "We might as well be."

"And anyway, he couldn't have been one of us. Well, he *could've* been, but he still would've needed some sort of time machine or wormhole or something to get him back to nineteen fifty-eight so he could publish the book. And *then* there would've been *two* of him in nineteen fifty-eight . . ."

"Maybe there were." He grins. "Did I ever tell you that you were the brainiest girl I ever knew?"

"Amn't I still?"

"Try not to say 'amn't,' rabbit. You'll date yourself."

"Splendid! I sound like a crone for using proper grammar."

"Strange, isn't it?" he murmurs. "How she brought you here, and you hated her for taking your future away. She brought *me,* and I couldn't have thanked her enough."

Mary sighs. "It doesn't matter now."

"What would you have done, then," he says slowly, "if the second experiment hadn't worked?"

She doesn't say anything for a long time. "Don't ask me that, Teddy."

7:02 P.M.

MOTHER OF A modern God? (Mother of a *post*modern God?) No, no, mother of no one. This body will never know the pains of labor. "It isn't possible," she tells him.

"You don't know that," Teddy says. "And you may not remember, but I told you a long time ago that delaying starting a family is a tricky business."

"We have—what's the most optimistic number? Four years? I don't think—"

"You might still be capable, though. That's what I'm trying to say. We ought to be . . ."

"We ought to be what?"

"Careful."

"I'm sterile as a mule," Mary says. "Lucy told me so."

"Gray told me she had no way of knowing that."

"Is that so?" Mary laughs a hard little laugh. "I think she must have been making it all up as she went along."

"Granted, I wasn't acquainted with her for very long," Teddy says. "But I think you're probably right." He eyes himself in the visor mirror. "Do you think I look my age?"

She gives him a sympathetic glance before returning her eyes to the road.

7:15 P.M.

The North Sea Road ~ Cape Eden

World's End Bed & Breakfast
Ted and Kathy Morrigan, Proprietors

NO ADVERTISEMENT for en suite rooms with satellite television and wireless Internet access. You don't come out here for those sorts of luxuries. Only the address and telephone number appear beneath the hand-painted yellow script.

Teddy stands on the step and rings his own doorbell. Once the farmhouse had been white with dark green shutters, but they've painted the siding a pale yellow and the trim a slightly brighter shade of green. For all the snow the place still looks as cheerful and well-kept as it was eighty years ago.

A man one might call a very spry-looking seventy-five opens the door. "Hello and happy New Year! You must be Edward. And your bride?"

"Mary," Teddy says, resting his hand on her elbow.

"Hello, Mary." She blushes as the man—not her son, *not her son*—takes her hand and says, "Please, come in, come in!" There's no flicker of recognition as he looks upon this pair of tired revenants, just an interest that approaches the grandfatherly.

Ted ushers them into the hallway and hangs their coats on the empty wall rack. Beneath it is a low wooden shelf made for shoe storage. Mary looks over her shoulder: the parlor door is closed. To her left, the dining room has five round tables, each set for breakfast. Small black-and-white photographs line the mantel beneath a large beribboned holly wreath, fragrant even from the doorway.

They'll have to get a closer look at those photographs later on this evening. No, there have been too many photographs. *No more photographs.*

"Your snow boots go on the shelf there, if you don't mind." He smiles apologetically. "My wife's a real stickler when it comes to that sort of thing."

"No bother at all," says Teddy.

"Just for the one night, is it?" They nod. "I have a double, two queens, and a king," he says.

"Do you have a room with a view of the bog? I know there's not much to see this time of year," she says quickly.

"I have a room with a queen bed and a view in that direction. Nicest room we've got. I'll take you upstairs."

"It's a fine place you have here, Mr. Morrigan," Teddy says as they reach the second-floor landing. "We're so glad we made it out here."

"Thank you. So how long have you two been married?"

They glance at one another before Mary answers. "About a year and a half."

"We're just taking a drive past some of our old haunts before we move to New Zealand," Teddy says.

Mary freezes—will he ask them how well they know the Cape?

"New Zealand, how wonderful!" Ted points to the door at the end of the hall. "There's the bathroom, and this is your room. I suppose your work is taking you there?" Teddy nods as Mary opens the bedroom door. "I'll let you get settled. My wife and I are watching a program in the front room. Just let us know if you need anything."

Teddy pulls out his wallet as Mary looks around at the walls, the ungainly wardrobe, the frayed silk mums in the vase on the desk. "How much for the night?"

"Is sixty all right? Includes breakfast, of course."

"Sure." Teddy almost succeeds in hiding his dismay at the price, and hands him three crisp twenty-dollar bills before Ted closes the door behind him.

Mary sighs as she falls onto the bed. Nothing remains from the times she slept here, not furniture or pictures or wallpaper. Only the slanted ceiling and the cozy little window seat are proof it's even the same room. Teddy plucks a peppermint from the dish on the nightstand and crinkles the cellophane wrapper between his fingers. "I'll go bring our luggage inside."

She raises a hand from the bed. "Don't. We'll do it later."

Popping the mint in his mouth, he sits on the bed beside her. "Are you hungry yet?"

She shakes her head. "You must be, though. Have you eaten anything at all, since . . ."

"No," he says. "And I'm not particularly hungry. But I suppose we should try to eat something eventually. Should we go somewhere, in the meantime?"

"We could visit Saint Jude's, if you like."

"No," he says. "I'd rather not, if you don't mind."

"Of course. Sorry."

"Bender's Hill?"

"We could borrow a sled."

"What do you want to bet that your old Lightning Glider's still hanging in the barn?"

"With what money?" she laughs.

"I'm finding it easier," he says slowly, "to pretend he isn't the Teddy I remember. It's not as hard as I thought it would be."

"And what about the house?"

Teddy shrugs. "I've walked into each room thinking of the way it used to be, but then I just kept telling myself it isn't mine anymore. Never was."

From the parlor downstairs they can hear parade music playing on the television. "You said we shouldn't talk about it. So we won't." She pulls off her sweater and dungarees and burrows under the bedclothes, where she removes the rest of her garments. Shivering, he follows her into bed.

Outside the frosted window, silence settles upon the snowdrifts.

7:45 P.M.

World's End Bed & Breakfast ~ The Parlor

TED'S WIFE EMERGES from the kitchen carrying two steaming plates of vegetables with a pair of oven mitts. Mary stares at her: this is the crisply dressed young mother of those home movies on the attic wall. "Hello," Kathy says. "You must be the newlyweds. Do me a favor and open that door for me? Thank you, dear!"

Ted turns from the sofa in front of the television set as his wife places the plates on the coffee table. "We aren't always such couch potatoes," he says earnestly. "Spending four hours at a time in front of the tube—"

"That's right." His wife sits beside him on the couch. "Sometimes it's six or seven." Her husband chuckles guiltily as she looks up at the two of them standing in the doorway. "Would you like something to eat?"

The "newlyweds" eye the furniture, the walls, the rug on the hardwood floor. Nothing's the same except where Ted and Kathy have placed the Christmas tree. They've arranged their gifts to each other neatly under the boughs, plastic packages of wool socks, tins of green tea, and bottles of nutritional supplements (like Fisol and acidophilus) Teddy and Mary have never heard of. "Oh, thank you," Mary says. "But we couldn't impose."

"Actually," Teddy says, "we were thinking about doing some night-sledding."

"Oh? It's been years since I've heard anyone talk of sledding at night—or sledding at all, come to think of it. I hate to sound like a grouch, but it really is true," he chuckles. "'Kids these days,' you know."

Teddy laughs. "We were wondering if you had a spare sled you could lend us."

"Of course, of course. We'll just take a walk out to the barn."

Donning their coats, scarves, and boots, they trudge behind him through the snow. The barn door is unlocked. Ted pulls on a string and above their heads a naked bulb casts a faint cold nimbus around them. Teddy peeks inside some of the old horse stalls, now teeming with wood-cutting equipment and unfinished furniture. "You're a carpenter, I see."

"The cranberries don't pay the bills, I'm afraid. But I'd do it anyway. There," he says, pointing to the wall above the second stall on the left side. Mary opens the stall door and shimmies around the junk stored inside. "There are two on the wall there, but I'd take the red metal one. The Lightning Glider's too old."

She pulls her sled down from the wall hook and stands looking down at it with her back still turned to them. "It's in fine condition," she says, though this is not true.

"Take the metal one, Mary," Teddy calls. "My wife has a weak spot for antiques, you might say," she hears him saying to Ted. "She likes to make use of things until they disintegrate."

Slowly she replaces the Lightning Glider on the hook.

"Where are you planning to go?" Ted asks. "There's a nice hill down by the high school. That's where the kids go—when they go."

"We have another place in mind."

"Ah," says Ted Morrigan, as he pulls the light cord and closes the barn door behind them. "Well, enjoy yourselves. If you're hungry afterwards, there's a nice place in town called Mona's. Lots of vegetarian things, if you like to eat healthy."

With hearty thanks, they slide the old sled carefully into the backseat.

8:15 P.M.
Cape Eden

BENDER'S HILL is no longer Bender's. Instead, a haughty brick mansion with a four-car garage stands at the bottom of it. BMWs line the drive and lights shine brightly in every window. The hill had always been private property, but no sledders would have been arrested for trespassing in 1928. Two women in fur coats and high heels teeter down the icy sidewalk, and as the front door opens Mary and Teddy hear loud music and even louder laughter.

They stand at the foot of the driveway, the sled's yellow nylon rope slack in her hand. "A New Year's party," Teddy murmurs. "Now, why weren't we invited?"

Mary turns to him, as disappointed as a child. "Now what?"

"Do you want to go to the high school field?"

"I don't have the heart to go sledding now."

"We'll eat first. Then maybe you'll change your mind."

TEDDY SLOWS OUTSIDE Tommy Dolan's Bar & Restaurant. The parking lot holds two beat-up sedans and a pickup truck. "Is this the place?"

"Yes, but let's not go here," she says. "We went there, the night we got . . . we got you . . ."

He nods, and keeps driving.

They stop outside the restaurant Ted recommended—closed for the New Year's holiday. So is every other restaurant on Main Street, even the Chinese take-out joint. Tommy Dolan's it is.

Tommy has treated himself to a night off. A yard-high lawn ornament, Santa Claus winking as he checks his list, stands illuminated on the far end of the bar. Teddy orders a fillet steak and potatoes, and Mary, remembering Leonardo da Vinci, chooses the spaghetti. From the jukebox she picks three Nina Simone songs, thinking of Gray.

"Jesus," says the man behind the bar. "You look like you just got back from Iraq."

"I was in the military."

"Baghdad?"

"No," Teddy says. "But it's been a long trip."

"You want a beer?"

"Do you happen to have any brandy?"

"Let me check," says the bartender. "There may be a bottle in the back I can dust off for you."

After dinner they drive to the high school and take to the hill, for one ride only.

10:15 P.M.
World's End Bed & Breakfast ~ The Parlor

MRS. MORRIGAN'S davenport has been reupholstered in a darker velvet. Mary looks at Ted as she runs her hand along the arm. "You did this yourself?"

"That bad, huh?" He laughs.

"No," she says, growing red in the face at her blunder. "It's lovely." A jewelry box, hand-painted with gold-leaf trim, sits at the center of the mantel. Mary has never seen it before, but somehow she knows it was hers.

"That box belonged to my mother," Ted says.

"It's beautiful," she murmurs, turning to look at him. "'World's End'—I like the name, it's very apropos."

There are more photographs on the wall above the sofa. Teddy surveys each one with an interest that would seem idle to anyone but her, even looking at his own wedding portrait without emotion. Beside it, a family portrait from the winter of the snow lion: he stands above her in uniform, his hand on her shoulder, with an eight-year-old Teddy Junior wearing a sober smile at his side, along with his younger brother, Joe. A wide-eyed Lucinda grasps at the pendant around her mother's neck.

But most of the pictures are of children and grandchildren, a dozen grade school portraits of charming, neatly-coiffed youngsters, half of them smiling without their two front teeth. "Looks like you have quite a large family," Teddy says.

"Five children and eleven grandchildren." Kathy smiles like a buddha as she takes a sip of herbal tea. "They all went back to the city yesterday. School starts again Monday, would you believe it?"

Ted bends over a stereo cabinet in the corner behind the Christmas tree. "I don't suppose you have any children of your own yet?"

"Not yet," Teddy replies.

Not yet! Mary turns in her seat and studies the wall. Eleven grandchildren?

The twelfth portrait is older, from the mid-eighties. Lucy's six-year-old mug is unmistakable.

"Ted tells me you're moving to New Zealand," Kathy says. "You must be so excited."

Mary nods.

"What do you say, Kath?" comes the voice from the corner. "You in the mood for some Tommy Dorsey?"

"Sure."

"You'll have to indulge us old folks," Ted chuckles.

"Tommy Dorsey is one of our favorites," Teddy replies.

The first track on the CD *The Best of Tommy Dorsey and his Orchestra,* a song called "Marie" recorded in 1937, begins as Ted retreats into the kitchen to pour his wife another cup of tea.

Teddy stands up from the sofa and looks down at her with an impish smile. "You used to love this song."

"I've never heard it before."

"Come on." He offers his hand. "Let's dance."

Teddy twirls her around on the rug in her stocking feet, winding his arm around her waist and pressing his lips to her cheek. Outside the frosted windows the snow is falling again. She closes her eyes, smelling brandy and pine needles, as Teddy sings under his breath, "As you recall the moon in all its splendor . . . Ma-ryyyy." Ted delivers the tea tray and seats himself beside his wife, who eyes the newlyweds with a smile best described as polite.

11:22 P.M.

Second-Floor Guest Room, East Gable

TEDDY IS LAUGHING. "And how about the time you brought home that rotten honeydew from the farmers' market?"

"What?"

"*Surely* you remember that. It was right after we were married. Cecelia was so appalled at you. Said you were no niece of hers." He laughs again.

"I don't."

"God, Mary," he murmurs. "It feels like we're starting over nearly every time we converse."

Mary turns from him. She is suppressing a horribly vindictive thought, something like, *Yes, well, your body isn't all it used to be.* Come tomorrow she will atone for this, at a tiny neo-Romanesque church off Route 3 on their way to the airport.

"I know it isn't your fault, darling. It's just going to take a bit of getting used to, that's all."

"It could have been worse, you know." She manages a mischievous little smile. "She might have cloned me at the age of nine."

FRIDAY, 1 JANUARY 2010 ~ 12:45 A.M.
The First-Floor Bedroom

"IT'S A COINCIDENCE," says Kathy Morrigan as she turns out the bedside lamp. "Just a very peculiar coincidence."

"It was a coincidence at first," he says slowly. "Their names are common enough, and maybe I'm just imagining the resemblance. But . . ."

"But what?"

"Do you think that's what it is? A coincidence?"

Kathy sighs. "I've never believed in ghosts, and I'd rather not start now."

"But that song . . . You should have seen the way they used to dance to that song."

"He must be at least twelve, maybe fifteen years older than she is, wouldn't you say?"

"That's the thing I haven't been able to figure out."

"There's nothing to figure out, Teddy," his wife says quietly. "They're not your parents." She pauses. "You chose that CD on purpose, didn't you?"

He doesn't answer, and she is opening her mouth to say good night when he says, "I wonder if this is it."

"What?"

"Senility. The onslaught."

"If it is, then at least I'm in good company."

"I thought you said you didn't—"

From a guest room on the second floor a man lets out a scream to still the heart. The Morrigans leap out of bed, shrug on their terry-cloth robes, and hurry up the stairs.

12:48 A.M.

Second-Floor Guest Room, East Gable

"SHH . . . IT'S JUST a nightmare, gibbon. Shhh, I'm here. It was only a bad dream, Teddy."

Someone knocks at the door.

"I'm so sorry," Mary calls out as the Morrigans open the door. They stand at the threshold wearing their most concerned faces. "I'm so sorry we woke you. My husband was having a nightmare."

"What?" Teddy says, bolting upright in bed. "Oh, God—I'm so sorry I disturbed you, I—"

"Not to worry," says Ted. "We're just glad everything's all right."

"There's a box of chamomile tea in the cabinet above the sink, if you'd like a cup. I always find it helps me to sleep better." Kathy pauses. "Well, good night."

Mary and Teddy murmur their thank-yous as Kathy closes the door behind them. Her husband shoots her a meaningful look in the dark hallway, as if to say "I told you so."

HE CLINGS TO her beneath the blankets. "You're so tense," he says.

"You frightened me."

"I'm sorry."

"What were you dreaming about?" But before he can answer she says, "No, forget it, I don't want to know." Part of her wants to resist as he winds his arms tighter around her waist, for she'd been having a nightmare of her own, and he'd been in it. In mornings to come she won't stand his touch before she's seen his face.

"There's something else," he says. "Before I fell asleep my mind got to wandering, and I discovered this memory—I don't know if I can call it that; it feels like it must belong to someone else."

The flesh rises on her arms despite the stifling heat beneath these heavy blankets. "What sort of memory was it?"

"I was a child. I couldn't have been, but I was looking up at you, so I must have been very small. I was looking up at you, and you were dressed in black, a heavy black velvet dress with lace on the collar." He pauses. "You were crying."

"Are you sure it isn't a memory from when your father . . . ?"

He shakes his head.

"Memories play tricks sometimes. Afterwards we might add details that don't belong—"

"No, Mary. It isn't the same memory, because I have *that* memory, too. Besides, you look nothing like my mother."

She chuckles. "That's true."

For half an hour or more they lie silently beside each other, both of them thinking of Mrs. Morrigan. Should she tell him that his mother outlived him by only three years? For what good? She also decides not to tell him that she has the same memory—that she remembers seeing herself in that heavy black dress, not in the mirror, but from the vantage point of a small child.

Dimly she recalls something she'd read in one of those "outdated" textbooks, something that might explain why they have memories that do not belong to them. "Teddy?"

"Mmm?"

"Do you recall what mitochondria are?"

"What for?"

"I just want to know."

"Sleep now, rabbit." He lifts his face from the pillow to flash her a devious smile. "You'll get your biology lesson first thing in the morning."

When Teddy drifts off she slips out of bed, goes down the stairs, and opens the parlor door with as little noise as possible. She lifts the lid on the jewelry box on the mantelpiece—empty. After a moment's hesitation she slides open the little gilt-edged compartment at the bottom of the box and holds the object that was inside up to the moonlight coming through the front window. It is a bracelet made of human hair, with an elaborately woven tie closure in place of a clasp.

10:25 A.M.

25 University Avenue ~ The Study

LUCY FINDS A BOX of her father's old embossed stationery in the bottom desk drawer. How fitting.

Dear Uncle Ted,

I'm sure you'll be surprised to hear from me, so I might as well say first that I am truly sorry I didn't make a greater effort to maintain our familial ties. That sounds quite stiff now that I've seen it on paper—I'm sorry for that, too.

I would like you to have the house in New Halcyon. I have contacted my father's attorney and will be signing over the new deed tomorrow, which means you should be receiving a phone call from her later this week. I've left everything in the house as-is, so I think you will find it just as you remember it.

I have decided on a fresh start, but I didn't think it right to sell the house when you have as great a claim to it as I did. I may return to New Halcyon someday, but I don't think so.

Please pass along my best wishes to Aunt Kathy and all my cousins.

Yours,
Lucy

Sometimes a branch falls clean off the family tree, whether through a fleet of excessively pugilistic white blood cells, unfortunate sexual proclivity, or too many wars fought by ill-fated sons. In the end it doesn't matter whose grandchildren exist only in the imagination, for a gene belongs to no one, least of all the human race.

"Merry Christmas," she mutters as she seals the envelope.

MONDAY, 4 JANUARY 2010 ~ 9:30 A.M.
The Basement

LUCY, STILL WEARING THAT impassive face of three days ago, opens the door when he knocks, and he follows her into the gloom of the old wine cellar. The overhead lightbulbs have burned out within a few seconds of one another, and she has not bothered to replace them. Now the only light in the room comes from the computer screen, the narrow garden-side windows, and a small Tiffany lamp borrowed from the red drawing room. Gray glances over her shoulder at the screen, where a DNA sequence scrolls with dizzying celerity.

In the end he doesn't have to say a word. No "I'm leaving," no "I wasted more than four years of my life with you."

She wants to tell him that she *will* miss him, that she may not have loved him, but how could she have? One learns how to love from one's parents, and Ambrose had only taught her the virtue of obsession. Is it her fault that she's only now learning to distinguish one from the other? *Give me another chance,* she wants to say, but she cannot open her mouth.

They stand opposite each other, her arms tightly crossed, his hands hidden in the pockets of his corduroys. He considers his words for several moments before he speaks. "You have nothing to say?"

"I wish things could have been different."

"Something sincere?"

"I *am* being sincere."

"I don't believe you."

"Just go ahead and leave, then. There's no sense twisting knives."

"I didn't come down here to say anything that would hurt you."

She searches for something to end the awkward silence. "Where are you going?"

Back to the old dank apartment above Mrs. Tepplethwaite's garage—but why be honest? "Friend of a friend has an apartment above his carriage house."

She laughs. "Who are you trying to kid? You don't have any friends."

"You're a fine one to talk."

"I don't pretend I have friends."

"Look, I didn't come down here to trade barbs either. I just—"

"You just what? What more is there to say?" When he doesn't answer right away, an ugly sneer passes over her face. "You're the real hero, you know. The selfless one who doesn't get the girl even though he deserves her even more than the guy she's actually in love with."

The poor girl: left alone between what's commonly known as a rock and a hard place, driven to spite through a snowballing sense of desperation. That's not true, though—she'll always have Megan. But will Megan come with her?

"I want to part on good terms, Lu." He puts his fingers to her cheek, and when she doesn't flinch he leans in and kisses her. She bites down on his lower lip—not hard, but when he pulls away in surprise she inadvertently cuts him. She can see the blood on his mouth.

Blood glistens on her lower lip, too, and he gazes at her in horror. This is not one of those turning points when a man suddenly realizes his lover isn't who she pretends to be. That point has been turning slowly all along. She's far more depraved than all the "Jesus freaks" she so despises. "Do the world a favor, Lucy," he says finally. "Don't reproduce—ever."

MIDDAY
Upstairs

ONLY NOW THAT he no longer lives here does he notice all the cobwebs in the corners, all the dust caked in the moldings. Housekeeping was never her strong suit—though he ought to have helped once in a while. In the master bedroom he packs the suitcase he'll take back to Rome this summer. Seeing the wintry light coming through the window above the bed, he thinks of that first morning four years ago—Lucy's skin stained gold and blue, her sleepy serenity—and he decides he was bewitched.

Gremlins in the dining room, the tarnished crucifix over every doorway, the hall closet filled with dead people's overcoats—no, he won't miss any of it. After loading the Prius with his suitcase, a few crates of books and CDs, and his new quilt folded neatly in a zippered plastic bag, he drives to Mrs. Tepplethwaite's and finds his old key beneath the moldy mat by the side door. Once he's unloaded his belongings he returns the Prius to Lucy's driveway, opens the front door, and drops the house and car keys in the bowl on the hall table. He stands hesitating in the front hall, for he has forgotten one thing but would rather not see her again.

Of course he decides to risk it. Climbing the staircase as quietly as possible, he opens the attic door, steps over the neatly made bed on the floor, and seats himself at the rolltop desk. There is a cache of photos in one of these drawers (beside a roll of two-cent stamps), spare copies of Mary's graduation portrait, and he is going to keep one for himself. Still clutching the wooden armrests, he surveys the room—the shrouded furniture, her dresses still hanging in the gloom of the open wardrobe, her empty perfume bottles lining the windowsill. It's always easier to leave a place for the last time not knowing that it will be.

Before he leaves, he picks up her pillow and presses it to his face.

Gray closes the front door and walks back to his once and future accommodation. Two weeks later he will make the down payment on a cheerful two-bedroom bungalow within walking distance of the school, in the opposite direction from the Dearthing house. Future girlfriends will run their hands admiringly over the hand-pieced quilt on his bed, and when they ask he'll tell them he found it at a rummage sale. None of them will ever notice the dedication done in small, perfect stitches on the underside.

9:46 A.M.

The Basement

THE PROGRAM CHIRPS at her; the sequencing is complete. What's on the computer screen will surely disprove the contents of that ludicrous file.

She pulls a clean hankie out of the pocket of her trousers and wipes Gray's blood from her mouth. No wonder he thought she was psychotic, even if she hadn't meant to bite that hard—what in God's name had gotten into her? Stupid to think he'd remember that first morning in the shower, when she'd bitten him playfully on his lower lip as he lathered the small of her back. He'd found it endearing then—more than endearing.

Lucy turns to the monitor, seating herself at the desk before she lets her eyes focus on the words. A queer feeling trickles over her, as if someone has just cracked an egg on the crown of her head.

L. Morrigan *and* L. Morrigan,

100% MATCH.

This is not possible. This is *absurd.* With shaking fingers she fumbles through the yellowed clippings and other miscellanea in Fuller's file, knowing full well that every scrap of paper in that folder only confirms what's on the computer screen. She yanks the plug from the back of the monitor and stands there, in the darkness of the half-dismantled laboratory, with the cable dangling from her fist.

The woman who first read her *Grimm's Fairy Tales, Through the Looking-Glass,* and Wilde's "The Happy Prince"? Not Lucinda. The woman who drove her, terrified, to the hospital in the middle of the night as her throat swelled from some mysterious allergy? Not Lucinda. Who gave her bowls of sliced bananas drowned in cream for an afternoon snack?

Not Lucinda—*Mary.*

So *this* was why her father was absent in all her earliest memories. "I was there, Lu," he'd told her. "I was working too much."

"You must have been working *all* the time, then," she'd grumbled again and again.

That one part was true—he *had* been working intently, hadn't he? And in the end, he hadn't even had time to record a maudlin confession on videotape, hiding it somewhere with the instruction "Don't watch this until I'm dead." It all makes sense now, the intensity of his affection, those vise-like goodnight embraces that had both thrilled and frightened her as a young girl.

Now she understands, too, why the boys in the house she remembered knowing as a toddler had vanished like last night's dreams. Her father had even had the gall to tell her they were someone else's children.

The dearth of baby pictures, virtually none before the age of six (the early photos she *did* have were probably someone else's); hazy memories of her mother sitting beside a radio in the evenings, her face drawn, her eyes ringed in red; and why Megan knew the simwomb worked—she knew because Lucy herself had been born out of it.

Her old friend at the Bureau of Vital Statistics had also forged a certain birth certificate. The inscription on the *Grimm's* flyleaf, dated the first of November 1980? Not written 'til 1986.

This is the kind of revelation that bears the shock only of your own opacity, the sort of truth you find you'd known all along. Lucy spreads her hands out before her, half-expecting to find the dreaded liver spots. Her decline has begun, all right—it's just going to take longer. That DNA was fresh.

Worst of all, her own grandmother must have known. There's no way she couldn't have. And she took the secret to her grave.

TUESDAY, 5 JANUARY 2010 ~ 12:15 P.M.
(GMT + 12 HOURS)
New Zealand

BOSTON TO LOS ANGELES, L.A. to Auckland, Auckland to Christchurch. They take a taxi to what the driver calls a budget hotel on the Avon, where they sleep for thirty hours straight. In her dreams she is back at 25 University Avenue, wandering the corridors with her arms full of lilies. Children dart from room to room in pursuit of one another, the hunted ones squealing in terrified delight, all of them kicking up the dust bunnies under the hall consoles and chairs. There are so many of them—five, no, six!—three more than she had in her other life, six more than she'll ever have now.

One of the children comes up behind her and clings to the folds of Mary's skirt, and Mary reaches down to smooth the dark, glossy hair before she's seen her face. And when the child looks up at her, Mary recognizes that pale, defiant little girl without astonishment.

MONDAY, 4 JANUARY 2010 ~ 10:32 P.M.
25 University Avenue ~ The Study

SINCE SHE WAS FORSAKEN by everyone in the world, she went forth into the open, trusting in God . . .

She should never have made a new inscription. With a fountain pen she scratches it out with uncharacteristic sloppiness and replaces the book on the shelf. *Everyday Life in the Twenty-first Century* is still missing, presumably for good.

For a long time Lucy stands by the sofa in the center of the room, absentmindedly twirling the antique globe on the end table. She shouldn't even be touching it, but on a whim she gives it a brisk spin, closes her eyes, and lays her forefinger on the swiftly turning surface.

The globe stops spinning. She opens her eyes and peers at the location under her finger: the Tropic of Capricorn, three inches west of an African territory labeled, simply, HOTTENTOTS.

With a sigh she returns to her desk and fishes her checkbook out of the top drawer. She writes *your half of the Prius* on the memo line, erring on the side of generosity when deciding on the sum. She'll mail it to him in care of the Classics Department.

She had expected to feel more than this, some sense of either loss or liberation. Could she leave here tonight with nothing but a crate of bottled water and a change of clothes?

None of this belonged to her in the first place. She will go but everything will stay, from the antique furniture to the piss in the dining room decanters, their crystal stoppers flecked with mold. Every family photograph reappears on the foyer walls.

No, not everything will stay—she dismantles the lab. The equipment goes back to the university laboratories from whence it was pilfered, and all the papers and files will burn in an aluminum trash can at the center of the labyrinth. First she sorts through each file four, five, half a dozen times in the hope of finding a sealed envelope with her name written in his illegible scrawl, but there is no posthumous explanation to be found.

Claudine's skeleton will remain, but the notes and doodles on the blackboard will not. After a long hesitation, she erases every mark on the board, wiping it clean with a wet cloth.

10:35 P.M.

The Labyrinth

SHE CHECKS EACH file again before tossing it into the can beside the old fishpond. Above her, little licks of fire dance in the curve of every spoon.

So much for "First thing Monday morning"! At least it's some comfort knowing federal agents don't want to come back after the holidays any more than the rest of us. Oh, they'll arrive soon enough; she has no doubt of that. But when Fuller and the men in black come knocking—and when they find their way in through the back door—they'll find nothing of interest whatsoever. She just wishes she could be around to witness Fuller's tantrum when they tell him he's wasted their time.

Someone is walking through the snow outside the tall hedge; Lucy hugs an open file to her chest and listens. The footsteps draw closer, as though whoever it is has walked the maze before.

"Back the fuck off," Lucy shouts. "I've got an Uzi."

From twenty yards away Megan's laughter echoes off the glass wall of the conservatory.

"What are you doing here?" Lucy says coldly.

"What do you think?" Megan steps through the archway in the hedge. "I smelled the burning paper."

Lucy throws the file into the can and doubles over coughing, a wad of Kleenex pressed to her mouth.

"That cough doesn't sound good."

"It's just the smoke."

"It isn't the smoke." Megan pauses. "I just wanted to tell you that I submitted my resignation. I'm driving to Taos. I was hoping you'd come with me."

Lucy looks at her for a long time. Megan smiles uncertainly.

"You *knew,*" Lucy says. "You knew, and you never said a word."

"Knew what?"

"Don't do that. I'm not stupid, Meeg."

A flicker of recognition passes over Megan's face, and she averts her eyes. "I didn't know," she says quietly. "I had a suspicion, but I never asked him. I didn't want to know."

"Your friend's dying wife doesn't give birth to a six-year-old child." Lucy tosses the last file into the can. "You knew. And I deserved to be told." A thick piece of paper falls out of the file and into the snow. She bends to retrieve it: the last copy of that grisly family portrait of 1986. The file had been marked "miscellaneous."

"It . . . it wasn't my place—"

"It wasn't your place!" When Lucy looks at her now over the blazing trash can Megan knows this won't end with her forgiveness. "There's just one thing I haven't been able to figure out," Lucy says.

"It was one of her baby teeth."

"Which explains why I have no photographs of myself before the age of six." Lucy pauses. "And why I remember the A-bomb." She drops the photograph into the can and watches their faces turn to ash, hers and her parents'.

"Thank you, Megan," she says. "But I'm not going to Taos."

JANUARY 2010
Christchurch, New Zealand

THAT FIRST MORNING they walk hand in hand down to a café on Cathedral Square, where they order cappuccino and a full breakfast at a table out front. Teddy picks up a newspaper and opens it to the classifieds while they wait for their eggs.

"What are you doing?"

"I need a job, don't I?"

"Can't we pretend to be on vacation, just for the first few days?"

"I don't mean to be a spoilsport, but at the rate we're going we'll be out of funds in another two weeks, and what if it takes me longer than that?"

"Couldn't you apply at the city hospital?"

"With a medical degree from nineteen thirty-two?" He shakes his head. "I'd have to go back to school if I wanted to practice again."

"You could do that. I'm sure you could get another scholarship—"

"At my age?"

"Your age won't matter. You could go to the university here—or we could go to Europe—London, or Edinburgh?"

"Would it be worthwhile? Chances are I wouldn't live long enough to graduate."

"Don't say that."

"I have to say it, rabbit. It's the truth."

"You don't know that."

"I don't even know if we have enough money left for a trip to Europe."

Mary points to the Help Wanted sign in the front window. "I think I'll go in and apply."

"But you've never had a job in your life!"

"It does say 'no experience necessary.'"

Teddy shakes his head.

"Most women work now, you know. Not only as teachers or secretaries, either. Ivy League schools award advanced business degrees to more women than men." She pauses. "If I get a job at a place like this, you'll be free to look for something better for yourself."

And so Mary becomes a full-time barista while Teddy spends his days trawling for "proper" work. They secure a clean but shabbily furnished one-bedroom apartment six blocks from the café on a monthly lease. To her surprise, Mary likes the work; her feet and lower back ache by the end of the day, but she never tires of the fragrance of dark-roasted coffee beans. She begins to bake for the café, too; her fig cakes and pumpkin bread become the most popular items on the breakfast menu. She even learns a few Māori proverbs from one of the regulars (*Waiho mate tangata e mihi:* "Let somebody else acknowledge your virtues.")

"A lot of people I know would invite an American to dinner only if they could put him on a platter," says her new boss, a middle-aged man with diamond studs in both ears, "but I just feel sorry for you guys." He calls her "the refugee."

A week after their arrival in Christchurch, Mary writes to Megan in care of the university asking, cryptically, if she might provide them with a new copy of Teddy's transcript—with all the dates changed, of course, as well as any obsolete courses. And if a medical school transcript is out of the question, could she at least send proof of his bachelor of science?

She writes three times, adding their new address clearly at the end of each letter, but Megan sends no response. Lucy doesn't reply, either.

FEBRUARY AND MARCH, 2010
Christchurch

SOME SUNDAYS THEY take the bus to Lyttelton, the port from which all the great explorers sailed. Long-legged college girls in fluorescent helmets paraglide down the side of the mountain, tossing and spinning in the wind like maple seeds. What did she mean to him, anyway?

"Oh *no,* rabbit."

"What?"

"You're looking pensive again."

Just one extraordinary passage in his life, that's all she was. Perhaps he's already half-forgotten her. Perhaps he never even took the quilt out of the bag.

"There's a town called Paradise," she says.

"Where?"

"Somewhere south of here. We ought to go."

"Just because it's called Paradise?"

"They named it Paradise for a reason, dodo-head."

"Nah." Teddy tucks a stray lock of hair behind her ear, in just such a way that those who pass them on the sidewalk assume they are very newly enamored. "Who needs Paradise?"

APRIL 2010 ~ 11:47 P.M.

The Glow-Worm Dell ~ Hokitika

"THEY'RE CARNIVOROUS, did you know that?" comes a squeaky American voice somewhere a few yards to their left. "The glow results from the oxidation of the insect's waste products."

Teddy leads her farther into the woods, careful to keep the flashlight beam on the ground. "So much for a romantic night out in the middle of nowhere."

"Gibbon?"

"Mmm?"

"I miss the labyrinth."

"Don't think of it."

"Don't you miss it?"

"I don't think of it. Look *up,* darling." With his finger he lifts her chin. Hazy blue slivers of light inch almost imperceptibly along the branches, moonlight tracing the gossamer in their wake.

TUESDAY, 11 AUGUST 2010 ~ 4:45 P.M.

Buzzwick's Café ~ Cathedral Square, Christchurch

WHEN TEDDY RUSHES into the café, her first thought is that her letters have been intercepted. But as she lifts the counter panel and walks out to meet him, she feels a pang of foolishness at her paranoia, for whatever he has to say is obviously good news. He presses her close and kisses her repeatedly in his favorite place, between her cheekbone and the nip of her ear.

"Hey, refugee!" her boss calls from the kitchen. "You're not off for another quarter of an hour!"

Teddy presses his lips to her ear. "How would you like to spend your austral summer frolicking with baby penguins?"

"What . . . how . . . ?"

"I went to the international center down by the airport this morning to follow up on the C.V. I'd submitted *months* ago," he says, grabbing her hands and cracking her knuckles in his excitement, "and by a tremendous stroke of fortune it turns out that a team of biologists—Americans—they need a new field assistant!"

"So . . . ?"

"I got the job, Mary! We're going down!"

She throws her arms around his neck and shrieks with glee.

"Two full months on the ice!" he says. "It's just what you wanted."

"Where?"

"The Dry Valley. Oh, I do have to tell you—they're not actually working with penguins."

"Oh."

"Don't be glum, it's even better than penguins." He laughs. *"Worms!"*

FRIDAY, 15 OCTOBER 2010 ~ 2:15 P.M.
International Antarctic Centre ~ Christchurch

AT THE CLOTHING Distribution Center Mary realizes that most of the gear Lucy bought for her wasn't made for weather any colder or windier than a New England winter. The American program will provide them with more appropriate supplies, including snow boots with detachable crampons and crimson parkas with their new names written on Velcro strips in permanent marker.

NOVEMBER 2010
McMurdo Station ~ Ross Island, Antarctica

THEY HAVE SUCCUMBED to the inherent romance of a journey to the end of the earth, visions of southern lights and Emperor penguins and afternoon romps through pristine snowbanks, the two of them looking out at shimmering sundogs on the horizon through floor-to-ceiling windows at some swanky bar with a punny name, toasty-warm in their long johns and woolen sweaters as they sip hot buttered rum from hand-thrown mugs. Oh yes, a perfectly unconventional happy ending.

But walls of windows aren't terribly heat-efficient, rum's far too precious a commodity to waste in cocktails, and "Southern Exposure" is as punny as it gets. Though the tundra is even more beautiful than it looks in photographs, the buildings at the base are depressingly utilitarian, and the dormitories are more commonly known as "deprivation chambers." Their quarters consist of a set of bunk beds with thin bumpy mattresses (lovemaking might be more comfortable in the snow) and a shared toilet under a naked lightbulb. Visitors and residents alike are allowed to bathe only every other day, and even then the showers shut off after five minutes.

Teddy's nightmares continue, but only the girl in bed beside him hears them.

In two more weeks they'll be sleeping on the ice.

SUNDAY, 14 NOVEMBER 2010 ~ 7:55 A.M.
The Canteen

WATCHING TEDDY DEVOUR his boiled eggs and toast with such gusto doesn't exactly soothe her nausea. He looks up from his plate, a bit of yolk smeared on his lower lip. "Not hungry?"

She springs from her chair and rushes to the W.C. down the hall, where a young grad student is making a careful attempt at shaving her legs. Mary disappears into the stall and retches last night's meatloaf-from-a-mold.

"Looks like you're going back already, eh?"

"It's just my stomach," Mary mutters into the bowl. "I shouldn't have eaten that meatloaf."

"Nuh-uh," says the girl as Mary emerges from the stall. "You've got a bun in the oven."

"I'm not." Mary frowns. "I can't be."

"Nothing's foolproof, you know."

Still trembling, Mary cups her hands beneath the other faucet and brings the water to her lips.

"Hold on a sec," the grad student says, dropping her razor in the sink and rolling the leg down on her long johns. "I have what you need." A minute later she reappears with a small box labeled FIRST RESPONSE in pink letters.

"What is this?"

"A pregnancy test. Haven't you ever seen one?"

Mary shakes her head.

"Just pee on the wand. Two lines is yes, one line is no."

Someone knocks on the lavatory door. "Mary? Mary, are you all right?"

8:30 A.M.
Dorm Block C, Room 11

"IT'S MENOPAUSE."

"Don't be absurd. Even if we discount the fact that you are twenty-three years old, you don't have a single symptom."

"I have *liver spots,* for Pete's sake!"

He squints at the minuscule print on the instruction sheet. "It says here that the formation of the placenta releases a certain hormone—"

"Leave me alone in here, would you please? I'm not taking it with you hovering over my shoulder."

8:45 A.M.

Dorm Block C, The Lavatory

WAS IT SO NECESSARY for her to lock the door? "Rabbit?"

"Not yet, dear."

8:49 A.M.

"RABBIT?"

"Not for another five minutes, Teddy!" Seated on the toilet lid with the naked bulb buzzing overhead, the chain swinging to and fro in the sickly gray glow, she blinks at the indicator on the little plastic wand:

Two lines, stark as daylight.

Acknowledgments

I have filed away all the stories my grandparents ever told me. They're more like snatches than stories: glimpses of blue-collar Philly in the late 1940s, fleeting references to dreary foster homes in Illinois, just a minute or two about that landless year-plus on a destroyer in the South Pacific. *Mary Modern* is 100 percent fiction, but every truth within it has come from observing these four.

Kelly Brown encouraged me to write this, Ailbhe Slevin saw me through the first draft, and Aravinda Seshadri provided second-draft feedback. You three: I am so, so grateful for your enduring friendship and support. Other friends in Galway helped in slightly less monumental ways (mostly by cheerfully indulging my writerly neuroses!): Seanan McDonnell, Diarmuid O'Brien, and Christian O'Reilly. Same goes for my pals in New York, Jenny Leff especially.

I began writing *Mary Modern* in the M.A. in Writing program at the National University of Ireland, Galway, in the fall of 2004, and I very much appreciate the encouragement of my professors there. Adrian Frazier, I'm glad I didn't bet you that €20. Mike McCormack, you've been a marvelous friend and mentor to me. Thank you for being so generous in all ways.

I was also fortunate to have many extraordinary teachers growing up in Moorestown, NJ, some of whom went out of their way to nurture my first attempts at writing creatively. (Perhaps you've noticed that

I have begun naming characters after you. I hope this is a more artful way of expressing my gratitude than mentioning you all by name.) Megan Newman and Kathy Huck, you were the best bosses a girl could ask for, and everything I learned from you has made the whole editorial and publishing process that much easier.

And, of course, I owe quite a lot to those whose works I read for both research and pleasure: Elizabeth Abbott, Frederick Lewis Allen, Joseph Sheridan Le Fanu, Edna St. Vincent Millay, Kate O'Brien, Matt Ridley, Mary Shelley, Ben Shephard, Lee Silver, Marie Simmons, Studs Terkel, Sara Wheeler, and Keith and Sarah Winston. I used lines from lots of great songs, too, so I'd like to mention Irving Berlin, Richard Jones, Gus Kahn and Walter Donaldson, Terry Shand, Jimmy Eaton, and Mickey Leader, Nina Simone, Marion Sinclair, and Heinrich Suso.

I'm not just being effusive when I praise my agent, Kate Garrick, and my editor, Sally Kim. Kate treated me like an A-list author when I wondered if I'd ever make her a dime, and Sally has more than earned her reputation as one of the savviest fiction editors in New York (I think she's *the* savviest, but I might be biased). Working with you both has been an unmitigated pleasure. Hearty thanks go to Shaye Areheart and Brian DeFiore as well, and to everyone who corrected, designed, promoted, and otherwise handled this book with such care and enthusiasm: Christine Aronson, Cindy Berman, Jill Flaxman, Janet Fletcher, Jason Gobble, Kate Kennedy, Dan Rembert, Karin Schulze, Kira Stevens, and Barbara Sturman, just to name a few.

I return, as always, to my family. Kate, thank you for being my eyes in New Zealand, and in general for being the dearest little sister in the universe. To my parents and all the rest of my family: thank you for always emphasizing "*when,* not *if.*" I don't eat elephant, but I like to think I've learned the lesson all the same.

About the Author

Camille DeAngelis received a B.A. from New York University in 2002 and an M.A. from the National University of Ireland, Galway, in 2005. She is also the author of *Moon Handbooks: Ireland* (Avalon, 2007) and lives in New Jersey when not bumming around her favorite Irish city.

About the Type

This book was set in Adobe Garamond, a typeface designed by Robert Slimbach in 1989. It is based on Claude Garamond's sixteenth-century type samples found at the Plantin-Moretus Museum in Antwerp, Belgium.